D0149244

UNDER THE GOLDEN SUN

ALSO BY JENNY ASHCROFT

Meet Me in Bombay

UNDER
THE
GOLDEN
SUN

A Novel

Jenny Ashcroft

ST. MARTIN'S PRESS
NEW YORK

First published in the United States by St. Martin's Press, an imprint of St. Martin's Publishing Group

www.stmartins.com

Designed by Omar Chapa

Library of Congress Cataloging-in-Publication Data

Names: Ashcroft, Jenny, 1980– author.
Title: Under the golden sun: a novel / Jenny Ashcroft.
Description: First U.S. Edition. | New York: St. Martin's Press, 2022.
Identifiers: LCCN 2021046501 | ISBN 9781250274762 (hardcover) |
    ISBN 9781250274779 (ebook)
Subjects: GSAFD: Love stories.
Classification: LCC PR6101.S525 U53 2022 | DDC 823/.92—dc23
LC record available at https://lccn.loc.gov/2021046501

Our books may be purchased in bulk for promotional, educational, or business use. Please contact your local bookseller or the Macmillan Corporate and Premium Sales Department at 1-800-221-7945, extension 5442, or by email at MacmillanSpecialMarkets@macmillan.com.

Originally published in the United Kingdom by Little, Brown UK in 2020

First U.S. Edition: 2022

10 9 8 7 6 5 4 3 2 1

For my brilliant nephew, Leo

AUSTRALIA

January 1936

The dawn was hazy, dense with heat; that brooding wind blowing out from the red west. *A stinker,* they'd call it inside, when they woke. The homestead's white weatherboard walls beat gold and pink, the paint sweating beneath the force of the rising sun. All around, as far as Mabel's darting gaze could stretch, the Lucknow plantation spread: acres upon acres of grassland, scorched by summer, dotted by cattle and stockmen's cottages, their corrugated roofs glinting in the glare. On the horizon, thick pockets of palm and gum trees rose, swaying, shuddering in the breeze. Mabel could almost hear the rustle of their dead, dry leaves, feel the rough pressure of their bark behind her back. Was Richie still somewhere out there, hidden amid them, maybe looking toward the house, toward her?

She didn't know. She didn't know. . . .

Beside her, in the porch, the old hammock rocked, its ropes creaking, back and forth. Mabel didn't sit — not on that hammock, not on her packed trunk — even though her legs, swollen with pregnancy, ached. She stared down the estate's driveway, past the barn, through the languid clouds of dust rising from the gravel, toward the timber gate. Beads of sweat dripped from her forehead, making her eyes sting. Under her damp dress, the baby kicked and turned, quickly, jerkily, like it sensed her fear.

"I'm sorry," she whispered to it, her words swallowed in the instant by the beating air. She set her hand against her stomach, felt another kick. "Try not to worry, little thing." Her fingers shook. "We'll be gone soon."

They would.

The ute pulled up not long after, spinning to a halt at the gate. *He's here, little thing. He's here.* Mabel swallowed dryly, watching as he jumped to the ground, ran toward her: fast, heedless of the fierce heat. He wore the same clothes he'd been in when he'd left her the night before. They were crumpled now, his shirt stained with sweat, and something rusty, something she didn't want to see, something that looked like dried blood.

The mark grew larger the closer he drew, climbing the porch stairs, reaching for her trunk.

"Is it . . . ?" she asked.

"It's done." The words were sharp, breathless. "We need to leave. Now."

"Richie's . . . ?"

"He's gone."

The sob left her before she knew it was coming.

His face creased in pain. "Mabel, no," he said, abandoning the trunk, pulling her, for all their urgency, into a hug. "This is a good thing."

She dug her head into his shoulder, clinging to the familiar comfort of his body. He loved her. He'd always loved her.

I chose the wrong brother, she thought.

Inside the house, a door slammed.

"We need to go," he repeated.

"I'm scared," she confessed.

"You'll be fine. You'll forget all this . . ."

"I won't."

"You can try," he said, kissing her.

"I don't know how."

"Yes, you do. You'll manage. I know you will." Another kiss. "And the baby will never know."

ENGLAND

CHAPTER ONE

Saturday, 1 March 1941

The milk train from Exeter St. David's to Paddington was near empty, and at a standstill on the wrong side of the Devon border, thanks to bomb damage down the line. Rose, who'd got up before dawn to catch it, was on her way to the Goring Hotel in Victoria: a twenty-fifth-birthday afternoon tea with her uncle Lionel and older brother, Joe. (It wasn't her birthday, but since that fell on 29 February, it was as close as she was going to get to one until the next leap year, in 1944. *Another five minutes, and you'd have skipped the date entirely,* her parents could always be relied upon to write in a card from wherever in the world they happened to be based—Ceylon, for the time being—*just a fraction too impatient to arrive at your own party. Tiny, perfect, but with such a pair of lungs. The way you used them, we were sure you'd realized your blunder.*) She almost felt like wailing now, not over today's party—which she was relaxed enough about getting to, she didn't have to be at Victoria until three—but the much-needed trip to the shops she'd planned to squeeze in first, and for which she'd risen so painfully early. She hardly relished the prospect of Oxford Street's queues on a Saturday, but stockings, hard enough to come by in London, were as rare as bananas in Devon, and she was on her last pair. Shivering in the frozen carriage, she huddled into her coat, stared through the window, out at the fog of steam and morning mist, the sheep clustered on the icy fields, and thought longingly of her rickety bed, the warmth of her landlady's flannel sheets, and the extra hour she might as well have stolen between them.

The farmer opposite her—her only other companion in the carriage—huffed, then, for what was surely the hundredth time, got up, peering down the train's corridor in search of the harried conductor, who'd already informed them that he had no idea when they might be on the move again, and was now, quite sensibly, keeping well hidden. The farmer had told Rose at the start of their journey that it was imperative he wasn't late into Reading. *Imperative.* He was on his way to a weekend meeting of the regional agricultural committees. He'd sounded rather proud of the fact, and Rose had suspected he'd been waiting for her to ask him more about the day's proceedings. She hadn't. After an endless winter working as a secretary for the Ministry of Agriculture, holed up in a tiny, oh-so-quiet office on an old dairy farm, just outside Ilfracombe, she'd rather had her fill of talk of wheat quotas, arable-land allocations, and livestock provisions. She only wished that when, back in October, her uncle Lionel had tentatively proposed the role to her, offering to pull strings at Whitehall to help her secure it—a place she could breathe the sea air, he'd said, find some peace after the grim events of September, come to terms with the child she'd lost, or at least move on from her dismissal from the air force (she hadn't moved anywhere; five months in, and the thought of that horrendous disciplinary hearing still made her cheeks flame, in injustice, shame)—she'd listened to her brother's warning that she was out of her mind to consider it.

"It'll be grim," Joe had said, "the dullest of purgatories. You don't need peace, you need distractions, less time to think. Try the Auxiliary Territorial Service, why don't you?" He'd given her a smile, half teasing, half sad. "I've heard the army will let anyone in."

She might yet give them a go. She was fairly sure her unfortunate boss—the very elderly, very sweet, *very* polite Honorable Hector Arden—wouldn't stand in her way. He'd probably be glad to see her in khaki. That way he could have someone different working for him. Someone who could type, for instance. Or take dictation without having to ask him to slow down, repeat himself, just wait while she got the last bit right.

"No, no," he'd say whenever she apologized for her ineptitude, "you're doing quite splendidly. Truly. Quite, quite . . . well."

On the bright side, she almost never had to run off for an emergency cry in the milk sheds anymore. That felt like progress. Maybe there was something to be said for the sea air, after all. . . .

The train juddered into motion, pulling her back to the moment. The farmer opened his mouth, to say what, she never discovered, because they creaked to a halt again. His eyes bulged at her, incredulous, quite as though this sort of thing weren't par for the course these days.

"I'm sure it'll only be another minute," she said, more to placate him than because she believed it.

He clenched his teeth, not believing it either.

In the end, it was another hour before they were properly on their way again. Time enough for Rose to finish the book she'd brought, be forced into risking the train's arctic lavatories, and the farmer to scout the other carriages in search of a newspaper, return with *The People,* read it, and fill their own carriage with acrid smoke from a packet of Woodbines.

"Don't do that," he said, as Rose got up to open the window, "it's too cold."

"Just for a minute," she said, yanking down the pane.

He stood, reaching round her to shut it again. "I'll catch my death."

She stared at him, liking him less, but was too British—with her army chaplain father, and politician uncle—to do anything other than summon a tight smile and say, "Well, we wouldn't want that."

He narrowed his eyes, as though trying to decide if she was in earnest, then—obviously deeming the conundrum not worth his effort—sat, picked up his borrowed paper, and flicked ash on the floor.

So he continued the entire way to Reading. With nothing else to distract her, Rose's mind wandered, landing inevitably on her fiancé, Xander, and the nagging unknown of whether he'd turn up at the restaurant for her tea. He was a press correspondent, over from New York since the beginning of the war. She'd invited him, of course she had, but he hadn't committed, or even mentioned his plans in the short birthday wire he'd sent the day before. (*A quarter century* STOP *Looks like you made it* STOP *Here's to a kinder year* STOP) His evasiveness hurt. That wire had hurt. She was still smarting at its brevity, those words. Looks like you made it. She wasn't even sure anymore that she *wanted* him to come to the tea. Before September, she'd never have believed that possible. Before the baby, the two of them hadn't been able to keep away from each other.

She missed that, she really did miss it. . . .

She sighed unhappily, exhaling a frozen white cloud. The farmer ignored her. They were finally pulling into Reading station and he was on his feet, making a to-do about checking his coat, his ticket. Behind him, the smoggy platform swarmed with passengers waiting for their train, probably all the other delayed London services behind them, too. The clock above the Women's Institute's steaming tea stand read close to noon, and although that made Rose twitch (she was going to have to seriously race for Oxford Circus if she was to stand a chance of scouring out nylons *and* getting to Victoria on time), the farmer at least was leaving, and, in an eleventh-hour act of redemption, left his paper for her, thrown behind him on the carriage floor.

She swooped to pick it up, reclaiming her seat as others swarmed in.

"Christ," said a soldier, batting the smoke, "someone been having a fire in here?"

They left the window open the rest of the way to Paddington: a welcome relief from the damp smell of everyone's woolen coats, as well as the stale tobacco. And although the menacing tang of cordite joined the cocktail of scents as the fields gave way to narrow streets, strips of houses broken by rubble, smoke from the previous night's raid, with the press of bodies it was almost warm in the carriage. For all Rose was squeezed into a corner, jammed between a woman holding a carpetbag and the desolate view outside, she was about as comfortable as she'd been all morning. Nestled in her tiny space, she read the farmer's paper cover to cover, skimming the war news—most of which she'd listened to on the wireless the night before anyway: skirmishes in Libya, strengthening German presence in Africa, losses in the Atlantic, Britain's back against the wall pretty much everywhere after the loss of France the year before, all of it so horribly grim—lingering over the middle pages instead, much more than she'd used to in peacetime. It had become a habit of hers, though. She loved the normality of everything printed there, the humanity of the reviews of gallery exhibitions and theater shows, the readers' recipes and gardening tips. She found it comforting, a reminder that, in all the fear and death, ordinary life was going on, everywhere. There was one sweet tale, too, of a woman who'd found a photograph album of her long-dead parents in the remnants of their bombed family home. The woman had never known the album had existed, and said it was like being given her parents back, seeing their faces again. It made Rose smile, this unwitting gift delivered by Jerry. She wondered if the German bombardier would be happy, too, if he knew what he'd done. *Probably,* she thought, thinking of the laughing pilots she'd known at her old RAF base in Surrey, and her brother, a bomber pilot himself (although thankfully currently on leave). They were none of them monsters. *Just following orders.* It was all about the discipline, after all, self-control.

"Something you apparently have none of," her middle-aged wing commander had pronounced at her dismissal. His voice spiraled up out of nowhere. (It had a horrible habit of doing that.)

"I have plenty," she'd retorted, keeping her smarting stare fixed on his by an effort of will.

The wing commander had sneered, as though her having the temerity to defend herself had confirmed everything he'd been so certain he knew about her.

"You knew nothing," she told him now.

Pushing his mortifying disgust away, ready to taunt her another time, she determinedly returned to the article. Some of the recovered album's photographs had been printed alongside the commentary: grainy pictures of the woman's parents on their wedding day, a studio portrait of them holding her as a baby. Rose touched her fingertip to it, imagining the babe in her own arms before she could stop herself, feeling her muscles, her heart ache.

It was then, with all her old grief washing through her, making her raw, that she noticed the advertisement. It was wedged beneath the photograph, just a few lines surrounded by a black border, entirely inconspicuous, and yet, very quickly, it became all she could see.

Wanted: companion to escort a young, orphaned child to Australia.
All expenses as well as passage covered.
Interested parties to apply without delay to 32 Williams Street, Belgravia.

"Oh," she said, the word catching in her throat, more than it might have, had she not just been fixating on that photograph.

The woman beside her turned, like she might be about to ask what was wrong.

Rose hardly noticed. She was reading the advertisement over, wondering what could have happened to make this child an orphan (the war, probably), trying to imagine how terrified it must be, about to be sent to the other side of the world with a stranger. A *stranger.* She dropped her hand, resting it on her empty stomach. The poor thing.

Interested parties to apply without delay to 32 Williams Street, Belgravia.

But that was so close to Victoria. And they were almost at Paddington, in surprisingly good time. She turned to the window, her pale reflection staring back at her, brow creased beneath her felt hat, thinking. . . .

But no, *no*, what would the point be in going to see them? She had a life here. A *fiancé*. She couldn't travel to Australia.

Of course she couldn't.

This tragic little thing was really none of her affair.

Absolutely, categorically none.

She looked again at the advertisement.

How young was young? she wondered.

And where exactly *was* Williams Street?

"No idea," said the soldier who'd commented on the smoke, "but someone will know at Victoria. Ask one of the clerks."

She nodded slowly. She could ask, of course.

No harm in doing that.

When she got there.

And actually, if she gave up on her dash to Oxford Street (so tempting), she could even drop by at Williams Street before tea, perhaps arrange an appointment for later to find out more. Lionel had offered to collect her himself from Victoria and take her to the Goring, but she could just as easily walk. Maybe.

If Williams Street really was on the way . . .

It wasn't. But, having caught the Tube direct from Paddington, she got to Victoria with an hour to spare, and it was close enough as to make passing by barely a diversion at all.

It started to rain as she left the station, though—not heavily, not enough to justify an umbrella (which was fortunate, since she'd left hers in Ilfracombe), but an icy drizzle that the wind made a weapon of, whipping it horizontal, stinging her cheeks, sending discarded rubbish gusting along the grimy pavements. She walked with her head bowed, holding her hat on tight as she followed the ticket clerk's directions. She didn't consider giving up and heading straight for the Goring, despite the grim weather. If anything, the fact that she was now so cold and wet made her all the more determined to press on. She'd come this far. . . .

"Stubborn," her uncle had pronounced, when she'd stopped to telephone his office at Whitehall—where he was always working, Saturday or no—using one of the station's public booths to let him know that he shouldn't worry about collecting her.

"Interested," she'd countered.

"Impulsive," he'd said, in the deep voice he always used whenever he was trying to be stern. "Why not wait, we can chat it through over tea?"

"You just want to talk me out of it."

"I'm worried you'll get held up," he'd said, not denying it. "You don't want to do that. They've promised a wonderful spread. Mock-egg sandwiches with mock mayonnaise."

"Oh, that sounds *lovely.*"

"Go straight there, have a glass of something. There mightn't even be anyone in when you get to this Thirty-two Williams Street."

"Then I'll leave a note, tell them where I am."

"They'd probably prefer you sent a letter, gave them warning."

"The advertisement says to apply without delay."

"Rather rum to turn up unannounced, though, Rosie . . ."

And so they'd gone on, him throwing up obstacles, her knocking them down, gently, realizing he was only being so cautious because he cared. Loving him more than ever for that, she'd assured him that yes, she knew how far away Australia was, and no, she had no intention of getting sucked into an interview before tea, she absolutely wouldn't make any reckless decisions either. "Not without talking to you first."

"Don't make any reckless decisions at all," he'd replied, exasperated, making her laugh, in spite of herself. "Rosie," he'd said, not laughing, "tell me you realize that this child, however alone, can never make up for—"

"That's not what this is about," she'd said, too quickly, no longer laughing either.

He'd sighed heavily, far from convinced (for which she could hardly blame him), and had told her that if she was so miserable in Devon, he'd help her find something new, there was no need to go to such lengths, and there were other options beyond the damned army. She'd said she knew that, but needed to look into this first, she'd always wonder about the child otherwise. Then, hearing him emit another long sigh—picturing him in his paneled office, elegant as ever in a three-piece, his kind face puckered by heart-pinching concern—had entreated him to not worry.

"Not worry?" he'd said. "All I do is worry about you and your brother. That's my job."

"No, you have one of those."

"This? The War Office? Nothing but a byline."

"Does Winston know?"

"Of course."

"I'm just calling by," she'd said. "Honestly . . ."

"Go then," he'd said reluctantly. "Hurry. You don't want to risk missing your cake. I've ordered mock chocolate. The three of us can't eat it alone."

"Three?" She'd sat up straighter. "Xander's coming? Did he *call* . . . ?"

She'd never found out. The line, with excruciating timing, had pipped, signaling an end to her pennies. "No," she'd exclaimed, rifling through her empty purse, "no, no, no."

She was still kicking herself for not mentioning Xander sooner. Why hadn't she done that?

And had he *really* been in touch with Lionel to say he was coming?

Part of her would love to think he had. That—after that wire, the pain of their recent, all-too-scarce meetings—he actually *wanted* to put himself out for her again. It would be . . . nice . . . to think that was possible. But she was wary of believing it, bruised from how many times he'd now let her down; scared of being disappointed if he did it again.

Trying to stop second-guessing it, and braced against another gust of wet wind, she pressed on, turning at the road the clerk had told her to look out for. She passed a corner public house, a church, then turned again, and again, until she came to the short, leafy enclave that was Williams Street.

It was a beautifully manicured crescent: all stuccoed town houses, with large bay windows and polished front steps. A gentrified road, without doubt. The type where bankers and lawyers lived. She wasn't surprised to find herself in such a place. While she and Joe had spent much of their childhoods in a small Dulwich vicarage, and, after their parents had reluctantly moved abroad, between their army-funded boarding school and Lionel's tiny bachelor flat in Parsons Green—so small, they'd had to coin-toss every holiday for who got the spare bedroom, and who the sofa—she had enough school friends from this area to have expected something akin to this grandeur. The wealth didn't intimidate her. It wasn't *that* which made her pulse jump, as she carried on walking. No, it was the fact that she was, quite suddenly, here. About to become an *interested party* (possibly) applying without delay.

She'd been so busy rushing around—telephoning Lionel, battling the elements, worrying over Xander—that she'd given herself no pause to think. Now, though, in the solitude of the blustery street, with her heels clicking conspicuously on the wet pavement, her mind filled with how little she knew of the people she was about to barge in on (*nothing, in fact*, came Lionel's voice), and the enormity of what might follow if they really did ask her to come back for a proper interview, offer her the position.

Would she take it?

Could she seriously be considering leaving everything here—for months, at least—and doing that?

On a sunnier day, she might have halted at the question, wondered at herself for coming this far without being certain of the answer—or how the practicalities would even work: what kind of notice Hector would need; how Xander might react. . . .

But it wasn't a sunnier day. The rain, if anything, was intensifying, and it really didn't seem an appropriate moment for contemplation. Besides, she didn't want to begin searching for reasons not to press ahead. Impulsive she might be (*irrational even*, chimed another voice—Xander's this time), but she'd meant what she'd said before: she wanted to know that this child was going to be cared for. After everything she'd lost, it simply felt so very . . . right . . . that she should do that. The first right thing she'd done in months, actually.

What could be wrong about that?

Telling herself, *Nothing*, she picked up her pace and carried on.

There was no iron left on the street—no gates, nor railings, nor banisters down to the basement kitchens—all assuredly taken, like so much of the country's metal, to be melted for munitions. The house numbers had clearly gone the same way. None of the black doors had anything beyond modestly painted markings to identify them.

Until number thirty-two, that was.

"My word," said Rose, reaching its front steps.

This time, she did stop. Heedless of the now heavy downpour, she tipped her head back, staring. She'd never seen anything like it. Not only was the front door painted in vibrant fuchsia, but the pink was itself covered in countless, beautifully curled "32"s, all in gold. The house's window frames had been painted, too, and had boxes beneath them, filled not with flowers, but with pinwheels that spun frantically, spiking the gray day with even more color. The front path added yet another layer, resplendent in a warm yellow that seemed to glow beneath Rose's black brogues. . . .

"It's for Walter," came a low voice from the kitchen door below, making her start. "She did it all for him."

Rose turned, her astonishment deepening as she saw an elderly man peering up at her, dressed in the traditional tie, tails, and apron of an Edwardian butler. His eyes met hers, dark and appraising in his wrinkled, weathered face.

"I suppose you've come about the advertisement," he said, speaking before she could gather her wits to introduce herself, or ask who Walter was (the orphaned child? she wondered). His tone was weary, resigned. It seemed she wasn't the first person to call.

She was still trying to decide whether that was a good or bad thing when he gestured her downward.

"You'd better come in," he said. "I'm Lester. I'll take you to Miss Barnes."

CHAPTER TWO

The kitchen Lester showed Rose into was stiflingly warm after the wintry outside, heated by a vast fire that blazed in the grate, making her skin burn beneath the several layers of clothing she'd piled on under her bedsheets that morning. It was homely, too — with a scrubbed wooden table, copper pans hanging on hooks, all of that — and immaculately tidy, in a way that put the cluttered kitchen of Rose's landlady to shame. (She loved a knickknack, her collection of house-shaped teapots just the start of it. *Nothing like a bit of Royal Doulton.*) But, just as with Lester, the room was dressed from a different era. Really, with its blackened range and flickering oil lamps, it might have been a set for a costume play.

"Miss Barnes won't be able to give you long," said Lester, shuffling across the flagstone floor. "No more than an hour or two."

"I'm afraid I can't stay long myself," said Rose. "I was hoping to arrange a time for later."

"She won't be able to see you later."

"Not at all?"

"No."

"Oh," said Rose, deflated.

"Tomorrow will be difficult too," said Lester. "Can you come Monday?"

"I'm only here for the day."

He frowned. "Best speak to her. Leave your wet things on the rail there, and follow me."

Seeing nothing else for it, Rose did as she was told.

He was silent as he led her up the internal stairs, more pulling than propelling himself from step to step. She, seeing the effort it cost him, hung back, anxious not to come across as rushing him. Feeling it would be wrong to make him talk, too, she contained the many questions she was itching to ask (who Miss Barnes was, whether she was the "she" who'd decorated the house, how many other applicants there'd been . . .), and limited herself only to inquiring about whether Walter *was* the child in question, to which she got a short nod.

"He lives here?" she asked, once they'd overcome the final step.

"For now," said Lester.

"How old is he?"

"Four," Lester replied, reaching for the landing door.

"Four?" she said, overly loudly, too taken aback to conceal her surprise. Lester turned, clearly taken aback himself, at her decibel.

"It's so little," she said, by way of explanation. It really was. *Four.* She'd thought maybe seven, or six at the least. Hector Arden's granddaughter was four, for heaven's sake, all but a baby with her round cheeks and lisping words. She often came by the office to play on Rose's typewriter, scribble on her grandfather's blackboard, so carefree. It was awful imagining her being ripped from her small, trusted world. Even the evacuees around the village had their friends nearby, siblings; mothers who visited whenever they could. . . .

"He'll be five in May," said Lester.

"Will he?" Rose wasn't convinced that made it much better. Judging by the way Lester had spoken, as defeated as ever, he wasn't either. She found herself warming to him, for that. For the first time, she felt some hint of compassion from him for this little boy.

"Come along." He opened the door, revealing a large, polished hallway. Another fire burned, lifting the gloom of the dismal day. "Miss Barnes will have seen you coming," he said, heading, much to Rose's dismay, for yet another flight of stairs. "She'll be waiting."

It sounded rather foreboding. *She'll be waiting.* Had Rose not still been struggling to come to terms with Walter's age, she might have been more daunted. Instead, as she followed Lester, she looked around, searching for signs of the small Walter, finding them, sweetly, everywhere: a miniature pair of yellow Wellington boots by the porch (*He likes yellow,* she thought, remembering the brick front path), a toy lion hidden in a potted plant, more animals arranged over the base of the stairs: zebras chatting to elephants, giraffes to penguins. Lester didn't stoop to tidy the animals away, despite his meticulously kept kitchen. He stepped around them, leaving the mess just as it was for Walter, making Rose like him more.

She liked, too, that a trio of Walter's crayon drawings had been hung on the stairwell, in gilt frames of their own, right alongside obviously expensive pieces of art. Just as with the decorations outside, the animals below, it gave her a growing sense that he was treasured in this house, loved — much more than his being parceled off to Australia suggested. The first drawing was of a park (a green line for grass, blue for the sky), the second, what appeared to be a river (another blue line), and the third, a Christmas tree (lots more green). Each had a pair of stick people holding hands, one tall with squiggly curls, the other small, both smiling. *Me and my mummy,* an adult had written beneath the one of the Christmas tree, making Rose ache, *by Walter Lucknow.*

There were photographs on the walls as well, although none of anyone who could have been Walter, or his poor lost mummy. Rather, they were turn-of-the-century, fizzing with extravagantly dressed women, cigarette holders in hand, mouths wide in hilarity. Rose peered into their faces, trying to decide which, if any, might be Miss Barnes. *You'll never guess,* they seemed to say. She thought about asking Lester, then decided just as quickly against it. He was breathing very heavily.

She was so relieved when they finally reached the landing and came to a halt outside a closed door, she almost forgot to be apprehensive about the thought of Miss Barnes behind it. It was her heart that reminded her, racing uncomfortably in her chest. She had no opportunity to steady herself, though, or even think about whether she should have stolen a moment to visit the lavatory, attempt to do something about her assuredly bedraggled appearance, because Lester knocked on the door, then opened it without pause, and, before Rose knew it, they were both crossing the threshold of an ornately decorated bedroom

The scent was the first thing that struck her. It took her a second to place it, to filter it from the perfume of the room's hothouse flowers, the smoke that wafted from yet another fire (where did all this coal come from?). But then she had it, and within a breath she'd forgotten the coal, the flowers too, because the harsh, clinical mix of carbolic and sickness was all she could smell. It transported her, far too evocatively, back to that hospital ward, September.

She didn't let the memory of those hideous weeks take over, though. She'd finally learned how not to do that. Besides, Lester spoke, drawing her attention to an elderly woman in a wheelchair over by the rain-thrashed window—a woman who could only be Miss Barnes—and, to Rose's distress, it was painfully apparent that this time it was she who was gravely ill. Not only ill. Dying. Her frail body was simply too wasted for there to be any other conclusion. Her bones jutted pitifully from beneath her dressing robe, her face was nothing but hollows, and her skeletal hands were covered in bruises: the puncture marks of needles.

Her gray eyes alone had life within them. As they moved, seeking Rose's, Rose's mind raced, making awful sense of Walter's departure, the urgency of that advertisement. *Interested parties to apply without delay.* Miss Barnes couldn't keep Walter, of course she couldn't. She was running out of time. . . .

"Don't look so alarmed," said Miss Barnes, making Rose realize with a start that that was exactly how she'd been looking. Miss Barnes didn't seem offended by her expression, though. On the contrary, her eyes shone with warmth, kindness, reminding Rose that, ill as she was, she was also almost certainly the woman who'd hung Walter's crayon drawings on her walls, decorated the entire façade of her house for him. "It's like I tell Walter," Miss Barnes said, "I appear far more horrifying than I am."

"I'm not horrified," Rose said, a lie, but somehow she summoned a smile to go with it.

"Just soaking," said Miss Barnes, and smiled too, making Rose glad she had. "I must say you look like a drowned rat."

"It's a drowning kind of day," said Rose.

"Yet," Miss Barnes said, "you battled through it."

"I did."

"You're the first to call without an appointment, you know."

"I'm sorry," said Rose. "I came to make one . . ."

"The young lady has plans elsewhere," said Lester.

"I have to be at the Goring at three. It's my birthday . . ."

"Your birthday?" Miss Barnes's eyes widened in surprise. Or was it hope? "You came on your birthday?"

"Yes," said Rose. "But I — "

"Your birthday," Miss Barnes repeated. She looked past Rose, toward Lester. "Well, well."

She invited Rose to call her Vivian after that, and take a seat too. "By the fire, you need to dry off."

"I really mustn't stay long," said Rose, avoiding the fire (her layers), choosing an armchair beside Miss Barnes, *Vivian*, instead. "Where's Walter?" she asked. "It's so quiet . . ."

"He naps over luncheon," said Vivian. "We have a temporary nanny for him. Lester's cousin, as it happens. Her grandchildren are eager to have her back."

"They'll have her soon enough," said Lester, padding off — Rose hoped for a rest of his own — turning at the door to remind Vivian that her doctor was due at four.

"I'm always less than myself after his visits," said Vivian to Rose, "otherwise I really would ask you back this evening." She smiled. "I do envy you, going to the Goring. It's my favorite."

"My uncle's too."

"He has impeccable taste. They used to do the most delectable hazelnut ganache."

"It's mock chocolate cake today," said Rose. "I can't begin to think what that is."

"Perhaps it's best not to know, my dear. Now, bring that clock closer so we can keep an eye on ourselves."

She was very efficient with their limited time together. Although she became perceptibly more tired as the minutes flew by, she never stopped talking — afraid, Rose felt increasingly, sadly certain, to waste a single second — and refused all of Rose's offers to fetch her water or tea. "Plenty of opportunity for that later."

There should have been plenty of opportunity too for Rose to admit that she'd only come that day to make inquiries, be assured that Walter was going to be all right. *I haven't made my mind up that I can take him myself yet.* But Vivian seemed so ready to assume that she was prepared to travel, and was so very ill, that Rose (eyeing the clock anxiously, the closer three o'clock drew) couldn't bear to disappoint her, not in the way all the other applicants apparently had. She liked her too much.

"You're the thirteenth to call," Vivian said, "in a week."

"The thirteenth," echoed Rose, visualizing the long line of others in her seat, "that doesn't feel very lucky."

"It doesn't, does it?" said Vivian, with her smile that was starting to become familiar, and that Rose discovered made it a lot less difficult to picture her as one of the exuberant women in the stairwell's photographs. "Most of them needed passage for their other children," she went on, smile dropping, "money to help them set up over there. Certainly none came on their birthday. There was one awful girl who was chewing something . . ."

"Gum?" Rose suggested.

"I don't know," said Vivian, coughing, "but she wanted to be paid just for coming to perplex me. She didn't ask about Walter, just his pinwheels. She couldn't seem to understand them at all." She stared at Rose, kerchief to her mouth. "Do you understand them?"

"I suppose I've been thinking they're to try and make him happier . . ."

"Yes," said Vivian, coughing again, "*yes*, and less scared. He's always been horribly daunted by this house, mausoleum that it is." Another cough. She closed her eyes, in obvious pain, and Rose sat forward, ready to insist she should fetch a drink, but Vivian drew a rattling breath and carried on, talking of how pointless modernization would be, how she couldn't bear anyway to plaster over her memories. "Lester's just the same, you'll have noticed his uniform, but what does that mean to poor old Walter? We're a pair of dinosaurs to him. He never used to get off Mabel's lap when they called."

"Mabel?"

"His mother, my . . . great-niece. A darling." Vivian tried to smile again, but it twisted, crooked with grief. "She came from Australia just before Walter was born. I helped her . . ."

"I'm so sorry," said Rose.

"Yes," said Vivian, and dropped her head backward, silent for several seconds. When she spoke again, Rose could tell she was having to force herself to do it. "She was killed just over two months ago, on Christmas Eve."

"Oh," said Rose, picturing that crayon Christmas tree, *Me and my mummy.* "Oh no."

"We didn't tell Walter until the new year. We said she'd gone away. He still thinks she was killed at the start of January. I couldn't abide Christmas to be the time he lost her. . . ."

"I am so sorry," Rose said again, and to her mortification, felt tears in her eyes. She brushed them away impatiently. This wasn't her grief. She had no right to make it hers. . . .

And she wasn't going to ask how Mabel had died. It felt too intrusive to do that.

Vivian didn't volunteer the information either.

"There's no father, I'm afraid," was all she said.

"He fought?" Rose asked.

"In a manner."

"A manner?" said Rose.

"You'll muddle it out," said Vivian, shifting her bones in her chair. "You seem a bright enough thing."

Rose wondered whether Hector Arden would agree.

"Now," said Vivian, with a glance at the carriage clock (to Rose's horror, it was somehow twenty past three already, *twenty past three*), "we must get on. We have a deal still to discuss."

She left a pause. If ever there was a moment for Rose to insist it was time for her to go, or raise the many reasons why she mightn't be able to take the position herself (her life, Xander, and so on), that lengthening silence felt like it.

But she said nothing. Horrendous as she by now felt about the others waiting for her in the restaurant, she simply couldn't make herself cut the interview short.

She wasn't sure she wanted to.

And then Vivian was talking again anyway, asking her how soon she'd be able to move into Williams Street, if they pressed ahead. She'd been unwell for a long time, she said, but had recently become much worse. "I don't mind for myself," she insisted, "I'm at the end of what's been a wonderful escapade, but I'm terrified for Walter. This decision that can't be rushed, *must* be rushed, and I want whoever takes him to live here first. He knows we're looking for a new nanny, but not that he's going away. When we tell him, he needs to feel like he's leaving with a friend."

"Of course," said Rose, Lionel's voice blazing in her head. *Don't make any reckless decisions.* "I'm sure that wouldn't be a problem." *Are you?* Lionel demanded. "As a secretary, I don't have particularly big shoes to fill."

"That's entirely to your credit," said Vivian, stifling another cough with her kerchief.

She talked on stoically, telling Rose that she wanted her to think seriously about doing this, to which Rose found herself saying she would, very seriously, and knew then that she of course already was. "I had a feeling when I saw you arrive," Vivian said, gesturing at the pinwheel-bordered window. "I watched you looking at our yellow bricks. I'm so glad I wasn't wrong." She spoke of the part of Australia Walter was headed to, the large estate in Queensland Mabel had come from, and which Vivian's own late sister had bought with her husband when they'd first moved there, back in the 1880s. "An old sugar plantation," Vivian said, "although they farm cattle now. My sister and I led rather different lives." She said her sister was long dead, and there wasn't much of the family left anymore, just her sister's daughter, Lauren, and Lauren's two children — Walter's aunt and uncle — Esme and Max.

"Mabel's brother and sister?" said Rose, more and more drawn in.

Vivian coughed again, which Rose took as a "Yes," and was glad that Walter was at least being sent to relatives. It felt better that way, even if they were still strangers.

"Esme's married herself," Vivian said, "although there are no children."

"And Max?"

"No," said Vivian softly, "no. He's only recently home. He was injured in Egypt, much better out of it . . ."

"A soldier?" Rose asked.

"Pilot."

"Right." Rose couldn't seem to get away from them.

They talked more. Vivian wanted to know about the work Rose did for Hector, her background too, and Rose, who'd decided to stop looking at the time because it made her sweat every time she did, told her about her childhood at the vicarage in Dulwich, then how, when she was twelve, her father had been offered a post in the army, as a chaplain for the troops. "It meant him and Mum going overseas. Joe and I were crushed, Mum and Dad hated it too, but the army offered to pay for school for Joe and me. We'd never have been able to afford it otherwise . . ."

"So they went for you," said Vivian.

"They went for us," said Rose. "And wrote *constantly*. They actually spoke about giving it all up last time they were home on leave, coming back for good. But then the war started . . ."

"Oh, the war," said Vivian wearily. "Have you seen them since?"

"No."

"That's hard."

"It is," said Rose. Used as she'd become to the pain of missing them, she never missed them less than she ever had. It was the same for them, she knew. "Lionel's always been wonderful, though. I don't know what Joe and I would have done without him." She laughed uncomfortably. "He doesn't deserve me showing up so late today."

"I'm sure he'll forgive you," said Vivian. "You're the forgivable kind."

Rose hoped she was right.

"Now tell me about this school of yours," Vivian said. "Did you have fun?"

"Probably too much."

"As it should be. Your brother too, I hope?"

"Oh yes," said Rose, replaying the countless times Lionel had bemoaned yet another summons to Joe's headmaster's office, "don't worry about that."

"And how did a vicar produce such naughty children?"

"Well, he didn't do it alone. My mother was a chorus girl." Truth. The story went that she'd been coerced into bulking up the parish choir one Sunday morning, had caught Rose's father's eye over the communion wine, and that had been that. "Dad says Joe and I are her fault."

Vivian laughed, then coughed. "You went to university?"

"No, the army wouldn't cover that. Besides," Rose smiled, "a friend helped me get a job as a receptionist at a jazz club in Soho."

"Wonderful," said Vivian, closing her eyes. "Wonderful. But how did you go from that, to Ilfracombe?"

"Not entirely happily," said Rose with an uneasy frown, and no desire to go into it.

Thankfully, Vivian didn't ask her to. She exhaled and sank back further into her chair, spent.

"Ring that bell for me, would you?" she said, raising a finger at a cord to her left, seemingly too exhausted to move.

Exhaling herself, Rose did as she was asked, she assumed to let Lester know they were finished.

"I'm still waiting for you to say you'll come back," said Vivian.

"I know you are . . ." began Rose.

"But you're being sensible and thinking," said Vivian, finishing her sentence for her. "Consideration can be overrated, you know."

"Can it?" said Rose, smiling, but not for long, because she risked a look at the clock, and it was even later than she'd feared: almost four.

"I'm sorry," said Vivian, following her gaze. "I've taken advantage of your better nature."

"You have."

"And I'm about to do it again. I hope I'm the forgivable kind as well."

Rose frowned, unclear what she meant, then turned, hearing the door open behind her. It couldn't be Lester. It was too quick. She thought maybe the doctor . . .

But it wasn't a man at all. It was a gray-haired woman, who looked a little like Lester with her angular face, only she was smiling more. And to Rose's surprise, she had a little boy by the hand. A little boy who had rich, glossy curls, skin much darker than she honestly had been expecting of a nephew of Vivian's, and who wore a yellow knitted jumper. He was cherubic, absolutely beautiful, but so shy. He hung back, clutching a floppy rabbit, trying to hide behind Lester's cousin's skirt as she led him on, toward Rose.

Rose realized, as they approached, what Vivian had been talking about. *I'm about to do it again.* The bell had been for them, not Lester at all. *She wanted me to see him,* Rose thought, and although it *was* undeniably manipulative of her, she really didn't care. Walter was peeking up at her uncertainly, still clinging to his nanny's hand, and was quite the most lost-looking child she'd ever seen.

"Hello," she said, and, unable to bear that she was making him so wary, got up, crouching before him, just as she did with Hector's granddaughter. His cheeks were flushed. He smelled sweet, of laundry powder. "Are you Walter?"

"Yes," he whispered.

"I'm Rose, but you can call me Rosie. Everyone does."

His eyes held hers. They were blue. Bright blue in his dark face.

"Does everyone call you Walter?" she asked.

"Yes," he whispered again.

"I liked your drawings on the stairs. They're very good."

He stared a second longer. Then he smiled. It was small, and very hesitant—heartbreakingly so—but it *was* a smile. "They're of my mummy," he said.

"I know." She smiled too. She really couldn't help herself.

Oh God, she thought, *Lionel's going to kill me.*

And as for Xander…

CHAPTER THREE

Xander wasn't at the restaurant. The third Lionel had mentioned on the telephone turned out to be Sarah, Joe's perpetually on-then-off-again girlfriend: a pretty, no-nonsense Pitman's graduate, currently working at the Ministry of Information, with far superior typing speeds to Rose. (Would she be game for a move to Ilfracombe? Rose wondered.) Sarah kept breaking things off with Joe on the basis that he kept failing to propose to her, but couldn't ever seem to resist his entreaties to give him another chance. He'd had nine of those now, by Rose's count.

"I hope you don't mind me coming," Sarah said, standing to kiss Rose.

"I hope you don't mind me being so late," said Rose, fixing a smile on her face, refusing to allow Sarah, or anyone else—herself included—to realize how let down she felt by Xander's absence. She'd dreaded facing him the whole way there, knowing that Lionel would have said something about the advertisement, and that she'd have to tell them both what she'd just agreed to, but it felt so much worse that he truly hadn't come. Hard as she'd fought to keep her expectations low, she'd become all but convinced, on her sprint through the rain from Williams Street, that he'd be waiting. *Who else could it be?* she'd thought.

"He sent you this," said Joe, seeing directly through her, as he'd always been able to do, and holding up the remnants of a champagne bottle. "This too . . ." He rummaged among the detritus of empty plates to find a sealed envelope. It took him two attempts to pick it up. He was absolutely blind.

"How much of my champagne have you drunk?" Rose asked.

"Almost exactly one third," he said.

"And the rest," said Sarah.

"There might have been some wine too," said Lionel, swaying around the table to hug Rose, well lubricated himself. It should at least help *him* take her decision on the chin. "Happy birthday, my darling."

"Thank you," she said, "and again, I'm so sorry."

"For being late? Or doing the interview when you promised you wouldn't?"

"Both. I never intended either . . ."

"Excellent," said Joe, "'s how all the best things happen."

"You're not back flying tonight, are you?" she said.

"Let's hope not," he said, and laughed.

Sarah didn't. She looked like she was already regretting his ninth life. Rose could never be certain whether to really like her or not. She supposed Joe had much the same trouble, hence his lack of proposal.

"Course he's not flying," said Lionel. "Another week before that. Now don't disappear, I'm going to let them know to bring more sandwiches."

While he went, Joe upended the last of the champagne into a glass for Rose, and Rose opened Xander's note.

I couldn't come, he wrote, *not with Lionel and Joe there. I hope you understand. Swing by to see me later, kid. Miss the last train back. It's been too long. X*

She sighed, too upset to want to understand anything, and frowning at that "X." She never could make out whether he meant it as an initial, or a kiss.

"No scowling," said Joe, sloshing champagne as he held out her glass. His hands shook too much lately, even without alcohol. "Not on your almost-birthday. Drink up, and tell us all about this passage down under that Lionel's determined to talk you out of . . ."

Lionel didn't talk her out of anything. He made several attempts as they ate their mock eggs, then persevered through the cake ("Prunes," declared Sarah, "lots of beetroot too," confirming that, so far as the ingredients were concerned, ignorance was indeed preferable to enlightenment), but Rose wasn't having any of it.

"If you'd been there with me," she said, "met them all, you'd understand. It's desperate there, Lionel."

"That doesn't make it your responsibility."

"No," said Rose. "I've made it that. I can't tell you how . . . *liberating* . . . it feels to have chosen something again."

"You're definitely going through with it, then?" said Joe.

"Yes, as long as I don't mess it up with Walter when I move in."

"You'll be fine."

"I hope so," said Rose. Already, she couldn't stand the thought of letting any of them down. Walter especially. She kept reliving his tiny smile, the utter vulnerability of him, clinging to Lester's cousin's skirts, knowing he was going to lose her too. The way he'd clutched his rabbit, like it was a safety belt, dimples in his knuckles. His mother had given it to him, she was certain.

"When do you start?" asked Joe.

"Soon," she said. "I need to talk to Hector. I told Vivian I'd wire on Monday to confirm dates . . ." She turned to Sarah.

"What?" Sarah said, fork to her mouth. "Why are you looking at me like that?"

"Do you like Devon?" Rose asked.

Sarah didn't, and she wasn't game for a move to Ilfracombe either (no great shock), but did, it transpired, know someone who might be.

"Really?" said Rose, deciding she might like her after all.

"Maybe," said Sarah. "She's from somewhere south, I'm not sure *that* south, but I'll ask. She's stuck in a munitions factory at the moment."

"When do you sail?" asked Joe.

"Vivian says next month."

"What about the torpedoes?" asked Sarah.

"She'll go in convoy," said Joe. "It'll be safe once they clear the Atlantic. They'll go around the Cape, through Colombo. Yes." His eyes lit up. "You can surprise Mum and Dad."

"Now hang on," said Lionel, "*hang on . . .*"

But Rose wasn't hanging anywhere. "I've made up my mind," she said, refilling his glass. "I'm sorry, but I have. I'll be back by Christmas."

"That should sweeten it for Xander," said Sarah. "Honestly, I think you're mad leaving him. I could give you a list as long as my arm of girls who'd give their eyeteeth to take your place."

"Not you, though," said Joe, "obviously."

"Are you going to call by?" Sarah asked, ignoring Joe, and nodding at Xander's card, which Rose realized too late she'd left bare on the table.

Flushing, she reached out to put it in her bag, hoping that Lionel and Joe hadn't read it, especially the part about Xander not wanting to see them — or her staying the night, for that matter. "Yes, I'm going."

"Maybe I'll *swing by* with you," said Joe, letting her know he for one had read everything. "It'll make his day."

"You can help Rosie catch her last train," said Lionel, confirming he'd seen it all too. "Or perhaps I should come as well . . ."

"Of course you shouldn't," said Sarah.

"I don't think they were being serious," said Rose.

"You need to do something about your hair," said Sarah, absolutely serious. "You can't let him end things."

"Her hair's not that bad," said Joe, signaling at the waiter for another bottle.

And while Sarah turned her attention on him, telling him he'd had enough, Lionel picked up his chair and moved around the table, shifting her sideways, sitting next to Rose.

"Now I'm only going to ask this one more time," he said, taking her hand tipsily. "Are you *sure* about chaperoning this little chap?"

"I am," she said. "Completely."

He looked into her eyes, still needing, she could tell, to be convinced. She tightened her hold on his, entreating him to get there, to trust her as he'd used to trust her, and was relieved when at length he nodded, squeezing her hand back.

"All right," he said gruffly. "Tell Hector I'll make sure he's not left short-handed, even if this friend of Sarah's can't do it."

"Thank you."

"You have to have lots of dinners with me before you go, that's my condition."

"How brutal of you."

"I won't be moved," he said. "Now finish your cake. You're far too skinny."

Rose almost started to relax after that. She very much wanted to finish her cake, if only for Lionel. But the thought of Xander hung over her, making it difficult to stomach more than a few bites. She hated that he hadn't come. And she hated that he still didn't know she was going away. She kept thinking of what he'd said the last time he'd visited her in Ilfracombe, weeks ago: one of the few visits he'd made over the winter. *This distance is killing us. It's like you've come here to kill us.* That was with her in Devon. *Devon.*

She pressed her fork into her crumbs, remembering the day they'd met. He'd come by the jazz club she used to work at, just before the start of the war, she'd told him she liked his accent, it made him sound like a gangster, and he'd told her to come have a drink with him, he'd talk to her more. From that moment on, it had been nothing but easy between them, carefree. They'd gone dancing every night after her shift, shocked his doormen by going back to the hotel he was lodged at, racing up to his room. He hadn't been her first ("Floozy," he'd said), just the first she'd never imagined being without. . . .

She couldn't believe how rapidly they'd unraveled from that, to this endless round of hurt they caused one another now. She knew how it had happened. They *all* knew how it had happened: the grief and regret, so much regret, that had done it to them. She only wished she had the faintest idea how they were meant to find their way out of it.

"Well, it's not going to be with you disappearing off to a sugar plantation with some stranger's kid for the rest of the year," said Xander, a couple of hours later, "I'll tell you that for free."

"They farm cattle now."

"I don't actually give a damn, Rosie."

His New Yorker accent was always stronger when he was angry. He wasn't shouting, though. He was being very careful not to do that. They were in his hotel bar. She'd suggested they go there quite deliberately when she'd had the receptionist call him down from his room, knowing he'd have to remain on best behavior.

The hotel was as upmarket as the Goring: a plush Mayfair establishment that was, she'd gradually pieced together, no less than he was used to. Not that he paid for it. A New York broadsheet footed his bills, which, she supposed, meant he was really very good at what he did. Or that his family owned the paper. ("My family doesn't own the paper," he'd laughed, back in happier times.)

Lionel had driven her over in his chauffeured staff motor, insisting it was as good as on his way home. (It wasn't, not even at a stretch.)

"Try not to argue tonight," he'd counseled her, as they'd hugged good-bye. "You'll be the one who ends up most upset. Leave Xander's telling-off about today for another time." He'd given her a long look. "Don't rile him. . . ."

It had been sound advice. Generous, too, coming from him (who, after all, had done his own share of telling Xander off since September). She'd truly meant to follow it.

And yet now, faced with Xander's barely contained rage, the unfairness that everything that was wrong between them suddenly seemed to be falling at her door, she couldn't quite resist saying, "I got your wire, by the way."

"You didn't like it?"

"I loved it. The bit about me *making it* was wonderful."

"I didn't mean it like that . . ."

"How did you mean it?"

"It's a turn of phrase, I didn't think . . ."

"You're a journalist, Xander. You think about what you write for a living."

"I sent it in a rush, I'm sorry. I had to file copy last minute."

"There are these things called cards. People send them on birthdays, not at the last minute, because the post can take a while . . ."

"I'm sorry. Did you get the champagne at least?"

"Yes, thank you."

"Did you enjoy it?"

"Joe drank most of it. Sarah was annoyed."

"Sarah's back?"

"Seems to be."

"She's a survivor," said Xander, then frowned, running his hands through his brown hair. His shirt crackled with the movement. He always wore such crisp, white shirts. They suited him, with his broad chest, his strong face. So did the relaxed sweaters he wore on Sundays, the casual polos in summer. Everything suited him. Except, these days, her. "I don't want to talk about Sarah," he said. "And I don't wanna talk about Joe, who hates me . . ."

"He doesn't hate you."

"Well that's swell of you to say, Rosie, but he does, and it's kinda feeling like you do too."

"Xander . . ."

"We should be married." He reached across the table, taking her hands, running his thumb over the spectacular diamond he'd given her last July. ("Look at it," Sarah had said, "*look* at it.") Rose normally wore it around her neck because it was too loose, but had put it back on before coming since he hated it when she didn't wear it. "We should have been married for months."

"I know." They'd had the church booked for the last weekend in September.

"Then move back to town. Let me buy us an apartment, one with a shelter . . ."

"I can't, Xander."

"You can . . ."

"I've promised them."

He dropped his head, taking a deep breath, as though for strength. She watched his shoulders rise, then fall. He was still holding her hands. "I'm asking you to stay."

"I know that."

"But you're still going to go?"

She nodded sorrowfully.

He cursed. "Rosie . . ."

"I need to do it, for me as much as anyone. I think it will help . . ."

"So you keep saying."

"I'll only be gone a few months, no different to if I was still in the air force and got posted overseas. And you could be sent anywhere, any time. You're always saying that."

"Sent, though, Rosie. *Sent.* You're asking to go."

"You see, you are good with words," she said, trying for a joke, although she didn't know why. Nothing had ever felt less amusing. "Take more care with my wires in future."

"You still want wires from me?"

"Yes, I still want wires from you," she said. Then, thinking of Sarah's words earlier, *you can't let him end things,* "Do you still want to send them?"

"Of course I still want to send them."

"Good," she said, relieved.

She was sure she was relieved.

He filled his cheeks with another long breath, and expelled it. "Will you stay tonight?"

She hesitated. There wasn't any practical reason why she shouldn't. She didn't have plans for the following day, and could probably even stay another — she was owed leave, and there was no urgency to her speaking to Hector anymore, not now Lionel had promised he'd take care of things with her replacement; she could wire Vivian first thing Monday morning, tell her she'd be back as soon as everything was tied up. She was looking forward to doing that. Already she couldn't wait to be on the other side of her move to Williams Street, getting to know Walter. She knew her own mind about *that.*

Spending the night with Xander, though . . .

"Stay," he said, softer now, imploring, "please stay."

She looked down at their hands, still entwined on the table. She wanted to be able to say yes. In so many ways it would be wonderful to go upstairs with him, lie in his arms, not trawl across rainy London again for a cold, dark train ride home. But they hadn't been together like that for months, not since she'd come out of hospital, no longer carrying their tiny, unformed child. (No one had let her see it. "You don't want to," they'd told her coldly, "and it's already gone to the incinerator.") Her dismissal from the air force had come straight after. She'd fled to the promised peace of Devon, still so weak from the sepsis, her body no longer feeling like hers after all the pain, the doctors treating it like a specimen. . . .

"Rosie?"

"I have to go back," she said. "I'm sorry."

He smiled humorlessly, pushing her hands away. "Have it your way, sweetheart, you always do."

"That's not fair," she said, stung.

"Isn't it?" he said, and, to her disbelief, stood, slamming his chair back, striding from the bar.

People everywhere turned, martinis in hand, staring, obviously wondering what Rose could have done to make such a smart, handsome man behave like that. She set her jaw, burning cheeks working in humiliation, anger too, at herself as well as Xander, because she was so sick of being this disappointing. She refused to cry, though, in front of everyone. She reached under the table, fumbling for her bag, her hat.

She was still down there when she became aware she'd stopped being alone. She looked up, eyes stinging. . . .

"Come on," Xander said heavily, "it's late, there might be a raid. I don't want to make your uncle and brother even madder by letting you go out alone. I'll take you."

CHAPTER FOUR

He stayed with her as far as Paddington. They were painfully silent with one another for the bleak, wet walk to the Underground, then again on the crammed Tube journey. As they stood pressed together in the stale carriage — looking everywhere but at each other, their bodies rigid with forced intimacy — she reflected miserably that they always got to this point in the end: when neither of them knew what else to say.

Their goodbye on the platform at Paddington was stilted, stiff. They stood inches apart, both freezing, the train steaming beside them, neither of them mentioning what had passed in the bar, even though it was all she, for one, was thinking about. He told her to have a safe journey home, and she said he should do the same.

"I could come see you in Devon before you leave," he said.

"You don't have to," she said, knowing he wouldn't anyway. He'd been only three times since she'd moved, despite promising to come many, many more. She'd lost count of the trips she'd made to the station to meet him — makeup done, a nice dress on — only to watch the train he was meant to have caught slowly empty, before giving up, heading back for a hug from her landlady, Enid, then a wire from him the next day with some excuse as to why he'd let her down again. Work, normally; the impossible length of the journey. She wished he'd just admit he preferred to spend his weekends with his foreign correspondent set: people who made him laugh, and were happy, and didn't remind him—just by failing so badly at forgetting—of all they'd lost.

"This has been a terrible night," he said.

"Yes," she agreed.

"Another one." He sighed. "God, Rosie, I miss who you used to be."

It was hardly the first time he'd said it.

It still landed like a slap in the face.

I miss me as well, she wanted to say. *I miss me so much. You were part of this happening to me too, don't forget.*

But she didn't, because she felt perilously close to falling apart as it was, and she knew that if she spoke those words, they'd push her over the edge—they always did—and she couldn't let that happen, not in the middle of a packed concourse, not with hours ahead on the train still to get through.

He dragged his hand wearily around his jaw. "Maybe you're right," he said. "Maybe this time away will be . . . good . . . for you. Better, anyway, for us."

"Yes," she choked, and felt no triumph that he'd given in so quickly, within the space of only one, short evening. Only sadness. Perversely, she wished he'd fought a bit longer to keep her with him, a bit harder.

He'd never been going to do that, though. She realized that. He—who sent champagne rather than himself to uncomfortable afternoon teas, and avoided trip after trip to see her—liked easy, not difficult. It was why he'd never be able to bear it if she did as he asked, moved to London. *I miss who you used to be.* Neither of them could cope with being together, the way things were. She supposed if they could, she'd have thought a deal harder about going to Williams Street in the first place.

The conductor blew his whistle.

"You'd better go," Xander said.

She nodded. She still couldn't trust herself to speak.

He frowned.

They didn't touch.

He told her to take care, that he'd see her soon, then, without a happy-birthday, he turned, leaving her alone for the second time that night.

Only this time, he didn't come back.

"Were you all right getting home?" Sarah asked, when she telephoned Rose at the office on Monday morning.

"Not really," said Rose, keeping her voice low so that Hector —
mercifully slightly deaf, but less than a couple of yards away at his own
paper-strewn desk — wouldn't hear. "There were no seats left by the time I
got on the train, so I had to stand all the way to Reading." She'd bashed her
knee against a stack of trunks, tearing the skin, ruining her last pair of good
stockings; the pain had made it even harder to hold herself together. "We
were delayed again. The last bus had left by the time I got to Barnstaple."

"I don't know where Barnstaple is."

"Twelve miles from my billet. I had to hitch a ride half the way, then
walk the rest." It had been raining. Hard. "I kept thinking something was
going to jump out at me."

"Well, I won't say you brought it on yourself."

"I think you just did."

"Have you heard from Xander since?"

"Another wire," said Rose, glancing at it on her desk.

Hated leaving STOP You make me feel such a criminal STOP Have spoken
to New York and asked to go away myself STOP Could use a change of
this old scene STOP Let me know when you get back to town so we can
try at something nicer to remember STOP Even domestics must get the
odd night off STOP

"You should see him," said Sarah. "Don't leave it like this. Remember
how happy you used to be."

Rose laughed shortly. "Remember is all either of us do." Increasingly, it
felt like the only thing left keeping them together. "I'm hoping when I come
back, it'll be better . . ."

"Hmm," said Sarah skeptically. "And have you told Hector you're
going?"

"Yes, this morning."

"How did he take it?"

"Better than Xander," said Rose, glancing at him scribbling. "He's excited, writing a reference to send to Vivian, and a whole list of requirements
for Lionel. Your friend mightn't make the grade."

"Well, that's why I'm calling," said Sarah, and told Rose she'd already
got hold of her friend, Laura, and Laura was mustard-keen for a move. "She's
from somewhere in Cornwall as it turns out, but Croyde beats Birmingham."

"I'm in Ilfracombe, not Croyde."

"Same difference."

"It's not," said Rose.

"The point is," said Sarah, "her factory only needs a fortnight's notice. I've spoken to Lionel, and he's given me the nod to send Laura's details over, so look out for them."

"I will," said Rose. "Sarah, thank you."

"You do check the post carefully?"

"Once in a while," said Rose, smiling, in spite of everything. "And really, I'm very grateful."

"Well, you've had a horrible time. It sounds like little Walter has too."

"He has," said Rose, edging further into the liking Sarah camp.

"I still think you're mad," said Sarah, ruining it slightly, "but I've promised Joe I'll be supportive."

Everyone in the village inevitably had thoughts on Rose's move as well. As the news spread, the close-knit world of Ilfracombe—which over the winter had threatened to drive Rose quite as lunatic as Sarah believed her (*How's your American, lovely?* The question had followed her everywhere. *Busy again last weekend, was he?*)—positively buzzed with opinion.

Hector, who really had been encouraging from the off, became even more enthusiastic once Laura's résumé arrived and they discovered that she had seventy-five words per minute, excellent references herself, and could be with them on the eighteenth of March.

"You only need stay a day or two for handover," he said to Rose, once he'd made his first shouty telephone call to Laura, confirming the position was hers. "I'm sure Miss Barnes is impatient to have you with her."

Mary at the post office shared Hector's conviction on that matter.

"You're certain March the twentieth will be soon enough?" she asked Rose, leaning across the counter to watch Rose write her wire to Vivian.

"I think so," said Rose, pencil hovering, since she never had mastered the art of talking and writing at the same time. "I told Vivian I'd need a couple of weeks."

"Well don't leave her in suspense," said Mary, waving at Rose's pencil, "finish it off."

Whenever Rose called at the post office after that—which was often since she was back and forth collecting the stockings Sarah surprised her with (*make sure you tell Joe how nice I'm being*), replying to all the questions from Williams Street, agreeing on her wage, giving her full name for the shipping clerk—Mary had something new to ask: about Vivian's clothes, her house, oohing and ahhing when Rose told her about the pinwheels, all the roaring fires.

"Is the coal black-market, do you think?"

"I don't know," said Rose.

Mary was disappointed about that, and that Rose hadn't inquired as to what was actually wrong with Vivian.

"Pneumonia?" she guessed.

"I don't know."

"A growth?" Mary suggested.

"I don't know."

"Pleurisy?"

Rose really didn't know.

But she reassured Mary that Vivian was pleased rather than disappointed about the date of her arrival (*So very relieved* STOP), Walter thankfully glad (*As happy as he knows how to be* STOP), and told her that tickets to Brisbane had been reserved on one of the few liners still carrying passengers rather than troops, departing from Liverpool in the middle of April (*Will wait until you're here to tell Walter* STOP).

"The ship *will* stop at Colombo," said Rose, excitedly. "I'm really going to see Mum and Dad." It had been almost three years. . . .

"*Colombo,*" Mary said. "It sounds ever such a long way. Do you get seasick?"

It was another thing Rose had no answer to. She'd never been out on choppier waters than the Solent on a summer's afternoon crossing to the Isle of Wight.

Mary was really quite worried about that.

The following day, her two sons—both strapping, wind-weathered, and reserved from fighting since they were fishermen—called at the dairy farm, saying their mum had had a word, and they'd happily take Rosie out if she'd prefer to know what she was dealing with, seasickness-wise.

"Really?" she said dubiously, looking through the window at the stubbornly hideous weather outside. "I feel like this is a case where ignorance might be bliss."

"I agree," said Hector's daughter, Anne—the mother of four-year-old

Lottie, also present, eating a bun on Rose's lap. "Is there even anything one can *do* about seasickness?"

"Not much," said Steven at the hardware shop, who'd been a sailor in the last war, and came out onto the High Street that evening to give Rose his best as she returned to her billet. "But it won't last more than a few days if you do get it. It's the snakes you need to worry about, once you get to Australia."

"I heard it were the spiders," said Fiona, from Fiona's Ices, joining them.

Rose offered to let them know her verdict on the matter when she returned, to which they laughed and said, "If you make it," but then both became more serious, saying that riddled as Australia undoubtedly was with deadly creatures, they thought it a lovely thing that she was taking young Walter home to his family there.

"It's a wonderful thing," said Rose's landlady that same night. "If I'd been blessed with a child and was killed," she paused, lifting the kettle from the Aga, "I'd be happy knowing you were looking after it."

"Thank you," said Rose, spooning tea leaves into a lighthouse-embossed pot. "I wish you had had children, but I'm so glad you've not been killed."

"How long do you think you'll stay in Australia?"

"I'm not sure," said Rose. "I suppose just enough time to make sure Walter's settled."

"You're not going to like leaving him," Enid cautioned. "You'll have spent months with him by then."

"I know." The thought had occurred to Rose, too. "But if he's happy . . ."

"Yes," said Enid, smiling, "it'll be worth it. Little lamb. And then you'll have a lovely voyage home. I wonder if you'll go first class." She stared dreamily out through the lead-lined window. It was raining again. "Just think of the food . . ." And she was off, fantasizing about the bananas Rose would have once they reached the Cape, wondering, however, if the water on board would be quite safe to drink. "You'll need to get chlorine tablets. And be careful of your skin. I've heard it can be a bit hotter out of England."

"I've heard much the same," said Rose.

"Will you send me a card for my board?" asked Enid, gesturing at the large cork mat next to the larder. It was covered in postcards, most of them from Enid's church friends: greetings from Swanage, Harrogate, Norwich. . . . There was just a handful from abroad — most of them sent before Rose had been born — of cheerful Tommies waving from French villages.

Enid never let dust gather on any of them. They'd come from her husband, Bert, before he'd gone Missing in Action, aged just twenty, at the Somme.

"I'll send you lots," said Rose.

"Well now," said Enid, "*now,* won't that be lovely?"

The days, so endless through winter, passed with strange speed after that, propelling Rose toward her departure date.

I'm so busy getting ready to see you again, she wrote to Walter, in one of the several letters she sent him over the course of that fortnight: short, chatty notes that would, she hoped, help him feel less shy with her when she arrived. It had been Lottie's mother, Anne, who'd helped her come up with the idea, when Rose had asked her for advice on winning a child's trust.

"Let him get to know you like Lottie has," Anne had said, "a little bit at a time. Softly, softly."

I hope we can do lots of drawing together, Rose wrote. *What else would you like to do?*

She watched the post anxiously for a reply. "We're all doing that," Mary said. It came three days later, with a covering note from Lester's cousin, Catherine, saying what a surprise it had been for Walter getting a letter, it was the first one he'd ever received — *pleased as punch* — and, since he was still learning to write, he'd dictated his own message to her.

Thank you for my letter. It is raining here today. It is cold outside. I would like to go to the park to feed the ducks. I can show you how to do it if you don't know. Love Walter.

He'd written his name himself. It sloped across the bottom of the page on an angle. Rose could picture him doing it, the pencil clasped in his dimply hand.

I'd love you to show me how you feed the ducks, Rose wrote back, *and I was thinking we could go to the zoo too. Did you hear about the zebra who escaped last year in a raid and nearly got all the way to Camden Town?*

I wish I had seen that zebra, he replied, and drew a picture of it, next to a red London bus.

"What a clever boy," said Mary.

"I'll put that on my board," said Enid.

You're becoming famous down here, Rose told Walter. *There's a little girl called Lottie who keeps asking about you. I think you'd be great friends. She loves animals too.*

I haven't had a friend before, he wrote in reply, making her throat tighten with sadness, all the more because, however much she hated to acknowledge it, she knew too well the looks his dark skin must have won him in his short life. She could only imagine how protective his mother must have felt of her beautiful, wide-eyed boy. She kept thinking about his father, too — whether he'd been Aborigine, as seemed most likely (was that the word, though? There'd been an Australian girl at Rose's school; Rose was sure she'd heard her use it) — and what Vivian could have meant when she'd said he'd fought *in a manner.* Had he and Mabel been married? Somehow, she thought not. It was the way Vivian had talked about helping Mabel before Walter had been born. It sounded like she'd come to London alone.

I hope we'll be the best of friends, she wrote back to Walter. *And I happen to know my brother would love to meet you. He flies planes. I can take you to visit him, if you'd like.*

Can I see his plane please? Walter asked.

Of course you can, she told him, hoping to God it would still be intact. Joe's last week of leave was over; he was back on sorties, bombing German shipping convoys and targets in occupied Europe. Every morning, she tried to resist the urge to tie up his base's telephone lines by calling to see if he was all right, and every morning, she failed. The torture of that pause before the ops girl confirmed he was still safe; the relief when she said he was. *You'll like Joe*, she told Walter, picturing her brother's smile, hearing his laugh. *They have a dog at the base you can meet, too.*

Her letters to Walter weren't the only ones she sent. She wrote to her parents too, not telling them that she was Colombo-bound, since she was becoming increasingly excited about Joe's idea of surprising them, but letting them know that she was for Australia. She was resigned to them reaching a similar conclusion to Lionel about her motivation for going. (*Tell me you realize that this child, however alone, can never make up for…*) They knew about the baby, after all. Lionel had told them, since she'd been too ashamed to do it. They'd been wonderful, though, her mother desperate to come to her, only agreeing to stay in Colombo after Rose had sent countless telegrams begging her not to risk such a long, hazardous voyage on her account (*Lionel and Joe looking after me very well* STOP), wiring Rose daily instead, repeating the impossible advice that she wasn't to blame herself for what had happened, nor fret about anything beyond getting better. *Like Lionel and Joe, your father and I can't bear that you were left alone in hospital for so long.*

Perhaps this is about what happened then, Rose wrote to them now. *Maybe I do want to help Walter because we've both lost someone. Is that so wrong? But I also can't stand to think of him alone, or with someone who won't be kind. Not when he doesn't need to be . . .*

She wrote to Xander as well. A letter first, saying she was sorry she made him feel a criminal. *I don't want to punish you, I'm not sure how many more times I need to say that.* She told him she'd hated his leaving too, but was glad he'd decided to go away, *obviously, I understand your need for a change of scene.* She asked when and where he was going to go, *let me know as soon as you know,* posted that the Wednesday after she received his wire, and waited for his reply.

None came.

When more than a week had passed with nothing, beginning to worry, conscious of the ongoing raids, she wired him at his office. *Please get in touch so I know all is well.* STOP.

Again, silence.

Worrying more, on her last day in Ilfracombe, she telephoned his hotel. To her relief, the receptionist there told her that he was fine. Not in his room, but fine.

"I'll call again later," said Rose.

"No, don't," said the receptionist.

Rose frowned. "Why?"

"It's just . . . he's gone away. He'll be back in a few days."

"Really?" said Rose, frown deepening, trying to make sense, not of Xander's being out of town—he often went on stories, shadowing politicians and generals, even if Lionel and Winston made things more uncomfortable for him these days ("We don't," Lionel claimed. "They do," Xander insisted. "Please ask them to stop . . .")—but of his going without telling her.

And the receptionist's manner, too.

There was something disconcertingly guarded in her tone.

"Do you know where he went?" Rose asked.

"No," the receptionist said, still in that same defensive way.

"Did he go alone?" The question was out before Rose knew it was coming. She didn't know why she asked it. But she felt suddenly quite nauseous.

"I'm not sure," the receptionist said, with a pause that made Rose feel even sicker.

Was she lying?

Rose didn't push her on it. She couldn't bring herself to. Shakily, she thanked the woman for her time and, gripping the receiver far too tight, hung up.

Laura, who'd arrived the day before and was sharing her desk, looked across at her in concern, lightning-quick fingers hovering over the typewriter. Already, Rose liked her. She was warm and friendly as well as efficient, full of talk of how wonderful it was to be by the coast again. *A balm to my soul.* She was staying in a B and B, but Enid had already offered her Rose's room. Rose hoped Laura would take it. She felt awful, leaving Enid alone.

She wasn't sure why she was thinking about Enid.

"Everything all right?" Laura asked.

"I don't know," said Rose, her voice strained to her own ears.

Had Xander gone away with someone else? Someone he shouldn't have? No. *No.*

Who would he have gone with?

"Is there someone else you can telephone?" Laura, so very practical, asked. "His office?"

"I don't think so." It would be too humiliating.

"Put it from your mind, then," said Laura kindly. "We've got your party to enjoy."

Rose nodded. They did. Hector and Anne had organized the farewell. Everyone from the village was coming. Hector's cook had magicked up platters of sausage rolls, Enid had made many, *many* sandwiches, and Mary was contributing elderflower wine.

It was a lovely few hours. Despite Rose's worry over Xander, she really did enjoy it. With everyone there, laughing and talking and wishing her luck, it was hard to believe how lonely she'd been over the winter; she felt guilty, like she hadn't appreciated them all enough.

But she told them how much she'd miss them. She thanked them each in turn. And, as the purple spring dusk deepened, giving way to darkness, Hector raised a toast to her too, telling her how much *she* would be missed.

"Oh," said Rose to Laura, "it feels suddenly very hard to go . . ."

"Well, I'm glad you've left me this opening," said Laura, "if that helps."

"It does," said Rose, smiling. "It does."

After that, for her there was just one last walk back to Enid's house, one final night listening to the wireless in her front room, and one more creaking climb of her stairs to bed.

The next morning dawned sunny for the first time in what felt like weeks. Anyone superstitious, which Rose was, would have considered it a positive sign. ("It is," said Enid tearfully. "It is.") Lionel, incredible Lionel, had arranged a motor to collect her, proclaiming he and Winston agreed her worthy of the petrol. It arrived at seven, and, after a lingering hug with Enid, Rose was off, down the lane, turning in her seat to wave, and watch the house, the sea, and village disappear: a whole chapter of her life over, as abruptly as it had begun.

The journey into London passed without delay, and before Rose was fully ready, they'd swapped the gold-dappled countryside for the city's rubble and smoke. As they progressed through the traffic—past the BUSINESS AS USUAL signs, boys selling newspapers, everyone keeping calm and carrying on—drawing ever closer to Williams Street, her nerves bubbled. She tried to guess where Walter would be when she arrived. In his room? Out in the park? She thought about what she should say to him. She should keep it brief, she told herself, as simple as her letters. *Softly, softly.* They crossed the Thames, into Belgravia, and she touched her shaky fingers to the window, spotting the small pub and church she'd walked past in the rain back at the start of the month, becoming excited as well as anxious, impatient now to arrive, for the wait to be over. Waiting always was the hardest bit.

They slowed, turning in to Williams Street. Someone, somewhere, was cutting a lawn. She could smell the grass through the driver's open window. She took a deep breath, drawing the sweet scent in, trying to steady herself.

It didn't really work, and then they were there anyway, stopping outside number thirty-two. It was just as Rose remembered it, with its pink front door, its yellow bricks and pinwheels, the color even more vivid for the bright day. She stared upward, wondering if Vivian was at her window again, peering down at her. *I had a feeling . . .*

The driver shut the engine off, leaving them in sudden quiet. Birds sang in the trees. He got out, opening Rose's door, letting in the mild spring warmth, then turned, taking in the house himself. Rose had told him about the decorations on the drive.

"She did all of this for a little boy?" he said.

"All for him," said Rose, stepping onto the pavement. Her legs were cramped, not entirely steady.

The driver shook his head in wonder, and told her he'd fetch her things. Thanking him, she cast one more look at Vivian's window, clenched her jittery fingers into a fist, made her way up the yellow front path, and knocked on the fuchsia door.

Silence followed. It grew longer, torturously so. She turned, looking back at the driver, her two cases in his hands. She wondered if she should go down to the kitchen, see if she could find Lester. She was still deliberating when she heard a noise behind the door, what sounded like a key turning in the lock.

She watched the handle move, the door slowly open.

She filled her lungs with another deep breath.

Here we go, she thought.

CHAPTER FIVE

It wasn't Lester who opened the door to her that day. Or Catherine. Catherine, Rose was soon to discover, was no longer at Williams Street, despite her several assurances that she'd remain while Rose settled in.

"Don't be alarmed," said Vivian, once she'd broken the news to Rose. (Rose was a little alarmed.) "You'll be fine," said Vivian, "more than equal to the challenge, and one of Catherine's daughters has flu."

No, it was Vivian herself—not at her window, but up and about, despite being distressingly even frailer than before—who came. It was what had taken so long; she'd been edging her way out from the drawing room.

"Quite a performance, I'm afraid," she said, leaning on her walking stick, her breaths rattling in her chest.

"You shouldn't have done it," said Rose, too concerned not to.

"Absolutely, I should," said Vivian. She'd dressed up as well, in a silk gown that must have fitted her perfectly once, but now hung loose from her hunched shoulders. "I couldn't let Walter welcome you without me. Could I, Walter?"

It was then that Rose realized he was there too, hovering behind one of the hallway doors. He peered across at her, blue eyes wide, every bit as squeezable as she'd remembered with his round cheeks, his mess of wavy hair, but so shy still, in spite of their letters. Conscious of that shyness, she didn't go directly to him, much as she wanted to (*softly, softly*), but smiled, she hoped encouragingly, and said, "Hello."

"Hello," he replied. That whisper.

He held his rabbit in one fist, a bunch of daffodils in the other, clenched so tightly the stems were bent. *He's nervous,* she thought, and felt such a rush of pity for him, all alone in his neatly pressed shorts and pullover, more lost than ever without Catherine's skirts to shield him. Yet another person to vanish on him without warning.

I'm not going to do that, she wanted to assure him, *I swear.*

Knowing, though, how meaningless the words from her, a stranger, would be to him, she did then move to where he stood, and, pushing her own shock at Catherine's departure aside — realizing he hardly needed a nanny as anxious as him — crouched before him like last time and, forgetting the words she'd rehearsed in the motor, asked if the flowers were for her.

He nodded. His dark waves bounced up and down. "They're yellow."

"They certainly are," she agreed, gently taking them. "Thank you."

"You'll find a vase on your bureau," said Vivian. "And here comes your driver, too." She held her kerchief to her mouth and coughed. Rose stood, concern growing at the racking noise, but Vivian waved her hand, making out she was fine. "I'm sorry," she said, once she could speak again, "such a silly fuss." She directed one of her smiles at Walter. "Why don't you show Rosie to her room while I have a rest?"

He shifted on his feet, looking from her back to Rose, tempted, Rose felt, but still in need of coaxing.

"You don't have to," she said, "but I'd really love it if you did, and maybe we could find a game to play."

He studied her a moment longer, appearing to think.

Holding her breath, hoping she was doing the right thing, she offered him her hand.

His eyes moved, looking at it.

Still, she didn't breathe.

Then he slipped his fingers into hers, warm, tentatively trusting, and she exhaled.

He remained very quiet, though, long after he'd hesitantly led her up to her new bedroom — which, with its soft carpet, luxurious double bed, and bay window overlooking the garden below, was easily the nicest she'd ever had. He perched on her bed obligingly enough when she invited him to sit there, and waited politely while she bade her driver goodbye, then nodded just as politely when she asked if he'd like to show her his room next door so they could find that game, but never once spoke unless she spoke to him.

"Oh look, Walter," she said, taking in his shelves of picture books, his low bed with its embroidered eiderdown, the tubs of building blocks and wooden figurines. "What a perfect bedroom." Supposing everything in it must have come from his old house — that his mother had bought him the toys, tucked him in beneath that eiderdown — she hoped that they could take at least some of it with them to Australia; it would hurt him too much, surely, to leave all these things she'd touched behind. There was a studio photograph of a woman who could only be her by his bedside; it must have been taken recently, because Walter, in her arms, wasn't far off the size he was now. Mabel was beautiful, more like a magazine model than mother, with her oval face, high cheekbones, fair hair, and dark lashes. There was something unsettling about the look in her eyes, though. Rose narrowed her own, trying to make it out. She seemed guarded. Haunted, almost. Certainly not nearly as carefree as her smile was trying to suggest — or the beaming Walter on her lap.

"You look like you're about to laugh," Rose said to him, gesturing at the photograph, wanting him to be able to talk about Mabel with her, for so many reasons, not least that if he didn't, how would he, so young, ever hold on to his memories? "Had your mummy said something funny?"

He shook his head.

"The photographer, then?"

"He was telling jokes," said Walter.

"What kind of jokes?" asked Rose, smiling.

"He said I looked like I'd been in the sun too long, but it was cold outside."

Rose felt her smile stick. *Bastard*, she thought. "What a silly man," she said out loud, relieved that Walter at least had taken his words in jest.

"That's what Mummy said."

"I expect she did," said Rose, understanding her strained expression a little better. Deciding to move the conversation on before she gave away her own anger, she suggested Walter choose their game.

Again, he cooperated with pristine manners, showing her where he kept his favorite puzzles, all of which were of animals. As they knelt together on the rug, piecing them together, she racked her brain for things to talk about, telling him about her journey up from Devon, more of Joe, Lionel too. It wasn't until they'd finished a herd of elephants, a lion with her cub, and a giraffe that she, suspecting it must be nearing lunch, went back to her own room to check the time, and discovered the notes Catherine had left for her on Walter's routine, beside the clock on her mantelpiece. The stacked pages were more of a manual, really—with menus, activity suggestions, specification on layers to be worn in different weathers—and had an entire sheet dedicated to Walter's daily schedule.

7 o'clock: rise, visit the latrine (NB: ensure he flushes it; he doesn't like the cistern's noise, but can do it), dress (see clothing) and brush teeth (see bathing matters). Short play (see games).
　　8 o'clock: breakfast (see food). Pia will help.

Who was Pia? Rose flicked through the pages, but could find no clue.

9 o'clock until 11: play. (As mentioned in outdoor pursuits, there is a playground in the park by the church.)
　　11 o'clock: elevenses (see food. NB: he's a bandit for biscuits, so keep an eye on Pia's barrel.)

Pia again.

Noon: luncheon (see food), followed by a nap, which you must not allow to go on later than 3 o'clock, otherwise he will struggle at night.
　　Afternoon: play. Fruit snack at 4 o'clock.
　　5 o'clock: supper, which Pia will prepare.

Pia!

Bath, then bed no later than 7 o'clock. You must remind him to go to the latrine (NB: do this throughout the day).
　　If there is a raid, shelter in the cellar.
　　If he wakes up at night, settle him back to sleep in his bed.

Rose filled her cheeks with a long breath, glancing at the clock guiltily. It was past one. He should be napping already. Was he famished?

"Not really," he said, when she peeked her head back around his door to ask. He'd abandoned the puzzles and was sitting cross-legged playing with his animals.

"Are you sure?"

"It will be soup again," he said, as though that was all the answer needed.

"You don't like it?" she hazarded.

"No," he said, much as he might have admitted to breaking a precious ornament, making her smile.

"Well, I'm glad I know," she said, "but I think we'll have to tough it out for today. Let's go." She held out her hand, and although he still hesitated before taking it, to her relief he *did* take it again. "You can tell me on the way who Pia is."

Pia was an Austrian lady who came daily through the week to cook and clean. They found her kneading dough in the kitchen, with Lester, who was polishing his pans at the table. He rose creakingly to greet Rose, apologizing that his cousin had had to leave her in the lurch. It was the most Rose had ever heard him speak. She didn't have a chance to get out much in reply, though, because Pia crossed the room, and, seizing her hand in her floury one, pummeled it, saying how much they'd all been looking forward to her arrival, and that she'd come to fetch her and Walter earlier but hadn't wanted to disturb their playing. "Soup can always wait, can't it, Walter?" she said, ruffling his hair, getting flour all through it, telling him to sit down with Lester while she and Rosie fetched him a bowl.

"Come," she said to Rose, gesturing her to the range. Lowering her voice confidentially, she told her that anything she needed, she was to speak to her. "Lester's not so able to manage these days, but we never talk about it. He's very proud." She held up her dusty hands. "I pretend I do less than I do."

She filled Rose in on many other things besides in the time it took her to pour Walter a helping of onion-scented broth, Rose to slice him some bread, and locate the kettle to brew a pot of tea. Pia was a fast talker, even in a second language, and covered a deal of ground, moving from Vivian's illness — "Cancer," she said sorrowfully, "all through her" — to the doctor who now visited every evening to administer morphine — "He wants (vants) her to have a nurse," she said, returning to her dough, "but she won't (von't) in case it upsets Walter (Valter)" — on to Catherine, who Pia said was very kind, but stuck in her ways (vays). "His mother never made him eat so much soup."

"You knew Mabel?" Rose asked, quietly, not wanting Walter to hear and think she was snooping (which she of course was).

"For years," said Pia, with a slap of the dough, and went on, saying that she'd first met her when she'd arrived in England, a few weeks before Walter had been born. She'd stayed in Williams Street, but then Vivian had leased her a house in Pimlico. "No husband to speak of, no nobody. She was lonely, poor girl."

"Why did she leave Australia, though?"

"I don't know," said Pia, in a resigned tone that suggested she'd given up asking. "I think it must have been to do with Walter's father. She never spoke of him, or her family. Maybe you'll find out when you're . . ." She stopped, looked over at Walter, persevering through his soup, and mouthed, *There,* reminding Rose, as though she could forget, that Walter, so little that his feet didn't even reach the flagstone floor, still had no idea that they were going, or that his rocking world was about to be turned upside down all over again.

She didn't make him nap that day. It was so late by the time they finished lunch, there seemed little point. Besides, Pia said they could take the remnants of the loaf they'd been eating for the ducks at St. James's Park: the very thing Walter had said he wanted to do in his first letter to Rose. It felt like a better way for them to get to know one another than going to sleep. And Lottie never had a nap. She seemed fine without it.

"Do you think you will be?" she asked Walter, as he demolished one of Pia's Viennese biscuits. (Rose wasn't above using sugar to win him over. Where did it come from, though? "The same place as the coal," said Pia, tapping her nose.) "You're not tired?"

"I'm not tired," he said, still in that low whisper.

"Good," she said, keeping her own voice at a determinedly jovial level. Pia gave her a cheering smile. "Lester, please don't tell on me to your cousin."

"Of course he won't," said Pia, answering for him.

He carried on polishing his pans, like he was used to her doing that.

Before Rose and Walter left, Rose suggested they say goodbye to Vivian, but she was fast asleep, on a velveteen chaise longue in the drawing room, her wheezing breaths filling the still air. Someone (Lester?) had placed a blanket over her.

"She's poorly," said Walter.

"She is," said Rose sadly, since there seemed little point in denying it. Knowing too, though, that Vivian — who'd refused to hire the nurse she needed for fear of worrying him — wouldn't want him dwelling on the melancholy fact, she led him out of the room, and on to the latrine, which he told her he didn't need.

"I don't," he said, hopping from foot to foot at the door, clearly needing it very much, but feeling awkward, she guessed, at doing something so personal with her nearby.

"I'll stay out here," she said.

"I can hold it," he told her, with an edge of panic to his voice that sent a fresh wave of sorrow shooting through her at how abandoned he must be feeling.

Desperate to make it better for him, she broke another of Catherine's rules and said that if he went, she'd take care of the flush for him. "I'll do that every time."

"Really?" He stopped hopping. It changed things for him, she could tell.

"Really," she said, smiling.

And to her utter joy, for the first time that day, his cheeks lifted, his eyes lost some of their anxious watchfulness, and he smiled back. Not the small smile he'd let go at her interview, but a proper, wide, full-hearted one.

He had such a gorgeous smile.

Already, she wanted to see it again.

She didn't stop working all through that sunny afternoon, trying to coax another from him. And shy as he remained on their walk to St. James's, then around the lawns with their sandbags and trenches, he gave her one, he gave her several, each one seemingly loosening the next. ("Of course," Vivian would say the next day, in one of her lucid spells. "That child was born for joy. It's what makes it all so cruel.") They had, right up until the very end of that, their first outing, a surprisingly nice time.

On the way to the park, they stopped at a telephone box so Rose could call Joe's base, which she hadn't had a chance to do that morning. She held Walter up so that he could drop the pennies into the slot, trying not to let him see how nervous she was, then perched him on the ledge while the connection went through.

"Do they tell you straightaway if he's all right?" he whispered.

"They tell me straightaway," she whispered back, feeling her heart kick as the operator's voice came down the line, *How may I direct your call,* grip-ping the receiver harder for the few seconds it took the girl in the operations room to answer. Fearing it would upset Walter if there *was* bad news, she kept the receiver away from his ear, bracing herself to pretend all was fine if the ops girl (Bella; they were on first-name terms) told her the worst had happened. But to her shuddering relief, Bella confirmed that Joe was safe, currently kicking a football outside with his crew, and Rose grinned, stuck her shaking thumb up at Walter, mouthing, *Hurray.*

"Until tomorrow, Rosie," Bella said.

"You're a lucky charm," Rose told Walter, and, in her joy, forgetting Anne's *softly, softly,* tickled him on his tummy, making him squirm, and gig-gle, actually *giggle,* just a bit.

At the park gates, she gave him more pennies to throw into the cap of a music man, who played them a song with his accordion and tambourine knees. At the sun-dappled lake, she reminded him of his promise to show her how he fed the ducks.

"You remember my letter?" he asked, flushing pink, sweetly disbe-lieving.

"Every word," she said, handing him the bread.

And there it was again: that smile. "Well, you do it like this," he said, rotating his arm, releasing the crumbs, making the ducks squawk, flocking to gobble them up.

With the bread all gone, they went for a stroll by the palace—parts of which had been cordoned off, damaged by a bomb a few nights before—and Rose tried to get Walter to guess whether the princesses were at home.

"I don't know how to," he said.

"Well let's see if we can spot them," she said, crouching beside him, making a show of examining each of the windows in turn. "There," she said at length, seeing nothing, but pointing at the top floor, "look . . ."

"Where?" he said, eyes widening, standing on his tiptoes, craning his neck, too excited for the moment—much to her delight—to remain shy.

"Up there," she said. "I think I saw Margaret . . ."

"Really?"

"Yes, look. Can you see her?"

He stared harder. She saw how much he wanted to. "I think so," he said. "I think, maybe . . ."

"Definitely," she said. "So now we know where her bedroom is."

With the spring warmth turning chill, they headed for home. It was then, on their way back, that the one thing happened to mar the day. Walter was thankfully never aware of it, but Rose very much was.

Wanting to squeeze in a final treat, she suggested they stop at the playground Catherine had mentioned in her manual. The leafy square was packed with children tearing around, letting off steam before their tea, and Rose — noticing how Walter looked at them, eyes yearning, hand holding hers tighter, at once intimidated and desperate to join in — was tempted to grab one of the little hoodlums, ask them to let Walter play with them too. She might have, but then she saw the group of smartly dressed women with victory rolls and cigarettes, over by the roundabout. To her disgust, they were nudging one another, staring at Walter beside her, not nicely, but rather as though they, like that photographer, thought he'd been out in the sun too long. Rose stared back at them, heart hammering at their brazen hostility, more so when she saw a couple of them call out to their own children, beckoning them closer, as though Walter — *Walter*, hugging his rabbit close, enraptured by the games going on around him — could do such a thing as hurt anyone. *I haven't had a friend.* Rose had almost forgotten his words over the course of their lovely afternoon, but she remembered them now, and her pain at reading them in his letter, how she'd been struck by the protectiveness his mother must have felt toward him. She was overwhelmed by it herself. Acting instinctively, stealing his attention before he had a chance to register the children being kept from him and be crushed by it, she said she thought it might be a bit late after all for the park, and asked if he'd like a shoulder ride home.

"Aren't I too heavy?" he asked, heartbreakingly unsuspecting of her motive.

"Not for me," she said, forcing her voice normal, despite her rage, and, abandoning Anne's *softly, softly* once and for all, gathered him close, not hoisting him onto her shoulders straightaway, but cuddling him to her, leaving the women behind without ever letting him see them, certain somehow that Mabel — who'd forced a smile for that photographer so that her little boy might remain innocent, believe the man's nauseating words nothing but a tease, and the rest of the world as kind as himself — would have done the same thing.

I'll keep doing it, Rose silently promised her. *As long as I can, I'll keep doing it.*

Then, with a kiss to Walter's soft curls, and a final withering look back at those women — only one of whom had the good grace to flinch, avert her own eyes, ashamed — she hefted him onto her shoulders, and made a fool of herself by pretending to be a horse, all the way home.

CHAPTER SIX

Vivian was already up in her bedroom when they got in, sleeping again, this time with the help of her doctor's morphine. Pia had gone for the day too, leaving a stew in the oven, and Rose and Walter's tickets to Australia in Rose's room, half hidden beneath her pillow.

Keep these safe, she'd written on the envelope. *Your return fare is being held at the shipping office in Brisbane.*

Rose discovered them just as she was finally about to go to bed herself, exhausted, hoping that Walter would do as she'd asked and wake her if he needed anything, knowing she probably wasn't going to sleep a wink anyway, listening out for him and the siren.

Their evening hadn't been easy.

She'd started to let herself hope that he might be warming to her—he'd laughed on their ride home from the playground, and chatted at tea, playing along with her game of imagining Princess Margaret's bedroom—but then he'd turned worryingly quiet again at bath time, watching pensively while she'd run the tub, clearly as anxious about taking his bath in front of her as he had been over going to the latrine, asking to get out almost soon as he was in. He'd been even more subdued at bedtime, staring up at her from beneath his eiderdown as she'd tucked him in, missing Catherine, she was sure, his mummy more than anyone, making her feel like she must be doing it all wrong, and such a stranger to him still, however much fun she might have convinced herself they'd been having.

It was why seeing those tickets unsettled her. She stood in her night-dress, staring at them in her hand, only dimly registering their calling points (Cape Town, Bombay, Colombo, Melbourne . . .), the class (first; she'd have to tell Enid), because all she could really see was the date, 10 April. All she could think about was how little time there was separating now from then.

Three weeks. *Three.*

It felt like nothing at all, not for her to become someone whom Walter—reluctant to let her bathe him—could happily walk up a gangplank with: his only companion on a voyage to the other side of the world, and the home of a family he hadn't yet met.

She dropped down onto her soft mattress.

Three weeks.

She was terrified it wasn't going to be enough.

No siren came that night. Midnight arrived, and Walter still hadn't made a peep. Rose tossed, turned, listened to the house's creaking pipes, thought she should probably check on him, got up to peek at him sleeping, clambered back between her too-hot sheets, checked on him again, and, just when she'd given up on ever doing it, finally, groggily, fell asleep.

She didn't know how long she remained that way, but, in the midst of a dream of women in victory rolls morphing into the nurses on her old hospital ward, *I hope we're not feeling sorry for ourselves again,* she woke, then jumped in the blackness, because Walter *had* come to wake her, and was standing right by her bed.

"Walter," she said, heart pounding at the wrench into consciousness, "what's wrong?"

"I'm scared," he said, and, to her distress, was crying.

"Oh, Walter," she said, and sat up, pulling him onto her lap. He came easily, readily, desperate, she could feel, for comfort, any comfort. "How long have you been awake?"

"I don't know," he said, with a sob.

A while then, she thought, picturing him next door, cowering from the shadows, trying to muster the nerve to move. "I wish you'd called out sooner, I'd have come."

He sobbed again.

"What's scared you?" she asked.

"My dreams."

"Dreams are awful," she said, still half in her own. "What did you dream of?"

"I can't," sob, "remember."

"But it wasn't nice?"

"No," he said, and she held him tighter.

They sat like that for a while. She couldn't think what else to do. Slowly, his sobs began to ease, turned to tremors that shuddered through his warm little body, then sniffs. He rested his head against her. She felt him growing heavier, the tension in him easing. *Safe.* She closed her eyes in relief. She'd done that for him. She'd really done it.

It felt like a start, at least.

He sank further into her arms. He was slipping back off to sleep, she could tell. But while she remembered Catherine's advice about settling him back in his own bed, she didn't follow it. Not when he'd been so afraid. She held him with her, pins and needles forming in her arms, tired, so tired. His breathing became deeper, the noise soporific, and her head nodded, jerking forward. All she wanted to do was lie back down and sleep herself, but she waited, not moving until she was absolutely certain he wasn't going to wake. It was only then that she got up, carefully lifting him with her, carrying him back to his own room, where she tucked him in beneath his eiderdown, his rabbit under his arm, and the photograph of his mummy right by his side.

He woke her most nights after that, sometimes unable to recall what had upset him, other times beside himself because he'd been dreaming of Mabel and had forgotten she was gone. Rose, hating how inadequate a consolation she was, always let him fall asleep with her—which, in fairness to Catherine, did become somewhat of a rod for her own back, in that it seemed to have the effect that he woke her more. While she never begrudged the minutes she held him, warm and protected in her arms, and was so glad he felt able to come to her—that she, unbelievable as it still felt, could comfort him— she became incredibly tired. What with the siren that also often wailed, sending them dashing down to the cellar (never with Vivian, who, terrifyingly, remained in bed, too frail to dash anywhere), there to sit with Lester, listening to the roar of the Luftwaffe's engines, flinching at the crump of their bombs, the broken nights became as bad as ones she'd known on her old RAF base during the Battle of Britain. Before she'd got dismissed.

"Hopefully they'll ease before September, though," said Vivian, whom Rose, early on in her stay, mustered the courage to steal a few minutes alone with so that she might tell her about her dismissal, feeling it would be wrong to hide such a thing from her.

To her surprise and relief, Vivian already knew.

"My lawyer insisted on digging around," she admitted. "I'm sorry."

"You don't need to apologize," said Rose, skin burning from the ordeal of speaking about it.

"There are many who should," said Vivian, and, offering Rose one of the chocolates she kept stashed in her bedside drawer (was there no end to the black-market dealings of number thirty-two?), was so very kind, telling Rose that in another world, a better world, none of what had happened would have been allowed. *It mightn't surprise you to know I marched with the suffragettes.*

She counseled Rose to be kind to herself, keep her days with Walter simple for the time being, while they were having such disrupted nights and the two of them were getting to know one another. "The zoo can wait," she said.

Rose was inclined to agree. Assuring Walter that she hadn't forgotten about their promised excursions—not to the zoo, nor Joe's base—for that first sleep-deprived week, she kept their outings to Belgravia, and gradually, with Catherine's timetable gathering dust on her bureau, the two of them fell into a new, looser routine of their own.

Mornings always began with a trip down the road to telephone Joe's base. While Rose remained poised to protect Walter from bad news, she tried to make it fun for him, always lifting him up so that he could drop the coins into the call box's slot. On their third day, he raised his arms in anticipation of her doing it, which, even in spite of her anxiety for Joe, made her smile. With him perched on the ledge, she'd wait for Bella to answer, and, hearing those beautiful words, *safe and sound, Rosie,* would stick her thumb up at Walter, something he quickly started to do back at her, making her smile more.

After that, heady with reprieve, she'd invite him to take his pick of places to go, refusing to accept it when he said, "I don't mind."

"You *must* mind, Walter."

"I don't."

"Shall we just go home then?" She'd pretend to head off. "Ask Pia if we can help make more soup. . . . No?" She'd feign surprise at his small smile. "You don't want to do that?"

"Not really."

"So shall we go to the ducks? Or down to the river?"

Mostly, he wanted to go to the playground, so to the playground they went; Rose refused to let those victory-rolled women keep them away. She was relieved, though, when they were never there as a pack again, only individually, which made them a deal less shameless with their stares. Ignoring them as best she could, she tried to encourage Walter to talk to the other children there. He, clutching her hand, holding his rabbit in the other, watched them all laugh and play as longingly as ever.

"Go on," she'd say, "that little boy looks nice. All you need to say is, 'I'm Walter. Would you like to go on the seesaw?' I promise you, it's that easy."

He'd try to make himself do it; she'd watch him, heart melting at his bracing breaths. Sometimes, he'd even take a step forward, and she'd go still, willing him on. But in the end, he'd always turn back, ask, "Can I just stay with you?," and, hating it for him, wishing she could gift him the confidence — or a brother like Joe to grab him by the hand, make him never alone again — she'd tell him that of course he could, and, taking her best shot at being a Joe for him, would ride with him on the seesaw, the roundabout, faster, making herself feel sick, which didn't bode well for the voyage, but was worth it, because he'd laugh, all inhibitions gone, happy, *as happy as he knows how to be,* and it was impossible not to be happy with him.

They'd head home for lunch, which Rose and Pia agreed could be sandwiches rather than soup, and then, instead of a nap, he and Rose played: painting, reading, getting out snakes and ladders, often with Lester joining in. They'd go out again in the afternoon, and when they got back, so long as Vivian was awake, they'd visit her before the doctor's call.

"The high point of my day," she'd say, face alight, beckoning Walter into her room.

Watching Walter happily run to her, then clamber into the chair beside hers, Rose would recall Vivian's words at her interview: of how he'd never used to get off Mabel's lap when he visited. "It's like I tell Walter," she'd said, "I appear far more horrifying than I am." Vivian had convinced him not to be scared of her, it was clear, with her pinwheels and kindness. Rose would almost smile, seeing it, but never could completely, because it felt so unbearably unfair that, just as Vivian had won his affection, she was having to let him go.

Vivian still didn't break it to him that he was headed to Australia, though.

"We'll know when the right time is," she assured Rose, who never forgot, not for any minute of any day, that he didn't know. Rather, the better she came to know him, and the more she could see him beginning—inch by hard-won inch—to trust her, the bigger a deception the secret felt.

But she didn't push Vivian on the matter. It wasn't her place, and besides, she realized very quickly that Vivian knew what she was doing.

Because while she didn't yet tell Walter that Queensland was going to be his new home, she did speak about it to him, making it familiar, laying the ground for him to be excited about going there. *Softly, softly.* As the days passed, she told him stories of the vast cattle station her late sister had built near Brisbane, with acres of land, and thousands of cows. "And what do cows do, Walter? Yes, yes. They go, *mooooo*." She spoke of the beautiful homestead her sister had once lived in, "fifteen bedrooms, so I've heard," and which now belonged to her niece, Walter's grandmother, Lauren.

To Rose's surprise, Walter didn't seem to have heard of his grandmother. In fact, he listened to Vivian describe her kindness much as he might have to a fairy tale. It made Rose uneasy. She remembered Pia telling her that Mabel hadn't used to speak of her family, but she'd never imagined that could have extended to her concealing their existence from her own son. Realizing now that it had, she wondered afresh what could have happened between them all, and if it had had anything to do with Mabel's coming to London as she had, pregnant and alone. Deciding the answer was almost certainly *yes*—worrying that whatever *had* happened was something really quite bad, and that the welcome waiting for Walter in Queensland mightn't be as warm as Vivian was making out—she resolved to speak to Vivian about it, when Walter wasn't nearby.

For the present, though, she remained quiet, and Vivian talked more, moving from wonderful Lauren on to Mabel's equally lovely brother and sister, Max and Esme.

"Max is a war hero," Vivian said, wheezing into the new oxygen mask the doctor had given her.

"Is he?" Walter asked, eyes widening at that word: *hero*.

"He is," said Vivian. "He spent a deal of time here, for university, and then again to see me, long before you were born. He's very nice, and so handsome." Her eyes softened, fondly, sadly. "He got quite hurt, though, when his plane was hit in Egypt."

Rose winced, thinking of the pilots at her base who'd gone down and survived. Some had been unscathed, but many hadn't escaped the cockpits in time and had come back with skin so melted they hadn't even been able to feel pain. Not at first.

Had Max been burned too?

Vivian didn't say.

"He was in hospital in Alexandria for a long time," was all she told them.

"Will he have to go upstairs with my mummy?" asked Walter.

"No," Vivian said gently. "But he loved your mummy, so much. And she loved him."

Vivian talked about other things too, besides Australia. Breaths rasping, she reminisced about her own childhood in Hampshire, the roads with only ponies on them, and her trips to see the great ships her father's company had built. She said that her parents had gone when she was still a girl, "Upstairs to wait for your mummy, Walter," and while her sister had married and left for Australia, she'd come to London, filling her bright, young years with parties and plays, dancing, "so much dancing."

"Now, this I'm keen to hear more about," said Rose, and fetched the photographs from the stairwell so that Vivian could tell her which, of all the beaming faces, was her own.

"I should have guessed," said Rose, once she had. "Your eyes haven't changed at all."

Vivian pointed out another face, beside her own: softer, belonging to a woman called Naomi, whom Rose could tell, just from the way Vivian spoke her name, that Vivian had loved dearly.

"You remind me of her," Vivian said. "And Mabel."

"Oh yes?" said Rose, flattered, intrigued.

"Yes," said Vivian, sounding oddly sad about it.

It intrigued Rose more.

"What is it?" she asked.

"I'll tell you," said Vivian, patting her hand weakly. "One day, I'll tell you."

She never did, though. At least, not while Rose was still in England. She made her wait.

"How frustrating," said Lionel, when, a week after Rose's arrival at Williams Street, she put Walter to bed, left Lester listening for him, and went to meet her uncle for one of his conditional dinners, back at the Goring. *Even domestics must get the odd night off.*

Lionel looked shattered. He told her, as they took their seats in the candlelit drawing room, that things were fraught at the War Office. She'd known they must be. She still listened to the wireless every night, with Lester now instead of Enid, and had heard how badly it was going against Rommel in Libya; there'd been a recent spate of convoy losses to torpedoes in the Atlantic, too. (Waters she and Walter would, frighteningly, shortly be sailing through.) Lionel admitted, though, that the situation was even worse than was being reported. Talking sotto voce, walls having ears, he said how twitchy the Far East commanders were starting to get about a possible Japanese assault. "Not," he hastened to add, "that we need fret about your parents. Malaya and Singapore are the worry." They were requesting more guns, he said, more men, but there was precious little to give them with resources so stretched in Africa. "Added to which," he said, wearily picking up his menu, "Hitler's looking like moving on Russia, so we need to be ready to help there." He lowered the card. "If your fiancé could write some more articles urging his countrymen to get involved, that would be helpful."

"I gather he writes a lot of them," Rose said. "No thanks to yours and Winston's cold-shoulders."

"We're always perfectly civil."

She smiled unhappily, not wanting to talk about Xander, upset just thinking about him. He'd written to her at Williams Street, a few days ago now: a short note that, to her growing disquiet, had given no explanation for where he'd been all this time — or who he'd been with — just said that he had to rush off again. *I'll be back before you go. The paper's sending me to Cairo, but I won't leave for a few weeks.* That had been it. No forwarding address, no hint as to *when* he'd be back. She'd been so annoyed, she'd thrown the message in the bin. She was increasingly tempted to do as Laura had suggested in Ilfracombe: call the Whitehall offices he worked from and ask if they knew where he was. She still couldn't bring herself to go through that humiliation, though.

Trying to forget about it, she changed the subject, asking Lionel how Winston was being, what with everything going on.

"Difficult," he said, surprising her not at all. He'd been working with Winston her entire life — *she'd* known Winston her entire life; there was a photograph somewhere of her trying to pull a cigar from his mouth — and it was a rare day that he described him in anything other than testing terms, much as Rose knew he loved him. "Suffice to say," he said, "we'll be needing wine tonight."

He ordered oysters, too. Real, not mock.

"Thank God," Rose said.

It was as they were finishing them that he asked her if she'd yet discovered what had happened to Mabel.

"Yes," she said miserably. Pia had told her. "She was hit by a bus." She still couldn't absorb the brutality of it.

"Christ," breathed Lionel, struggling too. "This blackout . . ."

"It was daytime," said Rose, who'd made the same mistake. "She was out buying Walter's Christmas presents." Rose kept picturing the racketing bus, imagining Mabel's terror, how her last thought must have been of Walter, his presents flying everywhere. "I assumed it had been the war's fault. I don't know why it feels crueler that it wasn't."

"Because we like having something to blame," said Lionel.

"Perhaps."

"And what about Walter's father?"

"I don't know," said Rose, brow creasing. "I want to ask Vivian what happened to him, but there never feels like a right time. I think he must have been . . . Aborigine, is it?"

"Aborigine?" Lionel's eyebrows shot up. (So it was the right word.) "You've never mentioned that before, Rosie."

"Does it matter?" she said, defensive to her own ears, still sore from those victory-rolled women.

"Not to me," he said, steadily. "But it will to a great many people over there."

"No worse than here, surely."

"Possibly worse. They don't let Aborigines vote. They're not citizens. We still get reports of violence." He gave her a troubled look. "What did Mabel's family think of Walter's father?"

"I'm not sure," she admitted uneasily, replaying that *reports of violence*, recalling what Vivian had said about Walter's father fighting *in a manner.*

Had the Lucknows turned on him?

Had they . . . ?

No, *no.*

Vivian had spoken of them all so highly.

"Do they definitely want Walter?" Lionel asked.

"They do." That much she had managed to ask Vivian about. Vivian had assured her that the family couldn't wait to have him with them. *I'm happy you care so much, I knew you would, but you'll see, they'll love him every bit as much as he deserves. Max especially.* "I don't think Vivian would send him to them unless they did."

"Is there anywhere else for him to go?"

Rose frowned. She didn't have an answer to that.

Fortunately, the waiter appeared, distracting them both by clearing away their plates and bringing their main course, the new go-to for every ration-starved menu: rabbit pie. (Oh, the rabbits; they weren't having a good war.)

They left the matter of the Lucknows alone while they ate, and Rose talked instead of the week she'd had with Walter, smiling as she reflected on how much chattier he'd become, talking to her about his mother, passing on the smallest details, like how she'd used to make him cakes covered in chocolate and coconut on his birthday. She recounted how, just that day, he'd made her heart sing at the park by taking her hand without her first offering hers, then had sat much longer in the bath; so long that she'd had to remove the plug to convince him to get out. "We're not out of the woods," she said, cutting a flaky mouthful of pie. "He still wakes every night. But he lets me cuddle him. He's always so . . . *sweet.*" She looked across at Lionel. "He could have made it much harder on me. Plenty would have . . ."

He smiled. "I remember thinking the same about you and Joe."

She laughed at that. "We made it easy?"

"As easy as any twelve- and fourteen-year-old could have," he said. "Don't get me wrong, I still blame you both for my gray hairs. But you were never resentful. You never *tried* to get into trouble," he narrowed his eyes, "accomplished as you both were at it."

She laughed again.

"The trick is," he said, "you've always known you've been loved, and it sounds like young Walter has too. From my limited experience, that goes a tremendously long way."

The waiter came again, removing their dishes, and they talked more, of Joe in his cockpit, perhaps somewhere over Europe, even now—dodging flak, they hoped: his last night before a merciful break of ground rest—and whether he should propose to Sarah.

"She's been very nice lately," Rose said, thinking of her new stockings (which she had, dutifully, written to tell Joe about), and Laura. "I'm sure she loves him . . ."

"But he needs to love her," Lionel said. "And she's so proper. I'm worried he'll spend the rest of his life in a new-build house, with a perfectly trimmed lawn and a downstairs loo with matching wallpaper and hand towels."

"You're such a snob, Lionel."

It was only once the waiter had served dessert—baked apples, real apples, just apples; no mock crème Chantilly, or mock meringues ("The chef's had enough," said Rose. "Haven't we all?" said Lionel)—that Lionel once again raised the topic of Walter's new home.

"You're getting very attached, Rosie," he said, apropos of nothing, as though it had been preying on his mind. "I can see it in your face when you talk about him." He reached for her hand. "I'm terrified it's going to break your heart, leaving him, darling."

She stared across at him, her mouth full of apple, suddenly unable to swallow. She remembered Enid saying something similar to her in Devon. *You're not going to like leaving him.* Rose had reassured her then, she'd reassured them both. *I know, but if he's happy . . .*

She didn't try and reassure Lionel now.

She couldn't, and not just because of the apple.

She knew he was right. Or almost right. She wasn't *getting* too attached, she *was* too attached; after only one week with Walter. She didn't know how anyone could spend their every waking hour with a child as kind and warm and utterly vulnerable as he and not be. She thought about him, worried about him, all the time. Even through this meal, she'd been fretting over whether he'd stayed asleep, or if Lester had managed to get to him quickly enough if he'd woken. She adored him, utterly. She wouldn't change it, couldn't regret. There was nothing she could *do* about it.

But still, she was terrified it was going to break her heart leaving him, too.

CHAPTER SEVEN

The two weeks they had remaining in England passed so quickly, after that.

Vivian, to everyone's grief, only just managed to hold on through them. She came down with a chest infection, the same night Rose was out with Lionel, and Joe limping back with his crew over the white cliffs of Dover, having failed to entirely dodge flak, but struggling home with one engine anyway. Vivian's infection really shouldn't have been the end for her either — it was little more than a cold, but the last straw for her tumor-ravaged lungs, and deteriorated quickly into pneumonia. Her doctor, sadly pronouncing there was little to be done but make her comfortable, pressed her again to get a nurse, but she wouldn't hear of it, *not until Walter's gone*, so he called more often himself, twice, sometimes thrice, daily, entirely behind Walter's back, administering as much morphine as her shrunken body could take.

"Y-You mustn't let Walter guess I'm so unwell," Vivian stammered to Rose, when Rose left Walter choosing a story one evening and looked in on her. It had been raining, weak gray light filled the room; for once, the pinwheels outside were still. Vivian, horribly pale, lay swamped by her pillows, the duvet she shivered beneath. She had the photographs Rose had fetched from the stairs beside her; her memories. "He mustn't know I'm going," she said. "H-He has to leave first." Even her eyes had begun to fade. It was awful, heartbreaking to see. "I won't be another person to leave him."

"We need to tell him he's going," said Rose, containing her grief by an effort of will, knowing how much it would upset Vivian to see it. "We have to . . ."

"Soon," said Vivian. "Spend m-more time together first. You're becoming such a pair." She smiled faintly. "Take him to the places you promised . . ."

What could Rose do, but as she was told?

Uneasy as she remained about the fast-approaching voyage ("It's hideous," she said to Lionel, when she met him for another meal, nine days before their departure, "at this rate we'll be on the boat, and he still won't know what we're doing"), she left Pia surreptitiously packing, and took Walter and his rabbit farther afield than she ever had, often for the entire day, keeping him well clear of Vivian, who no longer wanted him to see her at all. *Not like this. I-I'll have a better spell soon.* He kept asking when he'd be allowed to. He knew *something* was wrong, Rose saw that from the confusion in his round eyes when he looked up at Vivian's door. She hated that she was now keeping even more from him, how much she had to disappoint him, putting him off again and again. *I'm sorry, little man. I am.*

Their days out together, though, they were something else. As soon as they left Belgravia—where, Rose realized belatedly, he'd been trapped too long, grieving—he became . . . different. He smiled even more, laughed, a lot, happy, *as happy as he knows how to be,* loving, to Rose's elation, all of it: the escalator rides down to the Tube ("I used to do this with Mummy," he said, reaching for Rose's hand and stepping carefully onto the stairs, just like Mabel had obviously taught him), the coffeehouses, the museums, and, most of all, the zoo. Quiet as it was—the dangerous animals had been rehomed at Whipsnade for the duration lest they, like the zebra, make a break for freedom in a raid—he found thrills everywhere, running from the llamas to the flamingos to the tortoises, map held in front of him (upside down), calling at Rose to hurry with an exuberance she'd never have imagined possible when she'd met him.

He was almost as excited on their several forays to the shops, especially when Rose took him to Hamley's, which was open for business despite having been bombed, the serving staff at the entrance in tin hats, ready to dash inside to collect orders. Rose and Walter took their place in the queue on Regent Street, Rose said to buy something small, but when Walter became fixated by a set of farm animals in the window ("Rosie, look, look"), she couldn't resist using the last of her month's wages to buy them for him.

"I love the cow," she said, playing Vivian's game. "It's like Uncle Max's in Australia."

"I'm a bit scared of cows," he admitted.

"Never mind," she said.

Oh God, she thought.

Panicking more at how little time they had left before they sailed (now just a week), she asked Vivian again, first thing the next morning, if they could please just tell him.

But, "He's so happy," said Vivian. Her oxygen mask fogged when she spoke. "I hear him chattering . . . when you come home . . ." She broke off, phlegm rolling on her chest. "Let him stay happy. Please. There's still time . . ."

"Not much," Rose said, hating to trouble her, but feeling her anxiety grow, and not only over Walter.

There was Xander too.

She'd heard nothing more from him since his note, and while he'd assured her then that he'd be back before she left, she was becoming increasingly worried that he mightn't be, and that rather than having a chance *at something nicer to remember*, they weren't even going to be able to say goodbye. And what, *what* would that mean for them?

She had no idea. But she couldn't keep waiting any longer, wondering where he was, and if he'd appear. It was torture.

Swallowing her pride, and doing what she probably should have done long ago, as soon as she left Vivian she asked Pia to watch Walter, and — running, since it was raining again — went down the road to telephone his office, only to discover from one of the secretaries there that, far from being somewhere in England, as Rose had assumed, Xander had flown, *flown* across the Atlantic, back to New York.

"He didn't tell you?" the woman asked, sounding as shocked as Rose felt.

"No," Rose said numbly.

"He left in a rush," the woman said, obviously trying to make her feel better, which only made her feel worse. "I'm sure he wasn't thinking . . ."

"Of course," Rose said, increasingly sure of only one thing: that Xander, who'd accused her endlessly these past months of punishing him, was now very much — and for all his fine talk of her *maybe being right* about going away — punishing her, for doing it.

It felt so unfair, especially given he'd lost no time before asking his paper to send him overseas as well, to Cairo. *I could use a change of this old scene.* Concerned as she couldn't help but be at what had taken him to New York (his family? had something happened?), she was angry too, furious that he was deliberately keeping so much from her—that he'd disappeared, even before New York, to she still didn't know where—and desperate to get hold of him, make him explain . . . all of it.

But the woman at his office had no more information to give her: not on why he'd gone home, nor when he'd be returning to London, nor even an address in New York.

So Rose had no choice but to keep waiting after all. Try her hardest not to think about it too much.

Walter at least helped: the most welcome of distractions. Not wanting to give away her upset, or risk marring his last week in England, Rose packed their days fuller than ever, with another visit to the zoo, more trips around town, and even a tour, courtesy of Lionel, of the Houses of Parliament, the buzzing subterranean corridors of the Cabinet War Rooms.

"Look," whispered Lionel to Walter, outside the smoke-filled map room, beckoning him closer, pointing in at where Winston himself stood, cigar in mouth, eyes narrowed on the wall, examining the Libyan line. "When you're old like me, you can tell your grandchildren that you once watched the British Prime Minister working out how we'd win this war."

Walter nodded solemnly.

Then . . .

"What's a prime minister?" he whispered to Rose, making her laugh, in spite of everything, which in turn made Winston jump, and Lionel roll his eyes.

"That'll teach him for showing off," said Joe the next morning, when, waking to a welcome burst of spring warmth, Rose did what she'd been most looking forward to, and—checking first that Joe's station really hadn't been the target of any recent raids—took Walter by train to the rural part of Bedfordshire he was based in.

It was 7 April. Joe and his crew's last day on the ground before they were back on sorties, and, although Walter *still* didn't know it, Rose's chance to say goodbye to Joe. There were now just three days left until she and Walter sailed, and they were to spend the night before at a hotel in Liverpool. Rose wouldn't see Joe again for months. She wasn't sure how she was going to bear not being able to telephone Bella to check if he was all right.

"Bella will miss you too," he said, when he met her and Walter at the sleepy village train station, and knocked Rose's beret sideways, hugging her on the platform. "But you don't need to worry, because I'll be fine."

"You look exhausted," said Rose, frowning at the shadows beneath his eyes, so dark, despite his recent break.

"I could look a lot worse," he pointed out. "You look quite well."

"Thank you . . ."

"Your hair's better than last time too," he said, messing it up by pushing her beret back on. "And this," he grinned downward, "must be Walter. *Hello.*"

"Hello," said Walter. The whisper was back. His eyes were fixed on Joe's air force blues. Rose could almost hear the word circling in his mind: *hero.*

"Let's go," said Joe, "time's a-wasting," and, never one for *softly, softly* anything, picked Walter up, throwing him onto his shoulders, making Rose exclaim, and Walter squeal, just as he had on the playground's roundabout, too delighted, in that moment, to hide it.

As they sped along the leafy country lanes— hood down, Walter windswept and smiling in the back seat, face alight with the novelty of it all— Rose made Joe promise not to take him too close to the bombers. "Please," she said, voice low so Walter wouldn't hear, "let him think they're normal planes. He's so little, I don't want him looking at guns."

"Absolutely," said Joe. "Completely agree."

And then, as soon as they arrived at the flat grass fields his base's runways were built on—pulling up beside the Nissen-hut mess, the airmen lounging and smoking on deck chairs—he turned, grinned at Walter, and asked if he'd like to see inside a cockpit.

"Yes, *please*," said Walter.

"You're so annoying, Joe," said Rose.

But she didn't protest further. Walter, scrambling from his seat, looked like he might be about to implode with excitement, so over to the distant Wellington bombers he and Joe went, the squadron's spaniel chasing at their heels.

The half hour Rose spent waiting for them that morning—watching while they larked about, talking through the cockpit's transmitter to Joe's bombardier, Charlie, who also came out to play — was hardly the only memory she'd keep from their visit. There were three more occurrences of note — the last, in the true spirit of all finales, being really fairly major.

Before that, though, came the happier first, which was that while Walter, Joe, and Charlie were over with the planes, Rose met Bella. She came out from the ops room to introduce herself, much more glamorous than Rose had somehow imagined, with rouged lips, shiny black hair, and an enviably curvy figure beneath her Women's Auxiliary Air Force uniform. Had Rose ever looked so poster-worthy in her own WAAF getup? ("No," said Joe, later, over lunch in a nearby beer garden, "afraid not.") Bella batted away Rose's thanks for putting up with all her calls, telling her she understood, she had a brother too, and that to make it easier for Rose, she'd wire her, on the ship or in Australia, the second there was anything to wire about. "So you know that as long as you don't hear from me, he's fine."

"Thank you," said Rose, touched, relieved. "That's lovely of you."

"It's no bother," Bella said, and glanced across the field, toward where Joe was lifting Walter up into his plane's undercarriage. For a moment, as her eyes locked on Joe, her smile shifted into something softer, something that made Rose think suddenly of Sarah, and how she'd feel, seeing Bella smiling at Joe like this. . . .

But then the moment passed, Bella turned back to her, asked if she'd like a cup of tea, so airily that Rose wondered if she'd seen that smile at all.

The second thing to etch itself in Rose's mind that day occurred at lunch. There were a few of them in the pub's sun-filled garden; Charlie, some others from Joe's crew, and the spaniel, Oscar, had also come along to drink warm beer and eat pie. (Oh, the rabbits.) While Walter was playing with Oscar — tugging a stick from his mouth, keeping his own rabbit clear of Oscar's teeth, laughing in a way that made Rose feel so happy — it came out that Charlie had not only served in Egypt the year before, but had done so with Walter's uncle.

"Max Lucknow?" Charlie said. "Yes, I saw him go down." He spoke with the same nonchalance Rose had grown used to all airmen using when talking of life and death, trivializing it, making the fear less real. "He flew a Hurricane, very well actually. It wasn't his fault."

"What happened?" asked Rose, as Joe's rear gunner turned on the bench, listening too.

"We were over the desert," said Charlie, "covering a ground assault, the fighters were covering us." He sucked on his cigarette. "Max took out a Messerschmitt, then one came at him, the sun behind him . . ." His forehead pinched, careless façade slipping, reliving it. Rose pictured it herself: the blinding sun, the staccato of the bullets, Max's plane spiraling into the dunes. "None of us could believe he lived," Charlie said. "His whole crate was in flames."

"His parachute didn't burn?" asked the rear gunner.

"No," said Charlie. "A miracle really." He drew breath, frown deepening, then flicked his cigarette and smiled, the façade back. "A good man. A very good man."

Rose nodded slowly, reassured by that at least: that Charlie as well as Vivian thought well of Max.

"Did he ever mention his sister Mabel?" she asked.

"Not that I remember," said Charlie, lighting up another cigarette. His hands, like Joe's, trembled. "I don't recall him speaking much of home at all."

"I gather Mabel didn't either," said Rose, more to herself than Charlie, feeling a by-now-familiar trepidation over why.

Walter came back then, flushed with heat, dark hair sticking to his temples.

"Here he is," said Joe.

"Have some water," said Rose.

"We've just been talking about your uncle," said Charlie.

"I bet he can't wait to have you living with him in Australia," said the rear gunner. "Not long now."

Rose stared.

They all stared.

The rear gunner most of all, in horror, as it dawned on him what he'd said.

"I'm going to live in Australia?" said Walter, turning to Rose, his hot face no longer smiling, but creased with horrible bewilderment. "When am I going to Australia?"

And there it was: the third, and final thing to happen that day.

Really. Fairly. Major.

"Fairly?" Vivian rasped, later that night, when Rose — beside herself with guilt, and exhausted with the emotion of all she'd had to try and explain to Walter — carried him, sleeping, to his room, and, with a long, bracing breath, went into Vivian's to confess what had occurred. "I . . ." Vivian coughed. "I'm not . . . sure there's anything . . . fairly about it."

She was smiling, though. Relieved, she said, to have it taken out of her hands.

High, too, on morphine, without doubt.

"I've been rather . . . a coward about this," she admitted to Rose, closing her eyes. Her lids were waxy, purple; all her veins on show. She was vanishing, before all of them. Every time she inhaled, her lungs, full of liquid, rasped, protesting against the air coming in. Her throat was closing, the doctor had said. The tumors were getting bigger. Rose, who only ever just managed to conceal her pain at Vivian's pain, didn't know how Walter was going to cope with the change in her, when he finally saw her again to say goodbye. They should have let him come before, she realized; allowed him to absorb what was happening to Vivian gradually. Given him more credit for managing the grief.

He'd taken the news about Australia better than she'd dared to hope for, after all.

She told Vivian about that too: how, once she'd sat him on her lap, given him the cordial the rear gunner had rushed off to buy, and reminded him of all the stories Vivian had told them of beautiful Queensland—not to mention the great big ship the two of them were going to travel on to Australia ("Yes, of course I'm coming, too," she'd said. "Where else would I be, but with you?")—his confusion had eased, she'd felt his muscles loosen, and his expression had become less panicked. "I wouldn't say he was fine," she said to Vivian, "certainly not *pleased*. He was very clingy afterward, and wouldn't even let Joe take him back to his plane." He'd hidden behind her skirts. It hadn't made her happy. Given the choice, she'd have had him clamber onto Joe's shoulders, no question. "He kept asking if I could stay in Australia with him."

"And what did you . . . say?"

"That he probably won't need me to," Rose said, trying not to think too much about her own words as they left her, or the increasingly awful prospect of their parting ahead. Walter hadn't liked the idea of it either. The way he'd looked up at her when she'd said it, eyes filling with fear all over again. "I've promised I won't leave him unless he says I can."

"What will your," another cough, "fiancé think?"

"I'm not planning on telling him," Rose said. She still didn't know if she'd have the chance. "I'm sure Walter will be fine, anyway, once he gets there."

"Yes," said Vivian, and, with another weak smile, closed her eyes once more. "I have the strongest feeling he's going to be."

Silence followed. Vivian's labored wheezing was the only noise.

Rose lingered, waiting to see if she'd open her eyes again, but she didn't.

"I'll leave you to rest," she said softly, turning to go. "I really am so sorry."

Still Vivian didn't speak. Not until Rose reached the door.

"You're the . . . forgivable kind," Vivian whispered then, repeating what she'd said back at Rose's interview, her voice slurring with sleep. "Very . . . forgivable. I do so hope I am . . . too . . ."

She'd said that at Rose's interview, as well.

Rose couldn't think what she meant by it this time.

She didn't ask.

Assuming it was probably just the morphine speaking, she crept quietly away.

CHAPTER EIGHT

She didn't think of Vivian's strange words again. Or at least, not in London. Not during those last frantic forty-eight hours. She had far too much else to occupy her mind.

Vivian, wanting to reassure Walter herself about Australia, finally let him in to see her, briefly, the morning after he and Rose returned from Joe's base, first asking Pia to do what she could with some rouge, which wasn't much, and didn't fool Walter at all.

"Are you going upstairs with my mummy?" he asked Vivian quietly, cutting to the point in a way that only children could.

"No," said Vivian, somehow managing to smile. "Not . . . yet. But," she wheezed, "I am so very . . . old. That's why . . . you and Rosie will have a better time in . . . Australia." She fought to breathe. "I . . . wish I could go . . . too." She tried for another smile. It didn't work as well this time. She coughed, attempted to swallow it, but that didn't work either, and she scrabbled for her mask. Moving quickly, Rose fetched it, pressing it gently to her face.

Greedily, Vivian drew on the oxygen, scalding fingers grasping Rose's hand.

"Rosie?" said Walter from the foot of the bed, his bottom lip trembling.

"It's all right," Rose said, torn between rushing to comfort him, and staying with Vivian, helping her.

"I'm sorry," said Vivian, her entreating gaze making Rose's decision for her, pleading with her to take Walter away.

So she did, carefully extracting her hand from Vivian's, scooping him up and carrying him out to the landing, where she was relieved to find Pia waiting, ready to sit with Vivian until the doctor came.

"Why was Aunty Vivian painted like a clown?" Walter asked, once he and Rose were back in his room, breathing air that didn't smell of sickness, with their lungs that worked.

"We thought it would be funny," said Rose. She didn't know what else to say. "We won't do it again."

They didn't.

Vivian refused to let him see her anyway, not until the evening they left, when it was time to say goodbye. She'd made him afraid, she said; she couldn't let that happen twice.

But he was afraid, and not only about whether she'd get better. As he and Rose went through the piles of packing Pia had been readying, checking—now that he knew what was happening—that he wouldn't be leaving anything he'd miss too much behind, he asked Rose again and again if she would change her mind about taking him to Australia.

"I'm scared you'll have to go away like Catherine."

"I know you are," Rose said. How could he not be? "But I swear, I won't."

"Definitely?"

"Definitely."

When they weren't packing, they were out saying their goodbyes: to the ducks at the park, Princess Margaret in her bedroom, and the swings (but not those victory-rolled women) at the playground. Rose telephoned Sarah at her office too, not mentioning her trip to see Joe—she didn't know why (Bella's smile?)—but thanking her for all she'd done, telling her to take good care, talking, she realized, like they might never see each other again.

"You're not dying, Rosie," said Sarah. "At least I hope not, and that you get to the Cape safely. The North Atlantic's looking less and less fun . . ."

Back at home, Lester indulged Walter with endless games of snakes and ladders, and Pia stretched her nose-tapping supplier to the limit, procuring sausages for tea, sugar for cakes, and even enough eggs to make custard.

Catherine was thinking of him as well. She wrote, her letter arriving the morning before their night departure for Liverpool, sending a storybook

for Walter, telling Rose how much she'd been wanting to call herself, but had
decided that she'd best stay away.

*It breaks my heart not to see him, but I don't want to unsettle
things for you. Please tell Walter his Catherine loves him, and if
you could write to let me know how he is, I'd be so pleased to hear
from you.*

P.S. Rest assured I don't mind a bit about his routine.

"There you go, Walter," said Rose, handing him the book at breakfast,
smiling at his delighted smile. "Didn't I tell you how much Catherine would
be missing you too?"

She asked Pia and Lester if they'd mind him that morning, since there
were a couple of things she needed to do. They agreed readily, and — first
promising Walter that she'd be back by lunchtime ("Definitely?" he asked.
"Definitely," she said) — she headed out into the warm April sunshine and
made for the Tube.

She might almost have enjoyed that walk along Belgravia's sun-dappled
pavements — the respite from the grief of Vivian's closed door, and the dread
of parting hanging over them all — had she not been so nervous. But she was
nervous. She was in all sorts. As she hastened to Victoria, then ran down the
Tube's escalators, she actually felt like she might be sick.

She made it to Westminster without embarrassing herself, and from
there to the House of Commons.

She met Lionel first, in the lobby: that was the easy bit, although still
horribly hard. They didn't have long to say farewell — things were grim in
Libya, where Rommel was advancing fast on Tobruk, then the Germans
had invaded Greece too, capturing Thessaloniki, so everyone was frantic, and
Winston was preparing to make one of his morale-bolstering speeches in the
House — just time enough for a hug neither of them could bear to let end.

"I'm proud of you, my darling," Lionel said, holding her tight, nearly
making her cry, right there in the midst of all the hurrying politicians. "I've
always been so proud."

"Not always," she said, mind moving, before she could stop it, to the day
he'd found out she was in hospital, and had appeared, as angry as she'd ever
seen him, on her ward.

"Yes, always." He held her tighter. "Please, don't ever forget that we're here to help you when you come home."

"I won't," she choked. Then, fearing that if she didn't leave, she really would start sobbing, she kissed him goodbye, told him to take good care, and forced herself away, not looking back, unable to bear the thought of him staring after her, needing to keep her composure just a bit longer.

She had someone else to see.

Someone who'd written the other letter to arrive at the house that morning, hand-delivered, waiting on the doormat first thing, asking Rose to please be at a coffee shop near the cathedral at ten. *Our usual spot.*

Someone who'd apparently returned to London the night before, and whom she spotted sitting pensively at a shaded table on the cobbles, looking down the crowded pavement, across the road, searching for her, just not in the right place.

Someone who wore a charcoal suit, one of his crisp white shirts that suited him.

But then everything suited him.

Except, maybe, her.

She placed her hand to her stomach, breathed in slowly, and carried on toward him.

He stood when he saw her, held out his hand to touch her, then stopped himself, she supposed because he didn't know if he should.

"Hello, Xander," she said.

They had less than an hour together. He was in even more of a rush than her, needing to get back to the House for Winston's speech. "If it was anything else . . ." he said, and let the words that he'd put her first trail off. Even he seemed to realize they'd be rather rich, given recent form.

They couldn't go on, she'd accepted that now, not even given *how happy* they'd once been. Maybe it had taken her too long to realize ("Just a shade," Joe had said, at his base), but Xander's long silence this past month had finally made her confront just how broken they'd become, and it tore her apart, it did, but she'd assumed that he, so absent, must have reached the same conclusion as her. It was why she'd been so nervous, coming to meet him. She'd been sure their time had come, at last.

Only, he didn't want to end anything. She realized that the moment he almost, but didn't quite, touch her.

It threw her.

As did his excuses for why he'd been gone. He had some very good excuses. His father had had a stroke, he said. He was getting better, but none of them had thought he would. "I was . . . scared," he said, staring across at her, eyes full of that fear, taking her back, with such speed, to how he'd looked when she'd woken him in his hotel room at the start of September, bleeding, in so much pain.

He'd taken care of her, that night.

He really had taken care of her.

"I didn't know if I'd get there in time," he went on, grasping her hand, not hesitating this time. She wasn't wearing her ring. She had it in her purse, ready to give him. Would he notice her finger was bare? "I wasn't sure I'd speak to him again."

"Why didn't you tell me where you were going?" she asked, but not as angrily as she might have, now she knew his father had almost died.

"I don't know," he said, so candidly that she could tell it was the truth. "My uncle had arranged a plane, all I thought about was getting on it."

"You could have written after. Wired . . ."

"I wanted to. I talked about you all the time, with my mom, my brother. They made me see what an idiot I've been." He gripped her fingers harder. "I missed you. Every day."

"Then I don't understand why you didn't write," she said, voice rising now, because he really was making no sense. "I was so worried . . ."

"I knew I'd messed up. I didn't know how to make that right in a wire . . ."

"So you just did nothing?" She bit the inside of her cheek to stop herself crying. She couldn't cry, she couldn't. "You've treated me like I mean nothing."

"You're everything," he said, "you've always been everything." Then, taking her utterly by surprise, he leaned across the table and — regardless of the fact that they were in the middle of Westminster in broad daylight — kissed her, in a way he hadn't kissed her since she'd lost their baby, with a tenderness that confused her even more.

"I'm sorry," he said. "I've said that too much to you. But please, give me another chance . . ."

She didn't speak. She couldn't think, not with his lips so close to hers.

"I'll never not love you," he said. "I just can't help myself. And I want you to put my ring back on." (He had noticed.) "I want you to write to me in Cairo, I swear I'll write back."

"Will you though?" she asked, and oh God, now she really was crying. She wasn't meant to be crying. None of this was meant to be happening. She'd *decided,* made up her *mind* to draw a line. It had been a relief, in so many ways. . . .

"I will," he said, picking up a napkin, wiping her tears.

How many times had he done that?

"You were away before New York," she said. "I called your hotel. . . ."

"I went to Scotland," he said, quickly, like he'd been waiting for her to raise it. "I was mad, Rosie, really mad still about you landing Australia on me. And, I don't know . . . *sad.* I went shooting."

"Shooting?"

"Yeah. I wish I hadn't."

"Shooting what?"

"Birds, I dunno. It didn't make anything better." He ran the back of his hand around her cheek, his knuckles brushing her wet jaw. "All I thought about was you." He kissed her again. "Come on," he said softly, "stop crying now, kid. We're gonna be fine."

Would they be fine?

She didn't know.

But she didn't break anything off that day, either.

After he left her at Westminster Tube—with another unsettling kiss, and a promise that he'd do his best to get back from Cairo, just as soon as she returned from Australia ("Don't hang around," he said. "Or I'll have to come find you . . .")—she couldn't even make up her mind about whether their time in the sunshine had been *something nicer to remember.* She almost wished they hadn't had it. It would have been simpler, in so many ways, to have left England purely angry at him.

But it was done now. All done. She still had his ring in her bag.

She wouldn't put it on again, though. She decided that as she returned to Williams Street. She was still upset, regardless of his excuses, and nettled, now she'd had time to reflect, by the too-quick way he'd said *Scotland* when she'd asked where he'd been before New York.

Had he been there?

Alone?

Should there even be a question?

She suspected not, and until she made her mind up about it, she couldn't bear to be reminded of him constantly, looking at his diamond on her finger.

She gladly buried her worry over all of it, as, nearing number thirty-two, she was greeted by a far happier sight: Walter, running toward her, yellow jumper glowing in the sunshine, Rabbit bopping beside him.

"You're back, you're back," he squealed.

"You were waiting?" she said, swinging him up onto her hip.

"With Lester," he said, and there Lester indeed was, hovering on the yellow front steps. "I wanted to make sure you were coming."

"Of course I was coming," she said, pressing her tear-stiffened cheek to his soft, warm one. "We need to get ready, don't we?"

They did. Their train left Euston at six that evening. Lionel was sending another motor to take them to the station at quarter past five.

They had mere hours now left to go.

And they passed. Slowly, they passed. Rose and Walter spent most of them in the kitchen with Lester and Pia, trying to eat the glorious lunch spread Pia put on — sandwiches, ham and piccalilli, cheeses — failing completely. With the sandwich crusts curling, Lester urged Walter into games of snakes and ladders, Rose brewed multiple pots of tea, and Pia baked yet another batch of biscuits for the voyage.

Walter was quiet.

They were all quiet.

As the afternoon wore on, the April sunshine ebbing, casting the kitchen in shadows, Walter kept needing to go the latrine.

"My tummy feels funny," he said.

"It's because we're waiting," said Rose, wishing she could only make it easier on him. "It's always the worst bit."

At five, the doctor came. He said he wanted to be on hand to help Vivian that night. *She's been holding on, just for this.* Not long after, Lionel's motor arrived, with the same driver who'd brought Rose up from Ilfracombe. It was Lester and Pia who helped him load the luggage. By that point, Rose and Walter were already up with Vivian.

"Leave quickly," Vivian had entreated Rose, earlier in the week, "take him away as fast as you can once we've said goodbye. I won't be able to stand it otherwise."

With her doctor's assistance, she'd got into her wheelchair to say fare-well. Rose could only imagine the pain it cost her to be sitting, but she'd been determined that Walter should go believing her on the mend. Her mask was on her lap. A fire crackled in the grate, but she shivered anyway. Her every breath filled the hot space with a sound Rose had never heard before, and never wanted to hear again.

She had a pinwheel in her hand. Weakly, she held it out to Walter. He took it, eyes brimming, too young, far too young, for all these goodbyes.

"I know," said Vivian, cupping his face, "I know. You can cry, my dear. There's no shame in tears." She didn't stammer. If it hadn't been for her shiv-ering, the sound of her breaths, Rose might almost have been fooled into believing she *was* getting better. "I want you to put this pinwheel in your new bedroom," Vivian said, closing Walter's dimply hand around the han-dle. "That way, you'll always have a bit of me with you."

"I want all of you," he said, so simple. "Please come and see us."

"I'll try," she said, and a tear slid down her papery cheek. Walter started crying too. It broke Rose's heart, but there was nothing to be done. *There's no shame in tears.* "You're about to go on the adventure of your life," Vivian told him. "You're a prince, a knight, a first-class hero . . ."

He almost smiled at that. "A hero?"

"A hero," Vivian said. "I'm afraid you'll meet some villains along the way. They'll try and make you feel small, less than you are." She stroked his dark cheek. There was blood on the back of her hand. The doctor must have just given her something. "I've had that myself. Don't let them do it." She drew a quick breath. "Never, ever, forget how wonderful you are, my darling boy. Promise me."

"I p-promise," he said, sobbing more.

"I love you, Walter."

"I l-l-love you, too."

She looked up then, caught Rose's eye with her swimming ones.

Leave quickly, that look said. *Do it now.*

And Rose — not crying herself by pure, jaw-clenched effort of will — moved, gathering Walter's sobbing body close. "I have you," she said, "I have you, little one." Stopping only to kiss Vivian, and whisper that she'd look after Walter for as long as he needed her, she hurried him downstairs, where Pia and Lester were waiting to hug him too — "Chin up," said Les-ter, his own cloudy eyes far from dry. "Write often," said Pia, embracing

Rose as well. "Go now, off you go . . ." — then out to the mild spring dusk, and the waiting motor.

The driver didn't ask them if they were ready to go. He knew. He kicked the ignition without hesitation, and sped them away.

As they went, with Walter still sobbing on her lap, Rose turned, waving at Pia and Lester on the pavement, then looked up, one final time, at Vivian's window.

"She's been holding on, just for this," her doctor had said.

She'd made it. She'd let Walter be the one to leave her.

She did finally go too, though, that night, *upstairs* to be with her parents, Naomi, all the people in her photographs, and Walter's mummy. But Walter and Rose were well on their way to Liverpool when that happened, Walter fast asleep in the blacked-out carriage, exhausted by his tears, head resting on Rose's shoulder, blissfully unaware that his aunt never would be able to come and see him in Australia after all.

He remained unaware for a long time. They both did.

When ignorance is bliss . . .

It was months before they found out. By then they were thousands of miles away, their journey on that pitch-dark train long behind them; their voyage, and so much else besides, too.

But that was all ahead of them.

On that train, they had no idea of what was coming. They were still at the beginning of their journey.

About to go, as Vivian had said, on the adventure of their lives.

TO AUSTRALIA

CHAPTER NINE

Rose did get seasick on the voyage. She got sick as the proverbial dog, within an hour of the convoy she and Walter were on departing Liverpool's blitz-torn docks: a flotilla of passenger, troop, and supply ships, all painted gray to camouflage them from subs and bombers, drenched by sheeting rain, crowned by barrage balloons, and flanked by battle cruisers. Her mistake had been eating the hotel's porridge for breakfast. She couldn't keep it down once they hit the thrashing waves of the North Atlantic. She'd barely been able to keep it down from the moment she and Walter had boarded their requisitioned P&O liner, the *Illustrious* (it really wasn't). As she'd clutched Walter's hand, following a steward in a faded, threadbare uniform up the steep, rocking gangplank, then through the swaying, ancient ship to their cabin — taking in the gilt-painted hallways with their chipped chandeliers; the grand stairwells' trodden-in carpets and peeling banisters; the rust-crusted door of the screeching elevator that took them to A Deck — the oats had churned in her stomach.

"Does our cabin have a bathroom?" she'd asked the steward uneasily.

"It does," he'd said. "A bit of deck, too. It's a nice one."

It was tiny, faded like the rest of the ship, with more worn carpets, sagging twin beds, a sun-bleached painting of the Taj Mahal, and a bath-room Rose could tell had been luxurious once (there were gold taps on the sink), but now had mold growing between its tiles, and stains on the enamel latrine.

She was to become very familiar with that latrine in the days that followed. She'd wonder, on the rare occasions that she managed to stop heaving into it long enough to think, just how old the ship really was. Certainly, from the view through the portholes, it looked like the oldest in the convoy. She supposed that anything in better shape would never have been given over for passenger use in the first place, but kept for the military. But oh, it smelled: of mildew, oil from the ship's engines, and—the farther they progressed through the Atlantic's sub-infested waters—vomit. It creaked as well, like Rose couldn't believe, groaning up and over the waves, the noise never louder than at night, when lights were banned (the subs again), and in the darkness, the creaking became all there was; that, and the wails of other passengers trying to keep on their feet long enough to race for a bowl.

"Can I come into your bed?" Walter, one of the lucky few *not* to get seasick, would inevitably whisper from his own mattress, in the depths of the night.

"I'm worried I'll keep waking you," Rose would whisper back, hair pressed to her clammy cheek, mouth sticking with dehydration.

"I don't mind," he'd say. In her nausea, she'd picture his blue eyes darting, unseeing, around the rolling blackness. "I'm a bit scared."

So she'd let him in with her, and hold him with one arm, a bucket with the other, which at least meant she didn't have to disturb him too much to vomit. Strange, but through all those long nights, unlike Walter, she wasn't frightened: not of offshore bombers, nor even of the subs. She was simply too ill to be afraid.

Every cloud . . .

Choppy, the stewards, who mopped the ruined bathrooms each morning, called the conditions.

Torture felt like a more accurate description.

Hardly anyone left their cabins for that first hideous week. There were hundreds of them on board—evacuees, WAAFs on foreign postings with the air force, women from the navy too, then families of diplomats living in the still-peaceful East—but the ship's battered promenade decks and once-splendid dining hall remained near-empty. Rose knew this because, unlike everyone else, she had no choice but to be up and about, since Walter, in the pink of health, could hardly stay trapped in their cabin all day. Besides, given how upset he still was over their goodbyes (he asked about everyone at number thirty-two constantly), Rose wanted to keep him occupied. Luckily, so far as distractions from grief went, being at sea turned out to be as compelling as the zoo, Hamley's, and Joe's base combined, magnified to the power of several thousand.

What did it matter to Walter that their ship was falling apart? To him, an almost-five-year-old on his first ever sea voyage, it was a palace, an endless array of doors to be opened, lifeboats to be peered into, stairs to be raced up and down. He loved being on deck, up where the stewards assured Rose it was safe, taking his pinwheel out to watch it whizz around in wind so loud they had to shout to be heard above it. He'd laugh in his yellow raincoat, Rabbit tucked under his arm, exclaiming in delight when he spotted a whale, an actual whale, over by that battle cruiser. "Rosie, Rosie, Rosie, did you see?" (She didn't. She'd been having a retch overboard.) He was especially intrigued by the empty, cordoned-off swimming pool they found ("Why does it smell like that?" he asked. "I suspect because I did something very wrong in a former life," said Rose), and over the moon when a steward fashioned a tarpaulin tent for him in the base of it, so that he could play out of the rain with his animals.

There were more kind stewards in the dining hall. "Our best customer," they'd chorus, whenever Walter arrived. Their only customer, really. What with their smiles, their encouragement that he eat whatever he wanted (there was too much food; no one could stomach it), it was small wonder he was always so eager to return. Frankly, if there was a hell worse than keeping yourself upright in the throes of seasickness to bounce from swaying wall to swaying wall, escorting a ravenous child to a room that sweated the stench of boiled potatoes and custard, Rose didn't want to know about it.

"My nerves are shot," she said to Walter on their third afternoon, as she emerged from the dining room's latrines to find him working his way through a bowl of spotted dick.

He stared up her, spoon halfway to his mouth. "You look like Aunty Vivian," he said worriedly.

"I know." She'd just made the mistake of catching her reflection in the glass.

"Do you want some of my pudding?" He proffered his spoon.

"You eat it," she said, pushing it gently away. "I'm sure I'll feel better soon."

She wasn't sure of anything, but Steven from the hardware store in Ilfracombe had promised her the sickness would be brief, *no more than a few days*, and she was holding on to that. Surely by tomorrow, things would improve.

But the next morning, just as she was washing her hair over the sink, the wind changed, sending the waves in a different direction, making her feel worse than ever.

"Oh God," she groaned, swiveling for the latrine.

"Are your nerves shocked again?" asked Walter from the door, which might have made her laugh, had she not felt so wretched.

"Completely shocked," she said, collapsing back against the moldy tiles. Through the thin walls, she heard a woman swearing she'd never sail again. It brought Rose no comfort that she wasn't alone. Dying a slow death from vomiting was hardly a case for misery-loving company.

Walter sat by her, resting his head on her shoulder. Weakly she put her arm around him.

"Would you like some porridge for breakfast?" he asked.

"Oh God," she groaned. *Porridge.* "Oh God . . ."

It reminded her of how she'd felt when she was pregnant: the permanently sour taste in her mouth, the hunger but not hunger; the utter, awful relentlessness of it.

But, just as had happened then, eventually — and far less traumatically — her sickness did finally pass.

By the time they were into their third week of the voyage, and the captain came into a much buzzier breakfast sitting — the African sun blazing through the dining room's salt-crusted windows, him silencing the chatter to give them the good news that the convoy had now cleared the most hazardous waters, and was progressing on a direct course for the Cape ("Still no lights at night, I'm afraid, we're by no means standing down our watch, but please know I'm resting a fraction easier") — she, eating a hearty helping of bread pudding, felt so much more herself again, it was hard to believe she'd ever been that poorly.

We've all been swapping war stories, she wrote on her first postcard to Enid: a picture of the *Illustrious* back in finer times, bought in the ship's convenience store, ready to post with her other letters when they reached Cape Town. *There's not much to do except sit on deck and chat. Don't worry, I'm not getting burned. I seem to be going brown, which Walter thinks is a hoot. We've been promised bananas when we dock. I'll send them your regards.*

They hugged the coast all the way to Cape Town, sailing slowly, cautiously, *keeping watch;* it took them a month to finally reach the busy port. A month in which the sun kept shining, Walter turned five, and the aging captain—who'd noticed him tearing around the ship and had kindly asked Rose what they were doing, traveling to the other side of the world ("Oh my," he'd said, when Rose had told him. "Oh dear . . .")—arranged a cake. He raised a toast too, to Walter, at dinner, calling him a natural seafarer, which made him beam with pride, even more when the captain broke into a round of "Happy Birthday," and the hundred or so others in their sitting joined in with gusto, making the dining room's peeling walls vibrate, everyone smiling, no one for a second thinking twice about the color of Walter's skin (or certainly not betraying it, if they did).

"Do you think Mummy was watching me blow out the candles?" Walter asked Rose, when she tucked him and Rabbit in that night.

"Absolutely she was," said Rose.

They reached Cape Town not many days later, but didn't go ashore. The sun-scalded docks were heaving, crammed with ships waiting to join their convoy to the Orient, and they anchored just long enough to re stock their larders and furnaces, shed their post and a handful of passengers, then they were on their way again. *With bananas,* Rose wrote to Enid, savoring her first one in almost two years.

They sailed so slowly after that, diverting clear of any reported threats, that it took them another two months to reach Bombay. The weeks stretched, ever hotter, so relaxed out in the open water, that—with no evening news bulletins on the wireless, no morning papers with headlines shouting about which new city had been blitzed—it was almost possible to forget a war was going on. Days went by without them seeing land, the children played quoits on faded, splintered boards, the grown-ups lounged and smoked and ate, and Walter, who was yet to take the leap into doing more than smiling shyly at the other children, kept on with his ship explorations, his sessions in his swimming pool den, and lost hours playing with the farm figurines Rose had bought him, sitting happily, Rabbit beside him, at her feet.

"I keep forgetting you're his nanny," a friendly WAAF, bound for Bombay, smilingly remarked one baking morning, as she and Rose drank tea in deck chairs, watching him.

"So do I sometimes," Rose confessed.

"I wish I'd thought of nannying rather than the services," the woman said, shifting in her chair. "It would be nice not to be told what knickers to wear, for a start."

Rose laughed, but didn't say how much she'd hated those scratchy undergarments herself. She hadn't told anyone that she'd been in uniform, mainly because she didn't want to go into how she'd come to be out of it. Confessing to her dismissal *for morals unbecoming of a woman in the air force* (that was, being pregnant, then nearly dying ceasing to be pregnant, all while being unmarried) was hardly a topic for relaxed deck chair conversation.

But surrounded by so many WAAFs, she found herself thinking more often of the people she'd left behind at her station. She hadn't been there long—she'd joined up in January of 1940, and left just eight months later, at the end of that summer of death and dogfights that had been the Battle of Britain—and had spent most of that time holed up inside the tense walls of her station's radar room; that and racing for the safety trenches when the Luftwaffe arrived to bomb and strafe them. She'd made some good friends, though. While she hadn't stayed in touch with any of them—it would have been too painful—she hoped they were all right. She wanted to believe they'd survive whatever else this war threw at them.

She thought about everyone else back in England, too. On top of her postcards to Enid, she wrote so many letters, to Joe—who she tried to hold faith was safe since Bella had sent no word otherwise—and Lionel, Pia, Catherine, Lester, and Vivian (hoping, *hoping*, that she might yet be clinging on), Sarah too, since she never could seem to leave her out (she rather missed knowing she was close by; it surprised her how much), and to Xander, of course.

Those were the hardest letters of all.

She didn't know what to tell him. She couldn't imagine him being interested in the detail she gave the others of her and Walter's days, so she spoke mainly about him, asking about his journey to Cairo, what his hotel was like, and if he'd been into the desert yet. *Be careful of the camels*, she wrote, then scribbled out, because he was a very good journalist, and as quips went, it wasn't funny enough. It wasn't really funny at all.

I keep thinking about the way you kissed me, she wrote instead on that same ruined piece of paper, in the stifling heat of late afternoon, the day before they reached Bombay.

> *I wonder if I should have let you kiss me like that more. When you were doing it, I felt like you really did love me as much as you say you do. I felt like I was enough for you, again.*
>
> *I wish I felt like that all the time.*
>
> *And I wish I could have believed you when you said you were shooting in Scotland, yet I keep remembering that pretty waitress in your bar: the one who always smiled at you, but not at me, and never made you feel like a criminal.*
>
> *You said you never noticed her.*
>
> *I wish I could believe that, too.*
>
> *I wish I could believe so many things that you told me, about being as upset as I was that we lost our baby especially. But I'm still not sure I do believe that. I can't forget that you wanted me to get rid of it. I've tried, so hard, to do as you've asked and forget, but I can't. So perhaps you've been right all this time. Perhaps I never have forgiven you. I wish I could.*
>
> *Like I wish I still trusted you.*
>
> *I wish that the most.*

All I want is to go back to when I never doubted you, or us, at all.

She never intended to send him that page. It was smudged, scored-through; too honest. But that night, the post officer came around to her and Walter's cabin before she'd been expecting him, and in her sweaty haste to stuff everything she'd written into the right envelopes, she forgot to discard that piece of paper, and sealed it up with all the other pages she'd labored over for Xander, scrawling the address of Shepheard's Hotel in Cairo on the front.

She only realized she'd done it the next morning. It came to her, quite out of the blue, with a sickening thud at breakfast, as the boat dropped anchor at Bombay, and she was spreading Walter's toast with jam. She belted for the post room, Walter, toast in hand, behind her, pumping his legs to keep up. But it was too late. The sacks of the ship's mail had already been carted down the gangplank.

"Oh no," said Walter.

"Oh no, indeed," she said, pressing her hand to her sweaty forehead, replaying her own words. *Perhaps I never have forgiven you....*

"Are your nerves . . . ?"

"They're shocked, Walter. Totally shocked."

Since there really was nothing she could do about it, though (other than hope her letter would get lost, preferably in a nonviolent accident that didn't engender any loss of life), she endeavored to try and forget her own stupidity, and, on the recommendation of one of the stewards, took Walter ashore, for the first time since they'd left Liverpool.

Her legs, after so long at sea, were as shaky as a newborn deer's once they hit dry land, straight into the thick of the shouting hordes massed on Bombay's pungent dockside. Walter couldn't walk straight either. With her heart in her mouth (the crowds!), she gripped his hand *very tight*, and — yelling that he should keep close, not let go, "if you can't see me I can't see you" ("I see you, Rosie," he yelled back, holding Rabbit just as tightly, "I see you . . ."), she led him in the direction the steward had told her, dodging the workers hauling sacks of what smelled like spices in the sunshine, weaving through the porters and troops and ox-drawn carts, then under the majestic stone arch of the Gateway of India, across the road rammed with rickshaws and army trucks, into the grandeur of the waterside Taj Mahal Hotel — which, with its marbled foyer and wafting overhead fans, was absurdly serene by contrast.

"Oh, I like it here," she said, her voice echoing from the high ceilings. A harp played, obscuring the cacophony of horns and rickshaw bells outside. "Shall we stay, Walter?"

"What about Uncle Max?"

"Ah yes," said Rose. "I almost forgot about him."

They found their way out to the al fresco tables of the Sea Lounge, where they joined lots of well-heeled memsahibs who appeared entirely at home, then several other women with children who looked sufficiently fish-out-of-water-like that they too must have come from the convoy. With the sun beating down, the Indian Ocean glistening beyond, they took a seat at one of the remaining tables and, beneath the shade of a parasol, ate ice cream from frosted bowls.

"Ohhhh," Walter said, closing his eyes at his first spoonful. "Ohhhhhh, my goodness . . . This was definitely worth it, Rosie."

It wasn't his last ice cream of the voyage. He had another four days later, this time beneath the swaying fans of the Galle Face Hotel in Colombo, in the joyous company of Rose's parents, Stella and Henry.

Rose never did get to surprise them at their barracks; rather, they were the ones to surprise her, by turning up in her and Walter's cabin, all smiles and open arms, just as she and Walter were preparing to leave and brave the Colombo rickshaws to find them.

"I can't believe it," Rose squealed, running into their hugs. "I can't, I can't . . ."

"Lionel double-bluffed you," laughed Henry. "He knew we'd never forgive him if you missed us, so he wired. We've been following your progress all the way."

"Counting down the minutes," said Stella, holding Rose tight. Rose breathed in her familiar scent, her love, nearly weeping, just in her happiness at being with her, with them. They somehow hadn't changed a bit in the three years since she'd last seen them. Her father, in khaki, was still a slightly younger version of Lionel, and her mother, in a turquoise silk dress, was as glamorous as she'd ever been.

Rose told her as much.

"Glamorous," said her mother, crying in earnest, wiping away her tears. "I'll be forty-seven next year." She pushed Rose back, stroking her arms, examining her with her bright green eyes that saw everything. "You look well yourself." Her relief was audible. "So well."

"She looks splendid," said Henry.

"I am," said Rose, desperate to reassure them, feeling a fresh wave of guilt at how much she'd worried them. Then, anxious not to exclude Walter—hovering shyly by his bunk with Rabbit—she beckoned him over. "My fellow explorer," she said, "who doesn't get seasick."

"What?" said Henry. "Not at all?"

Walter didn't reply, just stared at Henry's uniform. (*Hero.*)

"Not a bit," said Rose, answering for him.

"Champion effort," said Henry.

"You'll have to tell me your secret," said Stella. "How about over ice cream? Do you like it?"

"Just a bit," said Rose.

"Yes, a lot," Walter said, rediscovering his voice.

"Well, I know a perfect spot," said Stella.

And that was when they left, for the Galle Face.

They walked the short distance from the ship. The palm-fringed fore-shore was steaming, almost as busy as Bombay had been. The air, buzzing with noise, smelled rich: of heat, sewage, salt, and petrol fumes. As Rose's parents led the way through it all, they told her that she'd only just caught them; they were due to set sail themselves in another fortnight, at the end of July, for Malaya.

Rose faltered in her tracks. "Is it safe?" she asked, remembering Lionel's words in the Goring, about how jumpy the Far East commanders were get-ting over the threat that the Japanese, who'd already invaded parts of China, might turn their attention to British-held lands next. *Malaya and Singapore are the worry....*

"It's perfectly safe," said Henry soothingly. "But they're hoping to bulk up their forces, just to keep the Japs away, so off I go, dragging your mother with me . . ."

"*Dragging*," said Stella, with an arch smile: the one Rose and Joe re-ferred to as her chorus-girl smile. "Poor, poor me."

"I wish you were staying here," said Rose, still uneasy.

"We'll be fine," said her father, tucking her arm into his. "If anything does happen, which it won't, we'll move to Singapore. It's a fortress."

Rose nodded, wanting to be convinced, not spoil the afternoon. "A for-tress," she echoed, looking up at him smiling down at her, the sun behind him, creases around his eyes. "A fortress sounds good."

Not spoiling the afternoon, they left the subject alone for the rest of their too-short time together, eating their ice creams in the humid opulence of the Galle Face's ocean-facing veranda, speaking of nicer things instead: Lionel, naturally, then Sarah—whom Rose's parents hadn't met but were eager to hear more about.

"Is she as terrifying as Lionel says?" Stella asked, helping Walter to scrape the last bits of ice cream from his bowl.

"Yes," said Rose, "but she has a big heart, too . . ."

They talked of Xander, as well, but only in passing—Rose's parents hadn't met him either, and although they asked after him courteously enough, they didn't say half as much as Rose suspected they might have, had Walter not been present (thank you, Walter). More than anyone, they talked of Joe.

To Rose's intense relief, her parents had recently heard from him and he was well, still surviving, but apparently as useless as ever at writing letters, so they were desperate to know how he'd been when Rose had last seen him.

"Please," said Stella, "leave nothing out."

Rose didn't. She relayed his every last look and word when she and Walter had visited him at his base.

"He gave me rides on his shoulders," Walter chimed in, "like Rosie does."

"I used to do that with them," said Henry.

Walter smiled. He had ice cream around his mouth. "Joe told me you used to tickle his feet."

"Did he now?" said Henry fondly, and turned rather quiet for a little while after that.

The war came up, as it always did. Rose's parents updated her on how grave things still were for the Allied forces, pretty much everywhere — Greece had now fallen in its entirety after the loss of Crete, there'd been another awful Allied defeat against Rommel in Libya, then Hitler had at last launched his invasion on Russia, as Lionel had said he might, stretching Allied resources even thinner — and they all pontificated on whether the Americans would ever go beyond their financial support for Britain, and join the fight themselves.

"I think there're plenty who want to," said Rose, recalling all Xander had said on the matter, not to mention the American pilots she'd encountered who'd enlisted to help, even though they didn't have to.

"There's enough who don't," said Henry. "They lost a lot in the last war. I fear they're going to need something really very awful to push them this time."

"What kind of awful?" Walter asked.

At which point Henry changed the subject, looking at his watch and saying with a sorry sigh that they really had better head back to the port.

It was once they reached the ship that Henry whisked Walter off for a look at the fish, and Stella, alone with Rose for the first time, did what Rose was sure she'd been waiting to do all afternoon, and — delicate face taut with concern — softly asked her how she was feeling these days about her baby.

"Oh, you know," said Rose. "Sad." Heartbroken, always. *It's already gone to the incinerator.*

"Your father prays for it," Stella said. "Every night."

"Oh, *Mum*..."

"Don't *mum* me. I want you to know that he's keeping it well looked after, in his way..."

"Please don't," Rose said, voice catching, unable to stand the thought of it, so tiny, being anywhere she wasn't, all alone. She'd felt it kicking, just before it had all gone wrong; such little kicks, living kicks. . . .

"Come here," said her mother, wrapping her in her arms. "There'll be other babies..."

"Not that one," said Rose, her words muffled by her mother's silk shoulder.

"You'll love another just as much..."

"I might not."

"You will..."

"No," said Rose, pulling away, drawing a breath on her grief. She couldn't give in to it, especially not with Walter close by. "I told you, the doctors said I mightn't be able to..."

"And I've told you, they were just trying to scare you."

"Well, they succeeded."

Stella narrowed her eyes, angry, like Lionel had been angry, that day he'd arrived on the ward. "I want to scare them."

"Lionel did an A-one job," said Rose, "I assure you."

"I wish I'd been there," said Stella.

"It was certainly something to behold," said Rose, almost smiling, in spite of everything, at the memory of her uncle appearing, apparition-like, at the foot of her hospital bed, kissing her gently, *You'll be all right now,* then going absolutely apoplectic at the unfortunate registrar on duty. And that had just been the start. . . .

Stella reached for her hands. "Your father and I want you to come to Malaya after Brisbane. I didn't want to mention it in front of Walter, but we don't think you should rush back to England."

Rose sighed, her hot forehead creasing. "I don't know..."

"Please," said Stella. "Who knows how long Xander will be away."

"It's not just him," said Rose, turning to look through the crowds of returning passengers at Walter, beside her father, his dimply hands on his knees, curls flopping forward as he peered down into the murky, fuel-stained water. "I can't think that far ahead . . ."

"You don't want to think about leaving Walter," said her mother, following her gaze.

"I can't," Rose said, too raw from talking about the baby to be anything less than honest. "I'll never see him again." Her voice cracked on the awful truth. "I can't imagine not knowing what he's having for his tea. Or if he's crying, and needing help . . ."

"I know," said Stella, who of course did, better than anyone. Hadn't she left Rose and Joe? "But he'll be with family, like you were with Lionel . . ."

"I want him to be with me," said Rose, trying to smile, because she realized how ridiculous she was being, how impossible that was. The smile didn't work. Her cheeks wouldn't cooperate. "I didn't think it was going to feel like losing another baby . . ."

"Oh, darling . . ."

"I'm scared, Mum. I'm scared I'll have no one, after this."

"You'll have us," Stella said, squeezing her hands. "Let us look after you. Think about it, Rosie. Please."

"All right," said Rose, glancing back toward her father, who was studying them anxiously, clearly aware of what they were talking about. "I will, I promise."

Saying goodbye to them that day was horrendous, even with the thought that Rose might be with them again so soon. She was shaky enough from her conversation with her mother, but also so very upset to be leaving them. Now that they'd spent this too-short time together, it had opened her up, made her realize just how sorely she'd been missing them.

But somehow, after many hugs, they all managed to let the other go, and Rose, picking Walter up, needing to feel the comfort of him in her arms, headed up the same gangplank she'd walked down so happily, a few short hours before.

"You look like your mummy," Walter said, as they went.

"You think so?"

He nodded. "Why don't I look like my mummy?"

"You do," said Rose, without hesitation. She'd studied that photograph of them together too often to be in need of consideration.

"She had yellow hair, though."

"Blue eyes too, I expect," said Rose, breathless; it was a steep climb. "Just like yours."

"I forgot about that."

"There you go then," said Rose, dropping a kiss on his curls.

"Will Uncle Max have blue eyes?"

"I don't know," said Rose. "We'll have to wait and see."

They reached the top of the gangplank. The deck was full of smiling stewards welcoming them "home," and the other passengers, some back from expeditions to buy tea leaves and Oriental scarves they'd probably never wear, many more fresh to the ship—replacing the last of the servicewomen who'd disembarked earlier onto transport trucks—all of them looking around despondently at the *Illustrious*'s rusty railings and scabby paint.

Rose turned, Walter on her hip, and blew a kiss down to her parents, arms entwined on the packed foreshore. Around them, dockworkers blew whistles, and crowds of others waited to wave their goodbyes. Already, the other vessels remaining in the convoy—just three, after Bombay—had pushed back, horns blowing, heading for the open ocean. The *Illustrious* didn't take long to join them. In the ship's belly, the engines kicked into motion. There was a deep grinding as the anchor was pulled up. Down on the dockside, the workers yelled, running to unravel the great ropes that had kept them tethered to shore, and that was it, they were off, moving away from the port and Rose's parents, both of whom—her father in his khaki, her mother in her turquoise dress—were already becoming smaller.

"Goodbye," Rose called to them, "goodbye."

She and Walter didn't stop waving until the pair of them had disappeared, the palm-covered coastline of Colombo too, vanishing into the darkening dusk.

"There we are," said Rose quietly to Walter, staring into the blue-tinged blackness, picturing her parents' eyes staring right back at her, "our last stop."

It was to be their last sight of land too, other than tiny islets, for weeks.

They didn't see the bulk of a continent again for more than a month. The war continued, with Hitler's forces pushing hard on Russia, racing against time to complete their invasion before the onset of the Siberian winter, but on board, they played more quoits, spotted turtles and whales and dolphins amid the waves ("Look, Rosie, look"), and Walter tentatively started to do more than just smile at the other children, and talked to one of them too. Never had Rose's heart felt fuller than the first time she watched him edge up to a smiling blond little girl who'd boarded at Colombo, and say, "Hello, my name's Walter. What's yours?" It was Verity. Verity was also five, and from Brisbane, as was her mother Kate, and they were both very nice, very sad to have left Verity's dad, a tea planter, behind in Ceylon to enlist, but also very happy that Walter and Rose were Brisbane-bound too.

Kate was from the city itself. She'd only vaguely heard of the Lucknow cattle farm. ("Stations, we call them," she said, smiling. "It won't be anything like as small as your English farms, I can tell you that.") She wasn't like those victory-rolled women in the park; she never once alluded to the shade of Walter's skin. Verity, who'd grown up with the children of local Ceylonese tea workers, certainly didn't give a hoot about it either.

It was Rose who raised the matter—or rather that of Walter's father—a week or so into her acquaintance with Kate. She hadn't forgotten her misgivings over what had become of him, this man who'd fought *in a manner*; even with Vivian's assurances, she kept agonizing over what hand the Lucknows might have played in his disappearance, and, by extension, what that would mean for how they'd treat Walter. She didn't want to believe Vivian would send Walter somewhere he couldn't be happy, but at the same time, try as she might, she couldn't shake Lionel's question from her mind. *Is there anywhere else for him to go?*

It was her anxiety that compelled her to speak to Kate about it all, one morning while the children played in the swimming pool. She supposed she wanted Kate—the only person she'd met from Brisbane—to reassure her, tell her that she was worrying over nothing.

Kate didn't.

"I wish I could," she said. "I hope that whoever these Lucknows are, they'll be good to Walter, but honestly, if you want my opinion, Mabel left them at that station because she was forced to. Places like that aren't known for treating Aborigines well. Some do," she caveated, "but plenty don't . . ."

"They don't want them there?" asked Rose, dreading the answer.

"Oh they want them," said Kate, "they *employ* them, as stockmen, drovers, but for a fraction of what they pay whites."

"Right," said Rose heavily. "How fractional?"

"Pretty bloody fractional," said Kate. "Most of them have them living in these camps, completely separate." She shook her head. "Really, it would have been tough for Mabel to stay with Walter's father, even if she'd wanted to. I can't think an old cattle family like hers would've welcomed a marriage, and Queensland has laws . . ."

"Laws?" Rose felt sick now.

"Laws," repeated Kate. "Have you heard of a thing called 'White Australia'?"

"No," said Rose, with a certain sense she didn't want to.

Kate told her about it anyway, full of disdain as she relayed her government's policies prohibiting immigrants of *non-European* ethnicity from moving to Australia, filling Rose with horror as she talked of the means they used to keep their own non-white population in check — of which banning them from voting was apparently just the start.

"There's a Chief Protector of Aborigines," she said. "He controls . . . everything . . . about their lives. Their employment, earnings, property, and," she gave Rose a rueful look, "who they marry. Some states encourage mixed couples, there's this idea of 'breeding the Aborigines out,' " — she grimaced — "but in Queensland they don't like mixing." She sighed. "I'm afraid they just don't want to encourage children like your gorgeous little Walter."

Rose stared back at her, disbelieving.

What was she taking Walter into?

"People do travel to other states to marry, though," said Kate, talking on. "We're not all bad, I promise. There're those who hate the laws enough that they'll help Aborigines get around them." She frowned. "There must be some reason Mabel left home all alone . . ."

"I think something must have happened to Walter's father," said Rose, never surer of it than now. *They just don't want to encourage children like your gorgeous little Walter.*

"Maybe," said Kate, regretfully. "Or he, well . . . you know . . . wasn't someone Mabel *wanted* to be with, in that — "

"Don't," said Rose, interrupting before Kate could put that particular possibility into words. "I can't even think about that."

She couldn't.

As Walter peeked his head out of his den, smiling up at her, just checking she was still there, she tried to expel from her mind the idea that he could have been made in such a way.

It still preyed on her, though. All of it did.

And, as they traveled farther beyond the equator, the weather chilling into the Southern Hemisphere's winter, Walter became more unsettled too. He never strayed far from where Rose was, and, the closer they drew to Australia, started to say that maybe he didn't want to go to Uncle Max's after all.

"Why can't we just stay here?" he asked, as he and Rose drank cocoa outside their cabin one night, wrapped in blankets on deck chairs, the full moon bathing the icy ocean in silver light. "I like it here, with Verity and you . . ."

"You'll still be with me," Rose said, hoping so much that, whatever the Lucknows might have done in the past, they wouldn't make a liar out of her now, and would let her stay on until Walter was properly settled. She had enough money to keep her going. Before she'd left, Vivian had given her a stack of pounds to cover her wages up until September, then almost double the amount again. *Think of it as a thank-you.* "Haven't I promised I won't leave unless you say I can?"

"I won't ever say you can."

"We'll see . . ."

"We won't, Rosie," he said, hands wrapped around his mug, eyes wide. "We won't see . . ."

"All right," she said, unable to bear the panic in his face. "It's all right."

They sailed on, and the weather became even colder. Gradually, they all spent more time indoors—Walter and Verity eating every meal together, doing drawings and playing snakes and ladders on Walter's bunk—until, on a gray, foggy August morning, the ship's horns blazed again, and the hundreds of them on board rose, braving the cold to stand on deck once more, Walter back in his raincoat, holding Rose's hand, all of them watching as the rugged, windswept shores of Victoria slowly came into view.

"Is that it?" Walter asked Rose, quietly, reverentially.

"That's it," said Rose, just as quiet, apprehension snaking down her spine.

Australia had never felt quite real to her, until that moment. It had been an idea, a faraway concept, too distant to be tangible.

Now, though . . .

It felt real now.

The salt wind whipped her face. Ahead, waves crashed against Victoria's looming cliffs.

She drew a deep breath.

Beside her, Walter did the same.

She squeezed his trembling hand.

Please, she thought, *let him be happy, here. Let him be glad we came.*

She smiled down at him, wiped a tear from his watering eyes with her thumb.

Please, just let them be kind.

CHAPTER TEN

They reached the sleepy port of Brisbane on the lower reaches of the Brisbane River four days later, in the last week of August, stopping first at the
misty, industrial dockside of Melbourne, then, on a much clearer, crisper day,
at Sydney Harbour, where the dark blue water sparkled in the wintry sun,
the vast bridge glinted, and the city's sandstone buildings shone. (*Such a
show-off,* came Joe's voice.)

It was warmer again, up in Brisbane. Not Bombay warm, but balmy,
if threateningly cloudy, the narrow river's banks thick with tropical veg-
etation, dotted with palms, and the oddest-looking houses too, all built
on stumps, with red tin roofs; a couple of women in aprons came out of
them, children in tow, staring up at the *Illustrious* as they cruised past.
Other than them, though, the bankside was deserted. Rose, squinting in
the stormy glare, had read in a paper brought aboard at Ceylon how, back
in March, the US naval squadron had visited the city, sending everyone
wild with "Yank-mania," bringing record-breaking crowds to the river to
greet the fleet's dawn arrival. She struggled to imagine the furor now, with
everything so very quiet. It was as though the close, steamy afternoon were
holding its breath.

She'd brought Walter up from their cabin early for their arrival, wanting to be at the front of the rush to disembark. He'd been needing the

latrine constantly since lunch, just as he had when they'd been about to leave London, and it felt easier to be on the move than not. They were dressed in their best, their onboard luggage down with the porters in the hold, ready for off-loading. They'd bade their goodbyes to the captain and stewards, but not yet to Kate and Verity, both of whom joined them as the *Illustrious*—the very last ship remaining of their convoy after Sydney—crawled through the shallows, progressing cautiously, agonizingly slowly over the riverbed, toward the port's long wharves.

The harbor itself was smaller than Rose had been expecting, much more provincial than either Melbourne or Sydney, with weathered wooden jetties, timber dock sheds, fishing trawlers bobbing at anchor, and the low-rise city sprawling behind. There were seagulls everywhere: feeding off the trawlers' nets, perched on their boughs, circling above, dirt-white feathers melding with the gray sky. As the birds squawked, Kate made a joke about their Australian accents, at which Rose duly smiled, but she barely registered the movement of her own sweat-dampened lips. She wasn't looking at the birds anymore either. She'd spotted something else, something she couldn't stop staring at even when the *Illustrious* shook, dropping anchor, bashing sideways into the dock.

It was the noise that first drew her attention: a swell of excitement coming from a crush of people massed behind barricades at the end of the quayside, cheering, waving at the *Illustrious*, clearly come to collect their friends, relatives . . . five-year-old little boys. Unlike the empty riverbank, there were well in excess of a hundred crowded there—men in suits, women in bright dresses, wide hats protecting them from the sunless sky—too far away for Rose to see properly. She couldn't make out any of their faces, but all she could think about was where, in the thick of that noisy collection of strangers, the Lucknows might be.

The unknown nagged at her relentlessly, all through the rigmarole of disembarkation that followed: navigating Walter down the packed gangplanks, distracting him from his own nerves during their wait with Kate and Verity to have their papers stamped (*I spy with my little eye. . . .*), then propelling him through the hectic pushing of everyone collecting their belongings from the luggage bays.

"Hold my hand, little man," she shouted. *If you can't see me . . .*

Never once did it occur to her, during any of that rush, to doubt that the Lucknows would be waiting for her and Walter on the quayside. Vivian had assured her they would be. "The house is only a couple of hours inland," she'd said. "They know you're expecting them." Rose had no reason to doubt her word. Not yet. As she handed her luggage tag to one of the ship's porters, she believed absolutely that the only thing now standing between herself, Walter, and his family was the time it would take for the porter to return with their trunks.

That, and their goodbye to Kate and Verity, which they said right there at the bays, Kate and Verity's trunks having come out first. The parting was hard, a horrible wrench, but brief—it was too crowded on the jetty for the four of them to linger over anything—which at least seemed to make it easier on the children. They didn't cry; rather Verity kissed Walter on the cheek, and he flushed, kissing her quickly back, which was sweet, and lovely, and should have made Rose smile, only she couldn't. She simply couldn't. She was far too anxious.

"My nerves are shocked for you," said Kate, hugging her. "Remember, if either of you need anything, telephone. We're in the directory."

Rose hugged her back, thanking her, saying she was sure they'd be fine, determinedly hoping—through her trepidation—that they might be. That hope was all that was keeping her going.

She couldn't let it go.

She gripped onto it when, a quarter hour later, with her and Walter's own trunks finally collected, and him perched on the trolley atop them all, the two of them followed in Kate and Verity's wake, over to the barricades, only to discover when they got there that, contrary to all Vivian's fine words, the Lucknows *weren't* behind them. It threw Rose, of course, that they hadn't come. It surprised her, very much, to find a taxi driver called Lance waiting in their place—a placard reading W. LUCKNOW AND R. HAMILTON held aloft—but she refused to read anything sinister into their absence. Lance, who was brusque, but reassuringly friendly to Walter, winking at him (Rose managed a smile, when he did that), told her that he'd been sent by the shipping office, the account already settled in full, and even though he didn't have a name for who'd made the arrangement, Rose was sure one of the Lucknows must have, too busy in the end to make the trip themselves.

Yes, it seemed a *little* odd to her that they'd sent no message of explanation with Lance, but she didn't dwell on it. The shipping office could, after all, simply have forgotten to pass a message on.

"I'm glad it's going to be just us a bit longer, Rosie," said Walter, as she lifted him down from the trolley, letting Lance take it, on to where he'd parked his ute (whatever that was) on the road.

"I think I am too," she admitted, kissing him.

Now that the shock of the Lucknows' absence was starting to pass, this extra time before meeting them felt like a stay of execution.

"Best move," called Lance, frowning upward at the massing clouds. "There's a helluva storm coming."

Rose nodded, but didn't immediately follow. She turned, Walter on her hip, stealing one final glance across at the *Illustrious*. Its gangplanks were empty now, its walls dulled by the slate, purple sky, the water swelling an eerie turquoise beneath its hull. There very much was a storm coming. The old ship had no need to worry, though. It wouldn't be heading out to sea that evening, but into Brisbane's dry dock. ("Essential repairs," the captain had said, rather begging the question as to how seaworthy it had been, these long months.) Rose rested her cheek against Walter's curls, replaying those months—the weeks and weeks the two of them had spent together on board condensed into seconds—feeling a sudden, awful ache right through her, because they really were all over.

Then, hearing Lance call again for her to hurry, she dragged her eyes away from her and Walter's floating home, determinedly not thinking about what else the captain had said to her: that she'd perhaps find herself climbing back aboard before long, for her journey away from Australia. She simply couldn't stand that; sitting in the dining room Walter had had his birthday in, walking by that swimming pool. . . . Shaking the possibility off, she hastened on.

Afterward, she'd come to look back on that image of herself, hurrying after Lance, the first raindrops falling, dampening her favorite red dress, and be amazed that she'd been so quick to put one foot in front of the other. It would seem . . . ridiculous, really . . . that she hadn't had a keener sense of foreboding about what she was hurtling Walter toward. Felt some warning alarm of what was afoot.

But as the sky began to grumble, and she picked up her pace, she felt nothing beyond an old childish unease at thunder, the stitch in her side, Walter's warm weight in her arms, and the importance of getting him into Lance's ute (which was a truck) before the weather broke.

She was still nervous, yes, about meeting the Lucknows. Of course she was nervous.

Just not, it transpired, nearly nervous enough.

The storm raged through all their long drive to the cattle station. Before they even left the city, the rain was falling in sheets, blackening the day into premature night, the darkness fractured only by flashes of lightning on the flat horizon, and the glowing windows of suburban bungalows, corner shops called milk bars, and pubs called hotels. No blackout in Australia, yet.

Lance wasn't a talker. ("Gotta concentrate," he said, as, wipers flipping frantically, they swerved to avoid a pothole.) Rose, not much in the mood for conversation, was relieved. Walter, nestled with Rabbit beside her, was quiet as well: exhausted, she was sure, from the emotion of the day. Although at first he flinched at every crack of thunder, before long his head grew heavier on her shoulder, his eyelids drooped under the soporific percussion of the rain on the ute's metal roof, and by the time they'd swapped Brisbane's residential streets for the even darker bush-lined roads of the hinterland, he was fast asleep.

Rose rested her own head sideways against the window, tired too. And hungry. She'd packed a picnic of sorts before leaving the ship—apples, cheese, and bread—but in her rush, had left it in one of the bags in the ute's back. Trying not to taunt herself with thoughts of the unreachable food, she let her mind wander elsewhere, not to the Lucknows for once, but to everyone at home: Joe, and the agonizing question of whether he was still safe (it never left her), hoping she'd be able to wire him, now that she was here; Lionel came next—she missed him so much; then her parents, and if they were yet in Malaya; followed by Vivian, whom she was desperate to have news of too. As Walter stirred, shifting his weight against her, and Lance drove on, through the thick, swaying shadows of so many unfamiliar trees, she remembered Enid, and the postcard she owed her, then Steven from the hardware store (*It's the snakes you need to worry about*), Fiona from Fiona's Ices (*I heard it were the spiders*), and finally, inevitably, Xander.

It always came back to Xander in the end.

She frowned, subconsciously running her thumb over her bare ring finger. Her diamond, like the cheese and bread, was buried somewhere in the ute's rear. She hadn't so much as looked at it for weeks now. What would Xander think, if he knew?

Not much, he silently told her, his handsome face perturbed, hurt. . . .

Had he received any of her letters?

Had he received *that* letter?

Sent any of his own back?

She supposed she'd find out soon enough.

She glanced at the foggy clock on the dashboard. It was already past seven.

"How much longer will it be now?" she asked Lance, trying to move her numb legs without waking Walter, stifling a yawn.

"'Nother half hour," Lance said. "Mebbe more. Depends on this rain . . ."

The rain didn't stop, and it was more like a full hour by the time they finally crawled to a halt at the Lucknows' timber gate, shut, which hardly felt very welcoming. Rose stared at the drenched wood, her body so stiff it was numb, her empty stomach liquefying with fresh apprehension. Hail started to fall, bouncing off the black windscreen, making her feel worse. It was almost as though the weather was warning them away. Lance eyed the downpour, a dent in his craggy brow, clearly as loath as Rose felt to get out in it. But before she could offer, however reluctantly, to be the one to open the gate, he moved, hefting himself from the cabin, running to swing the timber wide, back at the wheel again within seconds, re-firing the ignition, shirt sticking to his skin, water dripping from his nose.

"You must be keen to get home," she said.

"Little bit," he agreed, flooring the accelerator, the cabin juddering around them as they passed over some cattle grids.

They bounced onward, and Rose sat up straighter, doing her best to breathe her pulse under control, and cushion a still-comatose Walter from the driveway's ruts. She thought about waking him, giving him time to come round before they met his family, and let him catch his first glimpse of the house. He was sleeping so soundly, though, his long lashes flickering in a dream. Beneath her hand, she could feel his chest rising and falling, his heart so regular, at ease. She couldn't bring herself to make him nervous like she was, not again.

Besides, it was difficult to see much through the storm, and the house, when it did eventually come into view, was a bit of an anticlimax. After all Vivian's eulogizing, Rose had pictured something epic, something like Margaret Mitchell's Tara in *Gone with the Wind,* but the simple, two-storied building that greeted her was rather different. Fifteen bedrooms? Rose didn't think so. There was perhaps space for five beneath the low, sloping roof. She almost smiled, replaying all Vivian's descriptions, realizing how much she'd exaggerated. She didn't mind the deception—not as she would come to mind Vivian's other lies (*I hope I'm the forgivable kind. . . .*); Vivian had only been trying to make Walter excited, Rose understood that. And the house, so far as she could see in the darkness, was still perfectly nice, with what looked like white weatherboard walls, and wide verandas running around the length of both floors. There was a set of wooden steps leading up to the shadowy front porch, a hammock just beside it, limp and sorry for itself in the wet, stormy air, but full of promise for sunnier times to come. Rose pictured Walter lying in it, the veranda flooded by golden light; him swinging, smiling. . . .

"Must have lost power," said Lance, cutting through her fantasy, peering up at the silent house himself, which was indeed almost entirely in darkness. Only one light burned, at a downstairs window, faintly, like it came from a lamp out the back. "Least you know someone's in."

"Yes," said Rose slowly, no longer thinking about hammocks on sunny days, but of whoever was inside—reading, or cooking, or doing whatever it was they were doing, by the glow of that flickering lamp.

Of one thing she was sure: they weren't watching for herself and Walter to arrive, because even when Lance pulled up and beeped his horn, twice, then three times, no one came out to meet them.

"Maybe they didn't hear," said Rose.

"Mebbe they don't wanna get wet," said Lance, beeping again, to no avail. With a resigned sigh, he threw open his door, filling the cabin with the hail's noise, and ran around to the back of the ute, lugging the first of Rose and Walter's trunks through the beams of his ute's headlamps, into the shelter of the veranda.

Feeling like she really couldn't stay dry and leave him to it a second time, Rose gently laid Walter horizontal, and, bracing herself, opened her own door, jumping out to help. She was soaked within a second of landing on the flooded gravel; hail hammered her head, stinging the bare skin on her arms, and it hurt, it was *cold*, but, as she ran to join Lance, he grunted in a way that suggested he was grateful she'd made the effort, so she supposed that was something. Between the two of them they got everything unloaded in no time, and then Rose was back at the cabin, gathering Walter's floppy body into her wet arms, running with him through the deluge, try-ing to keep him dry, and not slip as she climbed the porch steps.

Lance, *keen to get home*, didn't hang around for long. He did one final check of the ute, making sure Rose had everything (she did), then tipped his sopping hat, said goodbye, waved away her thanks, and, with a gruff ob-servation that Rose should get the little fella into bed, was off. Rose didn't blame him for beating such a hasty retreat; it would be hours, after all, by the time he got back to the city.

Still, it was a shame that he didn't stay a little longer.

Had he done that, Rose could have asked him to drive her and Walter somewhere else: a hotel that was really a hotel, for instance. Or back to Bris-bane, to Kate's house.

Anywhere, really, where they could have dried off, eaten something warm, and yes, got themselves into bed.

Because they weren't going to be doing that in any one of the Lucknows' five or fifteen bedrooms, that much became clear within just a few minutes of Lance driving away. No matter how many times Rose rapped on the porch's locked fly screen with her one free hand—holding Walter, stirring, but still miraculously sleeping, up over her shoulder with the other—nobody came to answer. She moved to the nearest window, hammering the glass there too, but . . . nothing.

There was definitely someone inside. A woman. Rose saw her through the window, or rather her silhouette, darting back from the doorway at the end of a floorboarded hallway, her quick movement shown up by that single, flickering lamp. It was the furtiveness of her that really panicked Rose. The woman had heard her knocking, Rose was certain, even over the noise of the storm. She'd heard, and wasn't coming.

Even worse: she was trying not to be seen.

Let them be kind, Rose had thought, back on the ship, staring at the waves thrashing Victoria's shore.

This was not kind.

She knocked again, so hard her wet knuckles felt like they might crack. Her other arm ached, muscles burning beneath Walter's weight. "Please," she called, too desperate by now to worry about disturbing him, "we've come a long way. Walter needs to go to bed. He's only five."

Silence.

Rose cursed, slamming the window once more, this time with the flat of her hand.

Why was the woman hiding?

And who was she?

Walter's aunt Esme, or grandmother Lauren?

Rose didn't want to think that.

She *couldn't* think that.

The woman must be a servant, or a neighbor: someone who'd been left in charge for some reason, and didn't know to expect guests so was afraid to answer the door. . . .

"Rosie?" said Walter, blearily, letting her know she had indeed woken him. "Are we here?"

"We are, little man," she said, moving her dead arm as he squirmed, helping him to get comfortable.

"You're all wet," he said.

She nodded. She was.

Emitting a ragged sigh, she turned, staring out through the water gushing from the edge of the veranda's roof, into the unknown blackness beyond. More lightning flashed, illuminating the vast swaths of rolling land surrounding them — the fields and distant cottages, scattered clumps of trees — and her mind worked, trying to devise what to do next. She couldn't let Walter know they were being kept locked out of the house, on that she was settled. It would devastate him. No matter what happened, she wouldn't allow him so much as a sniff of suspicion that he was anything other than welcome in his new home. Besides, he might yet be welcome. This really might all be some awful misunderstanding.

"I'm a bit cold," he said, burrowing against her.

"I know," Rose said, shivering too in her damp clothes. "We need to get you tucked up. But I'm afraid I've been a bit silly . . ."

"Silly?"

"Yes," she said, thinking as she spoke. "I've brought us all the way out here on the wrong day."

He moved his head, blinking dozily up at her. "How?"

"The ship was too quick." She summoned a smile. "Can you believe it? No one's going to be in until tomorrow."

He blinked again, absorbing it.

Please don't ask any more questions, she silently entreated him, acutely aware that there were many, *many* holes in her hastily concocted story: everyone else's families waiting at the port, for a start. *Lance* waiting . . .

Fortunately, Walter asked nothing. He simply smiled sleepily back at her, trusting her entirely, always so sweetly ready to trust: that beautiful innocence she was so desperate to protect. He was relieved too, she could tell. *I'm glad it's going to be just us a bit longer.* It broke her heart, how relieved he was. For a moment, tears swelled in her throat; she was too cold and hungry and exhausted to fight them. All she wanted to do was whisk him away, to anywhere, never bring him back to this dark, unwelcoming place, and keep him always happy, always with her.

But since he wasn't hers to do that with, and she had no means to do it anyway—and needed him to hold on to his smile—she swallowed hard on her tears, looked around once again, then, eyes locking on the bulk of a building within sprinting distance, said that they were going to have a bit of fun that night.

"Fun?" Walter said.

"Yes," she said. "We're going to camp."

Camp? demanded Lionel's voice in her mind. *Camp, Rosie?*

Steven followed. *It's the snakes you need to worry about.*

"It will be an adventure," Rose said, before Fiona could chime in. *I heard it were the . . .* "I loved camping at school."

"Where are we going to do it?" Walter asked.

"There," Rose said, pointing at the building she'd seen, which she hoped was a cattle-holding barn. They'd had plenty such things back in Ilfracombe. They were always dry, with hay inside. Perfect, really. "I've got some apples in my bag," she went on (thank God for the apples), "bread rolls too. We'll find a nice comfy spot and have a feast."

And that was just what they did, as soon as Rose had rifled through their trunks and extracted the food, some clean, dry clothes, and Mabel's eiderdown for Walter to sleep beneath. (The irony that she was using it to shelter him after they'd been barred from the home Mabel had fled from didn't elude her.) The barn was thankfully just what she'd hoped for. It felt like their first piece of luck that night. Feeling her way through the pitch black, whispering at Walter not to be scared (Oh God, were there snakes?), she found them a mound of stacked soft hay, and there they changed their clothes, ate their feast, then curled up together, surprisingly snug with the rain hammering down above, the air musty with the tang of animal sweat and warm milk.

Walter slept. He slept so well, within moments of Rose tucking him into his mummy's blanket and kissing him good night.

Rose didn't sleep. Drained as she was, she lay wide awake on the crackling hay, replaying the image of that woman hiding, ignoring her calls, her pleas. *He's only five.* The heartlessness of it plagued her. As did the thought of Lance, and the nagging question — which she now couldn't shake — of whether the Lucknows really had arranged for him to be at the port. Because if they had, then why hadn't they made sure everything was ready here at the house too?

It made no sense that they hadn't. Whichever way Rose looked at it, she couldn't make it make sense.

And she couldn't help her growing fear that Vivian had somehow arranged for the taxi instead, forced into it when the Lucknows had refused to pick Walter up themselves.

Or was she jumping to conclusions?

Would Vivian really have sent Walter all this way, knowing he was so unwelcome?

Is there anywhere else for him to go? (Lionel again. Bloody Lionel.)

"Oh God," breathed Rose, closing her gritty eyes.

She went in circles like that for hours, always coming back to the picture of that woman's darting silhouette, feeling her anger toward her grow more each time.

Had she simply been a neighbor, or ill-informed servant?

Rose wanted so much to believe that she had, and that the Lucknows would return on the morrow, full of apologies and embarrassment, ready to fix everything, make it all up to Walter. Fighting to convince herself, she combed over all the glowing things Vivian had said about the family, reminding herself too of the obvious regard Joe's bombardier had had for Walter's uncle Max. ("A good man," he'd said, back in that faraway beer garden, "a very good man.") But, somehow, it didn't help. None of it helped. In the darkness she became less rather than more convinced that the Lucknows would apologize for anything the next day, and ever surer that that woman had either been someone acting on their orders, or Esme or Lauren themselves. And much as that idea fanned her fury, it terrified her too.

Because if she was right, if the Lucknows were deliberately keeping

Walter away, then, contrary to all Vivian had said, they hadn't been waiting eagerly all these long months for him to join them.

No, they'd been dreading his arrival.

Hoping that he, so good and beautiful and sweet, would never arrive at all.

CHAPTER ELEVEN

Rose did finally fall into a sleep of sorts that night. She knew that, because she dreamed, strange dreams that she was back at her old RAF station, cradling a mug of tea, watching clouds idle across the sky, smiling distractedly at a joke one of the pilots cracked, trying to make out a sudden dart of gray spiking through the clouds, then dropping her tea as the siren wailed, running, the pilot beside her, so many others too, all of them throwing themselves into the field's slit trenches, bullets bouncing around them, spraying up soil. She tumbled forward, beside herself with fear, not for herself, but in case her fall hurt the baby. The drone of the planes filled her ears, so loud, so all-consuming that it woke her, her sore eyes jerking open with a start. She squinted, near-blinded by the sunlight flooding through the barn's slats, slowly realizing that, unlike her tiny, lost baby (*it's already gone to the incinerator*—it hurt, oh it hurt, to remember), the noise of the engines had been no dream; there was a real plane overhead, growing louder as it descended, coming in to land.

For a few disorientating seconds she struggled to remember where she was. Then, as it came to her, and the rest of the hideousness that had been the night before flooded back, she closed her eyes again, forgetting all about the plane.

Weren't unmanageable things always meant to feel better in the morning?

Nothing felt better to her.

She glanced sideways at Walter. He at least seemed content, still sleeping, burrowed beneath his eiderdown, curls sticking out. *A happy camper.* Tentatively, not wanting to wake him — not until she'd had the chance to wake properly herself, and marshal her wits for the return trip she had no choice but to make to the house — she shifted away from him, flexing the crick in her neck. She felt horrendous, horribly sad after her dream, and more tired somehow for having slept. Her limbs were so heavy, it was like they were pinning her to the ground. Her head was splitting, her mouth sandpaper dry. What time was it? She had no idea. She'd once had a wristwatch to help with such things, but had lost it months ago and never replaced it. At her guess, though, it couldn't be much past dawn. The light oozing through the barn's slats had the pink tinge of sunrise to it; the air felt early-morning crisp, fresh, after the storm. Nearby, birds sang: a strange cawing Rose hadn't heard before. Somewhere, a cockerel crowed. (That was more familiar.)

She reached up, pulling a piece of hay from her hair. God, her neck really hurt.

And she needed the loo.

What was she going to do about that?

Go outside, she supposed. Find somewhere concealed to crouch. She really didn't want the first thing she said to the Lucknows to be "Can I please use your latrine?" No, there was a deal else she wanted to say, starting with a question. *What the hell is going on?* Possibly, she'd phrase it more politely, but then again, maybe she wouldn't. She didn't feel very polite. She'd woken as furious as ever; more, even, now that she was so cold, and aching, and having to go for a wee out in the open.

Stiffly, she pushed herself to standing. Walter murmured softly, but otherwise didn't stir. Praying he wouldn't until she returned, she moved as quietly and as quickly as she could, shrugging a knitted cardigan on over the loose dress she'd slept in, tiptoeing to the barn's door, opening it just enough to edge through the crack, out into the yard.

She paused for a moment then, distracted by the house. It was much closer than her run through the rain had made it feel the night before: no more than fifty yards away. Now that it was light, she could see it properly, and while it was a little bigger than she'd first thought, with a small side annex attached to the main building, it was still nowhere near the proportions

Vivian had suggested. The annex perhaps added a sixth bedroom, but no more. The building was definitely well-kept, though, in a way that spoke of time and money spent. The weatherboard walls had been freshly painted; there were pots of vibrant flowers lining both verandas, and neat shutters at all the windows. Beneath the hammock, a tabby cat lounged, and really, Rose might have found the entire picture reassuringly idyllic, had her and Walter's trunks not still been standing stacked by the porch. The fly screen remained resolutely shut, too.

"Well, we'll see about that," she murmured, and, mindful of Walter, hurried on, splashing through the yard's puddles to the other side of the barn, searching out an adequate hiding place.

As she crouched behind a wheelbarrow (disappointingly the best shield on offer), she looked out over the grasslands surrounding her, at first to distract herself from how exposed she was, but very quickly because she simply couldn't help but be stunned — in spite of her mood, her discomfort at being in the middle of a farm with her drawers down — by their rich beauty. The pastures stretched endlessly, lush and glistening after the rain. Above, the sky was pale, clear, the clouds now gone, the sun edging upward on the horizon, heating her chill skin. Before her very eyes, the warm rays spread, inch by inch, tinting everything they touched with gold: the scattered cottages, the trees and grass, the cows that grazed, everywhere. . . .

And, oh God, there was a cow coming across the yard, toward her.

There was a cow coming, and she was still peeing. She couldn't stop. (She really had been bursting.)

Desperately, she tried to finish, the cow moving ever closer, its eyes on her eyes, seemingly intent on plowing her down.

"Please stop," she whispered at it. "Please . . ."

It didn't stop, not until it was almost on top of her, so close that she could smell the grass on its breath.

She stared up at it.

It stared back at her.

"Don't butt me," she entreated it, finally finished, but unsure whether she should risk moving.

It snorted, and stared more.

"All right, I'm going to try standing." She swallowed, cautiously rising. To her relief, the cow didn't charge her, but remained where it was. Not taking her eyes from it, she adjusted her knickers and pulled down her skirt.

"I need to wash my hands," she told the cow. There was a tap at the barn's wall. She eyed it, thinking of the uses she could make of it: getting clean, having something to drink, filling a bucket so Walter could wash too. She hadn't touched running water since leaving the ship and really didn't want to let a cow stop her doing it now. "I'm going to move," she said to it, edging past its shoulder, willing it not to follow her.

It followed her.

She walked faster.

So did the cow.

"I'm really not that interesting," she said, picking up her pace, then again as the cow followed suit. "I promise I won't hurt you, so please don't hurt me."

"She won't hurt you," came another voice, a male voice, breaking the dawn silence, sending Rose's already racing heart catapulting into her mouth.

She spun, wanting to see who'd spoken, but the cow mooed (*what do cows do, Walter?*), reclaiming her attention, moving even closer, sending her hurrying backward.

"Don't do that." That voice again. It didn't sound very happy. "She'll think it's a game."

"A game?" said Rose, not happy either, holding up her hands that needed washing in front of her, as though they'd be any good at holding the cow off.

"Just stay still, I'm coming . . ."

Seeing nothing else for it, she did as she was told, snatching another look over her shoulder to see the man the voice belonged to. He was coming around the barn in the opposite direction she had, it looked like from the fields below. (Oh, oh, had he seen her weeing? *Please not,* she thought. *Please not, please not . . .*) He was tall, broad, dressed almost entirely like a cowboy, in a loose shirt, wide-brimmed hat, and belted corduroy trousers, stained with mud. Only his thick leather jacket marred the picture: an airman's jacket, with a sheepskin collar and cuffs. The same jacket the pilot in her dream had been wearing just now. Dimly it came to her that this man must have been the one flying the plane that had woken her. Much more clearly, she realized that he was also Walter's uncle Max. It had to be him, she didn't doubt it, and it wasn't his airman's jacket that made her so certain.

No, it was his burns.

"So handsome," Vivian had said, back in Williams Street. This time, she hadn't been exaggerating. Rose didn't need to look twice to see how striking Max's features must once have been — before the war, before Egypt. Even now, the left side of his face carried the ghost of a rugged kind of perfection, all the more haunting for the livid welts that shattered it on the right, obscuring everything from his cheekbone down. Those cockpit flames Joe's bombardier had spoken of had done their work. *None of us could believe he lived.* The words came back to Rose heavily. As they did, she momentarily forgot her rage toward the Lucknows, overcome by pity for Max; the agony he must have endured. The scars were deep, stretching the skin on his jaw, his cheek, around his ear, down his neck, all the way to his open collar, so unrelenting that Rose could only suppose they covered his torso too. . . .

"They don't hurt," Max said, with a curtness that made her own skin burn. "Not anymore." Reaching the cow, he leaned against it, heading it off toward a nearby pen. "You don't need to look at them if they bother you."

"They don't bother me," she said, defensive to her own ears, because they didn't, and it upset her that he thought they did. Determined to prove him wrong, she kept her gaze fixed on his face, but then grew even hotter at the discomfort of her own forced focus. Really, now he was close, it felt as though she could do nothing appropriate with her eyes.

"Why is this cow out?" she asked, talking through her awkwardness, voicing the first thing that sprang to mind.

"My guess is because we've got a broken fence somewhere," Max said. "What I'm more concerned with," he shoved the cow forward, guiding it safely through the pen's gate, "is who you are."

"Who I am?"

"Yes. And what you're doing here, because it sounds to me like you're a long way from home."

"Quite a long way, yes."

"So . . . ?"

She frowned. "Are you joking?"

He locked the gate. "Is something funny?"

"Not really," she said. Not at all. "But you must know why I'm here."

"Nope," he said, turning to face her. "I most definitely do not."

She narrowed her eyes. "You are Max Lucknow?"

"I am," he said. "I have no idea how you know that, but I am." He leaned back against the gate. "Your turn. Who are you?"

"Rose Hamilton," she said, watching, waiting for him to give away some spark of recognition.

But he didn't. His expression remained as uncomprehending as before.

To her disquiet, he didn't appear to have heard of her at all.

It made no sense.

Nothing in this damned place made any sense.

"Your aunt wrote about me," she said. "She told me you replied. Vivian swore . . ."

"Vivian?" he said, cutting her off. The unblemished skin on his forehead puckered. "How did you know Vivian?"

It was a mark of her unease that she didn't notice his past tense.

"I've been living with her," she said, exasperated, "looking after Walter. She sent me here with him, we arrived last night. You were meant to have met us at the port. We . . ." She stopped.

She couldn't go on.

It was his expression, the shock that had come over him: no pretense, she was certain. No one was that good an actor.

"You really didn't know we were coming?" she said.

"No," he said slowly. "I really didn't know."

She stared, absorbing it, turning numb with shock of her own.

How many times had Vivian spoken of Max's excitement that Walter was on his way over? Rose didn't know. She'd lost count. . . .

"She promised me she'd told you. She promised . . ."

"Christ," said Max, taking off his hat, tugging his hand roughly through his hair. "He's actually here?"

"Yes, he's *here*," she said, voice shaking. "Only no one would let us in the house last night. We had to sleep in there." She gestured at the barn, feeling her rage return, growing with every word she spoke. "Think on that. A five-year-old little boy, at the end of a journey to the other side of the world, had to sleep with no dinner, on a pile of hay."

"I didn't know . . ."

"You didn't hear us?" she said, incredulous. "I was pretty loud. . . ."

"I wasn't here," he said. "I've been up-station . . ."

It didn't make her feel better. "You were meant to be *here*," she said. "Someone was. A woman was. She seemed to know we were coming, even if you didn't. She knew to keep us locked out."

He said nothing, just shook his head, jaw set, she thought maybe in anger too, but she couldn't be sure.

"Do you know who that woman was?" she asked.

"I wasn't here," he said again.

"Do you suspect, though? You look like you might suspect . . ."

He said nothing.

She took it as a yes.

"Your mother?" she guessed.

"I don't know . . ."

"But you *suspect*." That really did it for her. "What is *wrong* with her?" she erupted. "What is wrong with *you*? Why aren't you happier?"

"Happy?" he said, and it was his turn to be incredulous. "You want me to be *happy* about this?"

"Yes, I want you to be happy," she said, so upset she was almost crying. "I want you to be ecstatic. Walter is wonderful, he's beautiful and sweet, and loves yellow, and plays make-believe with animals, and has never, in all the time I've known him, hurt a fly, and you, all of *you*, are behaving like he's the devil . . ."

"I don't think he's the devil . . ."

"No? Really?"

"No. *Christ*." He turned, looking like he might be about to kick the gate. "Mabel didn't want him here. It's the last bloody place she wanted him to be. Vivian *knew* that. It's why Mabel went to her, so he'd never have to set foot here."

"Well, now he has, he's here, because you're all he has, and your mother locked him out in the rain. You haven't so much as asked to meet him. Your own sister's *son* . . ."

"Sister?" he said, and faced her once more, giving her the oddest look. A look that knocked the wind out of her, leaving her in no doubt that something else very unpleasant was about to head her way. "Mabel wasn't my sister."

And there it was.

It took her a second to hear it.

She didn't have time to absorb it.

Because Walter himself called out then: a painfully panicked wail from inside the barn.

"Rosie. Rosie, Rosie, where are you . . . ?"

"I'm here," she just about managed to yell back, stare fixed on Max, who'd gone very still at the sound of Walter's tearful voice. "I'm here, I'm coming . . ."

Desperate as she was to grill Max more, she went, running through the yard's dirt puddles.

Max didn't follow. He watched her go, though. She felt his eyes on her the entire way.

His eyes that she'd been looking into these past minutes, and which she realized belatedly were brown, not blue.

His words reverberated within her, beating to the time of her own slapping steps. *Mabel wasn't my sister.*

Mabel wasn't my sister.

What had Mabel been to him, then?

What had she been to any of them?

And what, *what* of Walter's father? The grim possibilities felt horribly endless now it was dawning on Rose just how deceptive Vivian had it in her power to be.

I'm hope I'm the forgivable kind. . . .

"Rosie, Rosie." Walter was outside already, running toward her in the sunshine, arms open, Rabbit for once forgotten in his haste, his panic. He threw himself against her. "You haven't gone."

"Of course I haven't," she said, holding him tight, like she had so many times before, feeling his precious heart pound. "It's all right," she said, kissing his head that was covered in straw, resting her cheek against it, "you're all right . . ."

"I was frightened you were on another ship."

"I would never do that to you."

"I was frightened," he said again.

"I know," she said, hating it for him, "but I'm here, I won't leave you like that."

"You mustn't leave . . ."

"Shhh," she said. "Shhh."

She didn't tell him that Max was close by.

She certainly didn't say that this hero he'd had dangled in front of him since before leaving London wasn't his mother's brother after all. She just continued to hug him, praying he wouldn't sense her own racing panic, waiting for the rigid fear in him to ease.

But as it did, and she set him down — smiling weakly, running her hands around his mucky, tearstained face — she couldn't help but agonize over what they were going to do next. Stay? Never had it felt less appealing. She was desperate only to go, give in to the same instinct she'd felt the night before and run, taking Walter with her, to as far away as they could get.

Mabel didn't want him here. It's the last bloody place she wanted him to be.

She glanced over in Max's direction. She saw how his eyes were glued on Walter. He hadn't moved at all since she'd left him. It was as though he'd been rooted to the spot at the sight of Mabel's beautiful little boy. Still in shock, certainly.

Confused, too.

As confused as her.

And — whether for himself, or for Walter — more than a little fearful himself.

CHAPTER TWELVE

Rose didn't know how long they stood there like that: her staring at Max, him staring at Walter. It was probably only seconds, but it felt much longer. She didn't expect Max to join them, when he finally moved. No, she assumed that he, so shaken, would probably be the one to turn on his heel and leave the yard. Even as she watched him gather himself, broad shoulders rising and falling in a deep breath, she stiffened, bracing herself to go after him, call him back. *Don't be such a coward.*

She supposed she forgot for a moment that he was a man who'd flown headlong into dogfights with German Messerschmitts beneath the blazing Arabian sun.

In any case, he didn't walk away from her and Walter.

He walked toward them. Toward his fear.

That was her first surprise.

Her second was the way he was with Walter. She'd been ready for more abrasiveness, at the very least. But he was gentle, startlingly gentle, setting aside his own obvious emotion and crouching before Walter — just as she had when she'd first met him — telling him he was sorry he'd had to wake up in a barn, "I think your mum would probably have cried about that too, mate," speaking so softly, with such quiet empathy for this stranger child before him, that it made Rose look at him afresh, remember Joe's bombardier's words all over again (*a good man, a very good man*), and wonder why he couldn't have been a bit nicer to her just now.

Oblivious to her surprise, Max offered Walter his hand. The skin on it wasn't scarred, she noticed. Clearly, no flames had touched it. She supposed if they had, he might not have lived; he wouldn't have been able to punch his way out of the cockpit. . . .

She didn't know why she kept thinking about his crash.

Certainly, though, his hand looked strong enough to break a Hurricane's hood. Tanned, steady, roughened by work, it dwarfed Walter's when Walter shyly raised it, giving it to him.

Max almost smiled, then. Rose was certain he almost smiled. It was the way the skin around his dark eyes creased, the slight movement of the left side of his face.

You're allowed to, she wanted to say to him.

Smile, please smile.

He didn't. He stopped himself.

A shame. It struck her that he must have had a very nice smile.

Once.

"Are you my uncle Max?" Walter asked him quietly.

"Yes," Rose said, speaking out loud this time, quickly, before Max could. "A hero, just like Aunty Vivian said."

"Not much of a hero," Max said, the terseness back now he was speaking to her again.

She tried not to mind.

She was relieved at least that he'd let the "uncle" go.

"There's a lot we need to talk about," she said.

"Yeah." He sighed, pushing himself back to his feet. "Reckon we've got a bit of catching up to do."

"Should we go to the house . . . ?"

"Not yet," he said, "you stay here." He turned, narrowing his eyes toward the far corner of the barn, the house hidden beyond, thinking, she was certain, of his mother and sister lurking within its white weatherboard walls, and whatever it was he was planning to say to them. (If Esme really was his sister. If there was an Esme at all.) "I'll let you know when it's time."

Waiting for him to return that morning was agonizing, and not made any easier by having to pretend to Walter that everything was absolutely as it should be in the world, and no, there was nothing strange at all about the two of them being left in an Australian barnyard while his uncle (or not uncle) went up to get things ready at the house.

"But why can't we go too?" Walter asked, letting Rose know, with that one question, that he'd already taken a shine to Max.

It worried her — how could it not? — but didn't surprise her. She'd probably have taken more of a shine to him herself, had he spoken to her half as warmly as he had Walter. She frowned, replaying his curt manner, really from the very off, trying to think what she'd done to turn him so immediately against her. Existing, it felt like. Being in the yard when he hadn't expected her to be.

God, but she really hoped he hadn't seen her weeing.

"Rosie?" said Walter, still waiting for an answer.

"He's asked us to stay here," she said, pushing the mortifying image of herself crouched behind that wheelbarrow away. "I think everything's just a bit of a mess up there."

That at least wasn't a lie.

Wanting to distract them both from waiting for his return, she decided to get them cleaned and changed, which she did, starting at the tap, then back inside the barn. Picking all the hay from their hair took a while, hers especially (what would Sarah have said, if she could have seen her?), and by the time they reemerged into the yard, Rabbit once more with them, the sun had fully risen, turning the winter morning as warm as any summer's day in England.

The surrounding fields had come to life as well. On the curve of one hill, figures cantered on horseback, driving cows toward the golden horizon. Closer by, more people ducked in and out of the scattered cottages, gardening, hanging laundry. Rose paid them little attention. She was much more concerned with scrutinizing the Lucknows' house: as silent as ever, and eerily still in contrast to the activity everywhere else.

What was going on in there?

The cat hadn't moved from beneath the hammock.

Her and Walter's trunks remained on the porch.

"Should we go and get them?" said Walter, looking at them too.

"No," she said. "Let's just wait for Uncle Max."

Surely he wouldn't be much longer.

Looking for more distractions, feeling the first pangs of hunger, she suggested a walk, foraging—for what, she truly wasn't sure, but it seemed as good a way to kill time as any—and led the way down the same craggy slope Max had come up, back when he'd first appeared.

His plane was parked on an angle, diagonally across the flat strip of pasture before them: a low propeller-driven kite, very like the models she'd seen used for early training, back in England. She'd never felt inclined to fly in one, not that she'd ever flown. The idea terrified her, frankly. The metal frames looked so flimsy, too insubstantial to be airborne. It amazed her, now she thought, that Max still flew anything himself. It must terrify him too, to smell the fuel, be confined in a cockpit. . . .

"Look, Rosie," said Walter, pulling her back to the moment. "There's a *kangaroo*."

"Where?"

"There. Behind the airplane."

So there was.

"Look at that," she said, eyes widening. She'd only ever seen one in picture books before.

"Oh my goodness," said Walter, hesitantly setting off toward it, half crouched, half poised to run, Rabbit held protectively behind him. "Can I touch it?"

"I wouldn't. A girl I went to school with told me they punch."

He stopped.

No one got punched.

And the kangaroo got bored of them first, hopping off into the surrounding trees. So, after a quick look at the plane—"Can I touch the propellers, Rosie?" She was fine with that—followed by a hopeless search for berries or apples or anything edible, they went too, returning to the yard where they braved the last of the ship's cheese, then drank more water (because of the soggy cheese), and clambered onto an overturned trough, trying to throw stones into buckets.

It was then, just as Rose had begun to despair of anyone ever appearing, that someone finally came.

Not Max, but a woman with wispy white hair combed into a bun, and a smudge of flour on one of her cheeks. Hannah, she said her name was, as she hurried around the corner of the barn, telling Rose and Walter to please come on, quickly now. *Quickly.* (Really, it was almost as though she were the one who'd been kept waiting.) For a tense moment, Rose thought she, not

Lauren, might be the woman who'd kept them out of the house the night before, but then she realized she couldn't be. She was too tall, and broader, her shoulders more rounded.

Had she heard them, though?

"Were you here last night?" Rose asked, needing to check.

"No," said Hannah, like it should be so obvious, "I live up there." She waved in the direction of the cottages. "I was on my way down when Max flew in . . ."

"But where is he now?" asked Rose.

"Dealing with his mother," said Hannah, "and some other things besides. Meanwhile, my bread is ruining. I've only just added the starter, but there was to be no delay, oh no, Esme wasn't having that . . ."

Esme. So she did exist.

"No patience, that girl," Hannah went on (it seemed a little rich). "Never has had. I tell you, this has been such *a morning*, Max wasn't even meant to be back, and he's *ropable* . . ."

"What's 'ropable'?" asked Rose.

"I'll show you," said Hannah, gesturing at her to get up. "Keep asking these questions, and I'll show you. . . ."

"No need," said Rose, standing, "I think I can probably guess. I'm sorry you had to come . . ."

"It's not all your fault."

It's not at all my fault, Rose almost corrected her, but stopped, noticing how anxious Walter was suddenly looking—like he *really* didn't want to find out what "ropable" meant—and pulled a silly face at him, trying to make light of Hannah's crossness, and make him smile instead.

It wasn't very successful.

"Come here," she said, lifting him down from the trough, "let's go and find Uncle Max." Then, holding his hand firmly in hers, *I have you,* she nodded at Hannah, who set back off, leading them urgently on.

She set quite a pace. It took them no time at all to reach the house: barely the space of a few hastily drawn breaths, which at least meant Rose didn't have the chance to become too apprehensive over what was about to happen. Mainly, she worried about Walter, still anxious, and very quiet again by her side. She didn't know what she was going to do with him when they at last got inside. There was so much she was afraid of him hearing, and yet where else could he go but with her? Clearly there'd be no sending him happily off to the kitchen to bake with Hannah, as he'd used to with Pia. Hannah, running up the porch steps with militant speed, hadn't even acknowledged that he was there.

And their trunks had disappeared.

Rose stalled, registering that.

It unnerved her. It seemed to suggest some kind of decision had already been reached.

She rather wanted to know what that decision was.

"This way, this way," said Hannah, enlightening her not at all, opening the fly screen (so easy), and forging on through the front door.

The entrance hall, like so much else, looked different in the light of day. Less foreboding, certainly, than when Rose had been peering in at it the night before. It wasn't large, but was airy, with a pale wood floor that reflected the sunlight, a wide staircase leading upward, and a clock that told her it was already after nine. She could smell Hannah's yeasty dough, a fruitcake too, she thought. The kitchen couldn't be far away. Walter must have smelled it as well, because she heard his tummy grumble. Anxiously, pitifully, he pressed Rabbit to his waist, trying to quieten the sound.

"Hungry, is he?" asked Hannah, who'd already crossed the hallway, and was standing outside a closed door. For the first time she looked, properly looked at Walter, her face pinching, although Rose couldn't tell whether in more impatience or the same concern she felt. "Max mentioned he'd had no dinner . . ."

"A shame he couldn't have sent breakfast then," Rose snapped, abruptly losing patience with how long Walter had been forced to wait.

"Don't be too hard on him," Hannah said. "It's been . . ."

" 'A morning,' " said Rose. "Yes, I know."

"I'll fetch you a tray once the bread's in," said Hannah, "if it's salvageable." And with that, she flung the door she was standing beside wide, revealing what appeared to be a drawing room, and bustled off, to salvage whatever she could.

The drawing room was much bigger than the hallway, and more thoroughly furnished, with a cream woolen rug, an assortment of armchairs all different shades and patterns of yellow and blue, like they'd been bought over the years to match, and a row of tall windows that opened out onto the veranda, letting the sunlight and warm air flood through.

The cat had moved inside. It lounged on a woman's lap, its tail hanging idly to the floor. The woman was about the same age as Rose, different again to the one she'd seen the night before, slender enough, yet curvier, and quite feline herself, with her dark hair, and slanting eyes. Esme, Rose presumed, as slowly, her grip firm on Walter's clammy hand—keeping him with her, since she really had no choice—she walked further into the room.

She refused to be cowed as Esme looked her and Walter over, her head on one side, an intrigued expression on her brittle, pretty face. Rose kept her gaze steady, and studied her right back, trying to work out whether she, unlike her brother and Hannah, had known about it when she and Walter were being locked out. *Maybe,* thought Rose. Although, maybe not. She didn't look quite hostile enough. Really, she appeared more entertained than anything: the type who might have let them in, if only for the show. . . .

Max wasn't far away from his sister. He stood by one of the open windows, his jacket off, arms folded, jaw set. This time there was no doubting he was angry, although at what, or whom, Rose could still only guess. She seemed to be part of it, though, because while Max's face did soften momentarily as he looked down at Walter, throwing him his first smile (it was a nice smile), unlike Esme he didn't look at her at all.

And she didn't keep looking at him.

More put out than was comfortable by his distance, she turned, so didn't notice the way his eyes moved as she did, quite against his will, nearly catching hers. She'd already caught sight of the other person in the room. A woman who could only be Lauren, also standing with her arms crossed, over by a window on the far side.

She was an older, sterner version of Esme, beautiful once, perhaps, only she'd frowned too much. Her disappointment showed in every one of the lines dragging on her pale skin. She was small, but stood straight, her gaze fixed somewhere around the point of Walter's rabbit. Her shoulders were back, her tweed skirt nipped in at the waist, her chest proud, constrained by the corset Rose would put money on her wearing. It was a posture Rose recognized.

She recognized it very well.

It amazed her that there wasn't a shred of shame in it.

"You heard me last night," she said, momentarily forgetting, in her white flash of rage, that Walter was listening. "You heard."

Lauren didn't respond. Not straightaway.

She simply arched a brow, like it was beneath her to speak to Rose at all.

Then, slowly, majestically, she unfolded her arms, clasped her hands before her, and, still without so much as a whisper of contrition, inclined her head in a single, cold nod.

For a few seconds, no one said a word.

Esme raised her hand, twirling her finger through her pearls.

Walter edged even closer to Rose, as far away from his supposed grandmother as he could make himself.

On some level, Rose registered Max drawing a frustrated breath.

And she, she just stared.

Already she regretted speaking as she had in front of Walter, but her fury was only growing. She'd never encountered someone so decidedly, so assuredly *rude*. Even her old wing commander had had the grace to turn a bit red in the face, a bit flustered when he'd told her how disgusted she made him at her hearing. Lauren, though, she didn't give a damn.

It became even clearer, when, breaking her silence, Lauren said, "He looks like his father," to whom it really wasn't clear. Then, with a hating look for Walter, another for Rose, and a hissed order to Esme that she leave her damned pearls alone, she left the room.

"Who was that lady?" Walter asked, making Rose even angrier, because he was on the edge of tears.

"She's a wicked witch, Walter," Esme volunteered, still twirling her pearls. "But you must only call her that when she can't hear you. Otherwise she'll turn us all into frogs . . ."

"Esme," said Max, warningly. "She's not a witch, Walter, mate."

"Oh, but she is," said Esme. "She's the bad one, and I'm the good one." She gave Walter a shiny smile. "So you must be very nice to me. And I'll be nice to you, like my mum needs to remember to be nice, because you and my brother could turn us out on our bums . . ."

"What are you talking about?" said Rose, picking Walter up before he really did start crying, desperately trying to think of some way to get him out of earshot while she got to the bottom of what was going on. "Is there some other way to do this?" she said to Max, before Esme could answer her question. "Because this isn't the way to do this . . ."

"I know it's not," he said. "Now, Walter" — he once again became gentler — "I'm sorry about this nonsense. I only got you in here because that lady you saw was meant to be saying sorry, too."

"And I was very keen to hear that, Walter," said Esme. "To my knowledge, she's never apologized for a thing in her life."

Walter eyed her. His lip was no longer wobbling, but he remained wary. It was clear that he, like Rose, was trying to work out what to make of his aunty who probably wasn't his aunty, Esme.

"It's a witch thing," Esme continued. "A bad-witch thing. Good witches like me have to apologize for things *all, the, time*..."

"Esme, please," said Max.

"Our luggage has been moved," said Rose to him.

"I took it upstairs," he said.

"We're not camping again tonight, then?"

"No," he said, and this time she didn't look away before his eyes met hers. "Not unless you want to."

"Not really."

"All right," he said, and held her gaze a little longer. She colored, she couldn't help it. She realized it hardly mattered in the scheme of everything else going on, but she just knew he'd seen her weeing behind that wheelbarrow.

"You've a room here for now," Max said.

Rose nodded, willing the heat in her cheeks away, becoming tenser yet over that *for now*, knowing, though, that it was hardly the time to broach the subject of her staying longer.

"I was going to show you up," Max said, "after my mother..."

"Failed to apologize," said Esme, smiling at Rose.

"Anyway," said Max. "I've written a few things down, as much as I understand, to try and explain. I left it with your things."

"Oh," said Rose, taken aback that he'd thought of such a thing ("Why, though?" demanded Joe's bombardier). "Right."

"I thought it would be easier that way," Max said, glancing at Walter.

"Yes," said Rose.

"I don't know." He frowned again. "I wasn't expecting any of this. I'm doing my best..."

"Yes," she said again. "I can see. Thank you..."

"Don't thank me yet," he said, making for the door. "Read my note first." His frown deepened. "I'm not sure you're going to like a lot of what it says."

CHAPTER THIRTEEN

They collided with Hannah on their way out into the hallway. True to her word, she'd prepared a laden breakfast tray: eggs, ham, bananas, milk, tea, and some of the cake Rose had smelled, but no bread.

"Don't talk to me about the bread," Hannah said.

Max asked her where his mum had gone, and she said, "Esme's." Rose didn't know whether she meant a house, or a room, but had already seen and heard enough to suppose Esme wouldn't be particularly happy about her mother's invasion of her space. Max and Hannah exchanged a look, apparently knowing it too.

Hannah offered to take Rose and Walter on upstairs. "I'm already in motion," she said, "easier to keep going than stop, as they say."

Do they? thought Rose.

Max didn't protest. He went, absently ruffling Walter's curls with his hand that had punched through a Hurricane's hood, telling him he'd see him in a bit.

"Where will you be?" Rose asked. "In case I need to find you . . ."

"Taking that cow you were playing chase with back to where it belongs," he said. "Then finding the gap in the fence."

"Sort your shoulder too," Hannah called after him.

He waved his hand back at her, disappearing out into the sunshine, the fly screen swinging shut behind him.

"What's wrong with his shoulder?" Rose asked.

"His horse threw him in the storm," Hannah said. "It's why he came back."

"Where's he been?"

"Mustering, health checks his mum arranged at the western end." Hannah carried on toward the stairs. "He wasn't happy, said they weren't due, but she'd already booked the vet so what could he do? I knew as soon as I saw his plane that something had happened. His skin tears, just the slightest knock and it needs treating." She shook her head. "He shouldn't be doing this work, but I doubt he'd thank me for telling you that . . ."

"He said it didn't hurt anymore," said Rose, following. "That sounds like it must hurt."

"I daresay it does," Hannah said. "I daresay it does."

"Poor Uncle Max," said Walter to Rose.

"Yes," she said, mind moving once again to Max's manner when she'd first met him in the yard, seeing his abrasiveness now in a slightly differing light. He must have been angry enough, after his fall: at himself, his burns. She'd have been angry. Then there she'd been, a stranger, staring; something else for him to deal with. *I'm doing my best. . . .* "Poor Uncle Max."

"Uncle," said Hannah with a sniff.

She didn't linger upstairs with Rose and Walter. She really didn't seem the lingering kind. She showed them the rooms they'd been given at the head of the stairs—spartan, but pleasant enough, with brushed floorboards, cast-iron beds, and windows overlooking the curved driveway, barn and fields beyond—said nothing about how long Rose was going to be made welcome to stay in hers, just added another unsettling "It'll do you *for now*," then set their tray of food down on her bureau, and pointed out the small washroom they could make use of across the landing.

"No bath," she said. "There's no space. You'll have to take yours in the kitchen. We've vats to fill it."

There was an unmistakable challenge in her voice. She was waiting for Rose to balk, Rose could tell. But while Rose hated to let her down (she didn't at all), she wasn't remotely perturbed at the arrangement. They'd had no proper bath at her parents' home back in Dulwich either, or in Ilfracombe. It was one of the many things that had maddened Xander about her staying in Devon. ("I'll get you a bath," he'd said. "I'll buy you a house with five baths.") She asked only that Hannah show her the vats before she went home that night, since she and Walter had only had the yard's tap to use that morning.

"It was cold," said Walter, who, to her relief, was rediscovering his voice. Maybe it had been Max ruffling his hair. Or perhaps it was the sight of the food waiting. . . .

"Was it now?" said Hannah with another sniff, and the same pinched look she'd got when she'd heard his stomach rumbling.

Was it impatience?

Hannah didn't give Rose the chance to decide. She left, telling them both to eat up. "The cook never likes the meal getting cold." Another expression Rose wasn't familiar with.

She did, though, intend to eat. As famished as Walter, she helped herself to a plate of food as big as the one she made up for him, then poured herself the tea she'd been craving, and, setting Walter up to eat on her new, she hoped to God not *too* temporary, bed — pillows stacked behind him, a napkin tucked into his collar — she fetched the folded note Max had left for her on the top of their trunks, and took it, and her breakfast, over to the room's faded window seat, where she promptly forgot to eat, she forgot to drink, and read instead.

Max had been right.

She didn't like a lot of what his note said.

She hated, really hated, the beginning.

You've said that Vivian sent you, he wrote, *but mentioned nothing of her illness. I'm afraid you don't yet know that she very sadly died. If this is the first you are hearing of it — as I suspect, now I've spoken to my mother, that it might be — I am deeply sorry. I don't know how close you were, or how much Vivian might have told you, but she'd been living with her tumors for a long time. We often wrote, I spent a lot of time with her, over the years — first, when I was at university, then when I was in London again in '34 — and in the last letter she sent, when I was in hospital in Alexandria, before Mabel died, she said she was getting worse, but hoped it would be quick, she was ready. I'm not sure if that'll give you comfort. I hate telling you like this — it feels cowardly, and I suppose it is — but I can't say it in front of Walter, not if he doesn't know. I'm sure you'll know much better than me how he should be told.*

She didn't know.

Her eyes swam, her hands shook, and she had no idea of how he should be told.

She couldn't even make herself accept that Vivian was really dead. *Dead.*

More tears came. Roughly, she brushed them away before Walter saw them. She shouldn't be this shocked, she knew. Vivian had been so very ill. She'd worried about her, all this time. It seemed ridiculous, now she knew the truth, that she'd ever let herself hope that she might yet be alive. But she couldn't bear that she, with her stories and her photographs and her love and her kindness—Rose didn't forget her kindness, not even now she was starting to realize her lies—was gone. She glanced over at Walter and couldn't bear that he—trying to peel an egg with his little fingers and not spill anything on the candlewick bedspread beneath him—was going to have to find out that, seven months after he'd lost his mother, five months after he'd lost his first nanny, and four months after he'd lost his home, he'd lost his great-aunt too.

Wiping her tears again, she forced herself to read on.

I have no doubt that Vivian loved Walter very much. I say this not only because of how often she spoke of him in her letters, but also because, aside from her property in London, she left almost her entire estate to him, including a great deal of the money she's made through investments over the years, and half of this old plantation, which she owned, and has owned since my grandparents asked her for help when it nearly ran to ruin during droughts at the start of the century. Did you know that?

"No," Rose breathed, hands trembling more, "I didn't."

I own the other half. It passed to me when my father died, and Vivian has also left me a sum of money, which I wasn't expecting, and never asked for. I'm to hold Walter's inheritance in trust until he turns twenty-one, and all of this I learned this morning. I'd have eventually discovered it, I'm sure, but until now, my mother has concealed Vivian's lawyer's letters and wires informing us of Vivian's legacy, confirming that you and Walter were on your way. It was he, it seems, who arranged your transport from the port. I would of course have come myself had I known, and

will certainly take you for your return journey. You must be very
impatient to get home.

"Not impatient," Rose said. "Not impatient at all."

I don't ask for your sympathy. I suspect you're not much of a mind
to give it, but please understand my shock. It seems Vivian wrote
to my mother months ago asking her to have Walter here. When
she refused, Vivian wrote again, then to myself and Esme — several
times, apparently — but my mother's admitted she threw out those
letters. I was not myself, when Mabel went. My plane went down
in October, and I was only discharged from hospital in December.
I arrived here just as the wire about her death came, and it seems I
have not been keeping a close enough eye on anything since. Esme
has her own concerns, and I believe her when she says she suspected
nothing. She wasn't here last night to help you — she lives in one
of our cottages — otherwise, I assure you, she would have let you
in. I was away, as I've said. It was all very neatly managed by our
mother. I'm deeply ashamed you were locked out. I don't know how
she thought she was going to keep hiding Walter's inheritance, but
there you have it: she believed you and he would give up, go away,
and that she could make what she didn't want, go away. She has
always tried to control much more than she can.

Rose stared at the words before her, so hard, her smarting eyes stung.
There was too much to take in.

On some level, she was relieved that Esme truly hadn't been complicit
in all Lauren had done. Lauren alone was enough of an enemy. And although
she didn't entirely trust Esme, not yet, she wanted to. She wanted them all
on Walter's side.

"I'll be nice to you," Esme had said to him, "like my mum needs to
remember to be nice, because you and my brother could turn us out on our
bums..."

Now, Rose knew what she'd meant.

Setting the paper down, she glanced over at Walter, who'd given up on
his egg and moved on to the cake. *This is his,* she thought, *it's half his.*

He was too little, surely, to have the responsibility of such a legacy.

Would he even thank Vivian for it, when he got older? *I'm a bit scared of cows.* Would he want to be a rancher, or a cowboy, or whatever they were called here?

Had Max wanted to be one, when his share had passed to him?

She turned to the window, searching him out, spotting him instantly, walking toward one of the boundary fences, his hand to his shoulder that he'd told her didn't hurt. They'd got off on the wrong foot, the two of them. Now she was reading his letter, she realized how much. She was warming to him. She could feel it happening. *A good man.* She didn't like the thought of him alone and in pain in that Alexandria hospital. It nagged at her. She knew how it felt. . . .

Dragging her eyes from him, she carried on reading.

That is all I know. There's much more I don't understand. I can't fathom why Vivian sent Walter here instead of to a good family in England, when she knew — and must have known even before my mother wrote to her, refusing to take him — how hard it would be for him to come. You've told me she said I was Walter's uncle. Maybe she believed you'd refuse to bring him if you knew the truth. You seem the type who'd have no worries about doing such a thing.

Rose blinked. Did she?

She didn't know whether to be affronted by that.

What she did know was that she didn't want to read on. Her legs, her whole body had started to tremble with unease, because she had a fairly good idea now of what was coming, and it wasn't good, it really wasn't good. . . .

I am not his uncle, Esme is not his aunt, and our mother is not his grandmother. Mabel was married to my and Esme's brother. She grew up in Sydney, with a grandfather she didn't get on with, and met my brother Jamie there back in '34, while I was in England, who she also didn't get on with, as they discovered very quickly. She'd already moved in when I returned, and it was obvious that she didn't belong here, that this place wasn't good for her. Jamie wasn't good for her. He wasn't good for anyone, least of all himself.

It was months before Mabel admitted to him that he might not be Walter's father, and when she did, Jamie made it impossible for her to stay. I'm not going to go into all of what happened then, there is nothing to be gained by it, and it's something I try not to look back on. But after Mabel left, Jamie killed himself. That was the last day we saw Walter's father too. He's gone, I took him, Walter has no family left here, and should never have come.

But what's done is done. Vivian's decided this will be his home. I cannot promise he'll be happy. This is not a happy place. What I can say is that I realize none of this is his fault, and I have no intention of letting a five-year-old child down. Angry as I am, I will not let Vivian, or Mabel, down. You can sail home with a clear conscience, knowing I will do my best for Walter.

And now I see you both coming with Hannah. My mother at least has accepted Walter must stay. I hope she'll make amends.

We shall see.

Rose closed her eyes. She pictured Lauren as she must have looked while Max had been writing, saw again her pointed, venomous nod, and had no hope she'd make amends for anything. Her son had killed himself, the child she blamed had been forced upon her. Rose — who'd never had less intention of leaving Walter and sailing anywhere — could only imagine Lauren would want to keep punishing him, in whatever ways she could find.

Vivian, she thought.

Oh, Vivian.

What have you done?

Impossible as it felt, she forced herself to tell Walter about Vivian's death there and then, knowing that putting it off would only make it harder. Unsteadily, she crossed over to where he sat and pulled him onto her lap, saying they had something very sad to talk about. She reminded him of how poorly Vivian had been, how in need of a really nice long sleep, then, crying again, because she was only human, and it probably helped him anyway to share his grief, and actually — as Vivian herself had said — there was no shame in tears, told him how Vivian had had to go upstairs with his mummy. She'd been up there all this time, looking over them on their voyage, keeping them safe from the torpedoes, singing "Happy Birthday" to Walter, clapping her hands with his mummy when he blew out his candles.

"I wanted her to come here, though," said Walter, tears rolling down his flushed, round cheeks, his napkin still around his neck. "She said she'd come . . ."

"She can't, Walter. I'm so sorry, but she can't . . ."

"Oh," he said. "Oh . . ."

Feeling she had to do something to make it better, she found herself talking more, using the news of Vivian's death to excuse everything that had happened that morning, telling him that Lauren hadn't meant to be so horrible, she was just so sad, so they'd have to leave her alone for a while, and not mind her too much, or Hannah, for that matter, because brisk Hannah was really struggling too. Even Aunty Esme just said some very strange things sometimes, because she was missing Vivian so.

Vivian would have been proud, Rose thought, of the lies that poured from her tongue.

The only thing she didn't speak to Walter about was his sudden wealth. Five really was too young to be made aware of such a thing. He wouldn't be able to absorb it. *She* still couldn't absorb it.

Max, she thought, would be the best person to speak to him about it all anyway, when the time came.

She went in search of him an hour or so later, once she was ready, once Walter was ready, determined to get him to agree to her staying on, not just *for now*, but something rather more indefinite.

The two of them ran into Esme on the veranda, playing solitaire, avoiding her cottage, she said, as her mum had decided to move in.

"I'd much rather have you, but Max says Walter has to stay here, so I suppose I'll be moving back myself. Good news for you, though, Walter." She flashed him a smile. "The wicked witch has gone."

Rose felt a rush of relief. She realized it wouldn't fix anything, not in the long term, but still, she'd choose to have Lauren out of the house over in it, every day of the week.

"So where are we going?" Esme asked, pushing her cards aside, standing, inviting herself along. "I've been waiting for you to resurface."

"I need to talk to your brother," said Rose.

"Oh, he'll like that," said Esme. Was she being sarcastic? "Come on then." She jogged down the porch steps. "I think he's over at the plane . . ."

The late-morning sun was high, its rays warm, although a breeze had come up, bringing a chill to the air that made Rose shiver, tired as she was, reminding her that it was yet winter here, on the far side of the world, for all she was wearing a sundress. As she followed Esme across the lawn, she wondered when summer would come, what that heat would feel like; whether she really *would* be permitted to stay long enough to find out. Breathing deep on the unsettling unknown—the earthy air softer than out at sea, so much cleaner than back in London—she told herself, *It will be fine,* and, squeezing Walter's hand, let her eyes rove over the station's hills and grassy plateaus, just as she had on her dawn pee, astounded all over again by the wild beauty. It really was impossible not to stare. Never, in all she'd anticipated and agonized over these past months, had she imagined she was bringing Walter somewhere quite so . . . spectacular. The sky was bluer than any she'd known, the grass deeper, more sumptuous. Blossoms had started to spring: at the house, down on the trees by the gate, in thickets surrounding the fields. She could smell the scent. With every shudder of wind, the pastures whispered, rushing through infinite shades of green and gold, wafting the perfume to her. Out on the fields, more men thundered on horseback. For a second, she wished she were with them, doing the same. Then she remembered Max, what she was about to ask of him. She started worrying again. . . .

And all the while, Esme chatted, full of questions herself, quite as though she'd spent the past hour compiling a list. Not about Vivian, or what Rose had made of her brother's letter—it seemed she had some restraint—but England, London's shops, the bombings, Rose and Walter's voyage, too. "*Bombay,*" she said. "What I'd give to meet a sergeant major who'd carry me off there." She wanted to know everything Rose could tell her about the port stops, then, tiring of Rose's preoccupied answers, moved her attention to Walter: still puffy-eyed, but too overawed, it seemed, by Esme's demanding chatter to do anything but cooperate with her inquiries, filling her in on their ice creams in Ceylon, the fish he'd seen with Rose's father, the whales he'd spotted, and his best friend Verity. . . .

"A girlfriend?" said Esme, as they crossed the barnyard. The wheelbarrow was still there. "Walter, good on *you*. Was she pretty? I expect she was. Your mum liked pretty things. . . ."

"My mummy was pretty."

"She was," said Esme, and, even in her distraction, Rose heard the sudden catch in her voice.

It reassured her, that catch.

It made her think that Esme might have liked Mabel, when she'd lived here. Even loved her, maybe.

And if she'd loved her, surely she could be trusted with her child for a few minutes. Not out of sight, just earshot. . . .

"Would you mind?" she said to her, when they reached the top of the slope down to the plane. It really would be so much easier, speaking to Max alone.

Esme didn't mind. "Why not?" she said with a shrug.

Walter was less easy about it. Rose saw that in the edgy way he looked at her. "Rosie . . ." But Rose assured him she wouldn't be long, and not far away.

"Just there," she said, pointing at the plane, "with Uncle Max." She could see him now, on his haunches beneath one of the wings, his back to them, working on the engine. "Come and get me the minute you want . . ."

"He'll be fine," said Esme airily, dropping down and patting the grass beside her. "Come on, Walter, I won't bite, I promise. I don't like the taste of little boys." Then, more helpfully, "You can tell me more about the ship's pool. Did you swim?"

"It didn't have any water," he said, perching, albeit hesitantly, beside her.

"That's very disappointing. Was there a tennis court?"

"I don't think so."

"Walter, what kind of ship was this . . . ?"

Rose left them to it, carrying on down the slope, the grass skimming the bare skin of her feet through her sandals.

Max didn't see her, not until she was almost upon him. She grew ever jumpier, the closer she drew, uncomfortably aware of how different she felt in the wake of all he'd written, how much she wanted them to be able to start again. How sorely she needed him to agree to her staying. She was ready to fight if she had to. Vivian had been counting on her for that, she was sure of it now. Their conversation in London, the evening she and Walter had returned from Joe's base, had come back to her forcibly. She'd told Vivian that she wouldn't leave Walter until he was ready, and Vivian had smiled: glad, Rose had thought then. Relieved, she realized in retrospect. She'd always wanted Rose to stay. Those extra pounds she'd given to Rose with her wages before she'd sailed only felt like further evidence. They hadn't been a thank-you at all. No, Vivian had wanted to make sure Rose could afford to remain here.

"I've taken advantage of your better nature," she'd said, at Rose's interview.

It seemed to Rose she'd been looking for someone she could do that to all along. She was still doing it to Rose, from beyond the grave, and sad as Rose was—touched, even, that Vivian *had* thought to provide for her—she was growing angrier again too, desperate to rail at Vivian for how much she'd lied and manipulated rather than trusting her with the truth. She'd gone, just gone, leaving Rose to pick up her pieces, and nothing but unanswered questions in her wake: about this, what in God's name she'd thought she was doing, sending Walter into such a nightmare—because Rose had to believe she'd had a motive beyond desperation—then so many other things, besides. Small things it had begun to dawn on her she'd never now know: about Vivian's life, her marches with the suffragettes, and Naomi in her photographs, what they'd meant to each other . . . what it had been about Rose that had reminded her of her so. "I'll tell you," Vivian had said. "One day, I'll tell you." But she hadn't. And now she couldn't. They hadn't even been able to say goodbye properly. It felt so unfinished. . . .

She drew a pained breath, pushing her fury and grief down before it overwhelmed her, determinedly fixing her thoughts on Max instead, studying him, trying to decide how he'd react to her request. It was impossible to gauge. He had his back to her, his hat tipped forward, loose shirt pulling against his muscles as he worked. Fleetingly she wondered if he'd dressed his shoulder. She wouldn't risk asking. She'd realized how little he wanted pity. She was sure hers was another part of what had riled him earlier, in the yard. She'd felt sorry for him, and he'd seen it, hated it. . . .

Determined not to offend him again, she kept her gaze steady when, seeming to sense her attention on him, he turned, his eyes connecting with hers. It was the unburned side of his face that came toward her first. For a second, that was all she saw—just him, as he'd been: sharp cheekbones, sun-darkened skin, firm jaw tinged gold by stubble. Then the rest of him followed. His scars followed.

Him, as he was now.

"Hello," he said, guarded, but then she supposed you didn't write a note as honest as his and not feel exposed. "Are you all right?"

"Not even a bit," she said, reciprocating his candor.

"I'm sorry."

"I'm sorry, as well," she said. "For — "

"Don't," he said, interrupting before she could speak of his brother, or any of it. "You don't need to."

So she didn't.

No pity.

"I've told Walter about Vivian," she said instead, "but not about what she's left him."

"Good," Max said, "that can wait."

She nodded, pleased he agreed.

She drew breath, about to ask. . . .

"I see you've brought Esme," he said, speaking first, distracting her.

"She brought herself," she said, glancing back at her and Walter on the bank. Walter was the one talking, Esme listening. It felt like the safest way around. "She told me she's moving back into the house."

"I thought she might," Max said, reaching for a rag on the plane's wing, wiping his oily hands. "It'll be better for her. She's lonely in that cottage."

"She said she'd like to meet a sergeant major."

"She'll struggle with that out here."

"Vivian said she was married . . ."

"Still is," he said. "To Paul."

It was the way he said *Paul.* "You don't like him?"

"He lost their house gambling, then enlisted," said Max, still wiping his hands, "so no, not much."

"Is he in the air force?" asked Rose, reflecting that the Lucknows really didn't make the happiest marriages.

"Army," said Max, throwing the rag aside. "I think he thought bullets would be easier to live with than Esme's contempt."

She had to smile at that. "I can see his point . . ."

And, to her amazement, he smiled too.

He really did have a nice smile.

"He's in Sumatra anyway," he said.

"No bullets, then."

"Not yet, no."

There was a short pause.

Over on the grass verge, Esme laughed at something.

Rose turned again, hoping it was something nice.

Walter wasn't laughing with her. But he was smiling. Just a small smile: the kind she remembered from their first outing to Regent's Park, when they'd tried to spot Princess Margaret's bedroom at the palace. Still, a smile nonetheless.

He never could help himself for long.

"That child was born for joy," Vivian had said. "It's what makes it all so cruel."

Oh, Vivian.

"I don't want to leave," she said, forcing herself to the point. "I can't leave him. I never wanted to leave him. But now . . ." She stopped, turned back to Max. "You said you can't promise he'll be happy, but I have to know he will be. Please, let me stay, just until he's properly settled."

He studied her, face set. He didn't seem surprised by her request. It felt like, on some level, he might even have been expecting it. There was a wariness to his expression, though, that she didn't entirely understand.

"Surely it will be easier for you," she said, "to have me here."

"Easier?" he said, like easy was the last thing it would be.

"I'll look after him," she said, "while you're all getting to know each other. You won't have to worry . . ."

"Aren't there things you need to get back to?"

"Not really."

"No people," he said, still resisting. It was a bit insulting. "Family . . . ?"

"Yes, I've family," she said. "I've got an older brother, a pilot like you, who I'm scared for, every day. Then an uncle, my dad's brother, who's going to be furious when I tell him I want to do this . . ."

"You should listen to him."

"Perhaps, but I really never do."

Something flickered in his eyes.

Was it amusement?

It looked like it might have been amusement, even if it was very reluctant.

She took heart. It felt like a positive sign.

"What about your dad?" he asked.

"He'll probably be a bit furious too," she said. "And my mum. She's expecting me in Malaya . . ."

"That sounds nice."

"Doesn't it?" she said, and didn't mention Xander in Cairo. He hadn't asked her about a fiancé. "Malaya can wait, though. My mum can wait. She'll understand. Let me stay. You want to. I can see you want to, deep down . . ."

"You can see that?"

"Not really," she admitted. "But I think you're too kind to make Walter sadder when he doesn't need to be. I think you know making me leave will do that. I can pay board. Vivian gave me——"

"Stop," he said. "Please, stop." He exhaled raggedly. "You don't need to pay board. Christ, Vivian's left me more money than I know what to do with. I'm not taking yours . . ."

Rose smiled. "So I can stay?"

"Yeah. If that's really what you want."

"I do want, I do . . ."

She wanted to run over, tell Walter, only she couldn't, because then she'd have to admit there'd ever been a chance of her going. Needing to do something, moving before she knew she was going to, she reached out, grabbed Max's hands, holding them in hers.

"Thank you," she said.

"It's all right," he said, and for a beat, he tightened his own grip around hers. Instinctive, reflexive, for that second, the warm pressure of his hands was all she felt.

Then they moved away from each other.

She wasn't sure who dropped the other's hands first.

Still feeling his touch, she curled her fingers into fists.

He set his palm on the plane's wing.

"I'd better get on," he said.

"Of course," she said, very hot—had she really just grabbed his hands?—but too elated to mind that she was now blushing in front of him for the third time that morning. "Thank you again. I'm happy . . ."

"Yeah," he said, "you look pretty happy."

Her smile grew.

She waited for him to return it.

She really thought he might be about to.

But he didn't.

He lifted his hand from the wing, ran it down his face, around his jaw, over his scars.

She watched his fingertips move, across the welts, the dents and furrows left by his Hurricane's flames. His forehead creased, his eyes became heavier.

It was almost as though he was reminding himself that the burns were there.

CHAPTER FOURTEEN

He had to fly away again, after that, back to the muster he'd left three other stockmen in charge of that morning. (*Stockmen*, that's what they were called, not cowboys, nor ranchers; vaguely Rose recalled Kate saying as much on the ship.) He told Rose about it as they crossed over to Esme and Walter, so that he could say goodbye. His tone was brisk, detached, making her wonder if his smile, their touch, had even happened at all. Seeming to have already forgotten about both, he said that the health checks his mother had arranged couldn't be postponed, not now they were in motion. *Easier to keep going than stop.* The cattle marked for inspection would only need to be rounded up again in another month's time if the appointment was canceled.

"I wouldn't leave otherwise," he said to Walter, once they reached him and Esme. "I'll get back as soon as I can. You'll have Rose here to look after you." He didn't call her Rosie. She wished he would. "She's not going anywhere, so you don't need to worry."

"Well, thank God," said Esme, pushing herself to standing. "No need for boarding school after all then, Walter."

"What's boarding school?" said Walter.

"It doesn't matter," said Rose.

"Esme's kidding," Max told him, at the same time.

"Oh he knows that," said Esme. "He understands me perfectly."

Walter stared up at her.

Rose wasn't sure he did.

"How long are you staying for?" Esme asked her.

"Always," said Walter.

"A while," said Rose.

"Well, well," said Esme, eyes dancing. "This really is turning into quite the morning . . ."

"I'm off," said Max. "Tell Mum I'm gone?"

"No," said Esme. "I'm not going near her until she's calmed down."

"Fine," he said, leaving. "She'll work it out."

Rose watched him go, jogging down the slope without a backward glance, head tipped forward beneath his hat.

"I still can't believe you've got a plane," she said to Esme. "You fly anywhere in England and you're practically in another country."

"Oh, I'd like that," said Esme. "I've never got beyond New South Wales."

"Don't feel too bad," said Rose, her eyes still on Max. He'd reached the plane, and was kicking the engine flap shut, climbing into the cockpit she was still sure must terrify him. "Before this, I'd never made it farther than the Isle of Wight."

"What's the Isle of Wight?"

"Nowhere you need to worry about missing."

"Aunty Vivian had some colored sands from there," said Walter.

"Did she?" said Rose, surprised. "She never told me she'd gone."

Another thing she hadn't known.

"She said her mummy and daddy used to take her," said Walter, enlightening her.

"Why are the sands colored?" asked Esme.

"The rocks, I think," said Rose. "Everyone comes back with jars full. My old landlady had a whole display . . ." She tailed off, fairly sure Esme wouldn't be interested in Enid's ornaments.

Max fired the engine and started taxiing down the grass, building speed, arching upward, into the eye-watering glare.

"How far is he going?" Rose asked Esme.

"Depends where the others have got to," said Esme. "He'll need to find them before he lands. Shouldn't take more than a half hour . . ."

"A half hour?" said Rose, turning. "How big *is* this place?"

"I don't know," said Esme, with an apathetic rise and fall of her shoulders. "Couple of thousand square miles."

"That sounds big," said Walter.

"It is big," said Rose.

"There are bigger," said Esme. "Much bigger. This is a very big country."

"Yes," said Rose quietly, struck, suddenly, by the vast size of it all around her. Already, Max had practically disappeared, his plane no more than vapor trails. Even the sky felt bigger than it had in England. Higher up, somehow . . . endless. *A couple of thousand square miles.* She couldn't picture it.

It took her a second to realize Esme had spoken.

"What's that?" she said.

"Mum," Esme said, pointing at a small figure standing outside one of the distant cottages, also looking upward. "She's working out he's gone . . ." Her face hardened, not smiling for once. "She'll be hating that he didn't say goodbye, feeling sorry for herself."

"Because of Aunty Vivian?" Walter asked.

Esme didn't answer. She was still looking at her mother.

"Yes," said Rose, speaking for her, absently, though, preoccupied by what Lauren could have done to make her daughter dislike her so.

Perhaps she'd ask Esme about it.

There was a great deal she'd like to ask her, now she thought. Max's note had brushed over such a lot — what had gone wrong between Mabel and Jamie; what Walter's father had meant to Mabel; what Max had meant when he'd said he'd *taken* him (what *did* that mean?). . . . The list went on. Rose was sure Esme must know the answers to some of it.

She would ask her, she decided.

Maybe after Walter had gone to bed one night.

It came to her then that she was glad Esme would be in the house with them. She still hadn't quite made up her mind about her, with her sharp looks and confidence that felt too careless to be real (one knock, Rose suspected, and it would shatter), and yet she was grateful to have found her rather than some other kind of Esme waiting. Odd as some of the things that came out of her mouth might be, at least she wasn't silent, or cold, or withdrawn. It would be nice to have her to talk to. Other than Kate, and that too-short interlude in Ceylon with Rose's parents, Rose had had no proper adult company in months. And this place was huge, *a couple of thousand square miles;* relieved as Rose was to be remaining in it with Walter — and she was, she really was—Max was gone, Lauren despised her, and Vivian had dropped her in it utterly.

She really could do with a friend.

A telegraph arrived early that afternoon, while Rose and Walter began un-packing, setting Walter's picture of Mabel on his bedside table, her eider-down and Rabbit on his bed, filling the room's shelves with his toys, Vivian's pinwheel, doing their best to make the space feel more homey. It was the guest bedroom he'd been put in, Esme told them, standing by the window, keeping vigil for her mother to head off on her usual lunchtime rounds of the workers so that she could go to her cottage and pack a bag of her own in peace. Rose was in Max's old bedroom. It seemed he'd been living in the house's side annex for years, since long before he'd gone off to war. Rose didn't know what to say when Esme told her that, so she said nothing. It felt strange to her, though, that she'd be sleeping in his bed. After her sleepless night in the barn, she was desperate to climb into it, curl up between the sheets, but there was a discomforting kind of intimacy to the idea.

She wasn't at all sure Xander would approve.

She didn't mention Xander to Esme, though, just as she hadn't to Max. Instead, curious to know more about the station, she asked Esme how many people there were working on it.

"Lots," said Esme vaguely. "Gardeners, stable hands, Cook . . ."

"Hannah?"

". . . Bill. Hannah only works in here, he's got the station kitchen out back. He'll have sent lunch out." Esme tapped her fingernail on the pane. "They'll be breaking already . . ."

"And what about you?" Rose asked, throwing Walter a ball they hadn't seen since it had gone into the ship's hold at Liverpool, smiling tiredly at his smile. "What do you do?"

"The accounts, now I'm back. I'm good with numbers." Esme frowned, paused tapping. Rose thought she might be thinking about her wayward hus-band, Paul, and how he'd been less adept. "Max manages most of it, but Mum likes to think it's still her. It's why she goes out at meals, wants to make sure no one's slacking off, taking too long . . ."

"They must like that."

"Oh, they love it," said Esme.

Rose wanted to ask her if there were any Aborigine workers, like Kate had mentioned there might be. She didn't know how to put it, though.

That was when the telegraph boy arrived anyway, on his bike: motor, not pedal.

"No one's going to cycle all the way out here," said Esme, turning from the window, all smiles again at the diversion. Was it how she survived here, existing from one distraction to the next? Thinking, *Probably yes*, Rose frowned, edgy suddenly, reminded too much of herself through her months in Ilfracombe; that restless unhappiness that was now such a distant memory, but that she was so afraid would be waiting for her, when she eventually got back. . . .

"Quick, Walter," said Esme, "run and grab the telegram before Mum hops on her broomstick and gets there first."

"I don't want to," he said, to Rose not Esme.

"There's no broomstick," Rose told him, and, needing to move herself, escape her own disconcerting thoughts, stood, beckoning him with her. "Come on, we'll go together."

It didn't occur to her that the telegram would be for her. As she led Walter down the polished stairs, across the hallway, opening the fly screen (that would never not remind her of Lauren locking them out), she felt no worry that it might contain bad news: about Joe, Lionel, Xander. She and Walter had only just arrived; not even the worst kind of news traveled that quickly. She assumed the wire must be for one of the Lucknows: something cow related, or to do with Esme's Paul in Sumatra—a possibility that Esme, calling breezily for them to wait, didn't seem remotely concerned about.

The three of them reached the porch steps just as the telegraph boy came to a halt. Kangaroos had multiplied on the lawn to either side of the driveway while they'd been inside, a couple just tiny, barely out of their mothers' pouches. There was a trio of colorful parrots, too, at the end of the veranda, pecking at some dense-looking breadcrumbs Rose could only presume were the remnants of Hannah's doomed loaf. Walter looked from the parrots, to the kangaroos, back to the parrots, like he couldn't decide which to get up close to first. Rose could almost hear him replaying her earlier warning about a kangaroo's punch, weighing up whether the pelt would be worth it.

She was glad he was distracted. It meant he didn't notice the not quite friendly way the telegraph boy—who was actually a middle-aged man with a sun-leathered face—removed his goggles and stared at him. Oblivious to his attention, he set off toward the birds (the pelt, it seemed, wasn't worth it), little fingers curled into half fists, Rose guessed in anticipation of stroking their vibrant feathers.

Sure enough, "Can I touch these ones?" he called over his shoulder.

"I'm not sure they'll want you to," she said.

Which for some reason made the telegraph boy (that was a man) smile, snidely.

Rose didn't ask him what had amused him.

Esme didn't either.

For Rose's part, she had a certain sense she didn't want to know.

She forgot all about it anyway when the boy-man said he had a wire for a Miss Rose Hamilton.

"That's me," she said, nonplussed.

"Good," he said, holding out the wire.

She took it, not thanking him (that smile), and paying him no more attention as he replaced his goggles and roared away. She was too busy opening the telegraph paper, fumbling, worrying very much after all that it might contain bad news.

But, to her huge relief, it didn't.

It was nothing more than a few lines from Vivian's lawyer, Mr. Yates, wanting to be sure that she and Walter had arrived safely.

Sincerest apologies for the taxicab STOP It was only after you left London that I received conclusive confirmation that no other transport would be made available STOP

Rose could only imagine the tone that *conclusive confirmation* had taken.

Disappointingly, Mr. Yates didn't expand on it. He told her nothing much else at all, just asked her to wire by return confirming that she and Walter were in a position to receive further correspondence.

Have had several wires returned to me by Mrs. Lucknow STOP Do not want to send letter until I know you can be in receipt STOP As soon as I hear I shall post directly STOP

"*Damn*," breathed Rose. Any letter from England would take months to arrive: at the very least the four she and Walter had been at sea for.

"How annoying," said Esme, unabashedly reading over her shoulder.

Rose drew an irritable breath. Lauren getting rid of her post as well as Max's and Esme's felt like the last straw. She was of half a mind to march over to Esme's cottage and confront her about it. . . .

"You'd better wire this Mr. Yates back," said Esme.

It was, undeniably, a more productive course of action.

Rose read the words on the paper over. *As soon as I hear I shall post directly.* She supposed she should get on with it. Queuing at a telegraph office was pretty much the last thing she felt like doing after so little sleep, but she could at least get in touch with the others while she was there — Joe, Lionel, Xander, her parents — let them know she'd arrived, and was staying. She should visit a bank, too, change some of her pounds. She needed money. . . .

"Where can I do all that?" she asked Esme.

"Town," said Esme.

"Brisbane?" said Rose, appalled. It was so far away.

It amused Esme that she thought so.

"You ever want to go to the pictures, or do some proper shopping," she said, "Brisbane's it. But Narrawee's not fa — " She broke off, looked over Rose's shoulder, distracted. "Here we go, Mum's out. She'll be wanting to know what's in your wire."

Rose turned, and there Lauren indeed was, standing at Esme's low front door, peering across at them. She moved as soon as she realized they'd seen her, striding around the back of the cottage to where there was a horse tethered, pretending, Rose thought, that she'd come out solely for that purpose. It almost made Rose feel sorry for her, furious as she was. She pictured her sitting inside alone all this time, upset that Max had gone, waiting for Esme who had no intention of showing up, perhaps grieving all over again for her lost Jamie, in this place that was so much the opposite of happy.

Her sympathy really was only an almost-pity, though.

She couldn't actually feel sorry for Lauren.

She didn't have *that* good a nature.

She'd intercepted her post, made her and Walter sleep in a barn. Rose was sure she still had bits of straw stuck in her hair. She *knew* she'd been bitten, on her back, her legs and arms, by God only knew what. She couldn't just let all that go.

"I'm going to grab some bits if she's finally off," said Esme. "See if Hannah's done anything for our lunch, will you? I'm starving."

"What about this wire?" said Rose.

"I'll drive you into town after," Esme said. "But," she glanced over at Walter, now kneeling by the birds, holding his head tipped to the side so that he could watch them eat, "it might make sense to leave him here. His mum hated it, I can't think he'll like it much more." She frowned. "Not when they work out who he is."

CHAPTER FIFTEEN

With Esme's dark words ringing in her ears, and still smarting from the telegraph man-boy's smirk (had he found the idea of the birds not wanting Walter to touch them funny? *Had* he?), Rose did try to talk Walter into staying with Hannah while she and Esme went out.

"You can play with your toys," she said. "Won't that be fun, after all this time?"

"Not without you," he said.

"I'm sure it will . . ."

"Not really, Rosie."

"Please, Walter . . ."

He was having none of it, though. Not a bar.

Hannah, as dour as ever, didn't help. Although she had prepared lunch in the kitchen — cold meats, a salad, and a pot of richly brewed tea that Rose remembered to drink this time — she didn't join them for the meal at the scrubbed table, but kept working, clattering around at the sink, sighing about whether she'd ever have the chance to eat herself before nightfall, then again when Esme came in the back door with mud on her shoes, then again when, head in the cold box, she realized she was down to her last tomato and would have to go out to pick more.

"This day," she said. "This day . . ."

"We could go," offered Rose.

"You don't know where they are," Hannah said. "Or which ones to pick. I've still got to get the eggs, too. And now apparently I'm to play babysitter, on top of it all . . ."

In the end, Rose couldn't bear to put her, or Walter, through it.

So to Narrawee with herself and Esme Walter went.

"I suppose it has to happen at some point," said Esme dubiously, when Rose sent him running upstairs to visit the latrine first.

"You have to help me there," Rose said, speaking quickly, before he returned. "If there's any staring, like that man earlier, we can't let him see, get upset . . ."

"That man was an idiot. Don't worry about idiots . . ."

"I don't. But I'm not five, I'm twenty-five."

"So am I," exclaimed Esme. "Just turned, last month. When's your birthday?"

"February the twenty-ninth."

"Ooh," said Esme, wincing.

"The point is," said Rose, not wanting to get into all that, "Mabel never let Walter realize that the way he looks matters. I haven't. It shouldn't matter. He shouldn't need to think it does, not yet. Not for years. It'll change him. He's still too little — "

"I know that," said Esme, cutting her off, more serious suddenly. Rose liked that she was. She needed her to take this seriously. Esme, for all her talk of boarding schools and witches, had, *had* to care.

"So you will help?" she said to her.

"You're worrying about the wrong thing," said Esme, not answering the question. "It isn't the way he looks that's going to get people going. Plenty won't much like that either, but not everyone's a racist . . ."

"I don't think they are," said Rose.

"Good," said Esme. "Because we're definitely not. Mum's not. I can't say much nice about her, but ever since we were kids she's made sure this place is fair. Everyone's treated the same, they get paid the same, live the same, eat the same . . ."

"So you do have Aborigines working here?"

"Yeah," said Esme. "Of course. Walter's dad was a stockman. Mum hated him, like a lot of people in town hated him, but that wasn't just because he was black. Definitely not for Mum. It was because . . ." She stopped, looked upward.

Because of what? Rose wanted, sorely, to ask her.

That and, *How about you, and Max?*

Did you both hate him?

But they'd run out of time.

Walter was racketing back down the stairs toward them, with Rabbit. She hadn't even been able to make sure Esme would definitely help look after him when they got to town. Much as she wanted to count on her, she still wasn't sure she could. Esme, so flippant one second, then in earnest the next, was as unpredictable as anyone she'd met, and while she might have been concerned enough about Walter's feelings to recommend he stay at home, Rose had no way of guessing if that would stretch to her publicly taking his corner in a place she'd lived in for twenty-five years. She'd known Walter barely five minutes. He was the child her brother had killed himself over. Rose frankly wasn't sure if she'd want to get out of the motor and be seen with the two of them on the street.

"I flushed the toilet," said Walter proudly, coming to a halt.

"Good boy," Rose said, smiling a smile she really didn't feel.

"And washed my hands," he said.

"Even better."

"A friend of yours, is he?" said Esme, pointing at his rabbit.

"It's a she," said Walter.

"It's a he," said Esme, insisting, for her own inexplicable reasons. "Now come on. Let's get this over with."

Narrawee really wasn't far away: less than a quarter-hour drive from the Lucknows' front gate, in the opposite direction from Brisbane. Esme drove them over in one of the family's utes: a dark green truck with an open back, and faded leather seats. There was something incongruous about the sight of her behind the clunky wheel, with her glossy waves, fine-boned face, and flowery dress, but she drove every bit as assuredly as Lance had the night before, much faster too, bundling them along the empty, woodland-fringed road into town. The air blowing through the windows was fresh, scented by the storm-dampened soil, and something else that Esme said was eucalyptus trees. The leaves created a canopy above, casting the woody floor in shadows, letting through only the most occasional dapple of golden sunlight. Once in a while, they drove past a house — bungalows with boarded fences and manicured lawns—but other than them, there wasn't much to see beyond more kangaroos in the undergrowth.

They didn't talk much for most of the drive. Rose, sitting with Walter on her lap, her head rested back against her seat, was too tired—and too impatient to do as Esme had said and get the entire trip over with—to think what to say. Outside, above the noise of the engine, she could hear birdsong and the screech of crickets. It made her think of her old fighter base, back in England. They'd had crickets in the fields there, too. It all felt very vivid in her mind today. Perhaps it had been her dream the night before, helping to bring it back. Max, and his plane, too . . .

Walter, apparently thinking of Max as well, was the one to finally break the silence, asking if he would have got to his cows yet.

"I'd say so," said Esme. "He'll be back on his horse."

"Can you ride a horse?" Walter asked her.

"I certainly can."

"What about you, Rosie?" he asked.

"Yes," she said, stifling a yawn. "There was a stables near our house when I was little. I used to go all the time." Lionel had used to take her and Joe riding at Winston's as well, but she didn't mention that with Esme there. People could be a bit strange, she'd discovered, when they found out she knew him. She'd never forget Xander's amazement, when she'd told him. She wondered sometimes if her connections had been part of her appeal. If they still were . . .

"My brothers taught me to ride," said Esme, wistfully. "I loved it . . ."

"Rosie's got a brother," said Walter. "He showed me his plane."

"He's a pilot?" said Esme, taking her eyes off the road to look at Rose.

"He is," said Rose. "Bombers."

Esme filled her cheeks with a breath, and let it go. "This bloody war."

Walter turned on Rose's lap.

"Esme did a swear," he whispered.

At any other time, his shocked awe would have made Rose laugh. Joe, she knew, would have laughed.

But she didn't. And not only because of the thought of Joe in his bomber.

She'd spotted a clearing in the trees ahead of them, the beginning of what looked like buildings: a very small, narrow strip of them.

"Is this it?" she said to Esme.

"Ye-es," said Esme, clunking the gears as she took them on, to the head of the strip. "This is *it*."

It wasn't what Rose had been expecting. In her mind, they'd been heading toward something like the old market towns of Devon and the Home Counties: cobbled alleyways, old pubs and squares, thick crowds that she could at least try and keep Walter anonymous in. But there were no cobbles here, or alleyways, and certainly no bustling throngs either. On the contrary, there were downward of fifty people out and about in the afternoon sun. Apprehensive as Rose had been before, she grew much more so now, realizing just how on show she, Walter, and Esme were going to be on the short palm-fringed street. (If Esme got out of the ute.) There was only the barest smattering of shops: a grocer, hardware store, butcher and bakery, then two pubs (hotels), and the bank and post office. The pavements were covered in corrugated awnings, and even as they drove by, people turned beneath them, looking to see who was in their ute. The shoppers were mainly women, some with children, but there were a few men too: in suits, workmen's overalls, others dressed like Max.

"This is the town hall," said Esme, maneuvering them to a halt outside the tallest of the street's buildings. There was a recruiting officer on its front steps, chatting to a boy who didn't look old enough to be out of school, let alone sent off to war. "They have dances, sometimes," said Esme. "I haven't danced in years."

"No," said Rose, who hadn't for a long time either, not since she'd found out she was pregnant. "That boy's not going to enlist, is he?"

"Hamish?" said Esme. "He's only sixteen, Barney knows that."

"Who's Barney?"

"The officer."

"Do you know everyone here?"

"Most of them," said Esme. "That," she pointed at a graying woman staring across at them from outside the hardware store, "is my *lovely* husband Paul's sister. His family own the shop."

"She doesn't look too happy that you're here."

"Oh, she won't be," said Esme. "None of them will."

"I didn't used to have friends, either," said Walter.

"Walter," said Esme, pouting, "that's very sad. But I never said I didn't have friends."

"Do you?" he asked.

"Well, I've got Max . . ."

"He's your brother," said Walter.

"He can still be my friend."

"He was a bit cross with you."

"He's cross with everyone these days."

"Hannah's a bit cross, too," said Walter.

"You just have to not take her seriously," said Esme. "But don't tell her I said that."

Walter said he wouldn't, Esme said she'd be keeping her witch's ear out, Walter gave her ear a concerned look, and Rose, who had been considering asking the two of them to wait for her in the ute, decided she'd better keep Walter with her after all. The cabin was hardly a good hiding place anyway. It was more like a podium than anything, with its high seats and large windows—windows that Esme's sister-in-law was still scrutinizing them through.

"Come on," Rose said, drawing a bracing breath, "let's go."

"If we must," said Esme, and didn't hesitate before throwing open her own door and jumping down onto the street.

It seemed to Rose, from the ready way she did it, that she really hadn't been considering doing anything else. It made her feel a bit guilty for thinking she might. ("Good," Esme would say to her later that night. "So you should.")

They didn't stay long in town, no more than the time it had taken for them to drive over. Even that was long enough. While not everyone they encountered was unfriendly—there were a couple who even nodded hello to Esme, asked about Max, *Tell him to come out himself one of these days, stop hiding*—most were. Their curious stares hardened within what felt like seconds of Rose lifting Walter down from the ute, all of them seeming to guess, or at the very least suspect, in no time at all, who he was. And it wasn't only him they stared at. Rose, doing her best to ignore their attention, nonetheless felt it in every inch of her clammy skin: how the women especially took in her worn-out sandals, faded prewar dress, and hair that possibly still had hay in it. Their cold appraisal made her feel such a foreigner—more somehow than she had in either Bombay or Colombo—and so deeply unwelcome. She hadn't known anything like it, not since she'd been admitted to that grim hospital ward: those nurses with their rough, pinching hands. *You brought this on yourself.* She'd hated their hatred, just as she hated this hatred now, but she refused to let it debilitate her as it had then.

She'd done that one too many times already.

She wasn't debilitated. Really, had it not been for Walter, she would have had no hesitation in spinning on her heel, facing up to these strangers, just as she should have to those nurses. She'd been too frightened, back in that hospital, too weak and desolate, but she was none of those things anymore. She was furious: at their judgment, the unfairness of it. Her anger of the past twenty-four hours came roaring back within her, making her feel even stronger. These people, with their nudges and whispers, they were the weak ones. She was choosing not to make a scene. She wasn't scared of one.

"You'll meet some villains along the way," Vivian had said to Walter, the night they'd left. "They'll try and make you feel small, less than you are. . . . Don't let them do it."

Rose wouldn't, not to Walter, nor to her. She smiled, talking to Walter, swinging his hand, keeping her head high. And Esme, unpredictable Esme, played right along, sticking right with them, making Rose feel stronger yet, and so much less alone.

It really was nicer, not being alone.

Esme even took Walter's free hand as they crossed the road to the bank, and, following Rose's cue, chatted along, saying that there was a milk bar, just around the corner, that did the most divine ice-cream floats.

"What are ice-cream floats?" asked Rose, her arm brushing that of a woman who'd stopped, deliberately it felt like, in her way.

"Oh, they're really, really naughty," said Esme. "Dollops of ice cream, and lots of pop . . ."

"I've never had pop," said Walter.

"That's terrible," said Esme. "What about toffee apples? Have you had those?"

"I don't think so."

"The grocer there makes them at Halloween," said Esme. "It's Mum's *favorite* time of the year."

"Did you get dressed up for Halloween last year?" Rose asked Walter.

"I don't remember," he said. "Why is that man by those rakes looking so angry?"

"I think he maybe has a sore back," said Rose. "He looks like he's in pain."

"He is in pain," said Esme. "He's married to my husband's mum, Walter. He's been in pain for almost fifty years. Now, look at this tree with the red flowers. I used to climb it with my brothers. Why don't we see if you can get as high as we used to while Rosie changes her money . . . ?"

"Thank you," Rose said to her, once they were on their way back to the ute, done with the stuffy, stale-smelling bank, and the busy, oh-so-silent post office, where Walter managed to knock over a stand of postcards. Rose bought one for Enid (*Hello from Wonderful Narrawee*) and sent her many wires: to Mr. Yates, asking him to pass on her best to Lester, Pia, and Catherine too, then to Joe, her parents, Lionel, and Xander. (*Here safe and sound* STOP *Not leaving yet* STOP *Walter still needs me so will be staying for the foreseeable* STOP) She didn't know how Xander especially was going to react when he got his. Or rather, she did know. She just didn't much want to think about it.

Not doing that, she told Esme how glad she was that she'd been there. "It would have been harder," she paused, glancing at Walter between them, choosing her words, "finding my way without you."

"Yeah, of course," said Esme, like it was no bother at all, only she touched her hand to her waist as she spoke. Her fingers trembled a little. The ordeal had shaken her, much more than she wanted to let on.

Seeing it, Rose felt even more grateful. She wasn't clear what had made her come down so decidedly on Walter's side over what felt like almost all of Narrawee's, but she was resolved on asking her about it, that very night, along with everything else she wanted to know.

Esme, she was becoming certain, would tell her whatever she could.

"Can we please have an ice-cream float?" asked Walter, as they reached the ute.

"Another time," said Rose.

"We can make ice cream at home," said Esme, unlocking the door. "Hannah can, anyway. We have enough milk. We have lots and lots of milk. And fizzy pop. We've got everything. Bugger the milk bar." She shot Rose one of her shiniest smiles. "Bugger them all. And that, Walter," she threw her door wide, "really was a swear."

Hannah didn't make ice cream that night.

"I'm not in the mood for jokes," Hannah said, when they got back, and Esme filled her in on the plan. "You can take that right upstairs too," she said, as Esme threw her handbag down. "I'm not having all your clutter on top of me again . . ."

"It's never really *on top* of you," said Esme.

"Don't start," said Hannah. "I've had your mum here packing, ropable. I need to be at home, with a gin . . ."

"A mother's ruin," said Esme.

"I'll ruin you," said Hannah, batting her off. "Mark me, I shall ruin you. Go, do your sheets as well. Now, you," she said to Rose, as Esme left, "you might want to get on with drawing your bath." She pointed at the vats and cast-iron tub she'd left beside the range. "It's not a quick job."

It wasn't. And Hannah helped not at all with the filling and boiling and lifting of the vats. With dusk falling outside, and the crickets in full chorus, Rose sweated, hefting pail after pail from the range, trying not to spill it, because Hannah—mixing something in a bowl—sighed every time she did, and she really didn't want to give her that satisfaction. Walter stuck close to her, checking and double-checking in whispers that Hannah would definitely be gone by the time he had to get in the bath.

Hannah was.

She left before Rose had finished filling it, asking first whether Rose knew how to make such a thing as an omelette (Rose did), and setting a tea towel over her bowl. "I want to find a tidy kitchen in the morning," she said, by way of a goodbye, "no crumbs. And tell Esme that this bowl here is another starter. She is not to touch it."

"Why would I touch her starter?" said Esme, when—after Rose had lifted Walter, flush-cheeked and scrubbed, from his bath—she returned in her nightgown, with cold cream on her face, and rollers in her hair.

"I didn't ask," said Rose, buttoning up Walter's flannel pajama top. "I think it would have finished her off."

It was Esme who made the omelettes in the end while Walter played with the cat under the kitchen table and Rose took a bath of her own, concealed by the very same type of screens Enid and Rose's parents had had all that way away in England. The water had already started to cool. She could smell the ham Esme was frying in butter. She didn't stay in the tub for long, but, as she sank beneath the soapy water, feeling the grime and the stares of those strangers lift from her, she thought it might just be the nicest bath she'd ever had.

They all ate together that night, clean and warm, with the cat— Chamberlain, he was called; it made Rose smile: the opposite of a bulldog— purring between their legs. Esme suggested she and Rose partake of some of their own mother's ruin, and Rose agreed it was a very good idea. There was no thunder, nor pelting hailstorm, and while there was still so much that was awful, Rose pushed it all temporarily from her mind. Because she and Walter were inside, they were dry, with beds to sleep in that night, having a nice enough time with at least one of his pretend relatives. For the moment, it was enough.

But she didn't forget about everything for long.

Wrung-out as she was with exhaustion, and slightly drunk from the gin, as soon as they'd all moved into the drawing room, and Esme had put on the wireless — turning the dial away from the World Service's news that Germany was bombing Moscow, and finding a musical program instead — she was poised, waiting only for Walter to fall asleep on her lap before she finally asked Esme everything she was bursting to.

It didn't take Walter long to nod off. In the soft lamplight, he was gone within the space of Glenn Miller's low, crackling "In the Mood." As soon as his body had grown heavy, Rose looked across at Esme in her armchair, and, changing the subject from her time at the jazz bar in London, said, "There's a lot we need to talk about."

"Yeah," said Esme, eyes shining, gin in hand. "I thought you might have a bit stored up. You look knackered though . . ."

"I'm all right."

"You're tougher than Mabel," said Esme. "She'd have been in bed by now. And she would have asked Hannah to fill that bath."

She didn't say it unkindly. Far from it.

"You loved her," said Rose.

It wasn't a question.

"Like a sister," said Esme, answering it anyway.

"I'm sorry," said Rose.

"Yeah," said Esme. "So" — she puffed out a short breath, as though to expel the pain — "what else do you want to know? Where do you want to start?"

"The beginning. What happened with Walter's father?"

"No," said Esme. "That's not the beginning."

"No?"

"No," Esme said, slowly shaking her head. "The beginning goes back a long way before then."

CHAPTER SIXTEEN

It was after midnight by the time they finally went to bed. The music played on, Esme poured more gin, fetched a box of Old Gold chocolates, cigarettes as well, and held nothing back, but told Rose everything she knew, the whole sorry story spilling from her, like she'd been waiting for this opportunity, any opportunity, to share it. She'd as good as admitted in Narrawee that she had no friends. Max himself had told Rose she was lonely. It was only now, though, listening to her talk and talk, that Rose absorbed how right he was. Esme, it seemed to her, was even more lonely than she'd been. It struck her that she'd been surviving, barely, on her own here, on this isolated station, for far too long.

"It's Jamie that it all started with," Esme said. "He wasn't . . . easy, not even when we were small. He was a bully, and sweet, and horrible, and happy, and sad, and you never knew which one of him you were going to get. But the sweet, happy bits were so good," she smiled, distantly, into her drink, "they kept you hoping for more." He'd been six years older than her, she said, but two years younger than Max, now thirty-three. "The middle, and Mum's absolute favorite." He'd been friends with Esme's husband, Paul, too. They'd used to drink together, gamble together, when Jamie was in a social kind of mood. "We'd call them his ups," Esme said. "But then the grog would bring him down. Paul didn't give a stuff. I don't know why I never saw that . . ."

"And Max?" Rose asked.

"Max gave a stuff," said Esme, "but they didn't get on. Drove each other mad. Jamie always used to say Dad had loved Max more. I don't know," she reached for her cigarettes, pulled one out, "I never knew Dad, he died at Gallipoli before I was born . . ."

Rose winced. It was hardly an uncommon story. She'd had friends at school who'd never known their fathers either. Still . . .

"I'm sorry," she said, "that's awful."

"I know," said Esme, "very dreary. I don't think Jamie really remembered him either, but he always acted like he did." She placed a cigarette to her lips, lighting it. "He hated that he left all this to Max, and that Max went to London, to university . . ."

"He couldn't go?"

"No one was stopping him," said Esme. "Vivian offered to pay for all of us, but I was too stupid to realize I should take her up on it, then I married Paul and it was too late. Jamie was just too lazy." She drew on her cigarette. "He went to boarding school in Sydney, like me and Max, but dropped out at fifteen. Never worked. Mum told him it wasn't his fault, because nothing ever was. She always used to say how hard it was on him, having an older brother like Max . . ."

"He was so bad?" Rose couldn't picture it.

"No," said Esme, making more sense. "That was the problem. He was great. Still is, when he lets himself be. But Jamie hated that, thought everything came too easy for him, with our dad, then at school, making friends. . . . He was even better with the horses." She frowned at her cigarette. "Sometimes I think he'd have been happy that Max got burned. . . ."

"Really?" said Rose, taken aback.

"Maybe," said Esme, getting to her feet, reaching for the bottle. "He would have hated himself for it, but he'd have been pleased something went wrong for him. That's what he was like, never as good as he wanted to be."

For a moment, it made Rose think of Xander.

"More?" said Esme, proffering the bottle.

"Go on then," said Rose, holding out her glass. (She'd regret it in the morning, she knew.)

As Esme topped her up, she talked on, saying how resentful Jamie had been when Max had gone to visit Vivian in London, back in 1934, leaving the rest of them to manage the station. "Jamie was always asking for the chance to prove himself here," she said, sitting back in her chair, folding her legs beneath her, "show how he could run things, then when Max finally gave in, Jamie panicked, said he couldn't cope, and vanished off to Sydney. Just went." She stared across at Rose as though to say, *Can you imagine?*

Rose, thinking again of Xander, this time of how he'd disappeared for all those weeks before she'd left London, found she could.

"Mum was beside herself," said Esme. "We all were. He just went completely silent and you could never tell with Jamie what that might mean. We only knew he was still alive because he kept drawing money from the account. Then he reappeared after, I don't know" — she picked up her drink — "two months, all smiles, laughing, in a new suit with this great big bunch of flowers for Mum, like nothing was wrong, and Mabel with him."

"Married?"

"Rings on both their fingers," said Esme, raising her glass to her lips. For the first time, Rose noticed she wore no ring on her own hand: another thing that the two of them seemed to have in common. Rose almost mentioned it, feeling a sudden pull to confide in Esme, just as Esme was in her.

But Esme, caught up in her own memories, talked on, telling her how full of stories Mabel had been when she and Jamie had first returned to Queensland, of all the things they'd done together in Sydney. "Dancing, dinners, days out at the beach," Esme said. "He told her he owned this whole place. She was a shop assistant, used to sell rich ladies stockings, and said she quite fancied wearing them herself." She laughed unhappily, lighting up another cigarette, picking tobacco from her tongue. "I don't know what she thought a cattle station was going to be like."

"I can guess," said Rose ruefully, remembering her own visions of Tara.

"Yeah, well, she was pretty shocked when she got here. You should have seen the things Jamie bought her before they came. All these beautiful gowns, silk shirts and scarves and high-heeled shoes. We couldn't afford it, he drained the account, and she never got to wear anything out anyway." Another hollow laugh. "Sometimes, we got dressed up to have our dinner in the kitchen. It drove Mum mad . . ."

"She didn't like Mabel?"

"She loved her," said Esme, expelling smoke, surprising Rose. She found it hard to imagine Lauren, so cold, loving any stranger. "But she was always really edgy around her. Scared, I think. She says she always knew she'd leave . . ."

"Because she wasn't happy?"

"I suppose so," said Esme, and spoke more: of Mabel's homesickness for Sydney's bustle, its beaches, her upset when she'd discovered Jamie had lied to her about owning the station, the size of Narrawee—"She was even more shocked than you," Esme said, "the first time I took her there"—then Mabel and Jamie's rows when Jamie had started going out drinking again, sometimes not coming home until the next day, or even the day after. "She used to say he was cheating on her, and he'd say, what if he was, and Mum would tell Mabel he never meant anyone any harm, and Mabel would get angry at her." She gave Rose a harrowed look. "It was *fun.*"

"And Max?"

"Max," said Esme, flicking her glowing embers into the ashtray. "Max came back, and made it all worse, because Mabel fell completely, head-over-heels in love with him."

Rose stared.

She hadn't been expecting that.

It unsettled her. She wasn't sure exactly why.

She looked down at her tumbler, trying to work it out.

She'd already emptied her gin.

It must be why she was feeling odd.

"Did he love her?" she asked Esme, carelessly, she thought. Only it didn't come out carelessly. It came out quite strained.

It confused her more.

She needed to stop drinking.

"I don't know if he loved her," said Esme, thankfully not appearing to notice her discomfort (she'd drunk a fair bit herself). "I've never asked him. No one ever said anything about it. I don't think he'd admit it if he had. She was Jamie's wife . . ."

"Of course," said Rose, and managed to sound more normal this time.

"Mabel stopped minding Jamie going out after Max came back, though. She just let him get on with it, and it drove him mad, so he went out more, and Max would have a go at him, saying he should be treating Mabel better, and Mum would tell Max to leave off Jamie, and I'd tell Mum to leave Max alone, and Jamie would say I always took Max's side, the two of us should just bugger off to London, and Max would tell him that he'd bankrupt the place if he left him to it again, and . . ." Esme sighed, turning her hand in a circle of it having gone *on and on and on,* the red stub of her cigarette moving round and round. "Max barely ever came into the house when Jamie was home, just stayed in the annex, or out on the station. They stopped speaking. Mum made it worse, because she wouldn't tell Jamie he was the problem . . ."

"And what did Mabel say?" Rose asked.

"Not a lot," said Esme, stubbing her cigarette out. "She didn't really speak much to me, once Max was back." She ground the cigarette down. "She only wanted to talk to him . . ."

Rose nodded slowly. She didn't ask Esme how that had made her feel. She didn't need to.

Even in her hazy state, she could tell it had hurt her, just from the way she'd decimated the remains of her cigarette.

She became surer of it as Esme talked on: of Mabel's quietness around the house, so much worse after her grandfather in Sydney had died, in the middle of 1935. She said how Mabel had refused to go to his funeral, no matter how they'd all tried to persuade her into it; Lauren had even offered to travel to Sydney with her, so had Esme, and Jamie in the end, when Lauren had pushed him to. "Mabel wouldn't have it, though," said Esme. "Said her granddad wasn't worth the bother, he'd never wanted her around when he was living, so why would he now he was dead . . ."

"What about her parents?"

"Her dad was at Gallipoli too, never came back, and her mum did a runner when she was born, never came back either . . ."

"God," said Rose.

"I know," said Esme, and moved her gaze to Walter, softly snoring on Rose's lap. "Seems like she was a better mum to Walter."

"She was," said Rose, and felt a stab of grief for her, because she had been, there was no question in her mind: always with Walter, tucking him into bed each night, teaching him how to ride escalators, *I used to do this with my mummy*, making him cakes covered in chocolate and coconut on his birthday, cherishing him, it seemed to Rose, every day of the four and three-quarter years she'd had him. Never had it felt crueler to her that she'd had that all stolen from her than now, learning how little love she'd had in her own life. She hadn't even had anyone besides Walter and Vivian in London. Pia had said as much. *She was lonely, poor girl. . . .*

"I think she regretted not going to the funeral," said Esme, talking on. "She was upset on the day, only wanted to be with Max. He was tagging new calves, down in the barn you and Walter slept in. She hung around there the whole time. I don't know what the two of them talked about, but Jamie went out drinking in the end, left them to it, couldn't stand that she wanted to be with Max, not him." She pulled out another cigarette, lit it. "He went on bender after bender after that, and Mabel started going on these long walks around the land. I'd see her when I woke up in the morning, just wandering around the trees." She waved her hand in the direction of the window, the distant pastures. "She'd have walked miles. She couldn't ride. I said I'd teach her, so did Mum, but she wouldn't take us up on it. She probably wanted Max to do it." She glanced over at the window, frowning. "I'm pretty sure she went on all those walks because she wanted to bump into him. But she met Richie . . ."

"Walter's father?" guessed Rose.

"Yeah," said Esme.

"What did he do?" Rose asked, finally getting to it, throat tight, now that she had, with trepidation. "You said earlier people hated him . . ."

"No," said Esme, guessing, without Rose needing to say more, what she was most afraid of, "it wasn't that."

Rose exhaled, sinking her dizzy head back against the seat. "Thank God," she said, perhaps too loudly, because Walter stirred, murmuring in his sleep. He raised his hand, setting it on her forearm. She wanted to take it, press his warm dimply fingers to her lips, overcome as she was by relief. *It wasn't that.* It hadn't been that. . . .

Her relief, though, was short-lived.

She only had to look back to Esme, see her leaden expression, to be reminded that, regardless, nothing had ended well: not for the Lucknows, nor Mabel, nor Walter's father, who'd fought, *in a manner.* . . .

Esme went on, confirming it, saying that even though Mabel had chosen to be with Richie, Jamie wouldn't have it. "He told everyone that he'd raped her. That's why they all hate Richie . . ."

"They still think he did it?" asked Rose, horrified.

"They know he didn't," said Esme. "I've told them enough, so's Max, so did Paul, in the end. That's one good thing he did do. But they hate Richie even more for it, because of what they all did to him, what Jamie did. No one talks about it. Everyone wants to forget it. Walter'll have brought it back for them today . . ." She broke off, looked down at her empty tumbler, and reached for the bottle, offering it first to Rose. "More?"

Numbly, Rose nodded, needing it.

She drained that glass, then another, as Esme told her the rest, starting with the brief liaison Mabel had had with Richie in the Queensland winter of '35, before Richie had ended things, scared, so Mabel had eventually admitted to Esme, of what would happen to him if Jamie ever discovered their affair. "He and Jamie were friends growing up," Esme said, "with Max too. Richie's dad was a stockman, and his grandad. The family were here before we were." She knocked back her own drink. "They've all gone now, moved when Richie went. Must have broken their hearts . . ." She said how Mabel had grown even more melancholy after Richie had cut things off with her. "I couldn't understand it. I didn't know what had got into her, but she stopped going on her walks, just stayed in bed, cried, lost all this weight . . ."

"Was she sick?" Rose asked, recalling her own nausea during her pregnancy.

"She said she was, but I reckon just really sad, too. I'm not sure she ever loved Richie, but she liked him. She told me in the end that he'd made her feel like she existed again, like she mattered. He was funny, good-looking, kind." She shook her head. "Jamie wasn't being kind. He was still drinking, and Max was working, all the time, avoiding Mabel, I suppose, trying to stop riling Jamie up. Paul was always round here when he wasn't drinking with Jamie, seeing me. That must have made her feel even lonelier . . ."

"Were you engaged?"

"Not then," said Esme. "He'd asked a couple of times, but I'd said no. I wasn't sure." She bit her lip, frowning. "I liked him, sometimes. Mum never did, never has. Maybe that's part of why I kept letting him call, to get at her." Her frown deepened. "She's never liked me much either . . ."

"I'm sure she has," said Rose, unable to sit silent while Esme made such a painful claim.

"No," said Esme. "She's always had me tied up in her mind with Dad dying. Jamie told me once I made it all harder for her. Anyway," she continued, expelling a short breath, clearly not wanting to dwell on it (Rose couldn't blame her), "she said that Paul was a bad influence on Jamie, which he was, and would get bored of me, which he did." She smiled an unhappy smile. "She was right about that."

"I'm sorry."

"It's all right," said Esme, which it obviously wasn't. "She left me alone anyway, once she guessed Mabel was pregnant. She was over the bloody moon . . ."

"Because she thought Jamie was the father?" said Rose, feeling the same almost-pity for Lauren as she had before, when she'd seen her standing alone outside Esme's cottage.

"We all did," said Esme. "It got so nice after that." Her smile became warmer. "Jamie stopped drinking, he and Max started talking more. Jamie was . . . excited, you know, about the baby coming?"

Rose nodded. She knew. ("There's a baby," she'd said to Xander, when she'd first told him about theirs. "An actual real-life tiny human, coming our way. Our baby. This is a nice thing. An incredible thing . . .")

"We were all excited," said Esme. "Even Mabel. She must have got caught up in it all, tried to kid herself that the baby really was Jamie's. Honestly, if you'd known her like she was then, when she forgot to be sad . . . she was chatty, joked. She had this laugh . . ." Esme's smile grew. "We went into Brisbane one day, looking for ideas for cots that the boys could build. Mum started doing all this knitting; that rabbit of Walter's . . ."

Rose's eyes widened. "No . . ."

Esme nodded. "Mum was going to make a little blue jumper for it . . ."

"Peter Rabbit," said Rose. A *he*. "I thought Mabel must have made it."

"Well, she didn't," said Esme, smile dropping. "But she went really strange again over Christmas. Started panicking, I suppose. Mum got out these photographs of Max, Jamie, and Dad, back from before I was born. They both looked like him, Max more than Jamie, but Jamie had the same hair, the brown eyes . . ." She reached for her cigarettes. "We'd all been trying to guess if Walter would be a boy or a girl, if he'd look like Jamie, or Mabel . . ."

"Yes," said Rose, "I think I probably would have panicked too."

"It was stinking hot as well," said Esme. "We get these westerlies in the summer, the temperature goes well over a hundred, even in the shade. The only place you want to be is in the ocean. Mabel wasn't sleeping, none of us were, but she was already pretty big by then, I think it all got to her. I don't know" — absently, she put her cigarette to her mouth — "maybe she wanted to get back at Richie too. She swore to me afterward she didn't want to hurt him, that she'd never meant to tell Jamie his name . . ."

"But she did?"

"Yeah," said Esme, taking her cigarette from her lips. "She did. It was a couple of days after New Year. I'd heard her up and down all night, going out to sit on the veranda, back into the house, to the loo, then, as soon as it was light, she went into her and Jamie's room, it was next to mine, and told him everything." Her brow creased. "How sorry she was about what she'd done, that he might be the dad, but might not be, that it was Richie she'd been with. I heard it all through the wall." She tightened her hold on her cigarette, bending it. "I couldn't believe it . . ."

"What happened then?" asked Rose, the question leaving her of its own accord, regardless of her cold, trickling dread of the answer. She felt very much as she'd used to watching the dogfights overhead in Surrey: that certainty of events ending horrifically; a complete inability to drag her attention away.

"That's when Jamie started saying Richie had raped her," Esme said, still holding her unlit cigarette. "He just would not have it that she'd wanted it, said he was going to sort Richie out. Mabel started crying, really crying, shocked, scared, you should have heard her. I went in to try and calm Jamie down." She looked across at Rose. "Richie shouldn't have done what he did with Mabel, it was wrong, they were both wrong, but he would never have laid a finger on anyone. He wasn't like that . . ."

Rose nodded, her own hand on Walter's soft arm, thinking of his gentleness, his sweetness, picturing Richie, an older version. . . .

"Mum came in," said Esme, "crying her eyes out as well, cut up, saying she knew Mabel would never have done anything like this to us, she could tell us the truth, she didn't need to protect Richie, and Mabel kept saying she wasn't, but Mum wouldn't hear it, Jamie wouldn't. He said he was going to get his mates, get Richie. Mum started panicking too, then, said he should go to the police, have Richie arrested . . ."

"Did he?"

"No," said Esme. "Course he didn't. Mum knew he wouldn't. I knew he wouldn't. I rode out, went and got Max . . ." She glanced at her cigarette, frowned, then fetched her matches. Her hand was shaking, just as it had been in town. "His face, when I told him everything. He couldn't believe it either. I still couldn't . . ." She shook her head. "He found Richie, though, told him to run, hide until they could figure out where he should go, then he came back here, went up and spoke to Mabel. I think maybe that's when they decided she'd have to leave too, go to Vivian . . ."

"They didn't tell you she was doing it?"

"No," said Esme, shortly.

Rose heard how much their concealing it had stung. How much it still stung.

"Mum went mad at Max when he came back down," Esme said, "accused him of taking Richie's side over Jamie's. He told her he'd always been on Jamie's side, then left, said he was going to find him. Fat lot of good it did." She struck her match. "Jamie'd rounded up his mates, lots of others too, all of them hell-bent on finding Richie. There were a few tried to help Max talk them down. Those people we saw today, the ones who spoke to us . . ."

Rose nodded. She remembered. They'd asked after Max. *Tell him to come out himself one of these days, stop hiding.*

"They went to Tommo," said Esme, "the police sergeant here, before he enlisted, got himself shot in Africa. Asked him to do something, but he stayed out of it. Paul did too. Probably couldn't be bothered with it." She cursed, dropping her match. It had burned all the way to her fingertips. "The rest of them were ready to kill Richie." She sucked her skin. "Took Jamie's word, straight up . . ."

"Because Richie was Aborigine?" said Rose, even though she hardly needed to ask.

There was no doubt in her gin-fogged mind that, had Richie been white, they'd all have thought harder before believing Jamie. It would have been the same in England. Probably the world over. Certainly those victory-rolled women in Belgravia wouldn't have questioned Richie's guilt. . . .

"Yeah," Esme conceded. She lit another match. "Jamie would have known he'd get away with it. He was never stupid. Just really ashamed, after . . ." She frowned at the flame. "He didn't come home, not until it was all over. I don't think he could face us. Max was hardly here either. He was getting Richie papers to go to a station in New South Wales, sorting Mabel's tickets out, wiring Vivian. Not that I knew any of that then." Her face creased in the lamplight, her eyes hard with remembered pain. "No one was talking. Hannah was crashing around the place, Mabel stayed in her room, Mum kept away from her. I did too. I was angry at her, for doing all that to Jamie, even though I was . . . *furious* . . . at him too." She sought Rose's gaze, entreating her to understand. "He'd been happy, for so long . . ."

"Yes," said Rose, needing no entreating, understanding completely. "I'd have been angry as well, if someone had done that to Joe."

"The thing is, though," said Esme, "I wish I had spoken to Mabel. I never got to again. She must have been really scared. Christ." Her match had burned her again. She flicked it out, cast her unlit cigarette aside. "By the time I decided to talk to her, tell her how I felt, it was too late. Max had taken her to Brisbane. They'd gone while Mum and I were asleep. Max said Mabel didn't want to see Mum. She'd told him to tell me goodbye, that she'd write."

"Did she?"

"Once," said Esme, "saying she was sorry, for all of it, and that Vivian had found her a house, given her a new start, she needed to leave all this behind, try and forget." She paused, gave a resigned shrug. "I get that . . ."

So did Rose.

And she could see, very well now, why Mabel hadn't wanted Walter here, in this place.

It baffled her, more than ever, that Vivian had sent him, into the thick of so much hate, so much guilt. *Everyone wants to forget it.* No one would be able to now. And Walter would find out what had happened one of these days. He'd have to. He couldn't stay protected forever. . . . Vivian must have realized that.

Oh Vivian, she thought.

Vivian, Vivian . . .

"When Max got back from the port," said Esme, "he had all this blood on his shirt. Jamie and the others had found Richie, nearly killed him, but Max and a couple of his mates had managed to get Richie away, over the border into New South Wales. Max reckoned they'd look after him at the new station."

"Was Richie all right?" Rose asked.

Please let him have been all right.

"I don't know," said Esme. "The station wrote he upped and went when the rest of his family got there. We never heard from him again."

"You didn't try to find him? When Walter was born . . ."

"I don't know how we could have," said Esme. "And I don't think he'd have wanted it." She studied her glass. "He must have been in a real state, when Jamie had finished with him. When Jamie came home, he was covered in blood, as well. I'm not sure if he already knew Mabel had left, or if it was just about Max helping Richie, but he *went* for Max, too, just went for

him on the driveway, Mum and me and Hannah trying to get him to stop."
She broke off, remembering.

Rose stared across at her, seeing it in her own mind.

"He didn't hurt Max," Esme said. "Max walked away in the end. He was
always stronger. Jamie yelled after him that he'd ruined his life." She paused,
took a breath, seeming to steel herself to go on. "That night," she said, "when
Mum and I were down here arguing again, I don't even know about what,
Jamie went upstairs and shot himself. We were both shouting our heads off,
then the gun went . . ."

Rose closed her eyes. "I am so sorry."

"It was the worst noise I ever heard," said Esme quietly. "Max was next
door, in the annex, but he knew, he came running." She paused, biting her
cheek, trying to stop herself crying. Rose recognized the gesture well. "He
was the one to go up and find him," Esme said. "By the time Mum and I
got there, he was on the floor holding Jamie." A tear broke from her, despite
her efforts, rolling from the corner of her eye, over the rim of her cheekbone.
"He'd been there, then he was just gone."

"Oh, Esme." If Rose hadn't been holding Walter, she'd have got up, gone
to her. She couldn't remember the last time she'd seen anyone in such desperate need of comfort.

But since she was holding Walter, she had to settle for telling Esme
again how sorry she was. "Every minute, I'm frightened for Joe. Every minute. And you had all that . . ."

"I don't know why we couldn't stop him," said Esme, another tear
chasing the first. "We all knew he'd do it one day. He'd been telling us he
wanted to for years. I always wonder if I'd said something to him" — she
wiped her eyes — "given him a hug, told him I was sad for him, not just
angry, maybe it would have helped . . ."

"Don't. You can't do that to yourself . . ."

"Mum told Max it was his fault. She said that if he'd taken Jamie's side,
been a better brother, he'd never have done it . . ."

"She said that?" said Rose, appalled.

"She regretted it," said Esme. "Really regretted it. God." She reached
unsteadily for the bottle. "She felt so bloody guilty when he was shot down. I
said to her, so she should. She made his life a misery before he went. And he'd
only ever been doing the right thing." She held up the bottle. "One last one?"

Rose hesitated. She was absolutely ruined already. When she glanced from the bottle to the mantelpiece clock, she couldn't make out which was the big hand, and which the small. She'd forgotten the wireless was even playing.

But . . .

"Why not?" she said, holding out her glass.

It really did feel like the least she could do.

And it wasn't their last drink of the night.

They had another two in the end.

But although Rose would come to regret the gin, she was never anything but glad that she stayed up so late with Esme.

As the wireless played, and the clock ticked incomprehensibly on, they talked and talked, a bit more about Jamie — Esme telling happier stories, reliving her eighteenth birthday when he and Max had surprised her, taking her into Brisbane to a dance at the Trocadero, then Jamie's love of the ocean, surfing, how happy he'd always been whenever they'd made time for a drive to the coast. "Not often enough," said Esme — and in turn, Rose told Esme more of her own family: Lionel, Joe, her parents.

She still didn't speak of Xander, she couldn't think what to say, but did admit to how apprehensive she'd been, arriving in Australia, her dread of eventually leaving Walter. As they worked their way through their last, last drinks, she confessed how worried she'd been that afternoon, about whether Esme would get out of the ute with her and Walter in Narrawee, and Esme threw a pillow at her (or tried to), asking her what she took her for.

"I haven't been sure how to take you," Rose admitted, franker than she would have been sober. "I couldn't tell what you made of us, when we arrived."

"I was still working it out," said Esme, just as candid. "It was a bloody great shock, you being here. But I liked the look of you. I loved the way you stood up to Mum. And Max had thought you were all right . . ."

"I'm not sure about that. I upset him."

"Course you did," said Esme, slurring a bit. "Because of your face."

"What's wrong with my face?" asked Rose, slurring too.

"Nothing."

"I don't understand," said Rose.

Esme wouldn't explain.

"Come and talk to me when you've worked it out," she said.

She spoke more of Paul, telling Rose that he'd asked her to marry him again just after Jamie's funeral, that she'd agreed because she needed to get away from the plantation — as Rose was learning the family all called the cattle station — and couldn't see any other way to do it. "I never thought I'd be back again, that I'd have to ask Max for a cottage. Paul was doing all right. He had his own place, ran one of the hotels in town. Mum wouldn't come to the wedding, though. Told me I was dancing on Jamie's grave. Max came . . ."

"He said he didn't like Paul."

"Can't stand him," said Esme, "he thought I was an idiot and told me so, but he still walked me down the aisle. He hated it. Half the people there he'd had to fight to get Richie away . . ."

"But he was there," said Rose. (*A good man . . .*)

"He was there," echoed Esme. "I felt like he was the only one who cared about me in the whole place. I wanted to run, actually, but I didn't know where to run to . . ."

"I've had that," said Rose. "I had it last year . . ."

"What happened?"

"Too much," said Rose, "I'll tell you about it another time." She couldn't go on, not about the baby. She was far too drunk to be able to talk about her, or him. "I ended up in this place called Ilfracombe . . ."

"Ilfra what?" said Esme, and laughed.

So did Rose.

Esme laughed harder.

"Ilfra what?" repeated Rose, laughing more.

For some reason, after all the sadness, it felt really, really funny.

"Shhhhh," Rose said, spilling her drink as she raised her finger to her lips, "shhhh, you'll wake Walter."

Eventually, once the wireless program had crackled to an end, and the gin and Old Golds were almost empty, they climbed lopsidedly to their feet and turned in.

Rose got Walter up the stairs, she was never afterward sure how, and, as Esme slid off to her new, old, room — adjusting her rollers, saying that at least there'd be bread for breakfast the next day — Rose settled Walter into bed, sending up a silent prayer to Vivian that for once, just once, he'd let her sleep through to morning.

"You owe me," she whispered to her, "you really do owe me, so please make it so."

Then, her exhaustion crashing in on her, she stumbled next door to her own room, and, fumbling in the darkness, got herself ready for bed and climbed onto Max's mattress, as she'd been aching to all day, slipping her heavy limbs between the soft, clean sheets, dropping her head on the pillow.

Unlike the night before, she fell asleep quickly. She didn't check beneath the eiderdown for spiders, or snakes, or comb over the long, strained day in her mind. Nor did she dissect all Esme had told her, agonize over what it would come to mean for Walter, fret about Richie's fate, or try to devise whether Max *had* loved Mabel: his brother's wife. . . .

No, she had plenty of time to do all that in the days ahead.

As she closed her eyes, head whirling, drifting toward unconsciousness, she imagined her telegrams landing in the hands of her parents in tropical Malaya, Joe, Lionel, and Xander. . . . She tried to picture Xander in Cairo: handsome, legs crossed, lounging in the baking, opulent splendor of a hotel just like the Taj in Bombay . . .

But she found herself imagining Max instead. Sleeping. Not on the soft pillow she was, but the earthy ground, stars shining above, a campfire dwindling to ash beside him, horses tethered nearby: shadows in the darkness. She saw his strong, tanned hands clasped on his chest, rising and falling with his breath. She wondered if his shoulder still hurt. . . .

She'd upset him.

She wished she hadn't upset him.

"Because of your face," Esme had said.

She still couldn't work out what that meant.

Her eyes grew heavier.

She turned on her side, confused, her body sinking on the same springs that had creaked beneath him.

I'll think about it tomorrow, she told herself.

It will probably make more sense then.

CHAPTER SEVENTEEN

When she woke the next morning with a crashing hangover, Walter tugging at her arm, telling her that there were parrots on the windowsill and more kangaroos outside (he'd slept until past seven; maybe Vivian had heard Rose's prayer), she'd forgotten that she'd fallen asleep wondering about Max at all. All she could think about was how she'd never touch gin again, and that there was no justice in the world if Esme wasn't feeling as ill as her. ("There's justice," said Esme, when she appeared minutes later, grabbing the doorframe, her rollers still in, all at odd angles.) She couldn't concentrate on anything beyond raising herself gingerly to sitting and begging Esme to be the one to go downstairs and brave Hannah, fetch them both tea.

"Not a chance," said Esme, sinking into the room's one chair. "I couldn't sleep after I went to bed, I decided to go down and make the bread for her. She's going to be *ropable*..."

By sheer brute determination, Rose forced herself from her bed, went down herself, and got through the rest of the morning that followed: trying not to heave while she boiled the kettle, enduring Hannah's chagrin over the bread ("She didn't make a bad fist of it," Hannah said, hands on her hips, staring at the loaf Esme had left on the cooling rack, "but it's the principle. She's never done as she's told . . ."), getting herself and Walter dressed, picking at a breakfast of sausages, then foolhardily venturing out with Walter for a walk while Esme, in her own world of pain, set to doing the workers' wages — which Hannah had taken visible delight in reminding her were due that day.

"Go on, off you go," Hannah said to Rose and Walter, batting them out of the kitchen. "I daresay the fresh air will do you good, I can't have you under my feet all day." She pushed Rose on. "You're giving *me* a headache . . ."

The sun outside was blinding. It did Rose no good at all. And the air — which was certainly fresh, cooler again than the day before — made her shiver, even with a cardigan on. She wrapped her arms weakly around her body, squinting outward, *still* getting used to the rolling space, everywhere; the idea that Walter now owned half of all she saw.

"Come on," he called, scampering ahead, enviably full of beans, past the chicken coops that stood behind the house, on in the direction of a low hut, that was apparently Bill's station kitchen, and from which a strong stew-like smell was wafting. "Hurry."

"In a second," Rose said, swallowing on her bile. Walter had Rabbit with him, as usual. *Peter Rabbit.* Rose stared at its bouncing ears, recalling the way Lauren had looked at the toy too, back in the drawing room, when she and Walter had first arrived. Rose had thought she'd simply been avoiding looking at Walter's face, but realized now she must have been completely floored, seeing the toy she'd made with such hope for her grandchild back in her house again. In Walter's hands.

"Rosie," he shouted. "You're not moving . . ."

"You can blame Aunty Esme for that," Rose called back.

"Aunty," sniffed Hannah, appearing from behind with an empty basket in hand, presumably off to gather more eggs, or tomatoes.

"Cucumbers," she said. "Now go on, get on."

Rose and Walter were off to find the river that ran through the Lucknow land. Hannah had given Rose directions at breakfast, and Walter some crumbs to feed the geese.

"Here," she'd said gruffly, handing him a brown paper bag. "It'll still be too cold for swimming, although it won't be long until you can do that. Have a look for nests for now. The chicks'll be hatching soon."

She'd even patted him awkwardly on his curls. Clearly, with his rampant appetite for the food she served up, *never letting it get cold,* he was inching ahead as her favorite.

Rose couldn't begrudge him it.

But she couldn't find the river for him, either. She hadn't really been paying proper attention when Hannah had issued her complex instructions about fences and middle fields and turnings that ran off turnings beside walls. She'd been too busy resisting the urge to lay her head on the kitchen table and fall back asleep. As a result, she and Walter walked and walked, through pastures where the cows remained thankfully distant, and the grass was long and dewy, dampening Rose's shivery legs, but never came across so much as a babbling brook. The sky above clouded over, with surprising speed, and they headed on, into a likely-looking patch of woodland, the leaves rustling, crickets clacking, but to no avail. All they came across were a couple of turkeys, who weren't very interested in Hannah's crumbs.

It was disappointing to Walter. He tried to like the turkeys, but he'd been excited about the geese, chatting as they'd walked about how feeding them might be *just the same* as when they'd used to feed the ducks back at "Princess Margaret's house" in London.

"We'll find them next time," Rose promised him, as they turned back.

"Maybe we should get Hannah to draw us a map," he suggested.

"I think that's probably a good idea," she agreed. "You'd better be the one to ask her, though . . ."

It started to drizzle before they were halfway home. Thunder grumbled, and Rose suggested they should run, try and beat the storm, even though her head split at the prospect. But as they set off, Walter tripped, his little foot lodging in a rut, and fell, twisting his ankle, grazing his knee on a stone, which made him cry, because he was only five, so Rose had to carry him the rest of the way instead. He'd grown since she'd done it for any distance in London. A lot. (She'd noticed his shorts were getting shorter.) He was *heavy*.

"I can hear your heart beating," he said, as she jogged through the damp pastures, sweating gin, feeling like her arms might drop off. "It's beating really hard, Rosie."

It was raining really hard too by the time they reached the house, every bit as torrentially as it had been the night they'd arrived. And while fortunately this time there was someone waiting to let them in — Hannah, looking almost anxious as she peered into the deluge from the porch — the day didn't much improve from there. Because Hannah had a scolding to give to Rose, for getting Walter so wet, and something else besides: a bundle of wires that had arrived for Rose in her and Walter's absence, care of three different telegraph boys (that had possibly been men): replies to the ones Rose had sent from Narrawee.

The wires didn't *all* feel like bad news.

All but one were really quite the opposite.

Rose read them in the hallway, dripping, shivering, Hannah rubbing Walter down with a towel beside her, asking him what on earth he'd done to his knee. The first she opened was from Mr. Yates: a message not much longer than his previous one, but far more encouraging, assuring her that his letter was now in the post and would, he hoped, help her understand much better all Vivian had done. He went on, making her smile, despite her throbbing head, by returning Lester and Pia's regards, and mentioning that both were still at Williams Street, Pia working, Lester living, since Vivian had left Lester the house in her will.

"You look pleased," Hannah said, handing Rose the towel.

"I am." Rose had been worrying about Lester and Pia. She loved that Vivian had looked after them like this. It reminded her, through all her confusion and still-prevailing anger, of Vivian's heart. It was nice, really very nice, to be reminded of that.

And even more wonderful to read her parents' and Lionel's messages, especially the bit in Lionel's that told her Joe had been with him when her wire had arrived, was still with him, on another spell of leave, *exhausted but hanging in there*. "Oh, thank God," she said, her eyes filling with tears of relief. "Thank God, thank God." Lionel was well too, safe since the raids in London had ceased back in May (presumably because Hitler was so consumed with invading Russia), and Rose's parents were also happy, settled in a beautiful bungalow in Penang. While they did request that Rose still join them, as soon as she was ready, neither they nor Lionel tried to persuade her against her decision to stay on in Australia. *You always have had the kindest heart*, Lionel said, *to go with your stubborn streak* STOP. Even Sarah had been in touch, Rose was amazed to see, opening the fourth wire. She'd been visiting Joe at Lionel's the day before too, *reminding Joe he has to keep coming home safely*, and sent Rose her love, told her how glad she was that she'd made it through the torpedoes, and entirely unsurprised that she was staying in Queensland.

I knew you would STOP

Remarkable, really, how she managed to say I told you so about something the two of them had never discussed.

Rose didn't mind, though.

She was glad that Sarah had been with Joe, reminding him to *keep coming home safely*. Rose would forgive her plenty, including a downstairs loo with matching wallpaper and towels, so long as she kept him coming home safe.

"Are you almost finished, Rosie?" Walter asked, invading her thoughts, his hair all tousled, rubbed to within an inch of his life.

"Very nearly," she said, feeling a tug of guilt at keeping him waiting for her, standing there on his twisted ankle, his grazed knee. "I'm sorry, little man. It's just been such a long time since I heard from everyone. Sit down on the stairs, why don't you? I'll make some cocoa soon . . ."

"I daresay I can manage cocoa," said Hannah, shuffling off. "I'll look out some iodine for that graze, too. Come with me, Walter."

His eyes widened in alarm. "Rosie . . ."

"I'll bring him in a second," said Rose, picking him up, carrying him over to the stairs to sit with her, where she opened the final wire.

The wire that rattled her for the rest of the day.

Xander's wire.

It always did come back to him in the end.

She read it quickly, acutely conscious of Walter beside her, the prospect of Hannah's iodine looming over him. It was a long wire, it must have cost him a fortune, and while she knew Xander could easily afford it, part of her — the part that still clung to her love for him — couldn't help but be moved that he'd taken so much time over it. Cared enough to stand in a crowded, smoky Cairo telegraph office, planning what he should say, even if she didn't like quite a lot of what he said.

He'd received the letter she'd sent in Bombay — it hadn't gone conveniently missing — and was obviously upset about it, and that he'd had several of his own returned to him this past month. *I told you I'd write all the time Rosie, I kept my word on that.* He swore to her that he'd never looked twice at that waitress she'd mentioned, *she didn't have an inch of your class*, and truly had been in Scotland before he'd gone to New York. *I swear on my father's life.* He told her he was sorry that she still hadn't forgiven him, but not surprised. *Have always known it.* He hated it, though, just as he hated that she was staying on in Australia. He seemed very certain that her doing that had nothing to do with Walter and everything to do with her no longer trusting him. He wanted her to trust him. He *needed* her to do that. *Let me kiss you like I kissed you back in London more* STOP *Come marry me* STOP. He told her how much she'd love Cairo, where it was hot and terrifying and fun and had no awful memories like back in England, just a beautiful suite in Shepheard's Hotel where the two of them could start again. *We can be happy here* STOP *Am driving myself crazy thinking how happy we could be if you let us* STOP *Come Rosie come* STOP. He sounded so certain it was what she should do, that, even though she knew she wasn't going to leave Walter and go anywhere, she was almost, *almost* drawn in. . . .

But then she came to his final lines.

The lines that would plague her.

Or maybe I should do like I said in London and come find you instead STOP Maybe that will prove how much I love you STOP Maybe if you don't come here I really should do that STOP Maybe then you will trust me STOP

"Rosie," said Walter, in a hushed whisper, "you did a swear."

CHAPTER EIGHTEEN

Rose couldn't get to Narrawee that afternoon, desperate as she was to wire Xander straight back, assure him she truly *didn't* want him to come to Australia. It rained on and on, the downpour so torrential it would have been madness to drag Walter out in it again. It was impossible to see more than a few feet beyond the drawing room windows. Esme—who'd done the wages and spent the rest of the day lying prone on a rug beside the log fire Hannah had lit—was pleased at least about the storm. She said the rain was good for the pastures, the phantom river's water levels.

"Everyone'll be happy," she said, speaking with her eyes closed. "Most of them'll be inside, having a rest."

"What about Uncle Max?" asked Walter from the sofa, his bandaged leg propped up. Hannah had insisted on the bandages. *Better safe than sorry, as they say....*

"He'll be fine," said Esme. "He's well used to it."

Rose, recalling how his horse had thrown him in the last storm, hoped he *would* be all right.

Then she thought of Xander again.

He took over.

He really was so good at doing that.

The dim hours inched by, thunder hammering, the fire crackling, Rose fretting. The electric went, so they couldn't even listen to the wireless for distraction.

And Walter started sniffling.

"Is it any wonder?" said Hannah, stoking the fire. "First camping, then getting rained on."

"You were the one that sent them off to the river," Esme reminded her.

"You know as well as I do it's not *that* far away," said Hannah.

"Try and have a nap," Rose told Walter, hoping it would do him good, of course, but also selfishly thinking that if he did nod off, she could do the same: sleep the sleep she was now so desperate for, and attempt to forget everything else for a while.

Walter didn't want to sleep, though. Esme did. She had a long, enviable doze on her fireside rug, but he remained wide awake.

"I don't feel tired, Rosie."

"Are you sure?" Rose asked, pleading to her own ears.

"Really sure." He sneezed. "Can we play something?"

"All right," she said resignedly, and dragged herself upstairs to fetch some games.

Eventually, Esme woke and joined in. She was a dab hand at snap, and even luckier than Lester with snakes and ladders, and through a combination of multiple rounds of both, then more omelettes for tea, they made it to nightfall.

"On a wing and a prayer," said Esme, washing the dishes while Rose dried. (It always felt like the short straw. *This day, this day . . .*)

"Maybe you'll think twice before drinking all your mum's gin again," said Hannah, an oilskin hat over her gray hair, heading for home in the still-hammering rain. "Make sure you put more iodine on that child's knee," she said to Rose, "and rub his chest with some Vicks."

Rose did it all. She got him to bed too, *on a wing and a prayer,* and lay next to him while he sniffled himself off to sleep, her thoughts still full of Xander, whether she believed him about that waitress, questioning whether he was right and they really could have another shot at happiness in Cairo, agonizing over whether she could learn to trust him enough again to try, or if he ever truly would take it upon himself to appear here first.

Now that she'd really considered it (and considered it), she didn't think he would. His career meant everything to him — she should know — and she was sure he wouldn't want to leave his post for so long. She was fairly confident he *couldn't*, not if he wanted to hold on to it. No, this was probably just an empty promise, like his promises to visit her in Ilfracombe had, more often than not, been empty. She didn't need to worry, not about that.

Walter's breath deepened, heavy with congestion. He turned over, wafting VapoRub, snoring.

She almost started snoring herself, but just about managed to drag her leaden body next door, where she remembered this time to check Max's bed for spiders and snakes before finally, blissfully, collapsing into it.

As days went, it really hadn't been very successful.

The one that followed was hardly much better.

It was still raining come morning, and although Walter had miraculously slept through the night for a second time (*had* Vivian intervened?), giving Rose eleven wondrous hours of rest, he woke even more bunged up, his eyes streaming, a now-racking cough and fever to go with it.

"How bad do you feel?" Rose asked him, worriedly pressing her hand to his hot head, his cheeks. "Really, very, or extremely?"

"I can't breathe in my nose," he said, eyes watering more as he tried. "And my throat feels scratchy. Maybe very . . ."

"Do you want to stay in bed?"

"It's worse when I lie down."

"Maybe the settee then," she said. "We'll prop you up, make you all cozy."

Which was just what they did: they didn't leave the house again that day, or the next two, not even when the sun reappeared, not even for Rose to wire Xander. They stayed in the drawing room, Walter falling in and out of sleep, never quite ill enough to seriously concern Rose, but bad enough that she felt awful for him, really terrible about having let him get—as Hannah had put it—rained on, and also like she might be about to run mad, trapped within the house with its ghosts everywhere, and not much except puzzles she'd already pieced together a hundred times to do. As Walter dozed, she spent hours at the drawing room windows, staring longingly at the world outside: a world across which the moving clouds cast scudding shadows, and that turned a different color with each movement of the sun, from palest gold to lushest emerald, until finally the sun set, bruising the vast horizon in a spectacular rush of red, pink, and purple. The beauty of it never ceased to stun her, no matter how long she stared.

She did, though, start to become more accustomed to the plantation's

ways, its comings and goings. How Hannah arrived each morning at seven
and left for her cottage again at six; the way Esme would flit in and out of
her office beside the kitchen, working on a clicking, whirring accounting
machine, getting in Hannah's way, making Hannah exclaim (not always un-
fondly, Rose came to realize) about how she shouldn't spill that tea, or those
crumbs. Then there was Bill, the Aborigine station cook; Rose saw him all
the time, heading up to the vegetable garden, out in his ute with great vats
of food, delivering everyone's lunch and dinner. She started to wave when
he passed her, because he waved at her, giving her a curious smile, and
observed the other workers, too: the stable hands and stockmen who resur-
faced once the rain had passed—out galloping, moving the cattle, carting
hay and feed—envying them their exertion. Lauren was often on horseback
with them. Rose watched her especially. Once or twice, she caught her looking toward the house, seeming to be staring directly at Rose staring at her.
Rose wondered what was going through her mind. Her expression, though,
was too distant to be readable. She couldn't make it out.

But, the longer she spent at those windows, the more she found herself
thinking, about things she really didn't want to think about, and mainly
the baby, her and Xander's baby. It was almost September, a year since she'd
lost it, and much as it was a pain, a physical pain inside her, to remember, as Walter snoozed fitfully on the settee, and her solitude lengthened,
she couldn't help herself combing over it all, wondering how—if—things
could have been somehow different.

She'd waited until she'd been almost three months gone to break it to
Xander that she was pregnant. He'd spoken too often of how little he'd wanted
them to rush into having children for her to have been in any doubt of how
unhappy he was going to be. It hadn't shocked her when, beside himself over
what the baby would do their lives, the *fun* they'd been having—the fun he'd
still wanted them to have, in their first years of marriage—he'd asked her
to have a termination. But it had upset her. It had *angered* her. Badly.

Even now, remembering it, she felt *angry.*

That August had been the first time they'd ever rowed. (And rowed. And
rowed.) He'd asked her to go to a clinic he'd been recommended, just to see
what their options were; she'd refused, gone mad that he'd even looked into
such a clinic; and eventually he'd given in, said they'd better bring the date
of the wedding forward if she was so set on motherhood, so that they could
marry before she really started showing.

Have it your way, sweetheart, you always do.

She pressed her fingertips to the Lucknows' windowpane, hearing his voice again, replaying the way he'd sat in the vicar's office, drumming his fingers on the armrest of his hard wooden chair, nodding tightly when the vicar had proposed they hold the ceremony the last weekend of September.

They still hadn't told anyone she was pregnant: not Lionel, nor Joe, nor any of Xander's family. Happy as she'd been about the baby, she'd felt embarrassed about the way it had happened, and had wanted to be married before admitting to everyone he or she was on their way.

Gradually, Xander had seemed to get a little happier too. He'd stopped sulking and, right at the end of August, had even felt the baby's tiny kicks with his hand.

He'd smiled, when he'd done that.

"Maybe it will be a girl," he'd said, "as beautiful as you," and adding as he'd kissed her, "let's hope not as stubborn."

She closed her eyes, picturing that little girl.

She remembered her creeping fear when the kicks had started to slow, and the bleeding had started. Such little bits at first; she'd tried to ignore them. Then one night, while she'd been on leave and with Xander at his hotel, it had got much worse. "A late miscarriage," a doctor she'd seen since had told her, saying that there could have been any number of causes—infection, a blood clot, some problem with the baby, no one's fault—but at the hospital Xander had rushed her to, holding her close in the taxicab, his arms steady but his heart racing in his chest, they'd all assumed that she, so far along, and already in the early stages of sepsis, had caused it herself, attempting to have the illegal termination she'd never considered having.

Xander had told them that she'd done no such thing. She'd heard him doing it—dimly, through the fog of her pain and fear and fever.

She heard him again now, in the sunny drawing room.

All she's wanted is to have this damn thing.

One of the doctors had sent him away, threatened to call the police unless he left, which he'd eventually done. Not without a fight, but he'd done it.

"I'm sorry, Rosie," he'd said, kissing her goodbye, "I am so sorry, but I can't let this get out."

His career, of course.

"I'll telephone every day," he'd said. "Get better now. Please, get better."

He had telephoned every day. He hadn't just abandoned her.

But he hadn't come back again, either. No one *had* called the police, although one nurse had taken it upon herself to report Rose to her wing commander, resulting in the disciplinary hearing that not even Winston had been able to save her from. Slowly, she *had* got better. Alone. Xander hadn't told Lionel or Joe where she was, not for a long time, worried, he'd said, that she, who'd kept the baby hidden from them, wouldn't want to involve them.

"Ashamed of himself, more like," Lionel had said. "For leaving you."

Maybe he'd been right.

Certainly it was what neither he nor Joe would ever forgive Xander for. Lionel had wanted to have Xander blocked from Westminster afterward. *See what that does to his career.* Winston had been ready to help. Rose had talked them down. It hadn't just been Xander's fault that she'd been alone, after all. She could have asked one of the nurses to call for Lionel or Joe. . . . She'd been tempted to, many times. She'd never quite managed it, though; too ashamed herself; convinced she was, in some way, to blame for the baby's going.

But, when Xander had eventually told Lionel the truth, once Lionel had found him at work, forced it out of him after he'd become worried about Rose's silence, she'd been so relieved. Lionel had arrived on her ward, wonderful and gentle and kind, taking her to a new hospital Clemmie Churchill had recommended, rescuing her from the staff's disdain, and she'd regretted, very badly, not having trusted his compassion enough to have sent for him sooner.

"I regret it too, Rosie," Lionel had said, softly. "I regret it too."

So much regret.

From Xander, as well, perhaps more than anyone. When Rose had finally seen him again, he'd been full of remorse that he'd left her in the hospital, and grief too, he'd said, that they never would find out if their baby had been going to be a stubborn little girl.

She sat down on the Lucknows' windowsill, seeing his bereft face all over again.

His grief had felt real, so real. . . .

Much as she'd struggled to believe it really had been about their baby—much as she still struggled to believe that—she could never have stayed with him if he hadn't worked so hard to convince her how sorry he was, over all of it.

"I love you," he'd said, when he'd visited her at Lionel's new hospital, on the very day they'd been meant to marry. "I can't let this be the end for us." He'd wept, actually wept. "Please, can we just try and get back to how things were . . ."

They had tried. They'd tried and tried. And then Xander had got tired of trying, of feeling guilty when Rose had failed to be happy again. He'd started doing things like *not* showing up in Ilfracombe, sending bottles rather than himself to birthday teas, and disappearing—whatever the truth of who he'd been with—to places like Scotland.

I miss who you used to be.

God. She pressed her forehead to the windowpane, closing her eyes, a tear rolling down her own cheek.

She'd missed her too.

And she hated, *hated*, remembering.

So impossible, though, to ever, truly, forget.

Fortunately, Walter didn't always sleep. It was better when he was awake, distracting her.

And the pair of them weren't *always* left alone through those three long days. Hannah was in and out, checking that Rose was still using the VapoRub on Walter's chest, if he had any appetite back yet. "I daresay I could rustle up some shortbread. I don't want him hungry again . . ."

Lauren, shockingly enough, came once too, on the second morning Walter was poorly, startling Rose by appearing in the drawing room's doorway, peering in at him asleep on the settee. He'd been coughing. She'd heard it from the hallway.

"How long's he been doing that?" she demanded of Rose. She was in a sweater and riding jodhpurs. Rather intimidatingly, she had a crop in her hand.

"Not long," said Rose, eyes averted from the crop. "He's got a cold."

She didn't add the *no wonder* Hannah would have, or remind Lauren that, long before she herself had got Walter soaked, Lauren had been the one to force him into camping in a storm. She was sure there was no point. Lauren wouldn't feel guilty.

To Rose's fury, she didn't seem to care about Walter at all.

She stared at him a second longer, stony eyes taking in his quick, feverish breaths, how he held Rabbit close, and, muttering something about Esme and a grain order, left.

But then, something unexpected.

She returned less than a half hour later, while Walter was still sleeping, a brown glass bottle in hand.

"Give him two teaspoons today," she snapped, sharply setting the bottle on a side table, "then with breakfast, lunch, and tea tomorrow. Tell Esme to fetch the doctor if he's not getting better by then."

And with that, she went again.

Rose stared after her, mouth agape.

"I wasn't expecting it," she said to Esme, when Esme came in not long after to see if she needed a loo break. "I literally could not have been expecting it less."

"It was probably the last thing she was expecting to do," said Esme. "She'll have made that bottle up fresh though. It's her own recipe."

"Do you think she *does* feel guilty?"

"Maybe," Esme said, sitting. "She won't say sorry, though. Witch's warning. You will never hear those words leave her lips." She blew out a long breath. "If you're not going to the loo, shall we have a cup of tea?"

They had many of those together. Esme came by more than anyone, as often as her work allowed, rescuing Rose from her solitude, playing snakes and ladders with Walter when he was awake. She was so funny with Walter: awkward still, not seeming to have quite worked out how she should talk to a five-year-old, but doing her best. As the pair of them rolled their dice, she asked him more about his girlfriend, Verity, and if they should plan a trip to Brisbane, once he was better, to visit her.

"I feel it's my duty as your aunty, Walter, to make sure she's good enough."

"She's very nice," he said snottily. "She's really good at playing with animals."

"A solid quality," Esme agreed.

She told Walter more about the animals they had on the plantation, feigning horror when he admitted he was scared of cows— "That's no good. That really is no good . . ."—describing her hunter, Bess, promising she'd take Walter up to the stables to see her, just as soon as she could trust him not to pass on his cold.

"Can horses catch colds?" Rose asked skeptically.

"Maybe," said Esme, moving her counter. "So I'm not risking it. Now blow your nose, Walter. You're sniffling again."

She kept Rose company at night too, after Walter had gone down. They kept each other company. Together, they'd sit upstairs in Rose's room, close enough to hear Walter if he called—which he never did, he really was sleeping so soundly suddenly—Rose on her bed (which she continued to check, just as she checked Walter's, for spiders and snakes), Esme on the chair, both of them in their nightgowns, Esme with her rollers in, drinking no gin, but leafing through Esme's magazines, chatting about whether they preferred Clark Gable or Laurence Olivier ("Laurence," said Rose, "without question"), Esme talking more of Brisbane, the shops she wanted to take Rose to, and Rose telling her, at last, about Xander and the baby, the words pouring from her in much the same way as Esme's had when she'd spoken of Jamie and Mabel. Rose realized, as they did, how much she'd needed someone to talk to, too.

And Esme couldn't have been more sympathetic or understanding.

"So that's why you went to Ilfratomb," she said, and just like that renamed a town, in Rose's mind at least, that had been around for she didn't know how many centuries. "And what about Cairo? Will you go there?"

"I don't know," said Rose. "I feel better, these days. Much better. I'm scared that will stop when we're together again . . ." Such an awful thing to admit. "I don't completely believe he wasn't with that waitress either. I think he probably wishes he hadn't been, but I don't believe he wasn't, not definitely . . ."

"Well then, he's obviously mad," said Esme, with a smile that wasn't shiny, or brittle, just *kind*. "My penny's worth is you shouldn't go anywhere that might not be right . . ."

"I don't want to."

"Good," said Esme, "so you just need to tell him that."

As Walter started to get better—his cough easing with each dose of Lauren's syrup, all but gone by the third night of his and Rose's confinement, their fifth in Queensland—the two of them spoke more of him, and Vivian's motivation for sending him to Australia. With the window ajar, letting the grass-scented breeze in, the squeal of fruit bats, the clack of crickets, and the low moos of the cows, Esme shared her theory that

Vivian—who'd been kind enough to leave Lester her house, and Esme *a whole wodge of money* ("I have to sign something to promise Paul won't touch it," Esme said)—had wanted to do what was right by Walter, leave him the land that had originally belonged to his father's family.

"I think she knew it was in his blood," Esme said. "I was watching him, when you and Max were talking at the plane. He kept looking around him, with this"—she waved her fingers at her face—"expression, just like his dad. I reckon he really likes it here." She fiddled at one of her rollers, adjusting the grip. "Maybe that's why he's sleeping so well. He knows this is home."

"It's a nice thought," said Rose.

"A smart thought," said Esme.

"Do you think we should tell him Richie was his father?" Rose asked. "He's never spoken to me about *having* a dad. I'm not sure Mabel ever said anything . . ."

Esme thought about it. "Maybe we should just try and drop Richie's name from time to time, not make a fuss about it."

"Softly, softly," said Rose, smiling, remembering Hector's daughter Anne's advice in *Ilfratomb*.

"Yeah," said Esme, "exactly. That's how I found out about my dad. I'd hate to have had it all suddenly dropped on me when I got to ten or something, just because some adult had decided I was old enough . . ."

"So we'll let him get used to it," said Rose.

"Tell him more if he asks," said Esme.

Rose nodded slowly.

It felt like a good enough plan.

They didn't put it into practice straightaway, though, but agreed they should wait for the right opportunity. And while Walter woke reassuringly buoyant the next morning, and made Hannah very nearly smile by eating all his breakfast, Rose waited too before suggesting they venture to Narrawee so she could wire Xander her long-overdue reply. Walter had been so unwell; she didn't want to subject him to another gauntlet of stares just yet.

Instead, she—relief of reliefs—took him out around the plantation again, snugly wrapped up in his pullover and Wellies, an old woolen hat of Esme's pulled over his ears, even though the weather was growing warmer again, hot at times, the Queensland spring springing. For the next two days, they were hardly in the house, but roamed free, starting with another trip to find the geese. Hannah didn't draw them a map, but took them herself (*if you want something done...*), leading them through woods nowhere near the ones Rose had gone looking in, then down a steep bank to a wide, sparkling river, more rugged than its willow-fringed sisters in England, but every bit as idyllic. Palms and trees that Hannah said were gidgees lined the water's edge, their leaves reflecting off the rippling surface. Geese, scores of them, dived in and out, squawking, flapping, gobbling up the fresh crumbs Hannah had armed Walter with. He leaped forward, throwing handfuls, then back again, laughing in fear and delight.

"Don't get wet," Hannah cautioned. "Do *not* get wet." Her brow pinched, in an expression Rose was becoming more familiar with, and which she no longer doubted was concern.

"You were upset, when we arrived," she found herself saying. "I don't think just about your bread."

Hannah sniffed. *Don't talk to me about the bread.*

Not put off, accustomed now to her bark being worse than her bite, Rose asked, "Was it because Lauren had locked Walter out?"

"I daresay it was lots of things," said Hannah, her eyes still on Walter. "I was cross at Lauren, but Mabel too. That girl broke everyone's heart."

"That's hardly Walter's fault."

"Well, I know that. But it felt like she was back here again, turning us all on our heads—*Walter!*" Hannah's brow creased more. "Walter, come back from the water." She turned to Rose. "I think we'd better give him more syrup when we get back." *Better safe than sorry, as they say.* "I just saw him get a splash . . ."

When they weren't down at the river, Rose and Walter were out in Esme's ute, which Esme declared Rose had better learn to drive if she really was staying for the foreseeable. "You'll go mad if you can't get away from here when you need to. Have you ever driven a motorcar?"

"Yes," said Rose, cautiously, because although she had—Lionel had taught both her and Joe to drive his, before the war—motorcars were small. Utes were huge. . . .

"You'll be fine," said Esme. "It's easy. Now come on."

Walter *loved* those lessons, he loved them so much. He'd sit sandwiched between Esme and Rose in the cab, beaming as Rose lurched along the driveway, often stalling, always trying to avoid the kangaroos, one time accidentally flooring the accelerator, making Esme squeal and grab the wheel.

Hannah spectated from the veranda, apron on, her arms folded. "Be careful," she yelled out, more than once.

Lauren watched as well, from up outside Esme's cottage, thinking her unfathomable thoughts.

Rose wondered if she was happy her medicine had helped Walter.

She hoped she was. She really hoped. . . .

"Watch out for that bush turkey," screamed Esme. "Rosie, eyes on the *road*."

"Rosie," Walter said, laughing, "*Rosie . . .*"

It was on the second evening after he was back on his feet that, as a reward for Rose making it half a mile down the road to Brisbane and back without stalling, Esme took them both to meet her hunter Bess, up in the station's warm, echoing stables, where there were in excess of twenty other horses in stalls, grunting and snorting and munching hay. He loved that treat most of all. Rose did too. The sounds of the horses, the soft scent of leather saddles and sawdust, took her right back to the stables in Dulwich. It had often been cold and damp there, but here the air was golden, illuminated by the evening sun that oozed through the barn's slats. The horses were beautiful, especially Bess. Walter stared up at her, bit his lip, clenched his dimply fingers. . . .

"Yes," said Esme. "You can touch her." She gave him an apple to feed her too, instructing him to hold it up with the flat of his hand. "Don't curl those gorgeous little fingers, though, or she will *bite them off . . .*"

Some stockmen came in while they were there, both Aborigine, both full of g'days, and smiles that grew when Esme told them that Rose was a rider herself.

"Do you think she could use Leon?" Esme asked them.

They thought Rose probably could, and introduced her to him, another bay hunter in a stall several down from Bess's, then showed her his tack, his feed.

"You know how to care for horses, missus?" one of them asked.

"I do," said Rose, stroking Leon's silky neck. She'd looked after three of them back in Dulwich, every weekend for years. "What do you say, Walter? Should we come and see him again tomorrow?"

"Yes," said Walter. "Yes, yes, yes."

So they did. They spent the whole morning with him and Bess, changing their straw, their feedbags, and (Walter's favorite) brushing them down. Then, before lunch, Rose made him even happier by taking him for a ride, borrowing a pair of Esme's old breeches and some boots. They didn't go far, or fast. It made Rose nervous, having Walter perched before her in the saddle with no hat on; she didn't dare push it further than a slow trot down to the house and back. But he sat so proudly, beaming, little hands clutching Leon's reins.

"Good boy, Leon." He clicked his tongue. "Giddyup."

"Like I said," said Esme, also with them, on Bess. "In his blood." She smiled across at Rose. "I bet you're itching to have a proper gallop."

Rose smiled back. She was.

"How about it, Walter," said Esme, "would you stay with me this afternoon and let Rosie do that?"

"Maybe," he said, not entirely certainly.

"Oh come on," said Esme. "If you're really nice to me, I might even take you back to the river, we can see if the goslings have hatched."

Eventually, she won him over, and, later that day, off to the river they went, with Hannah in tow ("I think that would be for the best," said Hannah), *not* so that Rose could gallop, but so that she could finally — one week on from Xander wiring her — brave the drive to Narrawee and reply to him. It had been worrying her, a great deal, that she still hadn't done that.

"It's worrying me too, actually," said Esme. "Do it so we can all relax, please."

Rose enjoyed not a single moment of the drive into town. Rather, she had her heart in her mouth the entire way, dreading that someone would come haring down the narrow, shaded road in the opposite direction to her, or that a kangaroo would hop out of the trees, forcing her to veer off and possibly turn the entire ute on its head.

Fortunately, that didn't happen. The ute remained unscathed, and so did she. While her entire body was slick with sweat by the time she pulled up outside the post office, she did pull up, and ran in to send Xander's wire quickly, desperate now to get it over with. It didn't take her long to write most of it down. She'd planned the words so often in her head that, much as the thought of his hurt when he read them pained her, they flowed freely from the end of her pencil, telling him that she wouldn't be coming to Cairo, she was so sorry, but she couldn't, and he shouldn't talk again of coming here, not when it was impossible for him to do that, and she had no intention of leaving anyway; certainly not until Mr. Yates's letter had arrived, and she'd seen Walter through his first Christmas, when he'd miss Mabel most.

It was then, as she finished writing about Christmas, that she paused, unsure, suddenly, how to go on. She could do one of two things, she knew. She could promise that she'd consider joining him *after* Christmas, wherever in the world he might be; have one more shot at putting all their grief and hurt and mistakes behind them. Or she could finally close the possibility of them doing that—draw the line ending their relationship that she'd meant to draw back at that Westminster café, before she'd left London. After he might, or might not, have been away with that waitress.

What if he hadn't been away with her, though?

What if he'd been telling the truth, about that?

It would be too cruel, surely, to end things by wire.

She still couldn't be fully sure she *wanted* to.

In the end, she didn't.

I hate disappointing you, she said truthfully. *I have always hated that* STOP *I want to stop doing it* STOP *I'm sorry that can't happen just yet* STOP.

"A long one, isn't it?" Tina, the unsmiling woman who worked behind the post office desk, said, taking the paper from Rose.

"It is," said Rose. She hadn't scrimped on the cost either, even though, unlike Xander, she hardly had an unlimited supply of money. Vivian's was only going to stretch so far. . . .

Tina raised her eyebrows, told Rose the exorbitant charge, and Rose paid her, trying not to flinch as she handed over the coins, then, feeling like a weight had come off her, as well as her purse—it was done, *done*—left, returning to the ute, and the plantation.

She was more relaxed on the way back. She came across no oncoming traffic, or kangaroos, and, confidence building, drove faster, reaching the Lucknow gates just as the afternoon light had started to ebb, the sun sinking, bathing the long driveway, the lawns, and weatherboard homestead in its usual explosion of color.

The house was silent. No one returned her call of "Hello" when she walked in through the porch. Deciding that they must still be at the river, she briefly considered going to find them, but then, thinking of Leon, the gallop she could yet have, impulsively ran upstairs, changing back into Esme's old breeches and boots, tying her hair up in a scarf.

She jogged to the stables and tacked Leon up just as quickly, keen to get off and back before the others returned. Breathless from her hurry, she rode Leon out into the balmy, pink dusk and kicked him on, feeling the rush of air on her cheeks, in her hair beneath Esme's scarf, and, still heady with the relief of having wired Xander, laughed, just at the release of it.

The half hour she spent that evening in the saddle was the most fun she'd had in what felt like forever. Leon was a wondrous horse to ride; his legs stretched out beneath her, responding to every nudge and command she gave him, his hooves beating on the earth, throwing up clods of muddy grass. She cantered, then galloped, past the cottages, climbing the hillside, smelling earth, the scent of the spring blossom, and smoke from Bill's grill, snaking upward from his kitchen hut below. She went faster, pulsing with exhilaration, then slowed, getting to a steeper incline, patting Leon on his sweaty, silky neck.

She stopped when they got to the top of that hill, looking down, the plantation spreading before her in miniature, so small she felt as though she could have reached out and scooped it up into the palm of her hand. Some of the lights had begun to go on in the cottages. Children she hadn't met yet were playing in one of the gardens. She saw the Lucknows' house, her own bedroom window ajar, and didn't notice that there was a light on as well in the annex, because she spotted Walter, Esme, and Hannah walking back from the river, Hannah and Esme talking, Walter running ahead, one hand held out before him, like he might be pretending that he too was riding Leon.

Rose smiled, seeing it.

Leon shifted beneath her, and she closed her eyes, raising her face to the stars breaking out in the sky, breathing long and deep.

She wasn't sure what it was that first made her realize she wasn't alone.

A sound?

The grunt of another horse, the movement of its hooves?

Or just the weight of his eyes on her.

But she turned. She saw him, not far away, on a horse of his own, his hat on, reins held in one gloved hand (his hand that had punched through a Hurricane's roof).

"Hello again, Rose," he said.

"Hello, Max," she said.

Then she smiled.

It happened without her knowing it was going to.

Strange, but she hadn't realized, until that moment, just how much she'd been waiting for him to get back.

CHAPTER NINETEEN

He returned her smile. He did, however quickly he dropped it, cross with her, *again,* this time for riding out so far at sunset.

Rose didn't mind that he was cross, not like she'd minded it the day she and Walter had arrived. No, she was too pleased to see him. As he kicked his horse on, riding to join her, telling her that she needed to be more careful, he'd been worried she wouldn't be able to find her way back in the dark, she found she quite liked the idea that he'd cared enough to come after her; smiled, before he could help himself.

"He's cross with everyone these days," Esme had said.

Rose wasn't going to take it personally.

"Do you know what time it is?" he asked her.

"No."

"No?"

"I don't have a watch," she said. "I lost it." At the hospital, as it happened. They'd taken it off her when she'd gone in, never given it back. She hadn't had the heart to get another.

"It's almost seven," he said. "Too late to be out on your own . . ."

"I'd have been fine. I've been getting to know my way around."

"I can see." He came alongside her, eyes shadowed by the brim of his hat. "Who taught you to ride like that?"

"A very nice lady in Dulwich."

"You don't ride much like a lady."

She laughed.

He'd joked.

She liked that he'd done that, too.

"Come on," he said, turning away before she could see if he was tempted to laugh with her, "let's go back."

He walked his horse slowly along with her as they headed through the deepening dusk, down the hillside toward the stables. He hardly looked at her as they went (what was it Esme had said about her face bothering him? Rose couldn't remember; they'd been so drunk) but didn't entirely ignore her. He talked to her, a shade stilted at first, near strangers that they still were, his low voice carrying over the clod and slip of their horses' hooves, the twilight noises of the plantation — the cows, the fruit bats and cicadas — asking her how her week had been. She told him, a little awkward suddenly herself (out of nowhere, she'd remembered her pee in the yard, the cow he'd had to rescue her from, then the way she'd grabbed his hands before he'd flown off), but gradually relaxing the more he questioned her, enjoying the low warmth of his voice, the welcome surprise of his interest, until she found herself chatting almost freely, about her and Esme's trip to Narrawee, Walter's illness, Lauren's syrup ("Mum did that?" said Max. "She did," Rose said), and then all the fun Walter had been having since he'd got better. "Esme says this place is in his blood."

"It's a nice idea," he said.

"That's what I said."

"Sounds like you've been getting on with Esme."

"I have," she said, and, encouraged by his slanting smile, talked on, telling him about their night draining Lauren's gin, laughing at the loaf of bread Esme had made afterward.

He laughed too, when she told him about that. Such a low, husky laugh, it made her look at him twice, wish that he'd give in and look at her. It was odd, riding so close with his gaze so decidedly averted.

Or was it his scars he was keeping from her?

With his face in profile, she couldn't see them at all.

He'd thought they'd bothered her, back when they'd first met.

They don't bother me, she wanted to assure him. *They really don't bother me at all.*

It was he, though, who spoke, asking her what Hannah had said about Esme's bread.

"That she hadn't made a bad fist of it," said Rose, smiling again, distracted by the memory of how Hannah had stood, hands on her broad hips, staring, incensed, at the near-perfect loaf on the rack. "It was delicious, actually . . ."

"Hannah'll have liked that," Max said.

"She didn't seem to like it," said Rose.

"She never seems to like anything," said Max.

"Yes," said Rose dryly, "I'm getting to know my way around her as well."

He gave another low laugh, but still didn't turn toward her.

He didn't do that their entire ride back.

In response to her questions, though, he told her more about his week: the other stockmen he'd been out with, how fine they really had been, riding through the storm, then the relief of the vet's checks being clear.

"Does that mean those cows can go to market now?" Rose asked.

"Soon enough."

"Poor cows," said Rose.

"You feel sorry for them?" he said, an amused note to his voice, letting her know he hadn't forgotten about the cow who'd chased her in the yard either.

She felt her cheeks grow warm. It came to her that that had happened a lot the last time she'd been with him.

He had a knack, she realized, for making her blush.

"Where's your plane?" she asked him, talking through her discomfort.

"Not here," he said, and told her he'd ridden home, the plane was still parked thirty-odd miles away, he'd have to get someone to drive him out first thing to fetch it.

"I will," Rose found herself offering.

She wasn't sure why she'd done that. *Thirty miles.*

"It's a long way," he said, thinking of the distance too.

"It's fine," she said.

Was it?

"It'll be an early start." He sounded as uncertain as her. "I need to be back by sunup."

"I don't mind," she said, and really couldn't decide whether she wanted him to take her up on it or not. "It's better I'm home before Walter wakes."

"He won't mind being left with Esme?"

"He's stayed with her today," she said, but before she could add that she should probably check he'd be happy doing it again, Max—still obviously far from convinced of the plan himself—said, "All right then, thank you," and it seemed to be agreed.

They rode in silence for the remainder of the short distance to the stables, Rose for herself absorbing what she'd committed to, trying not to let her panic about her thirty-mile off-road drive home escalate, too caught up with the effort to wonder what was making Max so quiet. The balmy blackness had closed in by the time they drew the horses to a halt, but the moon was full, bright, lighting the stables' slatted walls, the stony forecourt, turning the water in the troughs silver. Max dismounted, then took Leon by the bridle, holding him steady while Rose too dropped to the ground.

"You go home," he said. "I'll untack Leon."

"I can manage . . ."

"You don't need to manage," he said, leading both horses on. "Go and have dinner, get an early night."

"You're sure?" she said, taken aback, touched.

You don't need to manage.

She couldn't remember the last time someone had said that to her.

"I'm sure," he said. "Tell Esme and Walter I'll see them once we're back tomorrow." He carried on toward the stables. "I've a few things to catch up on tonight."

"What time do you want to leave in the morning?"

"Five, if that's all right."

"Fine," she said. *Five.* "See you then."

"See you then, Rose . . ."

"You can call me Rosie."

"Wear something warm," he said, not calling her anything. "It'll be cold, so early."

It *was* cold. Even beneath her old Fair Isle pullover and tweed trousers, Rose shivered as she silently stepped out onto the black veranda the next morning, her cheeks tingling from the water she'd hastily splashed on her face, her ears still ringing from Esme's borrowed alarm clock.

Upstairs, Walter and Esme were sound asleep. Esme, who'd been inexplicably buoyant at dinner about Rose and Max's drive, had told Walter that he mustn't worry about staying home with her again. Happily, he—delighted at the news that his uncle Max had returned—really hadn't seemed too worried, but had agreed with reassuring speed that he would wake Esme if he needed anything. *Just so long as you're definitely home for breakfast though, Rosie.* He and Esme had had a whale of a time at the river, apparently. Esme had helped him build a fort.

"I've taught him some of my spells too," Esme had said, nudging him, smiling beside her at the table.

"I'm nervous about the drive home," Rose had admitted, failing to smile. "I got in a bit of a state going to Narrawee."

"But you made it," Esme had said, reaching for the salt. "How were you coming back?"

"Better."

"There you go."

"I was on a road though."

"Who needs a road?"

"I think I might," Rose had said.

"You don't," Esme had said, "you'll see, it'll be a breeze." She'd waved her hand, breezily. "Max'd never let you do a drive he didn't think was safe."

"What if I get a flat?"

"We'll find you eventually."

"That's very comforting," Rose had said.

She pressed her hand to her waist now, heading across the veranda. She wasn't tired, for all it was still nighttime dark, just jumpy, keen to be on her way and back again, laughing with Esme at what a breeze the return leg really had been. She'd grown increasingly apprehensive about the drive *to* the plane as well. Now that she'd had the night to consider it, she'd become very . . . aware . . . of all the time she and Max would be spending together. *Thirty-odd miles,* just the two of them . . .

Filling her tight lungs with the cool, black air, she walked on. Beyond the veranda, the pastures stretched in inky rolls. Slender silhouettes of palm trees swayed, leaves tapping in the breeze; crickets clacked everywhere. She was a few minutes early, but even so, Max was waiting, sitting on the veranda balustrade, looking out across the sleeping plantation, his flying jacket slung beside him. For once, he didn't have his hat on; his dark waves shone in the lingering moonlight, skimming his collar as he turned at the sound of her steps, seeing her.

"You look like a farmer," he said, with a slow smile.

"I used to work on a farm," she said.

"Did you now?" he said, in a way that made it sound like she was full of surprises.

Was she?

Not answering her silent question, he asked her if she was still all right to do this, which could have been her get-out, only it didn't occur to her to take it.

"I didn't get up this early not to," she said.

"Fair enough," he said, and, picking up his jacket, told her he'd drive on the way there, then jumped to the ground, waiting while she ran down the porch steps to join him.

A ute she hadn't seen before was parked on the driveway. His, she guessed.

"Very good," he said, opening the passenger door, taking her elbow, helping her into the cabin. She felt the warmth of his touch through her thick sweater, her shirt underneath.

She kept feeling it, even as he slammed her door, heading around to the driver's side, throwing his coat and hat in. She sat quite still as he swung himself up next to her, then fired the ignition, flooding the darkness before them with the ute's headlamps, catching moths in the glare.

"Ready?" he said, leaning on the wheel, looking at her sideways.

"Ready," she said, and still felt that heat in her skin.

Briefly, she noticed he again had the scarred side of his face hidden from her.

Then he shifted them into reverse, placed his arm around the back of her seat, moving so close that she caught the scent of his soap, and she forgot his scars. Before she knew what was happening, he spun them in a backward semicircle, forward again, flooring the accelerator, making her squeal, taking them up onto the grass verge and into the blackness.

"Can you see where we're going?" she asked, reaching for her seat belt.

"Just about," he said, with a quiet laugh, ignoring his own belt. "You're safe, Rose."

"Rosie."

"I've done this drive a thousand times," he said, speeding on, over the uneven ground. "But if you want me to slow down . . ."

"No, don't," she said, clicking her belt into place. "It's fun, as long as you keep on not killing me."

"I'm not going to kill you," he said.

He didn't slow down either.

And, as they roared onward, pelting across the pitch-dark land, she found herself letting go of her belt, unclenching, just a fraction, in her seat. *You're safe, Rose.* She studied his strong hands on the wheel, the stick — his smile lingering in the shadowed concave of his cheek — and felt her muscles loosen a degree more.

They didn't speak for a while after that. She adjusted her weight, trying to find a way to sit that would stop her juddering about so much. A couple of times, she glanced at him, wondering what he, so quiet, was thinking about. Once, he looked at her at the same time, and she turned, smiling self-consciously, caught out, fixing her attention on the windscreen instead, searching the glowing headlamps for landmarks to guide her home. All she saw, though, was grass, the odd rock and tree, too uniform to her foreign eyes to be memorable.

"I have no idea where we are anymore," she confessed, partly to end the silence before it became uncomfortable, but also because it was true, and concerning. "How am I going to find my way back?" An unwelcome possibility occurred to her. "Please don't say a compass."

"A compass."

"Seriously?"

"No," he said, with another smile.

She smiled too, in spite of her anxiety, enjoying the tease. "Then . . . ?"

"There's a track," he said, "near where I left the plane, it'll lead you straight back. It's longer, but you won't get lost."

"Good," she said, marginally reassured. "A track sounds good."

"And you'll be able to see by then."

"It gets better."

He laughed.

She smiled more.

"How long until I *can* see?" she asked.

"Not long," he said. "Look." He raised his hand, pointed over the wheel to the paling horizon, the hint of dawn Rose now realized had begun to bleed into the black sky, touching the earth below with the softest sheen of illumination.

She stared, her smile stilling on her lips, absorbing the glow, how it started to spread before her eyes, brightening the night. She thought of the sun, creeping upward; the madness it had been shining on in Europe, Africa, the serenity it was coming to here, now. . . .

"First light," she said, hearing the voices of the pilots at her old base again. They'd spoken of it, so many times; their early sorties, dawn attacks. She'd always been too busy in the radar room to see it herself.

"First light," Max echoed.

"I can't believe I miss this," she said. "Every day . . ."

"My dad used to wake me up for it," he said. "He'd take me out riding."

"Did he?" She pulled her gaze from the horizon, turning to him, surprised by the confidence, moved at the thought of him, so steady and assured, as a small child, riding out with his father who'd never come back from Gallipoli. "That's lovely."

"I didn't think it was lovely." He leaned back in his seat. "I used to moan . . ."

"But he kept making you do it?"

"He kept making me do it," he said, and Rose, seeing the way his dark eyes shone, didn't need to ask if he was glad that he had.

He drove on, taking them over a cattle grid, a bridge — maybe thinking about his father, maybe about something else she couldn't guess — and she, feeling no compulsion to fill the silence this time, tucked her legs beneath her, and watched the light continue to grow, extinguishing the stars, painting the fields and trees a misty blue. Cows morphed into being around her: scores of solidifying shadows; fences became distinguishable from hedges, blades of grass from budding spring flowers. It was all so effortless, so quietly, undemandingly spectacular.

Caught up as she was in the magic of it, it took her a moment to realize that Max had slowed to a halt beside a thicket of trees.

"Look," he said, his low voice drawing her attention to a trio of sleepy koalas in the branches. "Ever seen one before?"

"No," she said, meeting their dozy, fur-lined stares. *Can I touch them?* (She really wanted to touch them.) "Walter and I have been searching."

"We'll have to find him some."

"Yes," said Rose, smiling at the bears' slow blinking. "We will."

He sped up again, the miles left to his plane disappearing beneath their wheels. The sky outside brightened and they stopped being so quiet, talked more instead: of Walter, everyone back at Williams Street. Max said how happy he was that Lester had inherited Vivian's house (Rose was happy he was happy), and made her laugh by telling a story about the two of them going for a beer at the corner pub Rose had passed so often, and where Lester had shown himself to be an incredible snooker player.

"Lester?" Rose said. "Really."

"He thrashed me," said Max, letting the wheel spin through his hands. "He'd bet me twenty shillings he wouldn't . . ."

"Are you sure it's not that you weren't very good?"

"Yeah, I'm sure."

"I'm almost a professional," she said.

"Are you?"

"I am actually," she said. "I beat my brother all the time," and, remembering she hadn't yet told him that Joe's bombardier was Charlie, who'd served with him in Egypt, she told him about that.

"A good bloke," he said, grinning. "A very good bloke."

"He said much the same about you," said Rose, and didn't add what else Charlie had told her, about having watched Max's plane going down in flames. *None of us could believe he lived.* She wasn't about to remind him of all that. "He was well, anyway."

"And he's got your brother for his pilot."

"He has. Hopefully they'll be each other's lucky charm."

"I'm sure they will," he said, so kindly, so warmly, that she, who probably hadn't had enough sleep, felt her eyes sting and thought they could do with a change of subject.

It was then, anyway, that she spotted the plane, its propellers and wings a muted pink in the distance.

"We're here," she said, surprised (how it had happened so quickly?), and a little deflated too, although she didn't give herself pause to think too much about why, because her own journey home was about to start and track or no track, that was rather daunting.

Wanting to know more about it, and whether the track would be sufficiently road-like as to make driving it a "breeze," she asked Max where it was. A simple question, she thought.

And yet, he frowned.

"You sound worried," he said.

"No," she protested.

"Yes," he said, frown deepening, "and now I am too."

"I'll be fine. I've had lots of lessons with Esme . . ."

"Lessons?" He blanched. "You've only just learned?"

"No," she said quickly, "I meant lessons in the ute. I've driven a motor. Quite a few times."

She said it to reassure him.

He didn't seem remotely reassured.

"A few times?"

"Yes."

"When?"

"What?"

"How long since you last drove a car?"

She thought about it, casting her mind back.

"Right," he said, the longer she thought. "A while ago."

"There's petrol rationing in England," she said defensively.

He looked even more appalled. "It was before the war?"

"Well, yes . . ."

"Rose, why didn't you say . . . ?"

"I'll be fine," she repeated. "I got all the way to Narrawee and back yesterday."

"By yourself?" he said, and, since he didn't ask what she'd been doing there, she didn't mention that she'd gone to wire Xander.

"Yes," she said, and left it there.

"That's insane," he said.

"Esme wasn't worried."

"Esme's been driving since her feet could touch the pedals," he said. "Anyway, Narrawee's, what, eight or nine miles? This is more than thirty, on a dirt track."

"I can manage."

"You don't need to manage," he said, just as he had back at the stables when he'd insisted on untacking Leon for her.

Only she wasn't so grateful this time. She wasn't remotely grateful, not when he told her how he intended to get her home instead, and that it involved him flying her.

"Oh no," she said. "No, I don't think so . . ."

"I do."

"I've never flown," she said.

"Until today," he said, closing the remainder of the distance separating them from his flimsy, flimsy plane.

She shook her head, eyeing it, not wanting to admit how afraid she was, not given what he'd been through — not after they'd just been talking about Joe and Charlie — but nonetheless feeling very, very afraid: a thousand times more so than she had been about a dirt track. Her mouth had gone completely dry. "I'll be fine driving. We can't leave your ute here . . ."

"We've plenty of utes. Someone can pick this up anytime."

"That's ridiculous. You might as well have just driven out without me."

He pulled up at the plane, turned off the engine, the silence so still that she could hear the wind wisp over the kite's fragile metallic wings.

"What'd be ridiculous," he said, removing the keys from the ignition, "is me letting you head off, nervous, then something happening to you."

"It won't . . ."

"No," he said, opening his door, "because you're coming with me."

"Max . . ."

"Rose . . ."

"Rosie . . ."

He didn't hear. He grabbed his jacket and hat, jumped out of the ute and slammed his door, then came around to open hers.

"Max," she began when he did, legs shaking now, seeing how resolved he was, gathering herself to insist he leave her to take her chances on the ground.

"Rose," he countered before she could, "I'm not giving you the keys. And you don't need to worry about the ute . . ."

I'm not worried about the bloody ute, she screamed silently.

"I need the plane to check on some herds this morning," he went on, "so either you let me fly you home now, or we sit here until you agree to let me fly you home." His dark eyes held hers, unwavering. "Please, I've a lot to do, so just come now. You're not going to win this one."

"I — "

"No."

"But — "

"No," he said. "So, are you coming?"

She stared, then exhaled, the oddest noise leaving her.

"I'll take that as a yes," he said, and smiled, threw her his jacket. "You'd better wear this."

She tried not to let him see how scared she was. As she followed him over to the plane, then took his hand, feeling the firm grip of his fingers around hers, pulling her up onto the wing, she fought to distract herself from what was about to happen by wondering what Joe would say if he could see the gibbering wreck she'd devolved to. *Buck up*, probably. She tried to, willing her hammering heart under control, forcing her lips into a courageous (she hoped) smile. She straightened her trembling legs on the wing, opened her mouth to ask Max if he definitely didn't need his jacket, then nearly choked, feeling the metal flex beneath her.

"Is it meant to do that?" she yelped, grabbing Max's arm with her other hand, stomach lurching, shivery with fear; it was all she could do to stop her teeth chattering.

"Yes," he said, holding her steady. Did he squeeze her hand? A reassuring squeeze?

She was too beside herself to tell.

Or to feel awkward about how close they were forced to sit in the tiny, tiny cockpit, her on his lap since there was nowhere else for her to go, his legs firm, as tense as she felt, beneath her. His warm arms came around her and he flicked on the controls, tapped the fuel gauge, then started the engine, sending the propellers spinning to life. Dimly, she was aware of him telling her the flight would only take them a couple of minutes, she'd be home with Walter even sooner than she'd thought; much more consciously, she smelled petrol fumes filling their minuscule glass shell.

Did the flammable scent terrify him, as she'd always assumed it must?

She wouldn't ask, and not only because she feared the question would upset him. *No pity.* She couldn't ask.

She couldn't speak.

And he didn't ask her this time if she was ready to go like he had before they'd set off in the ute. Maybe he guessed after all how deeply unready she was. Again, she was past caring, because without another word he started taxiing, his cheek all but skimming hers as she shifted backward in alarm and he reached forward, pulling back the throttle, speeding them over the shorn, makeshift grass runway.

Oh my God, she thought, her eyes wide on the blurring green blades. *Oh sweet Jesus and God and anyone who's up there, please let this be all right. Pleaseletthisbeallright.*

It wasn't all right.

Not at first.

He accelerated faster, the plane roaring, the force of it shuddering through her bones, making the cockpit glass rattle until it seemed like it might shatter. They lifted, arched upward, and she clenched her eyes shut, feeling nauseatingly like she'd left half of herself behind, her head growing lighter the higher they climbed.

But then his voice, in her ear.

"You're missing it," he said. "Open your eyes, Rose."

"I don't know if I can."

"You can."

Somehow, she forced herself to, then felt worse seeing how high they already were, much higher than she'd imagined they'd be this quickly. Briefly, terrifyingly, it made her feel like they might drop, any second, to the ground. Only they didn't drop. She became more conscious of the strength of Max beneath her, his arms around her; how little he seemed to be worrying. *You're safe, Rose.* Wanting to believe it, she risked a look downward, then stared, chest swelling through her fear, absorbing the infinite acres of mist-covered land, reaching out, out, and out. She'd thought the view she'd seen on Leon the night before had been beautiful, but this, this was something else. For the first time in her life, she was able to see, actually *see* the earth as a sphere, the sky a great dome. She felt like she, not the plane, had wings.

Turning, pressing her fingertips to the cold cockpit roof, she stared back at the ute. It was the size of a toy. The trees were, too. The cows and bounding kangaroos dotting the fields looked like Walter's figurines. She watched them, her heart pounding as quickly as ever, just differently, delightedly, and, in the same moment, the sun at last appeared, its glowing red curve breaking the horizon, flooding the sky and cockpit with its rays, making her close her eyes again with the sudden rush of brightness, then open them just as quickly, *you're missing it*, drawing breath as everything became bathed in gold: the clouds, the land below, her own skin, Max's tanned hands on the throttle, his jacket around her.

"I'm worried you're cold," she said, rediscovering her voice, raising it to be heard above the engine.

"Not cold," he said. "Are you all right?"

"I'm fine," she said. "Happy."

"Yeah," he said. *You look pretty happy.* "We're going down now though."

"Already?"

"We're here," he said, and nodded to their left. She felt rather than saw the movement; the warmth of his cheek beside hers.

She craned her neck, looking downward, and realized he was right. There was the river, glistening rosily, the house where Walter and Esme were probably still sleeping, since it couldn't be much after six; all the cottages, their corrugated roofs winking in the sun's glare. A couple of stockmen were out, walking toward the stables.

"I don't want to go down," she said.

"You didn't want to come up," he said, laughing.

"Please," she said, "can we just have another minute?"

He didn't make her ask twice. He veered, their wings tilting, and made the engine roar, taking them past the river, the stockmen, and the road to Narrawee, until the plantation was all behind them and she was almost certain she could see the sea ahead.

"The ocean," he said. "It's the ocean here." Then, it sounded like impulsively, "You wanna do something fun?"

"Always," she said.

And he laughed again, took them upward, up and up, her ears filling, his arms coming around her tighter, holding her close, closer than she'd been held in such a long time. . . .

"Here we go," he said.

"Here we go, what?" she asked, only she didn't need to, because then he showed her, spinning them in a barrel roll, making her scream, laugh, her blood roaring in her ears, to her head, eyes streaming with delight, shock.

"Enough?" he asked, once he'd brought them level, wings steadying, his arms loosening again.

She took a shallow breath, then another, chest bursting with adrenaline. "Enough," she said.

"You're sure?"

"No."

"Then let's go again," he said, and they did, her blood roared once more, she laughed and she laughed and clung to his arms, telling him that that had to be it, otherwise she'd be sick. "I have a history . . ."

"All right," he said, "all right," and veered again, slowly taking them down from the boundless blue sky, the earth growing larger, coming up to meet them as they neared the barn Rose and Walter had camped in, its yard with its damned wheelbarrow, and the patch of grass below it, where Rose had grabbed his hands the first day they'd met, and where he landed again now, softly, no bumps, taxiing to a halt.

He got out first, jumping to the ground from the wing, then turned, reaching up to help her.

"I'm shaking," she said, landing on the grass with a thud, smiling, feeling the tears still on her cheeks. "I'm really shaking."

"Still wish you'd driven?"

"No," she said, taking his jacket off. "But I'm so sorry that someone else has to for me." She grimaced. "I feel a bit of an idiot . . ."

"Don't."

"I do."

"It's fine."

"I hope so." She held out his jacket to him.

He smiled, took it, his fingers closing around the fur that had been pressed to her neck.

For a moment, he continued to look at her, she at him.

She realized they were standing in exactly the same spot as they had the last time they'd been here.

She didn't reach out for his hands this time, though.

And she was the one who, thinking of Walter, reluctantly said, "I'd better get on."

"Yeah," he said, his eyes leaving hers, looking in the direction of the stables. "So had I."

"Walter really wants to see you," she said. "I think Esme does too."

"I'll come by. Once I'm back later. I need to get up to the stables now, refuel too, before I fly . . ."

"You will be back, though?" she said. "You're not going away again?"

"No," he turned to head off, "I'll be around a while."

She smiled, pleased.

He didn't see.

He was already walking away, his jacket that she'd worn in his hands, head dipped, like he might be looking at it.

"I really loved that," she called after him, needing to have it said. "Thank you, Max."

"You're welcome, Rose."

"Rosie."

His shoulders moved.

Was he laughing?

She watched him a moment longer, trying to make it out, then, not managing to, set off herself. Realizing how hot she'd become, she pulled her thick pullover over her head, the static catching on her hair. Her face was warm, tingling from the sun's rays, the burn of the rising sun; the memory of the almost-touch of his cheek against hers, up in his plane.

CHAPTER TWENTY

True to his word, he did call by to see Esme and Walter later that day — only one of whom had still been asleep when Rose had returned: Walter, curled up in his bed, snoringly oblivious of Esme hovering at his door, anxiously listening in case he woke. It was Esme who told Rose about Max's brief visit, just before tea, describing Walter's beaming smile when Max had appeared in the kitchen doorway, how he'd hung back, then run to Max when Max had crouched and told him to come on over here, mate, ruffling his hair, promising they'd spend lots more time together soon. Rose, wishing she'd been there for the call herself, only hadn't been because she'd been up in the vegetable garden with Hannah, trying to ingratiate herself by learning how to tell which tomatoes were safe to pick. ("So as long as they're red, not green, they're fine," Rose said. "That's about the long and short of it," said Hannah.)

She was to spend precious little time with Max over the days that followed. He was busy, visibly busy, off in his plane keeping an eye on the herds, flying to another station to inspect more Esme said they were considering buying with the money Vivian had left, then galloping around the fields closer to home, mustering with the other stockmen, catching Rose's eye as she sat on the veranda with Walter reading, or took him out on more rides of her own. He worked late, never returning from the stables until sundown. Rose would spot him then too, seeing him through Walter's window as she put Walter to bed, moving closer to look as he ambled down the dusky pathway in his loose shirt and corduroy trousers, running his hand tiredly through his hair, heading on to Bill's for dinner.

"You should come and eat with us," Rose said to him on one of the occasions they bumped into each other, on his second afternoon home, out in the sunny yard behind the house. She was hanging the laundry with Walter. Max was on his way to see Esme in the office. The white sheet Rose had been pegging billowed damply, and he bent, his leather chaps creaking, catching the sheet's corner before it skimmed the dirt floor, fixing it to the line for her. *You don't need to manage.* "It's got to be more comfortable in the house than down in Bill's hut."

"I like Bill's hut," he said.

"Come to us," she repeated.

"Yes, come," entreated Walter, squinting up at him, nose wrinkling.

"Maybe," he said.

"Maybe always means no," said Rose.

He laughed. "Not always."

But he didn't come to eat with them, not for dinner, nor any meal.

"Hasn't for years," said Esme. "Not since . . . Well, not since Mabel came."

Other things happened, though, in those early September days after he returned. Things like the sun continuing to shine, Hannah letting Rose and Walter pick more tomatoes *and* fetch the eggs for the first time, and Walter asking Esme, quite out of the blue over lunch, why she and Max had hair and eyes that were the same as each other's but not his mummy's— "Aunty Vivian said she was your sister too"—and Esme, brilliant Esme, not missing a beat before replying, "Oh that's just because your mum was our sister-*in-law*, married to our brother Jamie," like it was the most unexceptional news in the world (*softly, softly*). To Rose's astonishment, Walter asked no more, just nodded, seeming to accept it. She exhaled, Esme did too, and Hannah (brow pinched), declared that she'd make Walter his blessed tub of ice cream that night. "Don't expect it to become a regular thing, mind."

More surprises came quick on the heels of that ice cream: first from Lauren, who stopped by that same afternoon, demanding that she listen to Walter's chest ("It's fine," she said, pulling Walter's shirt back down gently, with startling care, glancing, just once, at his rabbit. "You can stop wearing Esme's hat, now, it's far too warm for that"), then from Kate, who telephoned the very next, inviting Rose, Walter, and, *yes, absolutely Esme,* to Brisbane for a visit, as soon as they could make it, but not from Xander, because he didn't reply to Rose's wire, not that day, nor any after.

"Is he ignoring it, do you think?" Esme asked.

"I don't know," Rose said. *Should there even be a question.* "He mightn't have got it. He could be away . . . I hope he's all right."

She did. Of course she did.

But she didn't agonize over his silence as she once would have. She really had done that too many times already, in the year that had been. There was only so much of it she could take. Slowly, she learned to stop watching the Lucknows' gate, wondering if, when, his reply would arrive.

Increasingly, she watched out for Max instead.

The habit grew so gradually, so stealthily, she hardly realized it had come upon her: how, as she roamed the plantation with a hatless Walter — taking him and Rabbit on more trips to see if the goslings had arrived, up to the stables to feed Bess and Leon, down to the pasture fences to try and get him used to the cows grazing (*I'll touch one if you will*) — she'd look around, searching Max out in the golden fields, the empty doorway to the annex, poised for the moment when she'd run into him again, and he'd smile, stop to chat. Maybe even call her Rosie.

She thought that perhaps he watched out for her as well. She realized she (perhaps) quite liked that he did that. The looks he'd cast up at her bed room window on his evening walks down from the stables, unknowing that she was already at Walter's window, looking down at him; how he'd turn on his horse when she glimpsed him out riding, the slightest movement of his hat giving away that he'd noticed her too.

Yet, no matter the attention they paid one another, it never ceased to take Rose by surprise when they *did* cross paths, like they had in the yard, and which they seemed to do more often as his first week home moved into the next. They did it all the time: colliding at the entrance to the stables, the door to Esme's office, out in the pastures, back in the yard, the vegetable garden; everywhere. They'd laugh when it happened, eyes meeting then dropping, speaking over one another to ask how they were, saying that they were fine, good, really good.

"I'm really good too," Walter would say.

Max would always leave too quickly, though, busy, yes, but also so persistent in making an excuse to go that, even given his smile when he saw

Rose—even given how much she'd felt that he as well as she had enjoyed their dawn drive, their flight—she couldn't help but worry that something about her (her face, could it really be her face?) still made him uncomfortable.

"It's his face, you wally," said Esme. "You've made him think too much about it, with your great big eyes. He *likes* your face."

"Oh no," said Rose. "Don't be silly. He told me I look like a farmer."

He mentioned her time on a farm again one warm morning in the middle of the month, when Hannah, off to do some shopping, asked Rose and Walter to clean out the chickens (*Do not leave the catch off the coop*), Walter left the catch off the coop ("Oh no oh no oh no," he wailed, running after the ecstatic, escaping chickens, "Hannah's going to be *ropable*"), Esme and Max, both in the office, rushed to the yard to help ("Stop running," Max said, "Walter, mate, stop running"), Rose swooped as they did, caught a bird in her arms, yelped at the force of its battering wings, then, seeing Max laughing, laughed too, and asked him what she was meant to do now. "Put it in the coop," he said, grabbing another chicken. "Call yourself a farmer?"

"No," she said, surprised, pleased that he'd remembered she'd lived on one. "I was a secretary for the Ministry of Agriculture, down in Devon." She crossed over to the coop, wrestling with the incensed chicken, shoving it unceremoniously back into its nest. "Not that I was very good."

"But the people were very nice," Walter volunteered. He'd managed to secure a chicken too. It was almost as big as him. He waddled to the coop, blinking at the feathers whacking his eyes. "They told her to be careful of spiders and snakes."

"She checks hers and Walter's bed every night," said Esme with a grin.

Max really laughed at that. "You don't need to check your beds for spiders and snakes."

"She won't be told," said Esme.

"Better safe than sorry, as Hannah says," Rose said.

"Quick," Max gestured at a chicken sprinting behind her back, "get that one."

Rose didn't know how long it took them to round up all the birds, the four of them chasing and grabbing and bumping into one another in the squawking yard, then racing up to the vegetable patch when Esme spotted a particularly determined chicken pegging for the gate ("Don't let it get the tomatoes," Rose called after Max, a stitch in her side, aching from laughter. "Hannah'll never speak to me again." "I'm not going to let it get the tomatoes, Rose"), but he stayed, doing most of the work in all honesty, catching the birds the rest of them missed, for once forgetting to disappear anywhere, not until the last chicken was in the coop.

"No muster to get to?" Rose teased him, smiling, head on one side. "No river to check on?"

"Yeah," he said, closing the coop's catch, the rim of his hat shadowing his own smile. "I decided they'd better wait."

And she smiled more, glad—really very happy, actually—that he had.

Happier again, when, a couple of days later, as she and Walter were walking back from the stables, he called out to them, and rode down to tell Walter he'd just seen some koalas.

"Yass," said Walter, hopping in his enthusiasm. "Where?"

"Down by the base field," he said, which meant nothing to Rose. He tried to explain, directing her to a grid, a hill, but that didn't mean much either.

"Could you show us?" she asked, fearing it would be the geese all over again if he didn't, but also because she wanted him to.

He hesitated.

"Please," she said.

"*Please*," said Walter.

"You don't want us getting lost on your conscience," said Rose.

"No," he agreed, "I could do without that."

"Then . . . ?"

He hesitated again, but only for the length of time it took him to glance at his watch.

"All right," he said. "Let's go."

"Thank you," said Rose. "Is it far away? Should I get Leon?"

"You're all right," Max said, dismounting. "It won't take us long to walk."

It didn't feel long. They headed back up to the stables, where he left his horse, then across the adjacent field into the dry, earthy shade of the woods, and as they walked, talking—him asking whether Hannah had guessed about the chickens ("No," said Rose. "Thank *God*," said Walter), whether Walter had enjoyed his ice cream, or got to know any of the other children on the plantation yet ("You should, mate," Max said, catching Rose's arm before she tripped on a rut. "They're about your age")—the time passed, as it always seemed to pass with him, in the blink of an eye. He held back branches for Rose and Walter to duck under, asked Rose more about her farm, and she told him, speaking of Hector, Enid, staring in disbelief when he said he'd been to Ilfracombe himself for a weekend back in '34, when he'd last visited Vivian.

"That's so funny," she said, nearly tripping again because she was still looking at him rather than at where she was going. "I wonder where I was that weekend."

"Not there," he said.

"No," she agreed, still absorbing that he had been visiting that place she was fated to know so well. "I'm sorry I couldn't show you around," she joked, or half joked. (She was truly quite sorry.) "What did you make of it?"

"I can see that a winter might have felt long," he said. "How did you end up there?"

"You don't want to know," she said. Then, before he could try and insist that he did, asked, "Why did *you* go?"

"To see the ocean," he said. "I'd forgotten how closed-in London could feel . . ."

"It must have after all this," she said, breathing the pure, woody scent of the trees, trying to imagine returning to that smoking, sprawling city herself.

Pushing the disenchanting prospect firmly aside, remembering his joke in his plane, she said, "You know it's the sea in Devon though, don't you, not the ocean?"

"I do know that."

"And while we're at it, we call Ilfracombe Ilfratomb now."

"Really?"

"Yes."

"Who says?"

"Your sister."

"Of course she does," he said, and she laughed, then stopped short, bumping into Walter, who'd found the koalas and pointed at them, low in the branches of a tree ahead.

"Wanna hold one?" Max asked him, before he could beg to be allowed to.

"I do," whispered Walter.

"Let's see if this guy'll let us," said Max, and, quietly approaching the tree, carefully lifted the smaller of the bears down. He did it expertly, as gently as he might have taken a babe from a crib, which in itself did something rather unexpected to Rose's heart in her chest.

As did the way he crouched, helping Walter to hold the bear himself.

"Not too heavy?" he asked him, before taking his own arm from beneath the bear's bottom.

"Not too heavy," said Walter. "Oh, he's cuddling me."

"He is," said Max.

"Rosie, look." Walter's eyes sought hers, aglow with wonder, the koala's head against his lemon knitted shirt. "Look at me."

"I'm looking, little man," she said. "I'm looking."

Max smiled up at her.

He'd forgotten to make an excuse to leave again.

"Wanna hold him too before I put him back?" he asked her.

"I do," she said, "I really, really do."

"All right," he said, and, lifting the bear from Walter, he came over to her, placed the warm furry thing into her arms.

"Oh," she said, echoing Walter, feeling its paws tighten sweetly around her.

"He likes Rosie," said Walter.

"He does, doesn't he?" said Max, and, as he ran the back of his finger under the indent of the bear's neck, she felt her heart skip again.

She started to watch out for him even more after that, never fully acknowledging to herself what she was doing, but doing it nonetheless: waving at him when she saw him out riding, waiting for the tip of his hat, his raised hand in return; anticipating, through entire mornings, bumping into him, those *collisions* when they'd stand in the sunlight, Walter between them, talking, Max leaving it just a little longer every time before saying he must go. She'd stave the moment off, telling him stories of her and Walter's day, smiling at some new irritation of Hannah's; how nice it had been to meet Bill at the vegetable garden.

"He took us down to his kitchen for soda bread," she said.

"Did you like it?" Max asked.

"Not really," she admitted, and he laughed.

She'd ask him what he'd been up to, and he'd tell her, setting down the saddle he'd been carrying, or the sack of feed, speaking of early musters, foals just born, the fresh herds they'd agreed they *would* buy from the station he'd visited, some new cows he'd discovered were in calf.

"How do you discover that?" Rose asked.

"You don't want to know," he said.

"Oh," she said. *Poor cows.*

Sometimes, when Rose was in the kitchen with Walter, he'd come through on his way to see Esme in the office, and would stop to look at Walter's drawing, or puzzle, and help Rose make tea, lifting the kettle from the range, passing her the tea leaves, *you don't need to manage,* leaning back on the counter, watching while she brewed the pot.

"What?" she said, one day, seeing his bemused frown.

"Are you timing it?" he asked.

She laughed, self-conscious. "How can you tell?"

"You count," he said. "Your lips move."

"They don't."

"They do," he said. "How long do you leave it for?"

"Two minutes until the first stir," she admitted, "and another minute after."

"You really need a watch," he said, then made her lose count anyway, telling her he'd had another escaped cow that morning.

"I'm glad I wasn't there for that one," she said.

"I'm glad for you," he said.

She smiled, peering into the pot.

"I was so shocked when I saw you," he said. "In that cardigan, all that hay in your hair . . ."

"I was pretty shocked seeing you," she said, and, speaking without thinking, finally admitted to how mortified she'd been that he'd caught her going for a pee — then wailed, because it turned out he hadn't known that's what she'd been doing at all.

"Seriously?" he said, laughing so much that Walter abandoned his drawing and joined in.

"Stop," Rose said, putting her flaming face in her hands, "*stop*. Please, can we never speak about this again . . ."

"What are we laughing about?" said Walter, still laughing.

"Cows," said Max, picking up the papers he'd been taking to Esme, setting off, "that's all."

Walter stopped laughing.

"What's wrong?" Max asked him, pausing.

"He's a bit scared of cows," Rose said.

"Just a bit," Walter said.

"That can't be very comfortable," said Max. "We're going to have to do something about that, mate."

He didn't say what, but did start to take Walter out riding himself, most afternoons, swinging him up into the saddle of his horse, head tipped back beneath his cowboy hat, dark hair brushing the collar of his loose cotton shirt. "You're taller than me now," he'd say, and Walter would laugh, then hoot, joyously, when Max climbed up behind him and took off, cantering around the fields closest to the house, so much faster than Rose could ever bring herself to dare when she had him with her. But much as she had her heart in her mouth, watching the two of them from up on the veranda with Esme, she didn't consider asking Max to slow. Not when Walter looked so protected, so tiny and safe in his arms; as safe as she'd felt, up in his plane. Not when Walter was so very happy. His yells of delight carried, it felt like, for miles.

Rose was sure that Lauren, who also watched them riding from up outside Esme's cottage, must have been able to hear.

Increasingly, remembering the tenderness with which she'd adjusted Walter's shirt, Rose wished that she really could get closer to her, see the expression on her grief-wearied face.

Certainly, Esme's was smiling enough.

"God, he adores it, doesn't he?" she remarked one day.

Rose nodded, but didn't smile with her. She'd found herself thinking not of Walter, or Lauren, but suddenly, discomfortingly, of Mabel, and how she'd have felt seeing her son in the arms of the man she'd loved. She wondered—just as she'd wondered when she and Esme had drunk all that gin—if Max, so gentle and good with Walter, *had* been in love with his mother.

She was tempted, sorely tempted, to ask Esme about it again.

She didn't, and not only because Esme had already told her she didn't know the answer.

No, she didn't want to give away to Esme that she cared.

She shouldn't care.

She knew full well she shouldn't care.

Not this much.

It set her awry, just thinking about it. She couldn't think about it. Not with Xander's ring in her suitcase upstairs.

She did her best to forget about it: impossible around the plantation, seeing him everywhere, but a little easier when, three weeks to the day after he'd returned, she, Esme, and Walter left for the day, off on their trip to Brisbane.

They called at Kate's parents' house first — a beautiful federation home by Brisbane River, in a place called Kangaroo Point — where they had the happiest of morning teas on the sun-dappled lawn, the children playing delightedly while Esme and Kate got to know each other, and Rose and Kate caught up, Rose managing not to mention Max too much, Kate saying how relieved she was that her husband Tim had been posted to peaceful Singapore. (*Just please let it stay that way.*)

They headed off to Brisbane next, taking the children on the ferry. As they crossed the glinting water, Walter and Verity standing on their tiptoes to see over the ferry's edge, just as they'd used to on the decks of the *Illustrious,* Rose watched them, and continued to keep the confusion of her own strange emotions buried at the back of her mind. She carried on doing that when they got off the ferry and ate takeaway fish and chips out of paper by the water's edge, the sun on their faces, glass bottles of pop by their sides. She helped Walter and Verity to squirt tomato sauce on their chips, stole one of Walter's, and really did think only of how happy they both were, how happy *she* was, and how much Enid back in Ilfratomb would love to be sitting with them, eating their salty, vinegary fried food.

She thought of Enid again when they went for a stroll along busy Queen's Street and she bought her another postcard. (*Greetings from the capital of Queensland.*) Kate treated the children to a comic each, and they meandered on, chatting, ignoring the recruiting officers, everywhere — the long lines of boys eager to sign up and be sent off to whatever the war had waiting for them — stopping for Kate to buy hair spray, then at a newsstand, where there was really no news whatsoever of what was actually going on in the war ("Dad says you can't get it," said Kate. "Only the good stuff. It's all censored. Probably why those queues to sign up are so long"), and still Rose didn't let her mind stray from the moment. Esme mentioned a haberdasher's she wanted to call at, and, as they headed for it — dodging the clunking trams, the motors and horse-drawn carts, passing stone buildings that might have felt provincial, coming straight from London, but seemed grand and impressive after the short narrow strip of Narrawee—Rose didn't even let some of the sideways looks Walter received bother her. Just as in Narrawee, his was the only Aborigine face on the pavements, but given he, trotting along talking nineteen to the dozen with Verity—Rabbit tucked under his arm, wholly caught up in the joy of being reunited with his first ever friend— noticed the attention not at all, Rose decided she wouldn't either.

At the haberdashery, Esme bought herself a new pattern, and insisted on treating Rose to fabric for new dresses too. ("Let me," she said. "Vivian said nothing about me not spending my money on you . . .") From there, they headed back to the ferry, passing the huge art deco Wintergarden picture house, which had posters on its walls advertising the release of Disney's *Dumbo* the following month ("Please, please, please, can we come," said Walter and Verity. "We'll see," said Kate and Rose), and Rose, enjoying herself more, felt only relaxed.

She remained so almost until nightfall: on the ferry, saying goodbye to Kate and Verity, through all the long drive back to the plantation, her and Esme taking turns at the wheel, Walter talking, reliving every moment of the day, asking when they could do it again, hardly letting either of them get a word in edgeways.

"You are a *chatterbox*, Walter," said Esme. "I never would have guessed when I met you, just how much of a chatterbox you are."

But then they reached the plantation. They turned through the gate, the house glowing in the ebbing light of the setting sun, and Rose, hearing Max's plane, seeing him take off from his patch of shadowed grass beneath the barn, stopped feeling so relaxed.

She felt deflated.

He wasn't home.

She wasn't going to be able to bump into him, tell him about the day.

"Where's he gone?" she asked Esme, once they'd pulled up.

"I don't know," Esme said, getting out of the ute, holding the door wide so Walter could scamper off to find Hannah in the kitchen for a snack. (Now when had he taken to doing that?) "Doing a recce for the new cattle maybe. The final papers arrived before we left." She slammed the door. "Max said he'll leave first thing to drive them down."

"He's going away again?"

"Looks like it."

"How long for?"

"About a week."

"A *week?*"

"Afraid so," said Esme.

She told Rose, as they walked up the porch stairs, that the upcoming drive wasn't the only thing Max had spoken to her about that morning. He'd also asked her if Rose had made any mention of how long she was planning to stay at the plantation.

"I told him you weren't rushing anywhere," said Esme.

"Was he all right about that?"

"Pretty all right," said Esme, "yeah. But," she stopped, turned to face Rose, unsure suddenly, "I'm sorry, I told him about Xander, that he's asked you to come to Cairo." She bit her lip. "I thought he should know. I hope you don't mind . . ."

"Of course not," said Rose, quickly, before she betrayed the jolt of confusion she felt at the news. "It's not a secret." Strange, that that was how it had started to seem. She hadn't been unaware that she'd never once mentioned Xander to Max, or to anyone other than Esme. He was so difficult to bring up, she hadn't even told Kate about him. "What did he say?"

"Nothing about Cairo," said Esme. "But he was obviously . . . shocked. And pretty annoyed when I said Xander hasn't been too . . . well" — she searched for the word — "reliable. He said you deserved better."

"He said that?" Rose said, heart quickening more.

"Yeah, he said that," said Esme, smiling, kindly. "For what it's worth, I think you do too."

He was gone the next morning, riding, not flying, with four other stockmen for the three days it would take them to get to the station the cattle were coming from. He didn't come to say goodbye to Rose and she, watching them all leave from her bedroom window, tried not to mind.

It was hard, though, him being away. Harder than she wanted it to be. She got on with life, with her and Walter's outings — up at the stables, down at the river with Esme, and increasingly, now they were getting to know him, in Bill's kitchen — but she couldn't make a pot of tea without thinking of Max passing her the leaves. She never went by the chickens without remembering his laughter. She and Walter always had such a nice time together, especially once the goslings hatched, especially with Bill, who, chopping onions one day, told Walter that he'd been friends with Richie, *dropping his name in* so neither Esme nor Rose had to think of a way of doing it. But, however much Rose enjoyed herself, however much she loved watching Walter listen to Bill's stories of Richie — his chin in his little hands, legs swinging at the kitchen bench, sweetly, heartachingly captivated by the revelation that he'd not only had a daddy, but a daddy who'd been funny and smart and kind with the animals, and so clever that he could have walked from one end of the plantation to the other with his eyes closed and not lose his way — it was only when, at the very end of September, that she, putting Walter to bed, looked up at the distant thunder of hooves, saw the approaching silhouettes of men galloping with more than a hundred cows in front of them and, realizing Max had finally come home, felt something other than . . . restless.

She struggled to sleep that night, though, quickly anxious about seeing him. She lay listening to the cicadas, remembering what Esme had said about him being shocked when she'd told him about Xander, worrying what he might have made of her own failure to mention her fiancé, hating that he might have come to think less of her; a liar. . . .

But to her relief, when he came to the kitchen at breakfast the next morning he said nothing about any of it. For all he'd left without a goodbye, he smiled at Rose, asked her how she was ("Good," she said, swallowing her toast, "really good"), ruffled Walter's hair, and, dropping a kiss on Esme's head, ruffled her hair too, just as Joe would have Rose's, then told her he was leaving some certificates on her desk.

"Well, there we are," said Esme, fixing her hair as he left. "That was fine, wasn't it?"

"Yes," said Rose.

It had been.

Really fine.

It was fine again when, a few hours later, Rose saw him up at the vegetable garden. He came past on his way down to the plane, his flying jacket that she'd worn slung over his shoulder, and while Walter weeded the cucumbers, Rose crossed over to him, asking him about his long ride, whether it had gone smoothly (it had), then, sensing he was about to say he had to go, talked on, telling him how mad she'd been driving Esme, being so useless learning how to use Hannah's Singer sewing machine.

"Esme's said she might as well just make my dresses herself."

"Well then, that's worked out," he said.

Still not wanting him to go, she told him about Walter's time with Bill, how much he'd been enjoying Bill's stories of Richie.

"Good," he said, "that's really good. I asked Bill if he'd tell Walter a bit."

"It was you?" she said, touched.

"Yeah," he said. "Bill grew up with Richie's dad. He was pretty happy when I told him Walter had come."

"Not like you," she couldn't resist teasing.

"Not at first," he said, with a laugh.

A laugh that was husky, and low, and reminded her how much she liked it, and was really very . . . fine.

But then he did leave, down to his plane, and as he went, he said, "See you later, Rose," still not calling her Rosie, which wasn't fine at all.

The last sun-drenched day of September gave way to October, and they continued to collide, and he'd smile, be friendly, but always walk away too quickly. Every night she lay in his bed—where there were never any spiders, no snakes—and thought of him in his annex, just feet away. She'd close her eyes, turn on her side beneath her thin, warm sheet, and fall asleep already looking forward to another chance at seeing him again, however briefly, the next day.

They were never alone. Esme was often there, so were other stockmen up at the stables; Walter always was, most of the time within earshot, tugging on Rose's hand, asking her what she and Max were talking about, why they were laughing, if Max could please take him for another ride. Mostly, it was Walter whom Rose and Max spoke about: how desperate it was that he was still so scared of the cows, how good that he'd finally started to make friends with the stockmen's children (*Hello, my name's Walter*), how funny that he'd accidentally let the cat into Hannah's cold box. Sometimes, they talked of other things—the growing heat, whether Rose had had any letters from home (not yet), what might be going on in the war (who knew?)—but never once, in any of those snatches of time Max allowed them to spend together, did they mention Mabel, or Xander.

Rose certainly said nothing of it when, at the start of October, Xander (who, it transpired, really had been away from Cairo, reporting from the desert) replied to her wire, disappointed that she'd disappointed him, asking her to swear she'd come find him just as soon as Christmas was over. *I can't prove to you how right we are unless we're together* STOP. She didn't admit to Max how wary she still was of swearing to anything, or say that, after much consultation with Esme, she'd wired Xander back promising only that she'd write soon. *Cannot keep talking about this by wire* STOP.

Max told her nothing that was private to him, either: what he thought about, for example, in the long evenings he spent alone, not eating dinner with the rest of them in the house; how much he found himself falling asleep, thinking of her. . . .

She wished he'd talk to her about himself. Like he'd talked to her when they'd gone to get his plane. As she'd felt him starting to talk to her, before he'd left on his weeklong cattle drive . . .

She wanted them to be better friends.

She still tried to tell herself that was all she wanted.

So she might have continued to convince herself, on and on.

So the two of them might have gone on, on and on: watching, passing, smiling, leaving, watching. . . .

But then he did something different.

Something quite out of the blue.

And nothing was ever the same for her again, once he had.

CHAPTER TWENTY-ONE

It was during that opening week of October that Rose first took to going out for her morning rides.

She'd been rising early for some time, up and dressed long before either Walter or Esme stirred. It wasn't the bright Queensland dawns that woke her, or the cacophony of the birds outside—even though she saw and heard both through her window, liking to sleep with her shutters open, for the breeze, the soothing sense of the stars spreading out infinitely, all the way to her parents in Malaya, Joe and Lionel in England. No, she'd be awake before even that all started. Ever since she and Max had gone to fetch his plane, with Walter still sleeping through until close to eight each morning—Rose didn't know whether thanks to Vivian (could it really be that?), Esme's claims that he knew he'd come home, or simple trust that no more change was about to come his way—she'd stopped needing to catch up on all the sleep she'd lost since moving to Williams Street. She and Esme normally had quite early nights. Even with the routine they'd got into of sitting up sewing after Walter had gone down, they always turned in by ten, and Rose often found herself up again before five o'clock had struck, sitting at her window, remembering her and Max's by now too-distant drive, watching, never less than mesmerized by the specter of the invisible sun creeping up the earth's curvature, brightening the huge, endless Australian sky from black to palest blue: that ethereal part of the day separating night from dawn which she'd always now associate with him, when she felt nothing less than at peace, anything seemed possible, and the whole planet seemed to be drawing its breath.

It was Esme who suggested at breakfast, the day after Rose had replied to Xander's wire, that Rose do something more than sit at her window for those predawn hours, and take Leon out instead.

"Make the most of it if you're going to be so uncivilized as to wake that early," Esme said. "Walter was fine when you fetched the plane. He knows I'm here, and that you won't be far, don't you, Walter?"

"How far will you be, Rosie?" he asked, spoon in hand, milk around his mouth.

"Not far," Rose said, liking the idea of dawn riding. Liking it very much. "You'll be able to spot me if you go to your window."

He thought about it, then nodded.

"I'll be all right," he said stoically.

"What a hero," Rose said.

He smiled. *Hero.*

She loved those rides. She loved them so much. From being in the stables even before the stockmen were, stroking Leon's silky face, feeling the warmth of him nudging against her, then saddling him up, taking him out into the creeping heat of the morn. She'd kick him on, feeling him come to life, the enormous pastures around them so silent that she could hear the earth moving beneath his pounding hooves. The closer the sun crept to the horizon, the hotter she'd become, breathless, sweat beading on her skin. She'd go faster, passing herds of grazing cattle, birds who stirred and flocked from the dawn haze in so many rushes of beating wings, and feel like she was the only person in the world. She'd wonder if she dared jump a fence, then she'd take that jump, her laughter, her elation, filling the humid air. She'd ride on and on, and she'd forget Xander, her fears for Joe, her parents, even about leaving Walter. The sun would appear, and she'd forget the war. The rays on her skin, her breath in her throat, and the beauty, everywhere, was all there was.

Until, there was Max, too.

Never on her rides. He didn't interrupt those. "You looked too happy, for me to do that," he'd come to tell her. She saw him at the stables when she returned.

Not straightaway. She'd been riding for almost a week when she first found him waiting for her when she got back. He was waiting, out of the blue, and it took her completely by surprise.

But before even that happened, there'd been the night before.

That Friday night when, for once, she and Esme stayed up later than ten, and went into Brisbane. Dancing.

Kate was the one who suggested the night at the Trocadero, telephoning that Friday morning to say that her mum had offered to watch the children so that she, Esme, and Rose could go out.

"Billo Smith and his dance band are playing," Kate said when she called, her voice crackling down the line. "Mum's said to tell Walter not to worry about stopping home with her, she's going to spoil him rotten and take him and Verity out for hamburgers."

At first, Rose hesitated, not because she doubted Walter would be fine — he'd be ecstatic at the idea of burgers with Verity, and he'd liked Kate's mum Ingrid the last time they'd visited; she'd given him and Verity lollies — but because she didn't know if *she* would be. It had been so long since she'd danced. . . .

"And me," said Esme, beside her in the hallway when Kate telephoned. "I don't know if I'll remember how."

"Is it something you forget?" Rose asked anxiously, putting her hand over the receiver while they had a quick conference. "Isn't it like riding a bike?"

"I don't know . . ."

"What would we even wear?" said Rose.

"Your white dress is just about finished . . ."

"I don't have any shoes to match, though."

"I could lend you some," said Esme. "I've got a pair that are a bit small." She frowned. "I don't know what I'd wear. . . ."

"I like your red . . ."

"Yeah," Esme nodded. "There's that. But, oooh, dancing. I don't know . . ."

"I don't know either . . ."

"Should we say another time?"

"Maybe . . ."

"Oh for God's sake," said Lauren, coming out of the office, making them both jump. Rose hadn't even realized she was in the house. She had a crop in her hand again. "*Go*," she said, waving it. "Go and dance. You're both too young to have forgotten how. Come on," she pointed her crop at Rose, then the telephone, "put that poor woman on the line out of her misery."

So Rose did.

She wouldn't have dared do anything else.

Kate was delighted.

"Fabulous," she said. "I'll see you at seven."

Walter was just as happy.

"Hamburgers in a restaurant?" he said. "An actual restaurant?"

"An actual restaurant," said Rose, pressing her hand to the base of her throat, still quite uneasy herself.

"Do you think they'll have ice-cream floats?" he wanted to know.

"Maybe," said Rose.

"Let's have a beer here," Esme suggested. "Bit of Dutch courage. The sun's past the yardarm somewhere."

They had a couple before they left (no gin), even though it was still so early; Esme turned the wireless on, filling the house with jazz, and Rose heated vat after vat of water, filling the bath too, so that they could wash and set their hair. Although there was one awkward moment when Max walked into the kitchen while Rose was in that bath ("Oh Christ," Max said, "I'm sorry. I came to speak to Esme." "She's upstairs," Rose said, splashing, grappling for her towel behind the screens. "Don't look at me." "I'm not looking," he said, laughing, *laughing,* "I'm going"), once she'd climbed out of the water, and was doing her makeup, pulling on silk stockings for the first time in weeks (Sarah's pair; *Thank you, Sarah*), she found herself becoming less nervous. As Esme sang in her bedroom, and Walter ran between the two of them, ready to go in his favorite yellow shirt, telling them to *hurry up* and be ready too, she grew excited instead.

More so when Esme told her the reason Max had come to speak to her before: he was going to drive them into Brisbane. He had an old RAAF mate who'd just returned home he wanted to see, one who'd also been injured in the desert air force.

"Will they come dancing?" Rose asked hopefully.

"We can ask," said Esme.

"Not a chance," said Max, once they were all finally ready and went out to the driveway to meet him, the five-o'clock sunshine beating down, making Rose self-conscious, dressed up as she was for nighttime. He, as ever, wore a loose shirt, his hat, and stood, leaning against the ute, glancing at her as she came down the porch stairs, so that she became more aware of the rouge on her lips, the click of her heels on the steps, the scent of oil from the bath he'd almost seen her in; her body in her own skin.

"You look like a farmer," he'd told her, when she'd appeared that dawn in her Fair Isle pullover and tweed trousers.

"You finished the dress then," he said now.

"Esme did," she said, and was impressed by how at ease she sounded.

"Isn't it pretty?" Esme said.

He looked at Rose a second longer, but didn't answer, because Walter ran toward him, and he bent, giving him his attention instead. Rose wasn't sure whether she was grateful or not, but as she watched Max scooping Walter up, throwing him in the air with such easy familiarity, she felt a small wrench at their happiness, how on the periphery of it she felt; how much she wanted to be part of it. . . .

She was still trying to digest the feeling when Esme reached the pair of them and smiled up at her brother.

"Do you remember when you and Jamie took me to the Troc for my eighteenth?" she asked him.

"Yeah," he said, pulling her into a quick hug too, "course I remember that."

He still refused to consider coming into the Trocadero that night, though. He refused to do that the entire way to Brisbane, him at the wheel, Rose with a bouncing, delirious Walter on her lap by the window, Esme laughing between them. Once they'd left Walter with Verity, picked Kate up (*Not too many lollies, Mum, please*), and reached the long twilit queues waiting to go into the buzzing, palm-bordered building that was the Trocadero, he drove straight off, with a beep of his horn and a "Be good" thrown out the window, Rose assumed at Esme. He left, just like that, so didn't hear Kate remark to Rose that he was a bit like heaven, "All Laurence Olivier in *Wuthering Heights*," or see Esme spot a client at the front of the queues (*Oh my God, look who it is*), getting them inside in no time.

Nor did he exclaim at the wall of heat that struck them when they all entered the noisy, pulsing dance hall, smell the perfume, the pomade, cigarette smoke, and aftershave. He didn't feel the sudden thrill of the press of sweaty bodies on the floor, the crash of Billo's band, or see Esme pause, sadly tracing her hand over a barstool Jamie had once sat on, then smile when Kate nudged her and pointed at the NO JITTERBUGGING signs on the walls, saying that rules like that were made to be broken. He didn't discover, like Rose and Esme discovered, that jitterbugging was just like riding a bicycle, and, as it turned out, all they wanted to do the whole night long. He didn't meet the battalion of fresh recruits who'd also come to the Trocadero (*the Troc*) that evening, bound — they guessed — for Singapore, or watch as Rose, Kate, and Esme jitterbugged with partner after partner, Rose, forgetting the wrench she'd felt in the driveway, getting a stitch instead, laughing until her stomach hurt, because it was so much *fun* to be thrown around and up and down to the swing of a band who knew just what they were doing with their drums, their trumpets, saxes and double basses, *in the mood*.

He was sitting on a dark veranda with his wounded mate, Simon, when that all happened, talking about Egypt, and too much of Rose, Simon failing to understand why he was so certain Rose would eventually leave Australia, choose to return to her fiancé, because Simon, blinded by his own injuries, couldn't see Max's scars.

"Maybe she doesn't either, mate," Simon suggested. "Not the way you think she does. Maybe she's choosing to stay here. Maybe you need to learn to trust that. Give this a chance."

Rose knew Simon said that, because Max, eventually, told her.

Just as she knew that Max arrived a little early at the Troc to collect her and the others, and stood — all but concealed by the dance floor's darkened doorway, his burned shoulder resting against the frame — looking for her.

She knew that he found her, because, just as she was letting the eighteen-year-old recruit she'd been dancing with (and who'd never kissed a girl before) kiss her goodbye on her hot cheek, she looked across the dance floor, breathless, smiling, and caught sight of him.

Was he as happy to see her as she was him?

She didn't know.

It was too dark for her to make out the look on his face.

But the next morning, after their long drive home to the plantation, Walter sleeping, Esme nodding off, and Rose doing the same — this time in the middle, pressed against the warmth of Max's body, her head dropping, before she could stop it, onto his shoulder ("It's all right," he said softly, "sleep") — she woke before dawn, more from habit than because she was ready, went for a ride anyway, loving it too much to miss the chance, and, when she got back to the stables, there he was waiting for her.

He wasn't surprised to see her, she could tell.

His pulse, she was sure, didn't jump at the unexpectedness of it.

She saw that he had a mug of tea in his hands, a mug that he said he'd brought for her, and realized that, incredible as it seemed, he'd come to find her.

"I thought you might need it," he said, raising the mug. "You were tired last night."

She smiled, nodded, too stunned to do more than say, "Thank you," as she dismounted, dropping stiffly to the stony yard floor, and took the tea from him.

"I brewed it your way," he said.

"With your watch," she said.

"With my watch," he said, laughing, taking Leon from her, walking him on to the stables.

"What time is it?" she called after him.

"Not even six," he called back.

"You're up," she said, pointing out the obvious.

"I'm always up," he said. "I see you riding . . ."

"You see me?" she said.

"Yeah," he said. "I see you, Rosie."

CHAPTER TWENTY-TWO

He was there, waiting for her at the stables, every morning after that.

He always brought her tea.

They never spoke about why he came. They were still weeks away from him admitting that, when he'd seen that soldier kissing her on the dance floor, he'd accepted what Simon had been telling him: that he'd been a fool, keeping his distance, all this time, not letting them be better friends, even if friends really was all the two of them could ever be; how, as they'd driven home, and her head had rested on his shoulder, it had struck him that he couldn't carry on keeping his distance anyway. Not as he had been. Not any longer.

"You slept on me," he'd finally say, too late. "I drove slower, just so you'd keep sleeping."

All of that—the awful realization of time, wasted—was ahead of them.

Back in that golden, sun-filled October, he sought her out every morning, he never let her down, and it felt like they'd have all the time in the world.

The first morning he came, they didn't even speak very much. Max simply led Leon on and told Rose to sit, enjoy her tea.

"Go on," he said, gesturing at a hay bale by the stable wall, "make the most of it before Walter gets up."

She did make the most of it. It was wonderful sitting there on that hay bale with the drink he'd brought her in her hands, picturing him in his unseen kitchen, timing the three minutes. She couldn't believe he'd done that. She couldn't believe he'd called her Rosie. *I see you, Rosie.* She stretched her sore legs before her, her eyes on the brightening sky, the softly whispering grass, and didn't think to follow him into the stables. She was still too busy absorbing that he was there at all.

But by the next morning, she'd had enough of sitting on her own.

When he took Leon from her, she went after him.

"I can drink my tea inside," she said, half expecting him to protest, send her away, or come up with an excuse to go himself, as she'd grown too used to him doing.

He didn't protest, though, or make an excuse.

"Come on then," he said, like he was pleased she'd followed, making her glad that she had. "Can you do the bridle?"

"I can do the bridle," she said, and set to it when they reached the stall, leaving her tea on the ledge to cool while he did the saddle, the two of them moving around one another, their feet rustling the hay, their arms brushing, Leon shifting between them.

Max told her, as they worked, that he'd seen her and Esme up at the cottages the evening before. They'd taken Walter to play tag with the stockmen's children. Max wanted to know if he'd been hallucinating, or if his mum really had also been there, watching the children too.

"You weren't hallucinating," Rose said, catching the brush he threw her. "When Walter dropped his rabbit, she picked it up and gave it back to him." Rose had been even more shocked by that than when Lauren had brought the cough syrup. "Esme said, 'Bugger me.' "

He laughed, pulling Leon's saddle off.

"What?" she said.

"You, your accent . . ."

"What's wrong with my accent?" she asked, smiling.

"Nothing," he said, patting Leon's back, his eyes shining, meeting hers. "Nothing at all."

She smiled more, and didn't know what to say.

But she felt something.

Something she still wasn't ready to acknowledge.

Something that was growing . . .

Trying to ignore it, she grappled for something else to talk about, and told Max she was off to Narrawee that day; she had to go to the bank. She didn't add how finite her supply of money was (she'd done her sums and, even with the extra Vivian had given her, only had enough to take her through to January, but that was another thing she was trying not to think about), just asked him if he needed her to pick anything up for him there.

"I'm all right, thanks," he said. "Wanna leave Walter with me?"

"I'm taking him," she said. "Hannah and Esme are coming too." *Strength in numbers, as they say.* "I can't let him turn into a recluse."

"Narrawee's not going to broaden his horizons."

"I know, but I don't want the people there to win." She walked around Leon, brushing his neck. He snorted, enjoying it. "Being scared of taking Walter in feels like letting them win . . ."

"Are you scared of anything?"

"Well," she said with a laugh, "your plane . . ."

"Ah, yeah." He laughed too. "Yeah, I could feel you shaking." His eyes were shining into hers again. "I felt awful for you . . ."

"Not awful enough to let me drive."

"I'd have felt a lot worse, letting you do that."

"And what about you?" she asked, speaking before she could decide not to, resting the brush on Leon's neck. "Does it scare you, going up in that thing?"

It was the most personal thing she'd ever asked him.

She couldn't believe she'd done it, now she had.

He looked taken aback too.

She started to become hot. . . .

But then he leaned back against the stable wall, still with Leon's saddle in his arms, and looked to the straw at his feet, brow denting, like he was thinking about his answer, but wasn't put out in the slightest that she'd raised the question.

"It did at first," he said at length, "but it scares me more becoming someone who can't fly." He raised his dark gaze to hers. "You were up there, with me. You saw it, felt it . . ."

"I did . . ."

"It would be like a prison to be afraid of that." He stared across at her. "Does that make sense?"

She nodded.

It made perfect sense.

"You're very brave," she said.

"No . . ."

"I think so," she said. "Is there anything you *are* scared of?"

He exhaled a short laugh, stood straighter, made for the stall door.

"One or two things, Rosie."

She didn't ask him to tell her what.

She felt like she'd asked him enough for one morning already.

Besides, he'd called her Rosie again. Trusted her enough to tell her what he had.

She bit her lip, carried on brushing Leon's neck.

It was really nice that he'd done all that.

He came by the house that evening to see how the trip to town had gone, ducking through the open kitchen door just as she'd turned on the lamps and was midway through filling Walter's bath. Walter wasn't there. He was in the yard getting eggs with Esme, being careful of the coop's catch.

"You survived, then?" Max said, taking the steaming vat she was holding and emptying it into the tub. "They all behaved themselves?"

"Almost all," she said, and went to fetch the next vat.

He took that one from her too, then went to fill both empties at the sink. "Almost?"

"Yes," she said, at a loss for what to do with herself now he'd taken over with the bath. (*I'll get you a bath. I'll buy you a house with five baths.*) "We had a bit of an incident at the milk bar."

He frowned, setting the vats back to boil. "What kind of incident?"

She sat at the table and told him: how Art, the skinny, sunburned proprietor, had tried to pretend he'd no ice cream left for Walter's ice-cream float. "You should have seen Walter's face," she said. "He'd been so excited about it. Art called him an abo." She broke off at the remembered slap of the word. "He said he didn't have ice creams for abos."

Max stared from beside the range, not surprised, but angry, very angry.

"What did Esme do?" he asked.

"Told Walter that Art was an idiot," Rose said. "I told Walter I had no idea what he was talking about . . ."

"I'll go and see him," said Max. "Talk to him myself . . ."

"I didn't think you went to Narrawee."

"I can."

"You don't need to," said Rose, but felt better, knowing he was prepared to. "Hannah came in, told Art he'd better have another look for the ice cream or she'd bring your mum to help him find it." *Strength in numbers, as they say.* "That did the trick."

He raised a brow. "Mum hasn't been into Narrawee since Jamie died."

"Really?" said Rose, taken aback.

"Really," he said. "She'll drive to Brisbane first. She hates Jamie's mates for what happened, almost as much as she hates herself."

"She was watching Walter again yesterday," Rose said, a few days later, back at the stables as they untacked Leon, her tea once again cooling on the ledge. Max had brought a mug for himself that day too. "I was trying to get him to feed the cows by the barn. He wasn't having it." Lauren had moved closer to him, asked him what was wrong, an unfamiliar hesitance in her voice. "She told him that Esme used to be scared of cows."

"She did," said Max, touching his hand carelessly to Rose's back as he passed her by. "Mum sorted her out in the end. I can't remember how . . ."

"Esme thinks she doesn't like her." He'd touched her back.

"Esme can be wrong about things."

"She told me Jamie said she made it harder on your mum after your dad died . . ."

"Maybe," said Max. "Jamie did, too, though."

She nodded slowly, thinking how overwhelming it must have been for Lauren: a widow with a newborn, a demanding six-year-old . . . She looked across at Max, realizing how quickly he must have had to grow up, at just eight, and how hard that must have been on him too, on top of losing his dad, who'd used to take him out at dawn, for the beauty of it. . . .

"Are you all right?" he asked her. "You look sad."

"I am a bit," she admitted. "Let's talk about something happy." She found a smile. "I'll start . . ."

And she told him about the bundle of letters that had finally arrived for her from England. Not Vivian's lawyer's one—that was still weeks away—but from Lionel, sent months before, then Joe—his brief, since he really was terrible at letters, but funny, saying how the station dog had ruined Sarah's dress when she'd visited him—another from Sarah, all cross because she'd also met Bella at Joe's base (*I've told Joe hourglass figures aren't everything, and he's told me he agrees, so I'm going to trust him.* Trust. Just like that. So

easy . . .), then Laura in Ilfratomb, who was loving life, loving being with
Hector and all of them, and had started courting the older of Mary's fisher-
man sons.

"I didn't know I was playing matchmaker when I left," Rose said. "I feel
quite smug. . . ."

"You look pretty smug."

"I expect they'll have a summer wedding, and a baby by spring."

She laughed as she said it. She was making light. . . .

Something of her own longing must have entered her voice, though,
because he didn't laugh, just asked, "You want children?"

"Yes," she said, without hesitation, "I'd love children," and might have
felt sad again, but didn't, because he took Leon's bridle from her, suggested
they finish their teas outside, which they did, sitting shoulder-to-shoulder on
the hay bale Rose had first perched on alone, their backs against the stable
wall, the sun edging higher, all of it far too lovely for her to be sad about
anything.

"Walter can go back to Art's any time he likes, by the way," Max said,
staring out at the horizon. "I don't know why he'd want to, but he can."

Rose turned, smiled.

"You went into Narrawee?" she said, hating that he'd had to, but liking,
really loving, that he had.

"I went into Narrawee."

The month ran on, the heat and humidity intensifying. They looked
after Leon, she asked him again, then again to come to the house for dinner,
until one dawn he stopped saying, "Maybe," smiled and said, "All right, all
right," instead.

She loved those evenings when he was there with her, Esme, and Walter,
chatting about nothing and everything, laughing, listening to Walter,
joking with Esme, the wireless playing, Chamberlain purring and whacking against their legs. He began to drop by more at other times, helping Rose
fill the bath again, seeking her out to show her a newspaper, full of censored
war news (more Allied pushes in Libya, successful RAF raids over Europe,
which she, chest tightening, could only guess Joe had been part of, navigating his crew through flak, nonchalant face fierce with concentration), then
lots of photographs of smiling diggers setting up tropical camps in Malaya,
No Japs Getting in Here, and one of the *Illustrious* steaming out of dry dock,
Colombo-bound.

"Sad to see it go?" he asked, setting the paper on the kitchen table.

"No," she said, feeling such relief that it had, without her on it. "Not sad at all."

At her suggestion, they went riding together with Walter, often, cantering alongside one another, racing, Walter hollering, Max outpacing her in the bright sunshine, grinning back over his shoulder. *That as fast as you can go, Rosie?* One day, they even took Walter mustering: a vain attempt to get him more comfortable with the cows. Esme tagged along, the four of them staying out until nightfall with the other stockmen, galloping farther than Rose had dared before, Esme getting sunburned, Walter hooting in delight, except when they got near a cow, which he never allowed Max to take him any closer than several feet away from.

"What are we going to do?" Max called to Rose.

"I have no idea," she called back. Then, to Esme, "What did your mum do for you?"

"Mum?" said Esme blankly, obviously having forgotten whatever it was, too. "I don't know. I could ask . . ."

"Do," said Rose. "Definitely ask."

She spent as much time as she ever had with Esme—she was very careful about that, not cutting her out, as Mabel had when she'd become friends with Max (oh, but it was harder and harder to think about Mabel becoming friends with Max), but going swimming with her and Walter in the river, on trips back to see a more cordial Art in Narrawee, buy toffee apples from the grocer for Halloween (Lauren's favorite time of year), then hatching plans to visit Kate and Verity again to watch *Dumbo*—but felt happy, dizzily happy, that her days were also now so full of *him*.

It was their dawns, though, that she lived for, when it was just the two of them, alone. Occasionally it was cloudy and rained, but they still met. She started coming back from her rides earlier so they could have longer together, but no matter how early she came, he was always there, waiting. They massed up hours on their hay bale, the sun rising, the pair of them filling in each other's gaps, making good the years when accidents of circumstance had conspired to keep them strangers: stories of her family, his family, the challenge of his own early days running the plantation—hard, but never unwelcome ("This is always where I've wanted to be," he said. "Wherever I've gone, this has always been home. . . ."), then her job in Soho, his economics degrees at LSE, Vivian, London . . . They talked and talked, of so much; far too much to remember, and yet, Rose remembered every word they shared.

He told her more about the people in town, those who weren't like Art, but old mates who'd been as furious as him over what they'd all tried to do to Richie, and whom he probably needed to try harder at seeing again. Then Tina from the post office, and her husband, both of whom had been first in line, trying to call everyone off their manhunt.

"But Tina's so unfriendly," said Rose.

"She's not happy," said Max. "I've known her since primary school. She used to tell us all she was going to be famous, a singer. And now she's stuck, on that street . . ."

He shocked her, saying that Aborigines weren't allowed in Narrawee's shops, its hotels, but had to drink in designated black pubs farther away. Going into more detail than Kate ever had, he told her about the huge reserves so many were compelled to live on; the Christian missions that stole children from their families, forcing their parents to let them raise them.

"Plenty are trying to change it," he said, resting his head back against the stable wall, making her care for him even more, just for how much he cared. "There are groups, the AAL, the APA, they work pretty hard for Aborigine rights." He drew a long breath. "They put forward a petition, not long after Walter was born, asking the King to create an Aborigine seat in the House of Representatives."

"But . . ."

"Yeah," he said, "it didn't work." He looked sideways at her. He had the burned side of his face turned toward her. He never hid his scars, like he'd used to. She didn't know when he'd stopped doing that. "They'll keep trying," he said. "We'll all keep trying."

"You don't have a camp here," Rose said. "Kate told me a lot of stations have Aborigine camps."

"We used to. My dad got rid of it, after my grandmother, Vivian's sister, died . . ." He closed his eyes. "God, he'd have hated what happened with Richie."

"Do you think your mum's sorry?"

"Yeah," he said, his chest filling with a sigh. "I think she's really sorry about a lot of things."

She wanted to ask him if he meant blaming him for Jamie's death.

So she did ask him. It was how it had become between them.

She'd come to feel that she could ask him almost anything.

And he told her that he knew his mum was sorry about that, because she'd written to him at the hospital in Alex, after his plane had gone down, saying so.

"Esme says she never says sorry," Rose said.

"Well, she said it to me." He stared into his mug. "She told me she'd never have forgiven herself if I'd died, and hadn't known. I didn't write back. I was in too much pain, and, I don't know . . ." His forehead creased. "I still think she was right . . ."

"No . . ."

"Yeah." He nodded. "Yeah. Jamie hated me, before he did it. I'd made him hate me." His frown deepened. "I'd made him think I hated him."

"He'd have known you didn't." Rose touched her hand to his. "He'd have known . . ."

He looked at her fingers.

Realizing where they were, she moved them, wrapping them back around her own mug.

"Anyway," he said, giving a quick, sad smile, "I told Mum when I got back here that we should forget it, put it behind us . . ."

"Can you?"

"I've been trying. She made it harder, doing what she did with Walter, but I'm trying. I want to forget."

She nodded.

She could sympathize with that.

Other mornings, he spoke more of Egypt, his time in the RAAF, the desert air force: his billet in the dunes, the endless sorties and raids and alarms, the terror and adrenaline and speed of his plane, the bullets that had so often missed him, until they hadn't, then the nights out he'd had with others like Joe's bombardier Charlie, drinking in the bars of Cairo and Alex, dancing, not sleeping, because what was the point in sleep when you didn't know if you were about to do that forever.

"I'm pretty glad you didn't do it forever," Rose said.

He stared upward at the sky he'd fallen from and said, "I'm pretty glad about that too." He smiled. "I used to fly over the pyramids, sometimes, at sundown . . ."

"Yes?" said Rose, tightening her fists on the impulse to reach out again, skim her finger along his cheek.

"Yeah," he said, and as he reminisced about those pyramids, the peace he'd felt, before the Messerschmitts had appeared, she leaned back, watching his face — the glow of the brightening dawn playing on his burned skin, accentuating the firm lines of his jaw, his cheeks — and, remembering the sunrise they'd shared in his plane, said how beautiful those desert sunsets must have been.

"Yeah," he said, turning to look at her, his dark eyes full of the memory: there again, high above the dunes, his wings casting shadows on the undulating sands below. For that moment, it was almost like she was there with him. "They were pretty beautiful."

She talked of her war too, her time in the WAAFs ("God, Rosie," he said, "is there any job you haven't done?"), Ilfratomb, and, without ever planning to, but because it was the way it had become between them, of why she'd ended up there.

He was so incredible, when she told him about that. He didn't become awkward when she spoke, haltingly, of her pregnancy, or impatient when she cried, saying how hideous it had been in that hospital. He just got up, fetched some cloth from the stables, then crouched before her, handing it to her so that she could wipe her eyes.

"I'm sorry," she said, pressing the cloth to her face.

"Don't say sorry," he said. "You don't need to say sorry for being sad about this."

"I feel . . . strange, that I've told you."

"Why?" he asked, softly.

"Because I wasn't married. I'm not married . . ."

"You think I mind about that?" he said.

He didn't seem to.

As she walked slowly back to the house that morning, she reflected that he really didn't seem to mind that she wasn't married at all.

But nor did he love her.

She didn't question anymore how she felt about him. She wasn't sure when she'd stopped trying to fight it — or if there'd even *been* one single moment of her giving in — but she *had* given in, finally accepted what it was that made her go to sleep each night in his bed thinking of him, wake again still thinking of him, and — no matter how much her body ached from so long in the saddle — drag herself up each dawn to go riding, because she just couldn't bear that he'd appear with her cup of tea and she wouldn't be there to take it from him. She loved *him*, of course she loved him: in a deep, drowning, unrecoverable way that she couldn't recall ever loving Xander, which was probably why, for all they'd come to share with one another, she still mentioned Xander to him so very rarely. Even though nothing had ever happened that Xander could take exception to, she knew, she *knew* in the core of her too-full heart that she was betraying him with every word and look she gave to Max.

If he could only see the things that happened in her dreams.

If Max could . . .

But Max couldn't.

He, she'd become heartbrokenly certain, wanted only to be her friend.

For weeks now, she'd been watching him, waiting for him to give some sign that he might welcome more than that. But he — who made her laugh and listened and smiled and teased and brought her cups of tea that were absolutely perfect, but had looked so odd when she'd touched him, and had never touched her, not since that day in his plane, not other than that care-less brush of her back — gave no sign at all.

So she was very careful not to give herself away to him.

She convinced herself that he really *must* have loved Mabel, that he still loved her, and she simply didn't measure up.

"Rosie, I don't think that's true," said Esme, whom Rose eventually con-fided in during their late-evening sewing sessions, knowing she'd go mad if she didn't talk to her about it. "You're beautiful . . ."

"*Mabel* was beautiful . . ."

"So are you," said Esme, snapping a thread, "and kind and funny and you dance really, really well, even if you are useless at making dresses." She smiled. "If I didn't like men so much, I'd be completely in love with you . . ."

Rose had to smile too.

But . . .

"He's not in love with me though, Esme," she said. "Maybe he wanted to try to be, when he first brought me that tea." God, it hurt, saying that. "Maybe he felt . . . I don't know . . . *obliged* to give it a go."

"Rosie — "

"No, Esme, I think he did, and has realized I'm not her, that I can never be her." She laughed, dipping her head so that Esme couldn't see how sad she really was, touching her fingertips to her forehead. "I know I'll never come close for Walter. I don't want to, I shouldn't. But, now there's Max, and I . . . Well, I feel like I'm falling short, all the time, of this . . . this ghost."

Esme reached out, taking her hand.

"You don't fall short for me," she said, squeezing fingers. "I don't know if that helps . . ."

"No," said Rose, joking, since there was little else she could do.

Esme laughed.

"Of course it helps," Rose said, squeezing her fingers back.

"Would you talk to him about it?" Esme asked.

"I can't," said Rose, "promise you won't either . . ."

"Not if you don't want me to . . ."

"I don't. I couldn't stand it coming between us."

"All right," said Esme, nodding, reluctantly. "Then I won't."

"Thank you," said Rose.

Esme kept her word. She never did mention it to Max.

And nor did Rose.

She couldn't stay away from him either, though. Being with him was the sweetest kind of torture, but one she couldn't resist returning for time and time again, morning after morning. Impossible as it was to sit with him, talk to him, hear his husky laugh and never move, as she yearned to move, thread her fingers through his — let her head drop once more on his warm, solid shoulder — it would have been harder to keep any kind of distance.

But she did do something else.

She finally wrote to Xander.

She'd been meaning to ever since he'd wired her, asking her to promise she'd find him after Christmas, and she'd wired him back, promising only that she'd send a letter, and he'd replied saying, fine, write. *Have it your way, sweetheart. You always do.* She hadn't forgotten that letter. She'd tried to finish it countless times, using up sheets of humidity-dampened paper, struggling to find words, any words, the deeper her feelings for Max had become.

One night at the start of November, though, after Esme had gone to bed, and Walter was sleeping, and she was sitting up on Max's mattress, hot and sticky, with only the faintest breeze coming in through the open shutters along with the moonlight, the wheeze of cicadas, the words suddenly came.

She realized, at last, what she needed to say, what she'd long needed to say: that, much as part of her would always regret the happiness they'd lost, they'd grown too far apart to be together again.

> *We've both wanted so desperately to get back what we had, but we're no longer the same people, so I don't believe we can. You've told me you miss the person I was. I'm not sure the person I am now is ever going to be enough for you.*

She paused, looking up at the window, toward the annex, tired, so tired, of not being enough.

You let me down, she continued, returning to the letter, *you let me down when you loved me totally, and it scares me what you might do, loving me something less. I've wanted to trust you. I've wanted so much to trust you, trust us, but I keep failing.* She thought of Sarah's words, about trusting Joe. So easy. *I've realized that it shouldn't be this hard. We both deserve for it not to be this hard.*

> *I want you to be happy. I want us both to be happy.*

> *I'm so sorry, I really am so deeply sorry, that we can't do that for each other.*

She was sorry. She wept as she finished, signing her name, seeing them together in her mind's eye: the nights out and fun that they'd had; him surprising her at her base, getting down on one knee in the field, giving her that diamond in front of all the pilots, *say yes, say yes;* the two of them racing up to his hotel room, kissing before the door was even shut.

Him cradling her in that taxicab on the way to hospital.

You're going to be all right, Rosie. It's all going to be all right.

It hadn't been all right, though.

It wasn't all right now. If it had been, she'd never have fallen as she had for Max. But she had fallen. She wanted to be with him all the time, in ways she wasn't supposed to, and she couldn't remain engaged to one man, longing for another.

She posted the letter the very next day, taking Walter into Narrawee alone since Esme and Hannah were both busy. She posted it, and, sad as she was, she also felt overcome by relief, which made her surer yet that she'd done the right thing.

She was certain she'd done the right thing.

It didn't occur to her, as she left the hot, silent post office, Walter's hand firmly in hers, that, unlike the letter she'd sent Xander from Bombay, this one really would never reach him.

She didn't suspect that Xander, already preparing to leave Cairo, to prove to her that he still loved her totally, wouldn't be in that crazy, terrifying city by the time the words she'd written arrived.

"How about we see if there are any toffee apples left at the grocer?" she said to Walter, and, smiling through her sadness, trusted, absolutely, that for her and Xander's story at least, that letter really was the end.

CHAPTER TWENTY-THREE

She didn't talk to anyone about the letter. Not Max (she didn't know how to bring something like that up without giving too much else away), nor Walter (who hardly needed to be bothered with it), nor Lauren, nor Hannah (obviously), nor Esme either.

Esme, as Rose was to discover when she returned from Narrawee that November morning, suddenly had her own not-very-romantic life to concern her, because Paul, whom Esme hadn't heard from in more than a year, had wired from Sumatra telling her that he needed to marry a local woman who was having his baby, so wanted a divorce. Esme couldn't sue him for adultery—the laws still didn't allow her, or any woman, to do that without also proving their husband had committed a crime (incest, bigamy, that kind of thing)—but Paul could sue her if she gave him grounds, which was exactly what he asked her to do. *Just a letter to my lawyer saying you have another fella* STOP.

"Bloody typical," said Esme, waving the telegraph at Rose from the veranda as Rose pulled up. "He cheats on me, and still manages not to take the blame."

She wasn't upset about it.

She was grinning.

"So bloody relieved," she said, doing a quickstep as she came toward

Rose for a hug. "I've wanted to not be married since the day we did it. I'd rather give him a divorce than him have to die."

Max wasn't quite so happy about the turn of events.

He exploded when, an hour later, he came into the kitchen while Rose and Esme were having a celebratory beer, Walter was playing with Chamberlain, and Esme showed him the telegram.

"Sue *him*," he shouted, making Chamberlain sprint for the door. He slammed the wire down on the kitchen table, as furious as Rose had known him. (He was even more Laurence Olivier, furious; she couldn't help but notice that.) "Sue him, Esme. Do him for cruelty, neglect . . ."

"It'll take too long," Esme said. "I just want it done."

"Not like this," said Max.

"Yes, like this."

"No . . ."

"Yes," said Esme, slamming her own hand on the table, the beer bottles clinking. "Just, *yes*. Now," she took a breath, "do you want a drink?"

Max didn't.

"I want to kill him," he said to Rose the next morning, after a day of him and Esme arguing about it, Lauren, fetched by Hannah, coming to join in, telling Esme that she couldn't let Paul destroy her reputation like this, he might have ruined Jamie's life, but he wasn't to ruin hers (*I will not let him carry on ruining yours*), and Hannah chiming in with her own tuppence worth, saying Esme, so impatient, shouldn't rush this, at which point Rose had taken Walter off to find his new little friends because Esme (highly impatient to be free, *free*) had exploded herself, yelling at her mum particularly that she was sorry she was such a letdown as a daughter, but she wanted this, she *wanted it*, and Lauren was just going to have to deal with it.

"You need to let it go," Rose said to Max now. "She's made up her mind."

"I don't want to let it go." He sat on the hay bale, his head in his hands, shoulders rising and falling in rage. "I've never wanted him near Esme. I've never trusted him, even when we were kids. She was fourteen when he started coming here to see her. *Fourteen*. He was twenty."

"At least Esme won't be tied to him anymore," Rose said. "She can meet someone else . . ."

"She hasn't *done* anything." He pressed his fingers into his scalp. "She's letting him accuse her of something she's never done. . . . If Jamie was here, he'd hate it for her . . ."

Rose wanted to put her arm around him.

She wanted to do that so much.

She pushed her hands underneath her legs.

"Esme's happy," she said. "She's going out later to get us gin for tonight." Rose didn't relish the thought. Truthfully, she was pretty daunted by it. Anyone else, and she'd have had no part of it. "Come and have some . . ."

"Gin?" said Max, raising his head, looking up at her.

"Gin," she said. "Come."

He didn't. He was still too angry.

And Esme wasn't the one to buy the gin in the end.

It was Lauren, full of surprises, who did that, coming into the kitchen to bash the bottle down on the table just as Rose, Walter, Esme, and Hannah were about to eat lunch.

"You're not a letdown as a daughter," Lauren said, looking a flabbergasted Esme in the eye. "I blame myself, for making you think that. I should never have let you marry Paul Butler . . ."

"You tried pretty hard to stop me," Esme said, voice cracking, audibly, with her shock. *You're not a letdown as a daughter.* "You said he'd get bored . . ."

"I never said that . . ."

"Yes . . ."

"No. I told you he'd get fed up, that men like him don't like feeling small. You've always been a hundred times the person he is."

Esme stared.

Rose stared.

Walter and Hannah stared.

"You're well shut of him," said Lauren. "We're all well shut of him, so you can have this," she gestured at the bottle, "on me. Another one on me."

And with that, she went.

"Bugger me," Esme said.

"Bugger me," Rose echoed.

"Bugger me," said Walter, popping a tomato into his mouth.

They all left Esme alone from then on. Even Max said no more to Esme about it, other than that Paul had better stay in Sumatra, not set a foot near her, or him, again. Rose drove Esme into town so that she could send Paul's lawyer word of her *fella*, and that night, once Walter was safely in bed, she took — in Esme's words — a teaspoon of cement to harden up and, toasting her friend's freedom, drank many, *many* glasses of gin.

"How are you feeling?" Max asked her, on the hay bale the next morning.

"Not good," she said. It was her turn to have her head in her hands. "I was so bad I forgot to check my bed for spiders and snakes."

"You don't need to check your bed for spiders and snakes," he said. "You know your hands are shaking . . ."

"I do know that."

"Where's Leon?"

"Inside. I couldn't take him out. Are you laughing at me?" She looked at him through her fingers. "You're laughing."

"Here," he said, still doing it, "take your tea. You should have stayed in bed."

"I didn't want to," she said, too hungover to remember she wasn't meant to be admitting to such things.

The creases around his dark eyes deepened.

He was smiling again, at least.

"You're not really going to Brisbane, are you?" he asked.

"I have to." She, Esme, and Walter were meeting Kate, Verity, and Kate's mum, Ingrid, at the Wintergarden at noon. Bloody *Dumbo*. Even Lauren was coming. She'd asked if she might the night before, as Rose and Esme had been getting stuck into the gin, saying she had some shopping to do. *Only if you don't mind.* "I can't let Walter down. He's been excited . . ."

Somehow, *on a wing and a prayer,* she didn't let Walter down. And nor did Esme, who surfaced at nine, rollers out, sunshades on, ready to go even though her hands were shaking too.

Lauren drove, pronouncing neither of them in any state.

"Fair enough," said Esme.

It wasn't the most comfortable journey. The ute's cabin was steaming hot, the November sun beating through the dusty windscreen, and, as Esme snoozed, Lauren sat awkwardly silent at the wheel, seemingly at a loss for what to say, crammed in such close confines with Rose and Walter. Fortunately, Walter, on Rose's sweaty lap, chatted the entire way, too happy to notice the tension, and they only had to pull over once for Rose to be sick. Rose felt so rotten as she heaved that really, Lauren's silence rather paled by comparison anyway. And she didn't entirely ignore Rose. She handed her a bottle of water, after she'd been sick, gave her shoulder a stiff pat.

"Better out than in," she said.

Kate wasn't in the best state either, when they arrived at the Wintergarden and found her, Verity, and Ingrid waiting on the baking pavement. As Lauren went off to do her shopping, and the children squealed and ran for another look at the *Dumbo* posters, Kate said she'd heard that morning from her husband Tim in Singapore, and he'd told her—in the loosest possible terms, trying to get his wire through the censors—that things were getting tenser, rumors spreading that a Japanese attack on the region was imminent, perhaps on its way before Christmas. She was very worried, as was Rose, for her parents in Malaya. While Ingrid tried to bat away their concerns, saying there was nothing in the papers about any invasion, it didn't make them feel better. As Kate reminded her mum, the papers would hardly report on such a thing.

"God," said Rose, "my head hurts too much for this."

"Let's go into the air-conditioning," said Esme, "get cool at least."

They all managed to perk up a bit for the children's sake, once they were inside the Wintergarden's plush foyer with its framed portrait of the King on the wall, and sweets called Fantales and Jaffas and Minties on sale. Esme bought Fantales, which turned out to be toffees, and Rose Minties (mints); then they carried on into the theater itself, just as an organ with an elderly man in top hat and tails at it rose from the stage, the man playing a short tune.

"Oooooh," said Verity and Walter.

Rose's mood improved in earnest from there, because during the brief newsreel that ran before the picture—so many crackling images of waving, sunburned diggers arriving in the supposed fortress town of Singapore, the jungles of Malaya, then laughing women in overalls working in British munitions factories, building bombs to send to Stalin in Russia—for a few seconds, Winston appeared on the screen, walking along the rubble of a London street, his fingers held up in his trademark "V," and Lionel, *Lionel*, was right behind him, his hair brushed back, three-piece on. His eyes looked right into the camera, smiling, like he'd known when he was doing it that Rose would be sitting where she was, looking straight back at him.

"Rosie," gasped Walter.

"That's my uncle," whispered Rose to Esme and Kate, failing to remember, in her joy at seeing him, that she hadn't told either of them who Lionel was, or that she knew Winston.

"What?" said Esme, not whispering.

"What?" said Kate, just as loud.

"Shhhh," said women sitting all around. "Shhh."

Rose didn't care. She'd seen Lionel, and she was happy, so, so happy. . . .

She remained so when *Dumbo* started. They all enjoyed the beginning: the chugging, heaving train of animals; the stork delivering Dumbo to his mummy. While Walter's lip wobbled precariously, watching Dumbo's mummy cuddling her new little boy, he assured Rose that he was all right, he didn't need to go outside.

But then Dumbo's mummy got taken away from him. Dumbo went to visit Mrs. Jumbo in her jail, and she rocked him in her trunk, singing "Baby Mine," never wanting to let him go, and Walter really did need to go outside.

It didn't surprise Rose. She wasn't far off falling apart herself.

"Oh, Rosie," he said, as she picked him up, tears pouring down his cheeks, "Rosie, I miss my mummy. And I don't want you to ever go. I don't want you to gooooo . . ."

"I know," she said. "I know, little man . . ."

"Shall I come?" Esme and Kate asked.

"Are you all right, Walter?" asked Verity.

"Sit down," came cries, everywhere.

"Oh shut up," Rose snapped at them all. Then, more nicely to the others, "We'll be fine, stay here."

They were fine.

Walter needed a cuddle, that was all: to hear Rose swear to him again that she had no plans to leave, not yet.

"Not ever," he said.

"All right," she said, carrying him down to wait for the others outside, not saying more about it, because it wasn't the time.

Lauren was in the foyer when they got there, knitting, having already finished whatever shopping she'd come to do.

"What's happened?" she asked, standing, shoving her knitting away.

Rose told her, Walter still sniffing in her arms.

Lauren listened, nodded, then said they should wait for a second, and went to speak to the ticket clerk. Rose, thinking she'd gone to ask for a refund, wanted to tell her it didn't matter, but then Lauren was back, and she hadn't been asking for a refund at all.

"That lady," she said to Walter, "has told me Dumbo gets back to his mum again, very happily indeed, at the end of the picture. She has promised me it's a nice ending. Don't you think it would help, Walter, to go back in and see that? Not sit outside in the hot."

He sniffed.

"I think it would help," Lauren said.

"I do too," said Rose, realizing how right Lauren was.

Another sniff.

"I feel very sure about it, Walter," said Lauren.

He looked up at her, face puffy, tearstains all down his round cheeks.

"Will you come too," he asked her, breath shaky, "like Verity's grandma?"

Lauren opened her mouth, then closed it. She didn't seem to know what to say.

Rose, nonplussed, didn't either.

Then Lauren did speak, amazing her more.

"Yes," she said, "all right then. As long as there's a seat."

"Walter can sit on my lap," said Rose, quickly, before she could change her mind. "You can have his."

"Well then," said Lauren, and off they went.

Esme was as stunned as Rose when she saw her mum coming in. She shot Rose a look in the darkness.

Bugger me, that look said.

"Do you want a Fantale, Mum?" she said, out loud.

Lauren nodded. "Yes," she said again. "All right then."

"You can have a Mintie, too," whispered Walter.

"Shhh," said everyone.

Walter, thankfully, remained happy through the rest of the picture, nestled on Rose's lap. ("I really don't want you to go anywhere," he kept whispering to her. "I'm not," she kept whispering back. "I've promised I won't until you say I can." "I won't, Rosie . . ." "Shhh," came everyone else.) Lauren enjoyed it as well. Rose saw that from how much she smiled.

She looked younger, when she smiled. More like Esme.

She cried, though, at the end, when Dumbo was reunited with Mrs.

Jumbo. Rose saw that too, much as Lauren tried to hide her tears, taking a handkerchief from her purse, pressing it to her eyes.

She wanted to say something to her.

It was Walter, though, who spoke.

"Are you all right, Grandma?" he whispered.

"Not really, Walter," Lauren whispered back. "But thank you, very much, for asking me that."

She became easier to be around from then on. There was no grand apology, but she smiled more, at all of them, took to coming by the kitchen for no apparent reason, *just checking how you are*, then up to the stables with more apples for Walter to give the horses, trying, in her own unexpressed way, to make amends.

"I suppose we'd better let her," said Esme at dinner one night, glancing at the drained gin bottle Lauren had bought. *You're not a letdown as a daughter.*

"I suppose we better had," said Rose.

"What did you do to her in Brisbane?" Max asked Rose, his dark eyes warm in the glow of the lamplight.

Rose really couldn't say.

She found it hard to think, when he looked at her like that.

At less distracted moments, she knew, though, that *she* hadn't done anything. It had been Walter who'd won Lauren over. Walter, whom Lauren had watched all these past months, worrying about his cough, his fear of cows, and just hadn't been able to bear—whatever her feelings toward his parents—to see upset.

She really seemed to love seeing him happy.

She never missed an opportunity to watch him play with his friends outside the cottages at dusk. She even brought them jugs of cordial to drink. Increasingly, she talked to Rose while she was there, cautiously at first—saying they'd have to start thinking about schools soon for Walter, talking of the several army procurement orders that had come in, the extra laborers they'd need to meet the deadlines—but then more freely, commenting that it felt like just yesterday that she'd been watching Max and Jamie play tag as the children were now.

"I can imagine," said Rose, softly.

"Just yesterday," said Lauren, shaking her head. Then, as though the simple act of remembering was too painful (which Rose was sure it was), she drew a sharp breath and asked Rose if Esme had been winding her up, or if she really did know Winston Churchill.

"Esme wasn't winding you up," Rose said, and told Lauren about how she and Joe had used to ride at Blenheim.

"And did you know how lucky you were?" Lauren asked.

"I think so," said Rose, feeling her own stab of pain at the memory of Joe as he'd been then: happy, utterly carefree, before he'd learned to fly, or heard of such a thing as a Wellington bomber.

Lauren asked about him, often, and Rose's parents, inquiring as to whether she'd heard anything more from them.

Rose had: worrying messages from her parents echoing Tim's words about the growing threat of a Japanese invasion (*Stay safe where you are for now darling* STOP), and even more concerning ones from Joe, who suddenly took to wiring her that November; strange wires that told her how much he loved her, how much he needed to trust she'd be happy, and felt too much like goodbyes.

"Tell him they're not," said Lauren. "Never leave a word unsaid, not with the world the way it is." She paused, and Rose, sure she was thinking of the letter she nearly hadn't got to Max on time, no longer felt an almost-pity for her, but something much truer. "Tell him."

"You should," said Max on their hay bale. Max who'd laughed, when he'd found out from Esme about Winston. ("Any more surprises?" he'd asked Rose. "No," Rose had said. Famous last words, as it turned out.) "He's probably too knackered to believe he can keep coming back," Max said now. "Make him believe."

Rose tried, sending Joe several wires of her own (*You will make it through* STOP *I need you to not give up* STOP *Never give up* STOP) and to Lionel and Sarah as well, saying how concerned she was, asking them to visit Joe and make sure he was holding up.

He's exhausted, sweetheart, said Lionel, *wrung out like everyone* STOP *Will keep doing everything I can* STOP.

Am as worried as you, said Sarah. *He told me to move on if anything happens to him* STOP *Have told him I would never move anywhere without him* STOP.

Thank you, Rose wrote back to her, *thank you so much for telling him that.*

She spent a fortune on it all, but didn't have to worry about that, at least, because Esme insisted on giving her more money, saying she'd spoken to her mum, and to Max, and they'd all agreed she was owed it.

"Not wages," Esme said, closing Rose's hand around the envelope of Australian pounds, "don't view it like that, but a thank-you, for being here. We'd never have managed without you, and I for one don't want you leaving because you can't afford to stay. Besides," she smiled, "Christmas is coming . . ."

Christmas was.

As December drew closer, and Rose kept up with her dawn rides, her trysts with Max ("G'day," he'd say, smiling, taking Leon's reins. "Hello," she'd say, dismounting, falling apart inside), the summer intensified, the days scorching at times: the kind of heat Esme had warned Rose of when she'd first arrived. *We get these westerlies, the temperature goes well over a hundred, even in the shade. The only place you want to be is in the ocean.* They didn't go to the ocean, because Lauren, worried that the lax petrol rationing laws would become stricter, should war really break out in the Pacific, asked them to be careful with fuel. They swam more in the river instead, not with Max — he never came, no matter how much Rose urged him to — but sometimes with Hannah in her thick woolen suit, even occasionally Lauren, all of them splashing and diving, the heat blazing down from the sun above, across from the center of the continent, so intense that parts of the drive melted, and the air hung in a wavering, shimmering blanket over the gold fields, the trees, barely even cooling at night.

"It'll be freezing in England now," said Rose, staring up at the moon one night at the start of December, sitting with Max on the porch steps, the hammock creaking in the stiff breeze behind them. It was another habit they'd fallen into, coming outside to talk on the evenings he stayed for dinner. Esme would join them at first, then make some excuse to leave. ("You don't have to," Rose would tell her. "I know that," she'd say.) "Maybe snowing."

"Do you miss it?"

"A bit," Rose admitted. "It's odd, being so hot, and Christmas on the way."

"Wish you were there?" he asked, in a way that made her turn, look him in the eye, and wonder if, maybe, *maybe*, he cared about the answer more than he was letting on.

"No," she said.

"Good," he said.

And for that second, just that second, as he smiled at her, and the thick, hot air blanketed her damp skin, she stopped feeling like she was in the shadow of a ghost.

She didn't feel like she fell short of anyone at all.

"And what happened then?" asked Esme, the next day.

"I realized it was probably just wishful thinking," Rose said, "and asked him what he wanted for Christmas."

"What did he say?"

"Nothing."

"He didn't answer?"

"No," said Rose. "He said he wanted nothing for Christmas. God—" She wiped her forehead. "It's so hot."

It was the morning of 6 December, and even at nine, they were both dripping with sweat as they walked Walter, scampering ahead, up to meet Lauren at a shed near the stables.

It was a familiar journey. They'd been making it every morning for some time, thanks to Esme finally asking Lauren, when they'd returned from *Dumbo*, how she'd got her to conquer her fear of cows, and Lauren had said, "With the calves, of course," like she'd been waiting, *waiting*, for someone, anyone, to ask her that very question. She'd had Walter up helping her bottle-feed the runts Max had separated from the rest of the stock ever since.

And Walter adored helping his grandma who wasn't really his grandma (but who he called "Grandma," because Lauren never told him not to); cautious as he remained of the big cows, he had no reservations (*no worries*) about sitting in the hay with their calves, their downy heads in his lap, Lauren leaning over him, guiding his dimply hand with the bottle.

It was strange for Rose, sitting at the edge of that oven-like shed with Esme, watching the two of them together. It wasn't just that it made her think of her own baby, seeing those tiny, vulnerable little things suckling their milk—although it filled her with such sadness, looking at them; such visceral longing—but, the more Walter smiled and nodded, listening to Lauren, giggling, she couldn't help but reflect on how all right he really would be without her now, in this place that no longer felt unhappy at all.

She knew he wanted her to stay, she never doubted that, but, if she had to leave tomorrow, he'd survive it, she was certain. He'd be fine with Esme, Max, and Lauren. More than fine.

Loved.

"Every bit as much as he deserves," Vivian had said.

She'd been right. She really had been right.

Rose couldn't be melancholy about it. She loved that he was loved.

But she didn't want to leave him either. Not tomorrow. Not ever.

She didn't want to leave any of them. She didn't want to leave Australia. Somewhere along the line, this land, with its lush beauty, its peace and gigantic sky, had come to feel like her home, too.

"Then just stay," said Esme. "Stay . . ."

"I can't," Rose said. It would destroy her to go on much longer, guest that she was, hoping to one day be enough for Max. What if he met someone, down the line? Someone who didn't fall short. What would she do then? "I need to get on, work out what comes next. I don't think I'll ever be able to do that here. I love it too much . . ."

"Well, you might have to keep loving it," said Esme. "If the Japs attack, it won't be safe to sail."

"It wasn't safe when Walter and I came over," Rose pointed out.

"It'll be even worse," said Esme.

Was she a witch?

"Maybe I am," said Esme.

It certainly felt like she had the sight, when, little more than a day after she'd spoken of a Japanese attack, with the Siberian winter storming, and the newspapers jubilantly reporting of a massive Russian counteroffensive against the Germans in Moscow, the news came over the World Service that the Imperial Japanese Army finally *had* made their move, and not only in Malaya, but Hawaii too, during their dawn of 7 December.

"Quick," screamed Hannah, from the kitchen, summoning Rose, who'd been upstairs reading with Walter, down. "There are ships on fire, *ships*."

"What ships?" said Walter, running after Rose.

"What ships?" said Esme, coming out from the office.

Then they stopped in the kitchen doorway, seeing Hannah by the wireless, stooping to listen at the speaker, her finger to her lips. The clipped British voice filled the hot kitchen, and Rose felt herself pale, hearing him tell of Japanese forces landed on the monsoon-whipped Malayan peninsula, bombs over Singapore, and a place called Pearl Harbor in flames, the American Pacific fleet under attack, ongoing efforts to rescue trapped men, so much bravery and determination from valiant pilots, sailors, doctors. . . .

The words kept coming, filling Rose with terror, for her parents in Malaya most of all. Were they safe? Near the fighting? The newsreader talked on, of huge numbers of American casualties, a meeting between Roosevelt and Winston, and she remembered her father's words, back in Colombo, about the US entering the war. *I fear they're going to need something really very awful to push them.* This was it. She had no doubt, this was it.

It was.

The next day, the US declared war on Japan, and Germany declared war on the US. Almost the entire American Pacific fleet had been destroyed at Pearl Harbor, and news from the British-held Far East was hardly better, where, to Rose's growing fear, the BBC reported that the Japanese were continuing to press on with their advance through Malaya, their assault on Singapore. None of them listened to jazz anymore when the news was on. Rose never missed a broadcast. As she sat beside the wireless's crackling speaker, often with Esme — Max, too, whenever work around the station allowed — she tried to picture the chaos unfolding in the jungle, the streets of Singapore, drained by foreboding for her mum and dad.

Stella wired, the same day that the news broke that the only two British battleships in the Far East — the HMS *Repulse,* and the *Prince of Wales* — had been sunk by the Japanese. She assured Rose that she was safely out of Malaya, in Singapore, and Henry was on his way, too, with his unit in a rear, still-peaceful section of Malaya, near the Singapore causeway.

Do not worry about the bombs STOP You survived them in London and we can here STOP We will be all right STOP

Rose tried to take comfort from that wire. And from the Australian newspapers' claims that the Allied forces would see the Japanese off in no time, helped by the shiploads of Australian recruits leaving for the region, sixteen-year-old Hamish from Narrawee among them. He'd gone into Brisbane, convinced a recruiter there that he was old enough.

"How the hell did he do that?" said Max, when Esme came back from town with the news. Paul's sister — fractionally friendlier since Esme had agreed to shoulder the blame for her and Paul's divorce — had told her about it.

"I don't think they're too fussy about age these days," said Esme, going to the sink, splashing water on her hot face.

"Christ," said Max. "What's wrong with him?"

"He's invincible, of course," said Lauren, also there. "He's sixteen."

"His mum's beside herself, apparently," said Esme, reaching for a towel, frowning. "I hope he'll be all right."

So did Rose. She hoped that by the time Hamish got to Malaya, the Japanese really would have been well and truly *seen off*.

It felt less likely with each new day, though, because the Allied army kept retreating, and the Japanese pushed closer to Singapore. There were no reinforcements to spare from Britain, with fighting still so intense in Africa and Russia; the Americans were still too far away to help either, and so much of their fleet had been destroyed.

"I'm scared," Rose said to Max. "I'm really scared Singapore's going to fall . . ."

"I know," he said, and didn't try to tell her it would be all right, not when they both knew that sometimes the worst really did happen. Like it had happened to him, to millions already, and to so many at Pearl Harbor.

Like it happened again, on another hot, hot evening, in the middle of December.

The wire came just as Rose had taken Walter to bed, and was heading out to join Esme on the veranda, already there with a jug of ice water. Max, who'd had a late stop mustering up-station for one of the new army orders, was on his way back to the house from his plane. It was him Rose watched — his silhouette against the dark bulk of the barn, the purple-blue sky — as the motorbike roared through the gates.

She feared, the second she heard its engine, that it was bad news. She'd been waiting too pensively for it to arrive to believe that it could be anything else.

It was what made her so hesitant, taking the wire that the man (discomfortingly, the same one who'd sneered at Walter) held out to her. She was terrified it was about her parents: a message from her mother, telling her that her father had been hurt, or worse. . . .

But the wire wasn't from her mother.

It wasn't from her father. Or from Lionel.

It wasn't from Sarah either.

And it wasn't from Joe.

Joe had said all of his goodbyes.

No, the wire, which Rose opened, then let flutter to the ground, was from Bella.

CHAPTER TWENTY-FOUR

It was the first time since they'd flown that Max held her, really held her.

Even as she let the wire fall, he was running toward her, catching her as she bent over, folding his arms around her, picking her up, cocooning her while she wept for her happy, brilliant, laughing, exhausted, terrified brother, who, like the rest of his poor, poor crew, was apparently never going to be safely home again.

> Shot down over enemy territory STOP Deeply regret to say no one bailed out STOP All engines and tail lost STOP Plane in blind spin STOP Rosie I am sorry STOP

He held her all night.

Esme stayed with them too, not leaving Rose's side, but telling her over and again that she needed to keep hoping, believe this mightn't be the end. It really mightn't be the end.

"They told us Max was dead, before we found out he was alive," she said.

"Really?" sobbed Rose.

"Really," said Esme. "Ten days, we thought he was gone."

"You've never told me that . . ."

"Now you know," said Esme.

"I was in the desert," said Max. "Walking . . ."

"You *walked?*" said Rose, crying more.

"You can get out of a spin," he said. "I've done it. It's possible . . ."

"With no tail?" Rose said, staring up at him through her tears, desperate to believe him. "Is it possible then?"

"Everything's possible," he said.

"In a Wellington?" she said, her fingers digging into his arm, forgetting his burned skin, entreating him to convince her. "Have you flown one?"

Say yes, she thought, *please say yes.*

"No," he said, not wincing at the pressure of her fingers. "I haven't. But it sounds like your brother's pretty good at it, to have survived this long."

"He must be," said Esme. "If he's anything like you, Rosie, he won't have given in. You've been telling him not to do that. Lots. I bet he hasn't. I bet he's hiding somewhere now, working out what to do. Don't you want to bet on that too?"

Rose did. So much.

But . . .

"No one bailed out. Bella said that." She pointed at the telegram, still lying on the floor. "No one bailed."

"No one saw, maybe," said Max. "What if it was dark?"

"I hate the thought of him scared," she said. "I hate it so much. I keep seeing him at the controls, his face, looking at the ground . . ." She put her hands over her own face. "I can't stand that he was scared."

"He won't have been looking at the ground," said Max.

"How do you know?"

"Because I wasn't," he said. "I didn't. I looked up, at the sky. He'll have been doing the same, getting the hell out of that plane, Charlie with him . . ."

"But no one bailed out . . ."

"Rosie, you don't know that," said Max. "You don't. And if he didn't give up, then you definitely can't."

She didn't tell him how much his holding her meant, that night, and he, who let her go at dawn, then stepped back, dipping his head, seeming to absorb their intimacy — that it had occurred — never attempted to hold her again.

Nor, though, did he stop refusing to let her believe Joe was dead. Esme didn't either. They would not allow her to do it. Lauren and Hannah — who'd grieved for Max, only to be given him back when they'd been told he'd arrived in hospital—were just as determined, and Walter, poor little Walter, who'd just about had enough of death, went right along with them.

Max was the one to tell him what had happened, insisting that Rose let him do it for her when she finally headed to bed that daybreak.

"Joe's not upstairs, Rosie," Walter said when he came to wake her at lunchtime, a cup of tea that had been brewed perfectly carefully balanced on a tray before him. She could hear Hannah moving around in the kitchen downstairs, Bill yelling out to someone to get him some onions. *Life,* going on. It felt so heartless. "His plane was really, really something," Walter continued. "You didn't see inside it, but I did, and I'm sure it kept him safe."

"Did Uncle Max tell you to say that?" she asked, her eyes swollen and sore.

"Yes. But I'm definitely sure, too."

"Thank you, little man," she said, taking the tea before he dropped it, hugging him. "Thank you. I'm glad you're sure."

Lionel was every bit as steadfast in his belief that Joe was on his way home.

They went down over France STOP, he wired, later that day. *France is a land full of heroes* STOP *Our men smuggled back all the time* STOP *On last radio contact Joe was still battling to get control of plane* STOP *We must trust he did* STOP.

Stella, still alone in Singapore, waiting for Henry, certainly trusted (*Will not believe he is gone* STOP *I have not held my son for the last time* STOP), as did Sarah (*Not moving on anywhere* STOP *Will go and find him if I have to* STOP), but Rose couldn't, and it made her feel so lonely, cut off by her grief, her abject failure to have any faith in her brother's welfare at all.

Only Xander seemed to accept he was really gone.

Xander, who'd read Joe's name in the casualty lists, and was devastated for Rose (STOP) but who hadn't got her letter, breaking things off between them, and never would, because he'd been at sea through all his long silence these past weeks, having left his newspaper (*left* it), he said to come to her, only then his ship had docked in Singapore just as the Japanese had attacked, and his newspaper had taken him back on, asked him to stay in Singapore awhile, report on the battles from the room they'd put him up in at Raffles.

"Does he always come up smelling of flowers?" Esme asked, when Rose numbly showed her his wire.

"Not always," Rose said, her voice flat to her own ears, thinking of how Winston and Lionel had tried to ostracize him after she'd left hospital. "A lot of the time, though." She read his wire over, trying to make sense of his newspaper having known he'd arrived in Singapore in the first place. "He must have contacted his editor," she said. "Offered to stay."

"Decided you could wait," said Esme.

"I suppose so," said Rose, and wanted to be relieved that he had, but felt odd, so odd, that he'd ever given up his post for her, sailed as far as Singapore.

Had he changed, as much as that?

Did he truly love her, as much as that (even if not enough to get all the way to Australia)?

The questions unsettled her. The thought of him so much closer, in the same city as her mother, believing them still engaged, unsettled her. Perhaps if she hadn't been so flattened by her grief for Joe, her fear for her parents, she'd have worried more about it, wondered what might come next for the two of them.

As it was, she thought only of whether Lauren would mind her using up some fuel to go to the post office, acknowledge Xander's wire, and reply to Lionel's, her mother's, and Sarah's as well.

Lauren didn't mind, but she wasn't having Rose driving anywhere alone.

"I'll take you," said she, who hadn't been into Narrawee since Jamie had died.

She was kind the entire way, not talking in the ute's sun-soaked cabin, just patting Rose's hand occasionally, which made it very hard for Rose not to cry. Walter wasn't with them. Max, who knew only that Rose had messages to send, but hadn't asked her who to—maybe he didn't want to know—had taken him down to the barn to help him tag the new calves. Rose wished *she* didn't know that's what they'd be doing. Even in the state she was in, she couldn't forget that Mabel had once sat in that barn with Max tagging calves, on the day of her grandfather's funeral. "She hung around there the whole time," Esme had said. "Jamie went out drinking in the end . . . couldn't stand that she wanted to be with Max." It was impossible for Rose not to torture herself with whether Max remembered her being with him there, too.

She supposed he must.

And it hurt.

It really hurt that while she was with Lauren, he was with Mabel's son, thinking of Mabel.

It hurt the whole drive through.

It was still hurting when, with Lauren waiting for her in the ute, she went into the busy, stuffy post office and, ignoring the long looks everywhere, scribbled out her various messages, leaving Xander's until last. She kept her reply short—thanking him for his, saying how odd it was that he was in the same city as her mother, telling him to please stay safe, *Am too sad to write more than that now* STOP—then handed it to Tina, and gladly let him, and her failed attempt to break their engagement, fall from her aching mind.

She couldn't think about it more than she already had. Certainly not in the post office, because Tina—rude, cold Tina—chose that moment to be nice for once, patting Rose's hand across the counter, like Lauren had patted her hand on the drive, only this time the gesture, so unexpected, really did make Rose crumble.

"I'm sorry," she said, tears streaming down her face. "I'm so sorry."

"Nothing to apologize for," said Tina, while almost everyone else continued staring, still too resentful to be anything but hostile.

Only one other woman stepped forward: one whom Rose hadn't seen before, but who handed her a kerchief, and Lauren told Rose afterward was sixteen-year-old Hamish's mum.

Lauren, who'd left the solitude of the ute, and was suddenly there too.

"Come on," she said, pushing through the stares she'd avoided for years, putting her arm stiffly around Rose's waist. "Come on now. Let's get you home."

That was the last time that Rose permitted herself to fall apart. She knew she had to keep going, if only for Walter, still so sweetly, innocently set on the idea that they'd hear any day that Joe was hidden in a French café, eating baguettes and cheese (Esme's story; it was a nice one). Rose couldn't ruin that for him. At Max's urging, she started riding at dawn again, not only to see him, as she *needed* to see him, but because when she rode in the heat of the rising sun, she felt closer to Joe. The faster she went, the more breathless she became, the less she believed he was up in the endless sky, looking down at her; she saw his face in her mind's eye instead, listened to his voice yell at her to keep her heels down, just as he'd used to back at Blenheim, and the strangest thing happened: she discovered hope.

"I prefer hoping," she said to Max, on their hay bale.

"I prefer you hoping too," he said, the touch of his eyes all she was going to get.

She'd resigned herself to that now.

He'd been so careful about never so much as brushing her hand since those hours he'd held her that it was hard to imagine he ever would again ("I wanted to," he'd eventually admit, too late. "But I still didn't know . . . And you were so sad . . ."); it made her sadder, but her hope, her hope for Joe, made her stronger.

She started managing to eat again ("Good girl," said Hannah), smile, sometimes, laugh, even: occasionally, guiltily. (*Don't be guilty,* Joe silently told her.) But much as she hoped, no telegram came saying that he'd miraculously been found. The Japanese pushed closer to Singapore, and no wires arrived from anyone, other than from Lionel, telling Rose how impossible it was proving to find out if her mother was still in the city, or had left on one of the ships now evacuating civilians, or if her father had even made it out of Malaya.

Complete chaos there STOP

Desperate, Rose wired Xander again, begging him to find her parents, send her news.

Will try, he said, STOP.

But after that, there was nothing from him either, and she grew afraid for him too. The silence, from all of them, was terrifying, made so much worse because she couldn't make head nor tail of what was actually going on in the battle. All through that strained, hot December, the news reported ongoing fighting in the jungle, but there was no detail, no information on what units were involved, or how bad the raids on Singapore itself had become. While Paul remained safe in still-peaceful Sumatra ("Trust Paul," said Esme), none of them knew how long that would last, and Kate's husband, Tim, who'd been moved to fight in Malaya, was shot at the start of the third week of December.

"He's coming home," said Kate, beside herself, down the telephone, "but I don't know if he'll make it. Dad spoke to someone, and they said that ships trying to leave harbor are being sunk. The planes get them . . ."

"He'll be all right," Rose tried to tell her, but the words caught in her throat, because all she could think about was the possibility of her parents being killed on one such ship. She couldn't lose them. She *couldn't*. She didn't want Xander hurt either. She never wanted that for him. . . .

And yet, haunted as she was by her fear, she *kept going*, like Kate kept going, like Lauren had in the last war, like millions did every day, *hoping* Joe and her parents were too. She didn't forget Christmas, or that Vivian had kept Mabel's death from Walter the year before so as not to ruin his for him. *I couldn't abide Christmas to be the time he lost her.* Rose was resolved that if she'd been able to brave-face it, so could she.

"That's the spirit," said Esme.

Together, they made paper chains to decorate the house, finished bright sundresses to wear on Christmas Day, and a new yellow shirt for Walter, along with some shorts that wouldn't be too short for him. Hannah knocked up mince pies, and Max and Bill went out to cut down a tree for the drawing room: a different kind of fir to the ones Rose was used to, much bushier, with a different scent, and insects lurking in its branches that bit her on the arm ("Only you," said Esme. "Only you . . ."), but a beautiful fir nonetheless. Lauren brought down boxes of glass baubles from the attic, and said that, since Walter was the youngest, he should be the one to put the fairy on the top of the tree. She lifted him up as carols played on the wireless, filling the blazing-hot room, and, once she'd helped him position the fairy, brought him back down, smiled, and pecked his cheek with a kiss.

Max caught Rose's eye, raised a brow.

She arched hers.

Esme pulled a face at them both.

Bugger me.

It was on another day that Esme and Rose took Walter with Lauren into Brisbane, burning another tank of fuel so that they could visit Verity and Kate ("Tim's ship's out," Kate said, running to greet them in the driveway, grinning. "He's really on his way." Rose was happy for her, she was), then heading into town to do their Christmas shopping. The city had changed since November. There were new signs up everywhere notifying of "brownout" restrictions to safeguard against Japanese air raids, and thick curtains for sale in the haberdasher's. The recruitment queues were longer than ever: packed with invincible-feeling boys who looked as young as Hamish, and several Aborigine men, one of whom they saw being turned away as he, with his skin, was, unlike the sixteen-year-olds, not wanted.

Some in the queue tried to stick up for him. "Come on, mate," they said to the recruitment officer, "let him." The officer was having none of it, though. "No black fellas," he said.

"Are you hungry, Walter?" said Lauren, pulling his attention from the argument.

"I am, yes," said Walter, always hungry.

"This way, then," said Lauren, and they went for afternoon tea in the very refined Lennon's Hotel, Lauren giving the maître d' a look that *dared* him to send Walter away, the four of them sitting down to scones in a dining room that had enough pressed tablecloths and shining silverware to rival the Goring's.

"I brought you here once, Esme," Lauren said.

"Did you?" said Esme, her mouth full of scone.

Lauren nodded, not looking at her as she spread jam and cream on her own scone. "You were about Walter's age. You smashed your cup on the floor."

"Oh," Esme said, and sounded so deflated, Rose felt awful for her. It was obvious she'd been hoping for a nicer story.

"You were a nightmare," said Lauren, disappointing her more, "you really were . . ."

"I'm sorry," said Esme.

"It wasn't your fault," said Lauren, and then did look at her. "I expected you to be too grown-up, right from when you were a baby. Walter's made me realize how little you were . . ."

"Oh," said Esme again, still with her scone in her mouth.

"It wasn't fair," said Lauren. "I wasn't fair to you. Now here," she reached out, placed the scone she'd been loading up with jam on Esme's plate. "Eat up."

"I think that's about as much of a sorry as I'm going to get," whispered Esme to Rose as they left.

"Is it enough?" Rose whispered back.

"It's going to have to be," said Esme. "I suppose it'll do."

"Would you ask your mum to move back into the house for Christmas?"

"Ooh." Esme pulled a face. "No, let's not get ahead of ourselves . . ."

Rose didn't push it. Lauren remained in her cottage, and life back at the plantation continued much as it had, just with Walter getting increasingly excited about what Santa (as everyone in Australia called Father Christmas) was going to bring him, and the party he'd been promised they'd have with all the workers on the station on Christmas Day. His excitement grew when a parcel arrived for him from London, sent back in July, full of tantalizingly wrapped gifts that Rose put beneath the tree, all of them labeled, "From Pia, Lester and Catherine, with our love." He never tired of sitting beside the tree, feeling those gifts, trying to guess what was inside, and wrote a thank-you card for Rose to send back to them all, complete with a drawing of a kangaroo and him, standing at a safe distance. Every morning, he opened the doors of the snowy Advent calendar Hannah had bought him, and each day he skipped along with Rose for their sweaty trips to the river, chatted with Bill in his kitchen, played with his friends, and helped Max deliver the runts—who were now strong enough to go out to pasture—back to the fields.

"Brilliant job, mate," said Max, lifting the calves over the fence with his warm strong arms that Rose imagined every night were around her. "You can do this again next year. Now, I've gotta go, but I'll see you at dinner." He looked at Rose. "See you then, Rosie."

She nodded. "See you then."

He was running off more, she'd noticed, busier than ever, he said, with all the dry weather, and the new army orders that kept coming in. He'd be away too for several days from Boxing Day, not for work, but an overdue checkup with a specialist in Sydney that he didn't like talking about, other than to say he needed to get ahead of it. She could see he *was* busy—galloping and hollering with the other stockmen, flying off to other parts of the station, making sure the cattle were getting enough water, moving them from pasture to pasture, tagging those ready for market (*poor cows*)—but she feared he'd grown to feel awkward with her again too, uncomfortable after the night he'd held her. ("Yeah, Rosie," he'd come to say, "I was pretty bloody uncomfortable.") He still made time to take Walter riding, though. And when he did, she always asked to go with them, unable to resist any chance to be where he was.

Whatever his discomfort, he always let her.

"Ready?" he'd say as she climbed up into Leon's saddle, smiling at her from beneath his hat, one hand holding his reins, the sun behind him. "Feeling all right?"

"Yeah," she'd say. "I'm all right."

And he'd tease her, telling her she was getting an Australian accent.

When he did that, smiled, she truly managed to forget, for the sweetest second, that Joe had vanished in a blind spin, bombs were falling on Singapore, and that it had been almost a fortnight since she'd heard a word out of that tiny island that probably wasn't a fortress at all.

But, before she knew it, it was 22 December, and still no news had arrived.

Two other letters of note did come that day, though.

The first was delivered early, for Esme, by courier: papers sent from Paul's lawyer, officially setting in motion their divorce.

"Yes," said Esme, running into the kitchen, where Rose and Walter were still having breakfast. "The very, very best of presents. More gin tonight."

"Absolutely not," said Rose.

"It'll do you good."

"It never does me any good . . ."

"It doesn't do either of you any good," said Hannah, coming in with a basket full of eggs and a sniff.

The second envelope that came that day was for Rose, and arrived much later, with the rest of the Lucknows' post. Rose was in the hammock with Walter when it came. She didn't pay much attention as Lauren sorted through the mail at the porch. She was engrossed in writing a letter of her own, to Joe, packed full of the things she'd realized she hadn't told him — about her life here, Max, what he'd done to her, for her — and which she was still trying to believe she'd never send, because it was too personal, but would tell him about instead. Walter, opposite her, was similarly caught up, coloring in his drawing pad: a Christmas present for Rose that she wasn't allowed to peek at.

"Here," said Lauren, pulling Rose's attention from her writing (*when I'm with him, I feel like anything is possible: so much happiness, adventures, babies . . . you getting out of that spin*), handing her the envelope.

"Oh my God," said Rose, setting her pen down, seeing the embossed London address on the seal. "It's from Vivian's lawyer . . ."

"Yes," said Lauren, tightly, "I saw that. I owe him a letter myself." She didn't say what about, but Rose, knowing her as she did now, thought that perhaps it would be an apology, even if not in so many words. "I'll leave you to read," Lauren said, with a pat to Rose's shoulder. "I hope it gives you something to make you smile."

Rose wasn't sure it would, but she sat up straighter, the hammock rocking beneath her, her hands trembling, impatient to see at long last what Mr. Yates had said.

His message was short, almost as short as his wires had been, but Rose wasn't disappointed. *His* letter, she quickly saw, wasn't the point. It was a mere covering note, apologizing for subjecting her to such a long wait — *the post is the post, and Vivian in any case wished this to find you only once you had had time to settle* — with another sealed envelope beneath it: thick, made of expensive parchment, bearing just two single words on the front.

Dearest Rosie.

Rose's eyes filled with ready tears, sure, even before she opened the envelope, that it had a letter inside from Vivian.

She wasn't disappointed in that, either.

Vivian hadn't just disappeared, left her without a word.

She'd written before she'd gone. Or, her doctor had, telling Rose in a covering note of his own that Vivian had dictated her letter to him over the course of the days leading up to Rose and Walter's departure, and her death. The date on his note was 8 April. Rose placed it easily. How could she not? It was just after she'd seen Joe for the last time at his base, come back and admitted to Vivian that Walter had found out about Australia, and that she'd promised him that she'd remain with him for as long as he needed her to.

"I'm sure Walter will be fine," Rose had said.

"Yes," Vivian had replied. "I have the strongest feeling he's going to be."

Rose looked across at him in the hammock, coloring, smiling, the sunshine seeping through the shade of the veranda canopy, illuminating his cherubic face, his black curls. It was just the way she'd pictured him the night they'd arrived in Lance's cab, in the hail and lightning. And here he was . . . Happy, really, really happy.

She reached up, wiped her wet eyes with the back of her hand, then, setting the doctor's message aside, turned to Vivian's.

I need to keep this briefer than I would like. There is much I want to tell you, to thank you for, but talking is so very hard, I will have to hold faith that you understand how deep my gratitude to you runs.

It runs very deep, my dear.

What I must not fail to do though, is explain. Not about why I have sent Walter to my family, his father's home, because I believe that by now you will have concluded what I am certain of: that it is the very best place he can be. I could have had him adopted by well-meaning parents here, but they might have ended up being the sort who don't believe in pinwheels and yellow brick roads, and I cannot tolerate that for him. I cannot die wondering if he will be loved enough. I will die knowing he is going to a place he will be cherished. It will take time, and I'm sorry for that, but I know you will help him through it. I feel sure that by the time you are reading this, you will have already helped him through it. I trust in you, Rosie. I trust in my family: my darling Max, and Esme who I feel I know, and Lauren too. For all she has refused to take Walter, she has written to me many times over the years, long before I had Max with me here, and I do not doubt her heart. I do not doubt that she will change her mind about caring for Walter, once she meets him. I believe she wants to have her mind changed.

"How?" Rose whispered, glancing across at Lauren, now opening the post at the veranda table, her head dipped, her expression unguarded; at ease. "How were you so sure?"

Vivian went on, telling her.

Mabel cared for Lauren, very much. Enough to have brought the rabbit she made with her here when she left Australia, giving it to Walter the day he was born. While she never forgave that Lauren didn't defend Walter's father, she spoke of her kindness often, telling me how hard Lauren had always worked to make her feel at home, and make up for Jamie's neglect. She grieved, endlessly, at the hurt she'd caused her, particularly Lauren's devastation over the grandchild she'd thought Mabel was giving her, and would, I am certain, agree with my decision to give Walter to her now. She knew Lauren loved her. I know Lauren loved her. It is this more than anything that convinces me she will be ready to love her son.

I also believe she wishes to make amends for what happened to Walter's father. Max wrote to me, saying how sorely she regretted her part in it, telling me she wept when he broke the news to

her of Walter's birth. Mabel became upset when I showed her that
letter, desperate to believe that Lauren truly did wish Walter well,
and so sad, too, that Max hadn't written to her. He never did. They
never wrote to each other, not after what happened between them
when Mabel left him at the port. Yet another regret...

Rose read those words twice, three times.

What? she wanted to demand of the letter. *What happened between them*
at the port?

I told Mabel, Vivian went on, shedding no further light,

that she should write to Lauren at least, admit how sorry she was
about Jamie, but Mabel couldn't accept that Lauren would want to
hear from her, or that she hadn't left it too late to say such things.
Rosie, my dear, it is only too late to change what you must once
you are dead, and since I for one am not dead yet, I have told Lau-
ren myself how sorry Mabel was for the heartbreak she left behind.
And whatever Lauren's resistance, I insist on granting her this
chance to right her own wrongs, make them good through giving
Walter the family he deserves.

What I cannot do is apologize to you in person for the truths
I have concealed, but please permit me do it now. I have only not
been open about where you are headed because I fear that if I was,
you would be horrified, and whisk Walter off with you, back to
Ilfracombe if you had to, and I believe so strongly that returning
to the life you were trapped in would be the very worst thing for
you, as well as him. I worry about you, Rosie. I have lived a long
time, and come across so much goodness that I know when I am in
the presence of it, and also recognize a kindred spirit in need. The
first day you arrived here, when I watched you getting soaked,
looking up at Walter's pinwheels, I felt such protectiveness toward
you. If I'd been stronger, I'd have run downstairs, hastened you in.
I still feel that protectiveness now. I hear your voice, everywhere in
this house, how wonderful you are with Walter, the happiness you
give to everyone around you, and yet how deeply sad you are, how
much in need of this chance to begin again.

I am an interfering old woman, but I adore that I have been able to give you this chance to begin again.

I told you once that you reminded me of Naomi and Mabel, do you remember?

"Yes," whispered Rose. "Yes I do."

It is because of your loneliness.

Another tear trickled down Rose's cheek. It hurt, that she'd been so obviously alone; that her sadness she'd wanted to belong only to her, had been so desperately visible to everyone else. She hated it: for herself, for everyone who'd had to watch her. Lionel, Joe . . .

How many times had Joe begged her to move on, be happy?

Too many . . .

Naomi and Mabel both lived their too-short lives prey to loneliness. I am growing tired, I cannot talk much more, but I will say that Naomi's parents wanted her to marry a man who could never make her happy, which she eventually did, and I never heard from her again, until I read her obituary, before she was even forty. I could never discover how she died. It tears me apart. Perhaps I will finally find out when I reach the other side. I will always believe, though, that, if she'd allowed herself to live happily, with friends she chose rather than in a way that others told her she must, she might yet be sitting with me. I believe that if Mabel had been able to shake off her regret, let others into her life, she would not have died either. Such a beautiful, kind, broken girl she was, I am convinced that when she failed to see that bus, it was because she was lost in her memories, her thoughts of a past she couldn't leave behind.

Rosie, we all have a past, it exists within us, and while forgetting may be impossible, learning to live with what is gone is so often essential to enjoying whatever is yet to come. I wish I had one of Catherine's rulebooks to give you for how one should move on

*from grief and loss, but there is no such book, yet I hope, I hope so
dearly that you are now finding your way forward. I have taken
advantage of you, convinced you to leave your home, your fiancé
and family and beloved brother to help me, so please let me give
you this one piece of advice in return: live, my dear. It really is the
one thing that is asked of us, when these bodies are given to us.
Live. Do that well. Do it joyfully. Please, I beg of you, let me look
down at you from the heavenly Goring I have every intention of
getting a table at, and watch you. Let me see you smiling, laughing, and I shall smile and laugh with you. I shall raise a glass and
enjoy your enjoyment enormously.*

> *Live my dear. Live, for me.*
> *Live, and love.*
> *Do not be lonely.*

Rose wiped another tear away. *I'm trying,* she silently told Vivian,
tipping her head back on the hammock, looking outward, turning her
swimming eyes to the blue, beating sky. *I've been trying.* She thought of
all that had passed since Vivian had last seen her; how much Vivian could
have looked down and watched her doing, enjoying her enjoyment: eating ice
cream with Walter in Bombay, Colombo; drinking gin with Esme; jitterbugging at the Trocadero; swimming in the river, riding at dawn; riding
with Max; talking with Max; walking with Max; laughing with Max . . . *I'm
getting better at it.*

But you're weeping, Vivian said. *Something is still holding you back, my
dear. What is it?*

Joe, of course, Rose replied. *My parents . . .*

It wasn't only them, though.

She didn't need Vivian to tell her that.

She knew very well that, even if she was to be given Joe back, and found
out today that her parents were safe, she'd still not be able to properly smile
and laugh without another person, too.

A person who hadn't written to Mabel again after she'd left Australia,
because of something that had happened between them at Brisbane port.

A person who was coming toward her now across the sunlit grass, removing his hat, running his hand through his hair. A person she'd been so
careful to hide her feelings from for so long.

Too long, maybe.

She looked back at Vivian's wire.

Live. Do that well. Do it joyfully.

She glanced again at Max, and wondered, for the first time, if she was being little better than a coward, not telling him how she loved him. As he drew closer, and raised his eyes, meeting hers, her heart quickened, and the possibility occurred to her that he might have been afraid all this time, too: of her love for Xander, the past she was learning to live with.

His past.

"It's his face," Esme had once told her. "You've made him think too much about it. He likes your face."

Did he?

Really?

Did she dare risk, finally, trying to find out?

She closed her eyes, drew breath.

Maybe she did dare.

Maybe, if he could fly headlong into bullets beneath the blazing Arabian sun, she could tell him she loved him.

Maybe.

Soon.

CHAPTER TWENTY-FIVE

She didn't do it that day.

Esme took over, appearing through the gates in the ute even as Max walked toward the house, back from posting her signed papers to Paul's lawyer, hammering up the driveway, wheels spraying gravel, beeping the ute's horn and grinding to a halt in front of the veranda.

"The Yanks are here," she yelled, throwing her door wide. "The Yanks are *here*."

"Which Yank?" said Rose, blanching.

"The *Yanks*," said Esme.

"The whole country?" said Lauren, still at her table.

"As good as," said Esme, jumping down to the ground. "Well, a few shiploads." She ran up the porch stairs, breathlessly telling them that she'd been leaving Narrawee just as Ivan from the grocer's had come back from the markets, and someone at the markets knew someone who'd been at the port, and they'd told Ivan that a convoy of US ships had arrived in Brisbane. "Ships that weren't destroyed by the Japs," said Esme.

"I guessed that," said Lauren. "What are they doing here though?"

"Ivan said they were meant to be going to the Philippines. The *Philippines*." Esme widened her eyes in an *imagine*. "They were diverted here, Ivan said, because it's not safe. Ivan said there's a big crowd at the river already, gone to see them. Ivan said he's going . . ."

"Ivan's had a lot to say," said Rose, her heart descending from her mouth now that she realized Esme hadn't been talking about Xander. (Not that she wouldn't have been happy to know he was safe.) She turned in the hammock, trying to get out of it with some degree of grace (impossible), conscious that Max too was on his way up the porch stairs.

"Here," he said, reaching out, holding the canvas steady, letting her clamber to standing, keeping Walter in one place.

"Thank you," she said, still holding Vivian's letter in her hand.

Max had been for a swim. She saw that from her sideways glance at his damp shirt, his wet hair. She realized that he must have gone down to the river knowing none of them would be there, and wondered how often he did that.

"We're going, too," said Esme.

"Swimming?" said Rose, instantly wishing she hadn't, because of course that wasn't what Esme was talking about.

"I think she meant Brisbane," said Max.

"Of course I meant Brisbane," said Esme, like Rose was an idiot. (She felt like one.) "I'm not missing this." She reached out, pushing Rose toward the house. "Go, go and get your things. Walter, run to the loo . . ."

"Esme," said Lauren, "the petrol . . ."

"Oh, I'll buy another container," said Esme. "It's still easy enough to get." Then, in a mark of her excitement, "You come too, if you like, Mum. Now, Walter, loo. Move. Rosie, stop just standing there. I want to see the ships before they up and go anywhere. Mum, if you're coming, come . . ."

"No patience," said Hannah, poking her head out of the drawing room window. "Esme, you have no patience . . ."

"Not today I don't," said Esme. "Everyone, come on."

Lauren didn't come. She said she still had too much to do before Christmas. Nor did Hannah, for the same reason.

Max did, though.

Rose, remembering Vivian's words in her hands (Live. Do that well. Do it joyfully), asked him to, and—to her delighted surprise—he, smiling, said, "Yeah, all right. I haven't got time, either, but let's do it."

He drove. Rose was in the middle, between him and Esme; Esme insisted on having Walter on her lap for once.

"Don't tickle me," said Walter.

"As if I'd do that," said Esme, tickling him, making him giggle.

The pair of them took up quite a lot of room. Rose's hip touched Max's hip the entire way to the city, her leg, his leg. There was nowhere for either of them to go.

Pretty bloody uncomfortable.

And yet also the most comfortable thing in the world.

She looked at him, the perfect left side of his face in profile. Had he noticed they were touching? He gave nothing away, if he had. He, one arm propped on the open window ledge, listening to Esme's and Walter's chatter about the upcoming party on Christmas Day — Esme saying that it would be their first one since before Walter had been born, "Just for you, Walter, Walter. You've brought the fun" — appeared only relaxed. (*No, Rosie. No ...*) Rose looked at his thigh, wondered how it would be if she reached out, set her hand on it. *Live well. Do it joyfully. ...*

"You look hot, Rosie," said Esme. "Let's stop for water."

They did, then had to stop again for Walter to go to the loo ("Not happy," said Esme, "not at all happy, young man"), and again for Esme ("Not h—" said Rose. "Don't," said Esme); night was closing in by the time they reached the city, which was in darkness, the lights in Brisbane's homes, its hotels and shops, blanketed for the brownout, hiding, they all hoped, from any offshore Japanese aircraft carriers. The sky was clear, though, full of stars, and the warm, silvery riverbank packed with Brisbanites come to see the already infamous Pensacola Convoy in dock. No one was meant to know it was there, a woman told Rose as she, Max, Esme, and Walter found a spot to sit on the rippling shoreline. The convoy's presence in Australia was absolutely top secret.

"Excellent," said Max, looking up and down at the massed crowds. "That's really excellent."

The ships shone no lights. No noise came from them to betray that, on board, the hearts of thousands of US sailors and soldiers beat. The only sound was from the soft lapping of the river shallows against their metallic bellies, and cicadas screeching in the bankside's undergrowth.

"Just think," said Esme, hugging her knees to her chest, staring across at the armored vessels, "they've come all the way from *America*."

"*America*," repeated Walter.

"What happens now, Esme?" Max said. "Is this it?"

"Shhh," Esme said, "I'm imagining I'm on one of the ships. Don't ruin it."

He didn't ruin anything. Esme continued to imagine, and he leaned back, elbows resting on the ground, stomach dipping beneath his shirt as he stared out across the silent water. Walter, hungry as always, set to eating the packed tea Hannah had thrown together for him before they'd left, and, as he munched, Rose lowered herself beside Max and told him about how she'd looked over at this very bankside they sat on, back when she and Walter had arrived in Brisbane in August.

"I was wearing my best dress," she said, looking into the darkness, seeing herself again as she'd been then. "I was all done up, ready to meet you all . . ."

"Are you trying to make me feel bad?" he asked.

"Always," she said, turning, resting her chin on her shoulder, meeting the deep shine of his eyes. "Is it working?"

"Pretty well."

"Why should Uncle Max feel bad?" Walter asked, mouth full of sausage roll.

"Who feels bad?" asked Esme, rejoining reality.

"You should," said Max, "for draining a tank of petrol so we could look at a few blacked-out ships."

"They're browned out," said Walter, spraying pastry.

"They look blacked out to me, mate," said Max.

Clearly, someone else on the riverbank decided they were all in need of additional entertainment too, because it was then that, out of the darkness, singing began: just one man at first, breaking into "Waltzing Matilda," but before Rose knew it, everyone else was joining in, hundreds, maybe thousands, of voices filling the still night air. Rose laughed, the music washing through her, imagining the men on board the ships hearing the song, too, coming to their portholes, onto deck, looking out, smiling; welcomed, so very far from home. Esme sang too, Max joined in, with his husky voice that was every bit as nice as Rose could have imagined, then raised his brow, seeing that Rose hadn't.

"Sing," he said to her.

"I can't," she said. "I don't know the words."

"Come on," he said. "The chorus isn't hard. Sing, Rosie . . ."

"I —"

"Sing," he said. "You can do it."

So she did. She sang.

Live. Do that well. Do it joyfully.

Walter took up the chorus with her, clambering onto her lap, resting his head back against her chest, belting out the words he didn't know either, just a fraction of a second behind everyone else, loving the moment, *enjoying it enormously.*

And, once all of them on the riverbank had finished, after a brief, hushed silence from the anchored ships, a single male voice broke from their invisible decks, carrying across the rippling water, filling the balmy night air with "You Are My Sunshine." Before Rose knew it, hundreds of other sailors were singing too.

As the lyrics rang out (*The other night, dear, as I lay sleeping, I dreamed I held you in my arms*) she turned instinctively to Max, only to find that he was already looking at her. Their eyes met (*You'll never know, dear, how much I love you*), and she felt a stilling, all through her, of hope, so much fear: at the precipice she'd decided to throw herself over; the lingering unknown of whether he'd catch her. . . .

Sadder words came: of someone leaving, loving another, *you have shattered all my dreams*, and still his eyes held hers. Hers held his.

Please, she thought, *please let him not shatter my dreams.*

His gaze on her softened, like he'd heard.

Then he smiled.

He smiled, his slow smile, and it felt like being caught.

She smiled at him, the sailors sang on, and her hope grew.

It didn't occur to her that she, not he, might one day be the person to walk away, love another, shatter him.

There on the riverbank, with him so close that she could have moved her little finger and skimmed it along the line of his body resting on the grass, she truly didn't believe that could ever, ever be possible.

CHAPTER TWENTY-SIX

Esme got a smile of her own as they left that night, and she, Rose, and Walter waited on the roadside for Max to fetch the ute, parked some distance away. The smile came from the tallest of a trio of US officers in crisp uniforms who passed them by, on their way to a waiting sedan and the city, all of them senior enough to have been allowed ashore and billeted in hotel rooms, which Rose and Esme discovered after Esme threw a "G'day, Yank" at the tall one. He turned, amused (more Errol Flynn than Laurence Olivier, but certainly very much like heaven), asked her if she had a name, which of course she did, as did he (Hank: Hank the Yank; it couldn't be helped), and so began Esme's Christmas.

"Right," said Max, when he pulled up and Esme, gabbling, filled him in on the thirty-year-old captain with two sisters, one brother, and a dog, who'd come from Arizona and had promised to telephone the house and arrange to take her out. "How long was I gone?"

"A lifetime," said Esme dreamily.

"When do you think he'll telephone, Esme?" asked Walter, polishing off the chocolate Hank had given him.

"I don't know," Esme said. "He might try to play it cool."

"Like you," said Max dryly.

He didn't play it cool. As keen as Esme (Rose approved), he called first thing the next morning saying he had the day to play with, asking if he could call by.

"We're two hours out of Brisbane," said Esme, grinning, twirling the telephone cord around her finger, not catching the way Lauren stopped on the way to the office, smiled at her.

Hank didn't care about the drive. He arrived as they were getting lunch ready, speeding from the city in his requisitioned motor, coming around the back way to the kitchen since he'd heard them through the open door, a big bunch of flowers in hand.

"No one's ever bought me flowers," Esme exclaimed.

"Oh my God," said Rose. "Really?"

"That's crazy," said Hank. "I'm bringing you more tomorrow."

"A good sort," said Lauren, once he'd gone, and who was very nice to him when he was there, coming by for lunch, asking him what he thought of Lennon's Hotel (pretty swell), whether his brother was serving (he was: a sailor, he'd been lucky enough to survive Pearl Harbor), how long he was going to be in Brisbane (a while, he hoped, but didn't know).

Hannah, being Hannah, was less cordial. She sniffed when she shook his hand, and that was about it, until she made a fresh batch of mince pies for afternoon tea.

"You're honored," Rose told Hank, while Hannah was busy pulling them out of the oven. "Really."

"I'll take that," he said, with his easy smile.

"She's never baked for Rosie," said Esme.

"Rosie let my chickens out," said Hannah.

"That was Walter," said Rose.

"*Rosie*," said Walter.

"How did you know about that anyway?" Rose asked Hannah.

"I know everything, young lady," Hannah said.

It was Max, though, more than Hannah, more than Lauren, whom Esme told Rose she was most anxious about approving of Hank.

"I need him to," she said, setting off with Hank to walk off Hannah's pies. "I really need to know he does, after everything with Paul, so if you see him, please tell him he has to . . ."

Rose did tell him, once Esme and Hank had returned from their walk, Hannah and Lauren had gone to their cottages, and she'd put Walter to bed.

She ran to meet him on his way down from the stables, passed on Esme's instructions, and asked him to come for a beer on the veranda.

"Remember," she said, "be predisposed."

"Predisposed?"

"Yes," she said, laughing, just because of the way he was looking at her. "He's very nice, and Esme's delirious, so you have to like him."

Max did like him.

"Genuinely," he told Rose the next morning, on their hay bale. "I was disposed."

Hank had stayed late. They'd all talked for hours: about Arizona, Pearl Harbor, then the desert, and Singapore, and Joe, and flying, and Walter, and *Dumbo*, and gin. . . .

"They're smitten, I think," said Rose, replaying how they'd hung on each other's every word. "They disappeared for hours when they went on their walk."

"Where did you go?" Rose had asked Esme.

"Everywhere, Rosie," she'd said. "We've been everywhere."

"I don't want to know what that means," said Max to Rose now.

And she swallowed the impulse to ask him to let her show him, *disappear with me*, because it was Christmas Eve, a year to the day since Mabel had died, and given Rose was still certain that—whatever his feelings had become, whatever might have happened between him and Mabel at the port—he *had* once loved her, it really didn't feel like the time to profess her own love for him.

They toasted Mabel that evening, back out on the veranda.

Lauren was there, but not Hank. He'd come again for the day, with more flowers, but had had to reluctantly leave before dinner, back to the city for a meeting with his CO. Walter wasn't present either, but tucked up once more for the night, sleeping soundly with Rabbit, his dreams hopefully full of nothing beyond Santa plummeting down the Lucknows' chimney, blissfully oblivious to the anniversary they were marking, raising their glasses to his mother in his absence.

"To Mabel," Esme said.

"To Mabel," they echoed.

Rose tried not to read too much into Max's set expression as he said it, but it was hard not to feel the pain of his set jaw, his strained voice, and feel her hope once again ebb; agonize for the thousandth time if she really ever could be enough for him.

Lauren raised another toast too, to Jamie. "I hope the pair of them are being friendly," she said, looking up at the stars. "I want to think they've moved on from what they did to each other, remembered how much they liked being together in Sydney."

"Let's go with that, Mum," said Esme gently. "Let's say they're swimming together off a heavenly Sydney beach."

Rose studied Max, waiting for him to say something.

But he, turning to look not at the stars, but at the driveway where Esme had said he and Jamie had last fought, said nothing at all.

"I think he was watching over you," said Lauren, looking at him now too, her face as soft as Rose had known it. "I think he did that from the second you enlisted, and panicked when he thought you were going to die, helped you get out of that plane . . ."

"You think that, Mum?" said Max.

"I do," said Lauren. "I think if he could, he'd come and sit with us all now, pick up a beer and tell you how happy he is that you're not in the state you were in this time last year. All those bandages . . ."

Max smiled sadly. Rose's heart hurt, physically hurt, imagining him in those bandages, watching him now, seeing how much he wanted to believe Lauren's words.

"I think Jamie'd do that too," said Esme.

"He'd tell me off as well," said Lauren. "He'd really tell me off, Max, for what I said to you."

"It's all right," said Max.

"It's not," said Lauren. "But someone was helping you, Max, in the plane, then the desert . . ."

"Dad, maybe," said Max.

"Both of them, then," said Lauren.

"I reckon both," said Rose.

He smiled again, less sadly this time.

Maybe I can be enough, she thought. *Maybe I really can be . . .*

"You reckon?" he said.

"Yes," she said.

"Oh, Rosie," said Lauren.

"Rosie," said Esme. "You really are turning Australian." She laughed, breaking through the grief that had been stilling the air. "What'd Winston think?"

In spite of the sadness of that evening, the weight of silence left by everyone not there, Christmas Day itself was happy, happier than Rose had dared to anticipate. No surprise wire arrived from Joe, or Singapore. No broadcast came over the wireless proclaiming that the Japanese were at last in retreat (on the contrary, they were told British-held Hong Kong had fallen to the Imperial Army). But the sun shone, the wind blew cool from the east, not hot from the west, and they all had . . . fun.

The day started early for Rose, not with Max, but Walter, who woke her at three, hopping because the empty pillowcase he'd left at the foot of his bed had become wondrously full—of oranges and nuts, the wooden toys and candy canes Rose had put in it. He upended it on her bed, blinding her with the lamp, refusing to go back to sleep.

"I want to give you your present."

"All right," Rose whispered, giving in, sitting up on her pillows, blinking herself awake. "Go and get it."

"It's not an it, Rosie," he whispered back, running off. "It's a lots."

"Lots of what?" she asked, when he returned.

"Lots of these," he said, and presented her with a stack of paper.

"Walter," she said, smiling, "you've made me a book."

"A picture book," he said, scrambling up next to her.

She took the pages from him, aching as she saw the bold lettering on the top.

Me and my Rosie: our hero adventures around the whole wide world.

"Hannah helped me spell," he said.

"Walter," she said again, quietly, lifting the sheet, revealing the pictures beneath. So many carefully colored drawings of all the things they'd done together since they'd met. "Oh, little man." Her tired eyes filled. She turned the pages, growing more touched with each new one: of them feeding the ducks in London, riding on the Tube, then at the zoo with the camels, on the ship, Rose with a green face . . .

"Because you were so sick," said Walter. "And," he turned to the next sheet, "that's me and Verity too, and," he turned again, "you talking with Kate . . ."

"Yes," she said, hugging him. "Yes, I see that."

"And this one," he pulled out another sheet, "is you and Uncle Max. Look at you smiling."

"That's a very big smile," she said.

"You're really happy."

"Yes," she said, "I see that too. Thank you." She cuddled him tighter, breathing him in, her lungs expanding with love, all her love. "I will cherish this forever."

She didn't show Max that picture of the two of them, but did tell him about Walter's book, just as soon as the sun had risen and she'd intercepted him as he left the annex on the way to the stables.

"I'm here not there," she called, beckoning him back to the porch.

They drank their tea on the porch steps that morning, Walter playing with his new spinning top on the veranda behind them, Max wearing the flying scarf Rose had made him for Christmas, setting the new washbag she'd bought him for Sydney by his side.

"You definitely don't have one already?" she said.

"Not as good as this," he said. "Want my present, now?"

"Yes, please," she said with a smile, and, seeing him pull a box from his pocket, realizing he must have been planning to give it to her in the privacy of their hay bale, felt her heart quicken in anticipation, curiosity. She took the box from him: too heavy for anything like a scarf, not heavy enough for soap. . . .

"Oh," she said, opening it, seeing the simple, delicate gold watch inside. "Oh, I love it."

She took it out, turning it in her hand, the gold catching the light of the rising sun, amazement soaking through her. He'd gone to a jeweler, just for her. Made time, stood in a shop, chosen the most perfect, perfect watch. He'd even had it engraved.

For happy times. Max.

No initial. No "X."

No confusion.

Only him.

"Thank you," she said, sliding it on to her wrist, loving how it fitted so perfectly, fearing the precipice waiting for her just a bit less. "I think," she glanced backward at Walter, "it might just be the second nicest present I've ever had."

He laughed.

She laughed.

Walter behind them, who never missed anything, laughed too.

"I feel bad about my washbag and scarf now," she said. "They seem a bit . . . small."

"You made me something, Rosie," he said, taking her empty mug, standing up. "Gave me something to start my day with." He smiled. *Enough.* "There's nothing small about that."

Hank arrived in time for breakfast, with the news that his CO had informed him his was one of the few units that would be staying on in Brisbane rather than shipping out to other parts of the country, while it was decided where they'd all go fight.

"Guess no one knows what to do with us yet," he said.

"Yes," said Esme. "Yes, yes, yes."

He was on rest leave until New Year, and had brought gifts for her too: real French champagne, another bunch of flowers, then a jewelry box that he'd bought on Queen's Street before dinner with his CO.

"The shops were all closing," he said, watching Esme unwrap it. "I had to beg the lady not to lock me out."

"I adore it," Esme said. "I adore that you did that."

"Now we just need to find you some things to put in it," he said.

"Well, she's always got her pearls," said Lauren.

There were more presents to come in the drawing room: lollies that Kate had passed on for Walter from Verity, all the books and toys sent from Pia, Catherine, and Lester in London, and a handful of gifts from overseas for Rose, too: more stockings from Sarah (Rose had sent her Old Gold chocolates), which, to Rose's sadness, Sarah had signed, *Love Sarah and Joe,* since he'd still been with them when she'd posted them, then rouge from her parents, a pen from Lionel, and a Smythson journal from the Churchills.

"Bugger me," said Esme.

"Esme," said Lauren, looking warningly at Walter, in the middle of opening her own gift.

"Oh my God, Mum," said Esme, once he had.

"Oh my *God,*" said Walter, staring, mouth wide, at his three new rabbits: Peter's sisters, Flopsy, Mopsy, and Cottontail.

"Can we all please start watching what we say in front of this child," said Lauren.

"Were they what you were making in the cinema?" Rose asked her, remembering that she'd been knitting when she and Walter had come out of *Dumbo*.

"It was, actually," said Lauren.

"I just," said Walter, "I just" — he sighed — "well, I really love them, Grandma."

"I'm very pleased, Walter," she said, flushing pink.

He'd got her a present too, care of Rose: a bottle of gin, then some perfume for Esme ("You've had enough gin," said Rose), and gardener's soap and hand cream for Hannah, which Hannah proclaimed very thoughtful, then gave him his new cricket bat, and surprised Rose with bath bubbles. "Since you like your baths so much."

At noon, the workers came down from the cottages bearing huge plates of cold meats, salads, and sausage rolls in their arms, ready to set up for the party on the trestle tables outside Bill's kitchen: the traditional do Esme had said they'd used to have every year, until Mabel had left, and Jamie had gone, after the last one in 1935. Lauren had baked lamingtons: the selfsame coconut-and-chocolate-covered sponges Mabel had used to make Walter for his birthday. She showed them to Walter when Rose brought him into the kitchen, ready to help Hannah carry the last bits down to Bill's.

"Come here," Lauren said, beckoning him over to see inside the tin she'd set on the kitchen table. "These are especially for you."

He looked into the tin, up at her, biting his lip.

"Aunty Vivian told me how much you love them," Lauren said.

"Can I please have one?" he asked.

"Yes, Walter," she said. "I'd like you to."

Solemnly, he reached his little hand into the tin for a square, and Rose felt herself ache all over again; that fierce, always growing, love. . . .

He paused before biting into the cake, as though preparing himself, then closed his eyes and took a mouthful.

"They taste just like my mummy's," he exclaimed.

"I taught your mum how to make them," said Lauren.

"Pretty much the only thing she knew how to make," sniffed Hannah, and perhaps added, *other than trouble*, although muttered it so quietly, it was impossible to be sure.

What Rose was certain of, as the day continued, and Walter ate more lamingtons and laughed and played in the sunshine with his friends, pulling crackers, wearing his paper hat, hopping from knee to knee—Lauren's, to Max's, to Hannah's, to Esme's, to Bill's—was that, after his year of loss, they'd given him a Christmas to delight in. One that Vivian, and hopefully Mabel, would have delighted in.

At dusk, Hannah and Bill both brought the pavlovas they'd been slaving over out from their respective cold boxes so that the stockmen could vote on whose was the superior meringue: another tradition resurrected from back in 1935.

"Hannah always wins," said Max, who, once the party had kicked off, stayed with Rose the whole afternoon through, the pair of them sitting with Esme and Hank at the end of a trestle, drinking warm wine in the warm sunshine, pulling crackers, eating too much. Hank had come in uniform. Max hadn't. He didn't wear his usual cowboy hat and corduroy trousers either, but a well-cut navy suit, a crisp, tailored shirt to rival Xander's, open-necked, with no tie, his dark hair brushing the white collar. *Like heaven.* "You wait," he said, topping up Rose's wine, "hers will be twice the size of Bill's."

It was indeed an epically proportioned feat of sugar, cream, and fruit.

"Not too bad, is it?" said Hannah, with a sniff.

Bill's efforts, which would have impressed Rose on any other day, paled sorrowfully in comparison.

"I still make the best bread," he grinned as Hannah tried not to look too jubilant at the unanimous vote in her favor.

Dusk turned to night. Rose and Esme fetched trayloads of candles in jam jars for the tables, Hank and Max carried down Lauren's portable gramophone, a couple of the stockmen brought out their guitars, and the children danced, holding hands and running around and around in circles on the dark grass, Walter's laughter vibrating through his entire little being: born for joy. The night became full of their singing, voices, music, the call of the nesting birds, and the cicadas' chorus.

"This could not have felt less like an English Christmas," said Rose, resting her elbows on the torn paper tablecloth, her cheek on her hand, breathing in the scent of candlewax and frangipani leaves.

"Where were you for it last year?" Esme asked, her own hand beneath the table, presumably holding Hank's.

"A really horrible bed and breakfast in the Lake District," Rose confessed. "I was meant to be at my uncle's, but I got to Paddington and couldn't do it. I telephoned and told him I was ill, and for some reason the

Lakes was where I decided to go." *Impulsive.* "It's odd, because I'd never actually been before. I was on a farm . . ."

"Another farm," said Max.

"Yes," she said, "and they *still* had powdered eggs for breakfast."

He smiled, sadly.

It was a bit of a sad story.

"Were you alone?" he asked. "The whole Christmas."

"No," she said. That's where the story got better. "I realized what an idiot I'd been on Christmas morning, telephoned Joe at his base, just to hear his voice, and then, there he was that afternoon. With Lionel."

Her eyes prickled, remembering their faces. The surprise of it.

"But not Xander?" said Esme.

Max shifted in his seat, looked across at the children. The candle threw shapes on his face.

"No," said Rose. "I didn't want to ruin his Christmas."

"Sounds like yours was pretty damned awful," said Hank.

It made Rose laugh, the bluntness of it.

She saw Max's smile.

"Ours was too," said Esme, "thanks to Max."

"You're welcome," said Max, turning back to the table.

"Mine was pretty good," said Hank.

"I'm really happy for you, mate," said Max.

"This one's better," said Hank.

"Yeah," said Esme, turning her smile on him. "It's pretty good, isn't it?"

The gramophone crackled into silence, the stockmen set down their guitars, then someone put another record on: the inevitable "In the Mood." Esme clapped her hands, pulled Hank to his feet, and the two of them were off, quite a few of the workers and their wives with them, jitterbugging on the grass, leaving Rose and Max alone at the table, the candle flickering between them.

"I'd have come to the Lakes," he said. "If you'd called me, I'd have come."

"I know you would," she said.

Then, because he'd said that, and because it was balmy and beautiful and her favorite song was playing and he'd given her an engraved watch and sat with her all day, and she couldn't be scared of Mabel's ghost forever, she edged a little closer to the precipice, almost over it, and asked, "Would you dance with me?"

He didn't answer straightaway.

She felt her body strain, just with the effort of waiting.

The beauty, everywhere around her, trembled, ready to shatter. . . .

But then, "I can't dance, Rosie," he said. "Not like that," he gestured at Esme and Hank, "not anymore." His eyes darkened with regret. "I wish I could."

She nodded slowly, remembering Hannah's words, *his skin tears, just the slightest knock,* hating it for him.

"Do you get hurt often?" she asked. "Around here."

"I do," he said, not cross, nor defensive; never with her, not anymore. "The doctor's going to tell me this week to stop, and I'm going to tell him I won't . . ."

"Then we won't dance either," she said.

He smiled, frowned, looked down at the jam jar, back up at her.

"I don't ever want you to not dance for me," he said, and, seeming to decide and move at the same time, pushed his chair back, stood, held out his hand.

She took it, his fingers closing around hers for the first time in too long, letting him pull her up.

"No jitterbugging," he said.

"I promise," she said.

She held her breath.

Was this happening?

He placed his other hand in the small of her back; the warmth of it through her dress. She gently touched her hand to the fragile skin on his shoulder, then rested her face against his chest, feeling it rise, fall.

The music raced, fast, and together they moved, slowly, smoothly, in-stinctively, as though they'd been made just to turn in each other's arms. He held her closer, laughter and voices ringing out, all around them.

"Happy Christmas, Rosie," he said.

"Happy Christmas, Max."

They danced on. His thumb moved on the indent of her waist. She closed her eyes, and the world retreated, disappeared.

She heard his heart, felt her own beat, beat, and for that small handful of moments, that was all there was.

Them, dancing, and her own pure, overwhelming happiness.

CHAPTER TWENTY-SEVEN

They didn't kiss.

Nothing was said.

Walter saw them dancing, came to join in, bringing the world back by grabbing both their hands, and that really was that.

"I need to speak to him about his timing," said Esme, when everyone at last turned in and the two of them sat in their nightgowns on Rose's bed with unnecessary second helpings of Hannah's pavlova. "I suppose all you can do now is wait for him to come back from Sydney."

"I suppose so," said Rose, drawing patterns in the pavlova's cream with her fork. He was sailing south, setting off for the port before sunrise by taxicab. He'd already bidden Rose goodbye, not privately, but outside the house, with Walter, Lauren, Esme, and Hank all there. *See you at New Year.* There'd be no tea for them in the morning, no hay bale. There'd be none of that for days. . . .

"I might take Walter to visit Verity," Rose said, scooping up a mouthful of meringue and mango, placing it in her mouth. It was sweet, too sweet now that it had sat for so long; hard to swallow. "Break the time up."

"Good idea," said Esme. "Hank and I are going to the beach tomorrow, too. Come with us . . ."

"I can't do that to you."

"You can," said Esme. "Mum's worried about my reputation, I've told her it's wrecked already, but she'd probably be happier if you and Walter chaperoned. Come . . ."

Rose didn't.

The morning dawned baking, much hotter than the one before, but, tempting as a trip to the beach felt, she thanked Esme for inviting her, then left her to disappear joyously off with Hank *everywhere* in his hoodless motor. For the rest of the day, while Lauren went out to the fields riding with the stockmen, back on duty, keeping her eagle eye on proceedings in Max's absence, Walter played with his new toys, and Rose helped everyone else clear up after the party, gathering the burned-out candles, picking shreds of paper hats and streamers from the sun-crisped grass, wiping sweat from her brow and folding the trestle tables away. They were all of them quiet, tired from the late night and wine, and Max was gone, already on his way to Sydney. It felt . . . flat, without him there. Like the joy had been sucked away.

Hannah hardly improved things. For some reason, as she and Rose washed up in the kitchen, Hannah scrubbing crockery and Rose drying (the short straw; *this day, this day* . . .), she decided to bring up the subject of the last time Max had made a dawn departure to Brisbane port, with Mabel.

"She cried," Hannah said, up to her elbows in suds, a careful eye on Walter through the window, pretending to be an airplane.

"How do you know?" said Rose, at once desperate to hear more, and fearful of what else Hannah might say.

"It's like I told you," said Hannah, prizing some congealed chocolate from a plate, "I know everything."

"And in this instance . . . ?"

"I saw them," said Hannah.

"Mabel and Max?" Rose asked, throat tightening on the effort of saying their names together, so casually.

Hannah nodded. "It was hot, a proper stinker, much worse than today. I hadn't been able to sleep, so was in my garden." She flicked the chocolate off. "I'd thought I might make some jam, but I didn't have enough strawberries. They were a few not ripe enough . . ."

Off she went, down a strawberry rabbit hole, until Rose, unable to help herself, interrupted, bringing her back to the point, asking where Mabel and Max had been.

"At the porch," said Hannah. "I saw the ute by the gate, Max hugging her, and thought, oh, ho, here we go . . ."

"Right," said Rose, heavily, taking the plate Hannah handed her, mind filling with the image of the two of them embracing. On the porch.

The porch she herself had sat on so many times with Max.

The porch she'd sat on only the morning before, opening his present. . . .

"He kissed her," said Hannah.

"Did he?" It was like a punch, right in the middle of her too-tight throat.

"On the head," said Hannah.

Rose paused.

"The head?"

That felt a bit better.

"She'll have wished it was more," said Hannah. "Probably told herself it meant more."

Rose had to ask. "You don't think it did?"

"Who knows?" said Hannah. "Maybe." She sighed. "Thick as thieves, they could be . . ."

"Yes," said Rose, distantly. Then, thinking of Vivian's letter, "Do you know what happened between them at the port?"

"Mabel got on a ship."

"No, Vivian said there was something else . . ."

Hannah shrugged. "All a long time ago now, whatever it was. A very long time . . ."

"Yes," said Rose, again.

It had been, she knew. Like she and Xander had been.

We all have a past, Vivian had written, *it exists within us.*

Rose would have to learn to make peace with Max's as well as her own, she realized that. It was so hard, though, still knowing so little of what had actually happened. How the present compared.

She needed to ask Max about it. She really did feel ready to ask him.

If he'd been there, she would have. . . .

But since he wasn't there, she did the only thing she could do.

She took the next plate Hannah handed her, and carried on drying up.

She missed him, every second, never more than when she came back from her dawn rides and found the forecourt silent, their hay bale empty. The weather turned and it rained on and off for three days: enough to make Lauren and Esme happy about the water levels, Hank to have to put the hood up on his requisitioned car when he took Esme out driving, and Rose and

Walter to be forced into too much time indoors. They drew, they read, they baked, Rose wrote more letters — to Joe, her parents, Sarah, Lionel, and everyone at home — but thought far too much, and not only about Max, but Joe and her parents, agonizing over whether they were safe, becoming floored by fresh grief for Joe and how long his silence had now gone on.

Buck up, she heard him tell her.

She did her best. As soon as the sun reappeared, the day before Max was due back on New Year's Eve, she took Walter to see Kate and Verity, just as she'd said she might. Hank chauffeured, dropping the pair of them for lunch at Kate's parents' while he and Esme went for more Fantales and a revival of *Gone with the Wind* at the Wintergarden.

"You reminded me of Scarlett O'Hara when I first met you," said Rose to Esme, smiling, *bucking up*, as she saw them off.

"I'll take that," said Esme, already catching Hank's turns of phrase.

Rose had high hopes of forgetting everything for just a short while, over that lunch. But Kate — expecting to hear within the week that Tim's ship had safely docked — was about as much use as Hannah in helping her do that. As the children played and they sat on deck chairs by the river, she told Rose that some of her friends had husbands and brothers who'd already started to trickle home from the fighting in the East. She was full of their horror stories of constant raids on Singapore, a pall of smoke hanging over the tropical city; lines of people trying to get on ships at harbor, before they were strafed.

"I hate to upset you," she said, "but I know you wouldn't want me keeping anything back."

"No," said Rose numbly, thinking that actually it might have been easier if she *had* held just a little back.

"Try not to worry that you haven't heard from them, anyway," Kate said. "I'm not sure it means anything. It sounds like chaos there."

It was just what Lionel had said.

Complete chaos.

It didn't stop Rose worrying. Quite the opposite. As she drank her tea, picked at the cake that Ingrid brought out, she tortured herself with pictures of her mum and dad in those strafed, smoke-blanketed lines at the harbor in Singapore. . . .

And, as though to prove things really could always get worse, when they all reached home that evening, it was to the news that Max had telephoned, and wasn't Brisbane-bound, as Rose had believed, but still, crushingly, in Sydney. Hannah had taken the call and vexingly asked very few questions, so only knew that Max's passage had turned back thanks to *some engine problem or other*, and he was now waiting for another boat to come from Melbourne, one that would see him arrive on the morning of the coming Sunday, the fourth.

"If he can get a berth on it," sniffed Hannah. "I gather they're all busy, with the 'vacuees coming from the Orient."

"Did he say that?" asked Rose.

"The wireless did," said Hannah.

"What else *did* he say?" Rose asked.

"That you're to have fun tomorrow night," said Hannah.

"She will," said Esme, who gave Rose a quick, sympathetic squeeze, then declared that she wasn't to even think about trying to get out of the Troc's New Year's Eve party.

Rose, who wanted to, didn't, and not only because she knew Esme was counting on her to keep Lauren happy about her late-night drive home with Hank. Kate had agreed to come along with them, and Walter was excited about another evening with Verity and Ingrid; Rose couldn't let them down. . . .

But she didn't have fun. She tried. She tried really hard. Although there'd still been no newspaper reports of the US *Pensacola* Convoy's arrival in Brisbane — or the deployment of various of its divisions to other parts of Australia, where the Americans still weren't officially meant to be — the sweaty, vibrating dance hall was packed with US troops, many of whom were, like Hank, excellent dancers, and Rose accepted every one of their invitations to take a turn. She even jitterbugged. Once or twice. But however much she swung and jumped and lost her breath, she couldn't keep her eyes from the doorway Max had stood in, back when he'd arrived to collect her in October, the night before he'd surprised her at the stables with her first cup of tea. She didn't stop thinking about him alone in Sydney, wishing he were with her so they could not jitterbug again. She never forgot her parents, or Joe, not for a single crash of a drum, until it felt wrong, so deeply wrong, that she was anywhere loud and noisy without knowing where they were.

Just before midnight, knowing she couldn't pretend to be happy a second longer, she slipped off, left Kate and Esme and Hank to cheer and clap, and saw 1942 in alone in a washroom stall, her head in her hands, crying, missing her silent family, so much.

"What can we do?" said Esme the next morning: the first that Hank wouldn't be coming, since his leave was now over and he was on duty until the weekend, drilling with his men. Esme was meant to be getting back to work too, but she told Rose the accounts could wait. "We need to keep you distracted. Shall we go for a ride? A swim?" Her eyes glinted. "Drink more gin?"

Rose tried it all. Nothing helped, though. Certainly not the gin.

Until, something did . . .

Something that arrived, like Hank, for the weekend, that following Saturday. Something that came by motorbike while Rose was finishing cleaning out Leon's stall with Walter, Hank and Esme were off for a walk, and that Lauren took, then — pale with anxiety — came running to give to Rose, pressing it into her suddenly cold hands.

Another telegram.

Not from Bella. Not from Lionel, nor Sarah.

Sadly, not from Rose's parents either.

She couldn't have it all.

Not that day.

But she, shaking all over, could have something.

Her eyes filled, racing through the miraculous, beautiful, heart-fixing words that swam before her, letting her know she *could* have something.

Bonjour Rosie STOP Safely home STOP I didn't give up STOP

She could have Joe.

She wept, almost as much as she'd wept at the news that he'd gone down, only this time Lauren held her, and Lauren wept too, smiling, crying, Walter beaming and wrapping his arms around both of them, saying, "I told you, Rosie. I *told you* . . ."

"Life can be good," Lauren said, dragging her hand over her eyes, the three of them standing in piles of hay. Rose knew she'd always now associate the sweet, dusty scent with joy. "Life really can be good."

They celebrated. Oh, how they celebrated. Esme cried as much as Rose and Lauren when she and Hank returned from their walk (*I was scared for him, Rosie, I didn't want you to know how scared I was....*), and Hank drove right off to buy more champagne, which they drank on the veranda that evening, Hannah joining in, bringing Walter ice cream, and everyone else on the station stopping by too, telling Rose how glad they were.

Almost all of Joe's crew had made it back, smuggled by the Resistance. Charlie was safe. Joe's copilot was safe. Only the poor rear gunner who'd told Walter about Australia had been killed, taken when they'd lost their tail. They raised a toast to him, of course.

"He brought me squash," said Walter.

"He did," agreed Rose sadly.

"May he be enjoying something just as good now," said Hank.

As the evening continued, growing darker, and Lauren and Esme talked of how much it all reminded them of the day they'd heard Max was still alive, how desperate they'd been to see him for themselves, Rose ached, more and more, to see Joe. Holding Walter on her lap, she rested her head back, staring up at the stars, picturing Joe, her laughing brother, warm and safe in Lionel's flat, Sarah and Lionel with him, doubtless with an open champagne bottle of their own. She breathed in the fragrant night air, and smelled not frangipanis, nor grass, but the wood of Lionel's open fire instead. She sent her thoughts reaching across the continents, stretching over the oceans to them all, until it really was almost as though she were in Parsons Green with them, sitting on Lionel's rug, Joe telling her to drink up, Sarah scolding her for ever doubting Joe would come home. She hoped they could feel her there. A tear of sweet sadness escaped her, and she hoped they knew that part of her was....

And she wished, as she'd wished so often now, that Max were here, with her.

Happy as she was, it would feel complete only once he was finally back the next day, when she'd be able to tell him not only about Joe, but about everything else she was so sorely impatient now to have him know.

He arrived just before ten the following morning, coming up the driveway in a low sedan that drove agonizingly slowly and glinted gray beneath the warm, cloudless sky.

Rose was waiting for him on the veranda. She'd been waiting since she'd woken, not even going for a ride. Hank and Esme had taken Walter for a swim. Esme had suggested it.

"You don't need an audience," she'd said. "Or any more interruptions."

Rose didn't.

Now that the moment was here, she was nervous. Petrified, really. She didn't know what to do with herself, watching the motor come to a halt several feet from the porch stairs; how to stand. She couldn't breathe properly. Her body felt too full, bursting with the words that needed to come out, but once let go, could never be taken back.

She set her unsteady hands on the porch railing, feeling her skin prickle with the heat, anticipation. She couldn't see through the motor's windows; they were all tinted.

It was such a smart car.

She hadn't expected it. . . .

The back door opened.

Breathe, she told herself, *just breathe. . . .*

Then she saw him, getting out of the car. He was wearing another suit, like he'd worn on Christmas Day. The memory made her smile.

The sight of him made her move, exhale, not so nervous anymore.

Not nervous at all.

She ran toward him, certain, suddenly certain in her euphoria at his being *there* that he'd catch her.

"Joe's alive," she called. "Max, Joe's alive, and I . . ."

He turned toward her.

She stopped.

Her voice stilled in her throat.

It wasn't that he didn't smile. He did.

But there was no surprise in it. He seemed to know already that Joe was alive.

It confused her.

As did how . . . removed, his smile looked. How guarded.

She opened her mouth to ask what was wrong.

Then someone else got out of the car, stopping her. He wore a US army uniform, which was strange, because she didn't know he'd joined the army.

The uniform suited him.

Like everything suited him.

"This has been a long time coming, kid," he said.

"Oh my God," she said. "Xander."

CHAPTER TWENTY-EIGHT

The two of them had met on the ship up from Sydney. Xander had boarded at Melbourne. He told Rose that as Max — with a short "I'll leave you both to catch up" — walked away to the annex, before she could think how to call him back.

"We got talking on deck," Xander said to Rose, them still standing by the motor. "He's a good guy. I've told him I can just about forgive him for keeping you hidden here all this time."

"He hasn't been hiding me," Rose said, too stunned by what was happening to pay attention to his choice of words, or what it might have done to Max, hearing them. She turned, watching the annex door swing shut, the knock of wood vibrating through the sticky, static air.

"Glad to see me?" Xander said.

"Of course," she replied, automatically.

She wasn't sure what she was.

She peeled her eyes from the annex door, leveled them once more on him. He was staring at her intently, trying to read her, she could tell.

"You don't seem glad," he said.

"I'm surprised." That much at least was true.

"I see that. Want another surprise?"

"I don't know."

"You do." He smiled. "You want it." He took a step toward her. "I've got your mom, Rosie. She's safe, in Melbourne."

She stared.

His smile grew.

She heard a strange noise break from her: of disbelief, relief. She barely associated it with herself. All she could think about was her mother. No longer in Singapore . . .

"She's safe?" she said. "Here?"

"Here," he said, and took hold of her hands, telling her that he'd left her in the care of a first-class clinic in Melbourne, recovering from the broken ribs and fractured arm she'd got falling down a flight of stairs in a raid just before they'd left Singapore. She was all right, he said, before Rose could ask, *gonna be fine*, and knew all about Joe. Lionel had wired the *swell news* after Xander had wired him, letting him know that Stella was out of harm's way, and that he was coming to fetch her, Rose.

"You wired Lionel?" said Rose.

"Yeah. Your mom was so happy about Joe. So, so happy. She can't wait to see you . . ."

"Xander, I — "

"Wait," he interrupted, "lemme tell you the rest," and talked on, burying her attempts to speak again, seemingly determined not to let her do it, but to relive all he'd done, which really was such a lot. He'd searched for days for her mother in Singapore, eventually coming across her at the packed Alexandra Hospital, the day he'd been due to sail out. He'd taken her away, "Carried her in my own arms," far from the overrun wards, the stretchers on the lawns, before the planes targeting the hospital could hurt her again. "I drove her straight to the harbor, Rosie, got her on my ship. She was pretty beaten up, but I took care of her . . ."

"Thank you," Rose said, absorbing it. "Really, Xander, thank you . . ."

"Rosie," he gave a baffled smile, "you don't need to thank me."

"I've been scared," she said. "So scared . . ."

"I know."

"I wish you'd wired . . ."

"I didn't have a chance."

"In Melbourne," she said. "When you wired Lionel. Or you could have asked him to . . ."

"I told him I needed to be here for you, to tell you myself . . ."

But what about what I need?

She didn't say it, not out loud. It would have felt sulky, thankless.

"Do you know where my dad is?" she asked instead.

"No," he shook his head slowly, "I'm sorry, Rosie. I tried and tried, but I think he must still be with his unit . . ." He held her hands tighter. "Your mom said the last he'd told her, he didn't want to leave them . . ." He leaned closer, like he might be about to kiss her. "I'm sorry. I couldn't get any word of him."

Rose took a step away from him, dropping her head, seeing her dad as she had when they'd last been together, in Colombo. His smile, on that busy harborside. *We'll move to Singapore. It's a fortress.* She clenched her jaw, not wanting to cry, to *give up*, but feeling horribly afraid for him. Because what good would getting to Singapore do him, even if he was still alive? The Japanese were going to take it, she was sure. They'd win, and what would they, who were bombing hospitals, *hospitals*, do to everyone left behind once they had . . . ?

"Rosie, come here," said Xander, and sounded so full of compassion, that she, overcome by sadness and fear, forgot she shouldn't let him hold her. She thought only of how he'd carried her mum to safety, *in his own arms*, and didn't fight his embrace, just sank into it.

It felt . . . familiar.

Nice, for a second.

But not nearly as nice, or warm, or *right* as Max's.

Max, who might well be watching.

Carefully, she extricated herself from Xander's hold, and looked up at him. He'd changed, she realized, since April. There were new lines around his eyes, shadows in his cheeks. He looked older. Tired.

It made her sadder, deeply, deeply sad at all he must have seen and experienced — in the desert, Singapore — and at what she now had to tell him.

"Xander," she began, not knowing how to go on, only that, hateful as she felt for the hurt she was about to cause — and deeply, deeply grateful — she couldn't go anywhere with him, as he'd come wanting her to. Not as his fiancée. She wanted only to be with Max. That hadn't changed. Plenty had changed, but not how much she loved him. Nothing *could* change that. "Xander, I — "

"No, Rosie," he said, and she heard from those words, the hardness in them, that he'd already guessed, at least in part, what she was going to tell him. Maybe he'd come all this way having already guessed. *Glad to see me?* He knew she wanted to remain here.

He knew, and had talked and talked as he had, because he didn't want to let her tell him.

"Can you listen to what I gotta say first?" he said, confirming it. "Please."

She stared sadly up at him, thought again of all he'd done these past weeks, the love she'd once felt for him — that she supposed she'd always now feel — and nodded.

Letting him speak a little more seemed like a small enough thing that she could do for him.

"Let's go for a walk," she said, conscious of how on show they still were; the possibility of Esme bringing Walter back. "Somewhere more private."

"Private," he said, with a crooked, heartbreaking smile. "Private sounds good to me."

They didn't go far. Rose led them down the slope to the right of the driveway, through the long grass to a flatter run of pasture, where Xander told her about his uniform, how he'd joined up at the request of a family friend, General MacArthur. It seemed he hadn't only come to Australia for her, but was going to be part of MacArthur's staff, based here on the continent. (*Does he always come up smelling of flowers?*) He'd be living in Melbourne for the foreseeable, another nice hotel, waiting for MacArthur and tens of thousands more US troops to arrive in Australia, which was to be the new headquarters for the Pacific forces.

"MacArthur loves that you know the Churchills," Xander said.

"Does he?" said Rose flatly, reminded of how much he'd always loved that she did too.

"I want you to meet him," said Xander. "I want you to stay with me in Melbourne and meet him. I'll bring you back here as often as you like to see Walter. I've told your mom I'll help her get back to London, to Joe, but it's time for us, Rosie. It's our time . . ." He stopped, turned to face her. "Marry me, Rosie. Please."

"Xander . . ."

"I love you," he said, "more than I ever have." He reached for her hands again. His face was tense, wrought with determination. . . .

She looked away, over toward a clump of distant gidgee trees. A kangaroo stared back at her.

"I know you haven't trusted me," Xander said. "I deserve that. But I swear to you, I wasn't in Scotland with that waitress from my hotel . . ."

"So you keep saying."

"I wasn't, Rosie. I . . ." He sighed, seeming to weigh up how to go on. "Well, the truth is . . ." Another sigh. "I was gonna be."

She laughed, miserably, dismayed, but not surprised. "Going to be?"

"I'm sorry," he said. "I was, I don't know . . . *beaten* . . . by how much you kept pushing me away. And she wanted to be with me. She really wanted it. . . ."

"I don't want to hear this, Xander."

"You have to," he said. "Rosie, look at me. Please look. . . ." He dropped one of her hands, touched her cheek, turning it, gently forcing her to do as he asked. "Nothing, and I mean *nothing* happened. Ever. We got to King's Cross, she was all keyed up, and so . . . *vapid* . . . and not you." His eyes bored into hers. "Rosie, no one is ever you. I don't know what the hell I thought I was doing, letting myself get as far as that station with her, but I gave her the money for a taxi and told her to go home."

She said nothing.

She wasn't sure what she was meant to say.

Did it hurt, that he'd got all the way to King's Cross with another woman? Please her, that he'd sent her home?

She couldn't tell.

She was pretty angry, actually. But overwhelmed still too: that he was here, at his honesty; how much he truly seemed to want to make it right . . .

"I'm so sorry, Rosie," he said. Then, repeating what he'd said in that café in London, "I've said that too much."

"I think we both have," she said.

He raised his other hand, took hold of her face. The insistent touch of his palms on her cheeks was, like his embrace, familiar. "I should never have left you in that hospital," he said. "In Egypt, I . . ." He frowned, creases forming on his brow. "I don't know. I guess I came to realize how wrong I've been, about what's important . . ."

"It's all right . . ."

"Don't," he said. "I know you know it's not. I need you to know I know it's not." His hands pressed against her. "I wanna go back, Rosie, to September. Force them to carry me outta that ward. I wanna catch trains every

weekend to see you in Devon, make it so that you never got to fall outta love
with me . . ."

"I didn't fall out of love."

Not then.

"Good," he said. "Because I love you, Rosie. I love you. We're right,
you and me." He breathed in, out. She felt the warmth on her lips. "There's
nothing we couldn't do, if you let us. So please, enough now. Let me take you
to your mom, and then marry me."

She wanted to say no.

She *needed* to say no.

Even if it hadn't been for the thought of Max, so close by, she wouldn't
have been able to say yes, take the leap he asked of her. For all he'd done for
her mother — and it was wonderful, it was — everything she'd written to
him in that letter he'd never got still stood. She looked into his entreating
eyes and felt no doubt that he, who'd almost betrayed her once, would do it
again, as soon as it came back to him that being together could sometimes
be hard as well as exciting. He'd remember that she really was no longer the
person he thought himself in love with, and it would make him miserable.

It would make them both miserable.

She was certain of it, yet she couldn't say it.

He always made it so hard for her to say.

And it didn't feel right to do it here anyway, in the middle of the Lucknows' land, with him looking at her like it would be the end of the world
if she did.

She was still set on telling him, though. Being honest.

She truly was intent on doing that.

When she said, "Xander, I need to talk to them all, here," she really
meant Max, whom she'd left alone now for too long, and was procrastinat-
ing, putting off the inevitable moment when she'd have to find the right
words to send him, Xander, away. . . .

Perhaps he realized, because he leaned forward and, before she could
dodge it, kissed her, full on the lips.

She stiffened.

"This isn't your home, Rosie," he said, softly, sympathetically, his lips
brushing hers. *Forcing her gently.* "You don't belong here. You need to come
back to me, where you belong."

And with that, he kissed her again and told her he'd go for a walk, come to collect her at noon.

"Pack, do what you gotta do . . ."

"Xander, I — "

"Our ship's at three, Rosie." His expression remained kind, but his eyes toughened. *Enough now.* "I got you a ticket, and your mom's expecting you."

"You got me a ticket?"

"Yeah, I got you a ticket."

Rose said no more.

She told herself there'd be time enough for that at noon.

For the present, she left him to his walk, set off back toward the house, and thought no more about him, or the ship.

She thought only of Max, the waiting precipice.

The one she was coming to, at last.

The one he held her back from when, just a couple of minutes later, she shakily knocked on the annex door, and he silently let her into his home.

"You don't need to say anything," he said, the instant the door was shut behind her.

"I do," she said, not looking around the small shaded kitchen she'd never been in before: not at the low table, the range; their mugs on the shelf. Only at him, standing just feet away, yet feeling unsettlingly farther away than she'd known him. Sunlight sliced through the window, drawing a luminous beam on the stone floor between them. "I do . . ."

"No," he said, his dark eyes unreadable, smiling, but still in that same removed way as he had by the motor. So different from how he'd been on Christmas Day.

It unnerved her, how different he was being.

Was it purely about Xander's having come?

Or had he guessed what she needed to say, and wanted to save her from it?

She stared at him, her pulse vibrating in her throat, trying to work it out. She couldn't, but swallowed, bracing herself to say everything anyway.

But then he turned from her, ran his hands down his scarred face, and, speaking before she could, shattered her, shattered her dreams, telling her she should leave, that day.

He told her he needed her to do that.

"But — "

"I want you to go, Rosie," he said.

And there it was.

He wanted her to go.

Wanted her to.

The pain of it was worse than she'd ever feared it could be.

CHAPTER TWENTY-NINE

She wasn't with him for long.

A few short minutes in the end was all it took for him to put an end to the life she'd been foolish enough to let herself imagine them having together here, with Walter. Max mightn't be going to be the one to leave, love another, but he was resolute that she should.

"This isn't your home, Rosie," he said, hurting her even more. It was exactly what Xander had said. "You don't belong here, I know that. There's so much more, waiting for you."

"Is there?"

Her own question made no sense to her.

She couldn't take in what was happening. She realized just how much she'd been hoping. . . .

"There is," he said, heavily, kindly, but without even a whisper of doubt.

It was then that she felt tears start to mass in her throat.

He'd made up his mind. Decided . . .

She wanted to stop looking at him. She couldn't stop. He'd taken off his suit jacket, had his shirtsleeves rolled up, exposing his arms. His arms that he never wanted to place around her again.

"I thought," she said, "I thought, maybe — "

"I could let you stay," he said, cutting her off. "It would be easy to do that. I have loved you, Rosie." His dark eyes held hers. "I've loved you . . ."

She said nothing.

Her voice wouldn't come.

He went on, telling her how he'd loved her. He was very generous about that, trying to make her feel better, she supposed, with his words that dropped hollow around her: of the night he'd driven slower back from the dance in Brisbane, just so that she'd keep sleeping on his shoulder; how much he'd had to fight against reaching out for her again, after the night Bella's wire about Joe had arrived; what it had meant to him, having her with him for Christmas.

"I've tried pretty hard not to love you," he said.

She said nothing.

She didn't tell him how much she loved him.

She was close, too close, to tears.

"I want you to be happy," he said. "All I want is for you to be happy." He smiled; that distant smile. "He told me you'd offer to stay. He told me you would . . ."

"I want to," she said, finally rediscovering her voice.

It shook, unsteady, full of shock; uncertain to her own ears.

"No," he said, "you don't. And you can't."

She realized then how hopeless it all was. She'd left it too late to speak to him. All of it was too late. He was sending her away. She'd run out of time to convince him not to. . . .

She didn't want to have to convince him.

"You don't want to stay here with me, Rosie," he said, trying to make her feel better again. "I'm not getting better. The doctor's said that this is as good as I get. There'll always be a chance of infection . . ."

"I could look after you," she said, trying to convince him after all.

"I have plenty of people to look after me."

"But I can—"

"I don't *want* you to."

Her eyes burned.

She hardly listened as he went on, saying that she looked after everyone and he wanted her to *live*, dance, not have to hold herself back.

"You should see me, Rosie. See what I'm like." He gestured at his chest, the skin under his shirt; that warmth she'd felt beneath her cheek. "You'd hate it . . ."

"How can you be sure?" she said, biting back her tears. She wouldn't be able to contain them for much longer. "Show me . . ."

"No," he said, and his voice remained so steady. *No doubts.* "I get to hide. I'm allowed. You're not . . ."

"I don't want to hide . . ."

"You shouldn't. And Xander will never make you do that. What he's done, coming here. The way he spoke about you on the ship. I didn't trust him before, but . . ." He paused. "He loves you. Really loves you, as much as you deserve to be loved."

Rose didn't tell him he was wrong, that Xander loved an idea, a shadow of someone he'd used to know; not her.

She didn't want to argue about Xander.

She only wanted to know one thing.

"What about you?" she said. "You said you've loved me. What about now?"

He hesitated.

Just for a second.

But a second that filled with the image of him holding Mabel. Kissing her. Grieving for her . . .

"I want you to go," he said. "I think you know you should too, deep down, which is why you're going to turn around now and leave with your fiancé. I can't give you what he can . . ."

He meant love. Her throat swelled, her chest burned, crushing her from the inside. *I can't give you what he can.* She knew he meant love.

A love like he'd felt for Mabel.

A love he'd tried, but couldn't quite manage to feel for her.

Nothing else would have convinced her to do as he asked.

But it did convince her.

She argued no more, but turned on her heel just as he'd said she would and, managing to contain her tears only until she was safely outside, went straight up to her room, that was his room, to do the very thing she'd dreaded doing since the day she'd arrived, and pack.

She was finished by the time Walter returned from the river with Esme and Hank, dripping, sun-soaked, calling out for her as he ran into the kitchen. "Rosie, Rosie, Rosie, is Uncle Max back?"

Rose caught him in her arms, becoming soaked herself, caring not at all, but forcing herself to tell him, quickly, all she had to.

It was, like walking away from Max, one of the hardest things she'd ever had to do.

It had to be done, though. This moment that had been coming for her, ever since she'd met him, was here, and she had to get them both through it. Her trunk was already in Xander's motor. He'd come back sooner than Walter and the others, and was, at Rose's request, out waiting for her with his driver.

"Whatever you want, kid," he'd said.

Had he been surprised at her decision to go with him?

She'd been too numb to tell.

But she couldn't have had him here in the kitchen, listening as she tried to explain to Walter, and Esme too, what she was doing: how much she loved them, how little she wanted to go, but how she truly wasn't going to be far.

"I don't want you to be far at all, Rosie," Walter sobbed, damp, chubby arms clinging to her neck. "I want you to be *here*."

"I do too, Rosie," said Esme. "Please don't do this."

"I have to," she said. "I am so sorry, but I do."

Lauren and Hannah stood by the kitchen doorway. Rose had already said her goodbyes to them. They'd helped her pack. Hannah had given her a handkerchief to dry her eyes, and together they'd all lifted her trunk down the stairs.

"I don't like this," Lauren had said, walking backward, Hannah huffing beside her. "I'm glad that you're not going to vanish for Walter. You're as good as a mum to him, and I want you to see him as much as you can. But this isn't the right way . . ."

"It's the only way," Rose had told her.

"It's not," Lauren had said. "You can have a home here. Always . . ."

"Stay in my cottage if you like," Hannah had offered.

It had made Rose cry again.

But she hadn't wavered. She needed to be gone. As far from Max as she could get. She wouldn't be able to bear seeing him after all he'd said; she couldn't stand to hear his voice. . . . Even now, knowing he was next door in the annex killed her. Lauren had promised that either she or Esme would bring Walter to meet her in Brisbane for their visits. Rose couldn't imagine ever coming back here. . . .

"I have to go with Xander," she told Walter now, hugging him so tight, fighting, *fighting* not to sob again herself. She couldn't fathom that she was saying goodbye to him at all. She'd never wanted to say goodbye. . . . "I'm not disappearing," she assured him. "I am never going to do that." Tears burned in her eyes, her throat. *There's no shame in tears.* "Do you understand? I'll come back to Brisbane to see you, just as soon as I've visited my mum . . ."

"Why can't I come with you now?"

"We don't have you a ticket, little man," she said, and then she was crying again. She couldn't help it. Max had broken her, and her heart was tearing all over again. Because however soon she might be going to see Walter, however *often*, he'd be going to sleep that night without her, waking up in the morning and running to Esme. He'd never wake up with her again. He wasn't *as good as* her little boy, he *was* her little boy, and now she was losing him too. She cradled him, tears soaking into his hair. It was hard, all too hard. . . .

"Come on, Rosie." Xander. He was back, taking her elbow. "We gotta get this ship." He didn't know, still. There was so much she'd yet to tell him. "We gotta go . . ."

"No, wait," said Walter, desperately grabbing Rose back, grappling to hold her. "I don't want you to go . . ."

"Oh, I have to," she said, but held on to him anyway, his precious little body trembling, and whispered in his ear again just how soon she'd see him, how close she'd be.

"You promise?" he said.

"Yes," she said. "Have I ever broken any of my promises?"

He shook his head.

"I won't break this one," she said.

"I'm scared, Rosie . . ."

"You don't need to be," said Esme through her own tears, taking him from Rose. "Aren't I here?"

"We're all here," said Lauren, wiping his cheeks with her hands. "So, come on now, you tell Rosie she's allowed to go. Otherwise she's going to cry the whole way to the city, and her mum . . ."

"All right," he said, through his sobs. "It's all right, Rosie." *Hero.* "You can go. I'll let you."

"Thank you," she said.

"Come on, Rosie," said Xander, his arm around her, steering her from the kitchen.

She caught Hank's eye as she went. He looked crushed for her, but smiled: his kind, easy smile.

"You got this, Rosie," he said.

She didn't know if she did, but she went with Xander. She let him help her into the car, sinking into the cool leather interior.

"Let's go," Xander said to the driver, quickly, probably worried she was about to change her mind.

She wasn't about to change her mind. Max had told her he didn't want her, but she still needed to live, as well as she could, and she'd decided, as she'd packed, how that was going to be, what that life was going to look like.

She felt no pull to stare over her shoulder as the motor roared away, down the driveway of the home she'd come to love. She couldn't bring herself to look at it, like she'd once looked back at Ilfracombe; another chapter of her life closing.

Besides, she had something else to do.

She turned to Xander, took a ragged breath, brought the diamond ring he'd given her from her purse, placed it into the palm of his hand, and finally told him what everyone else in the kitchen had known, and she'd long needed to have said.

"I can't marry you, Xander." She spoke with the same finality Max had. "I am so sorry, but I can't."

He stared not at the ring, but at her.

Hard.

He didn't move.

Maybe he realized that this time she wasn't going to be persuaded otherwise.

He still tried.

"What do you think you're gonna do?" he asked, at length.

"Stay with my friend in Brisbane tonight," Rose said. "Esme's going to telephone her. I'll wait for another passage down to see my mum, then I'll come back here."

"To Brisbane?"

"Yes."

He narrowed his eyes. He was growing more upset; angry, from the way he clenched his jaw. She watched him do it, trying to contain his emotion, like he had the night she'd told him she was coming to Australia.

Have it your way, Rosie. You always do.

She realized she always angered him most when she was following her heart.

"Are you staying for him?" he asked. "Your wounded pilot?"

"No."

"Should I get burned . . . ?"

"Xander, for God's sake."

"You feel so sorry for him?"

"I don't feel sorry for him at all. And I'm not staying for him."

He didn't want me to.

"For Walter, then? I've told you I can bring you to see him . . ."

"I'm staying for me. This is for me. I want to be here. I don't want to have to wait to be brought places. To have to *ask*. I don't want to leave what I've found here. I've been happy . . ."

"You don't know what happy is."

"Yes," she said, "I really do. I know exactly what it is, what it feels like." She almost started crying again, saying that, but talked through the urge. "I'll get a job, a flat . . ."

"A flat? A *flat*, Rosie?" He laughed. "I could give you the world."

"I want this world. And I want you to be happy too . . ."

"Then marry me."

"That won't make you happy."

"Well, this doesn't."

"I'm so sorry."

"So am I," he said, and closed his fist around the ring. "Guess I should have taken Allie to Scotland after all."

Rose smiled, joylessly. "Right."

"Guess I messed up there."

"Well, thank you for saying that, Xander."

"You're so welcome, Rosie."

"You've made me feel a bit better."

He laughed, just as joylessly, turned from her to the window, and said nothing else.

Not for any of the agonizing two hours they spent together in that luxurious motor car, getting to the port.

She tried at first to guess what he was thinking, if he was regretting how much he'd put himself out, helping her mother. She hoped he wasn't.

She wanted to believe he wasn't. And wretched as she felt over his hurt, his disappointment—she always did hate disappointing him—she couldn't keep worrying over it. Her mind was too full of her own grief. She thought of Walter, sobbing in Esme's arms, agonizing over whether he'd wake that night and cry again. She replayed every word Max had said to her in his kitchen, the resolve in him as he'd spoken, the pain—because it felt like pain, now she was looking back at it—in his dark eyes.

"He told me you'd offer to stay," he'd said. "He told me you would."

She glanced sideways at Xander, so good with his words, and frowned.

What exactly had he said to Max?

She didn't feel as though she could ask.

But, calmer now, no longer so blinded by her own panic, she struggled more to understand Max having been so adamant that she should go. She combed over their past months, replaying the thousands of words and looks and smiles they'd shared, trying to accept that they should be over.

Trying to accept that he *wanted* them to be over.

She couldn't do it.

The harder she tried, the harder it became for her to make sense of any of it. . . .

He'd held her so close, when they'd danced on Christmas Day. Given her a watch. Made her tea, just the way she liked it, morning after morning . . .

She was still turning it over when they arrived at the port, and Xander's driver unloaded her trunk onto the crowded, sun baked quayside. The ship steamed at anchor.

"I guess this is goodbye," said Xander.

The high-afternoon heat was relentless. There were no clouds, precious little breeze. Within seconds, Rose was perspiring. Her cotton dress, still cool from the motor, stuck to her clammy skin.

Xander didn't look hot. He looked as handsome as always in his smart, pressed uniform. He at least would get over his disappointment, she was sure. There'd be plenty of women to help him. He'd find another *Allie*, less vapid; it probably wouldn't take him that long.

"I want you to be happy," she told him again.

"I'll try and work that out," he said, and didn't say he wanted her to be happy too. "You're such a sucker for a sob story, Rosie," he said instead, turning to walk away. He laughed shortly. "I told him you were."

"Did you?" she said, but didn't laugh.

She'd remembered, suddenly, something else he'd admitted he'd said to Max on the ship, back when they'd both arrived.

I've told him I can just about forgive him for keeping you hidden here all this time.

"Yeah," Xander said, and wasn't laughing anymore either. "Guess that was a pretty low blow."

"I guess it was," she said.

He carried on, then paused, surprising her with one final kindness.

"You don't need to get another boat," he said. "Come see your mom now. I know how much you must want to . . ."

She did want to.

She really wanted to see her mum.

She hated the idea of her alone, waiting in hospital.

But she could telephone her. There'd be another ship to take her soon.

For now, she was thinking once more of her and Max's dance on Christmas Day.

Then, what else Max had said to her in the annex.

I get to hide. I'm allowed. You're not. . . .

She stood on the baking quayside that smelled of salt and oil, and those words were all she could hear.

"I don't want to hide," she'd said.

She stared at Xander, so smart, so perfect in his uniform that suited him, seeing him through Max's eyes, all the way up from Sydney.

I can't give you what he can.

Had he been talking about love?

Or something else?

Something like parties and jitterbugging and the carefree, privileged life she was almost certain now that Xander had painted for him as waiting for her.

And if he had meant that—if he loved *her* as she loved him, so much that he'd been afraid of her staying with him out of pity, being *a sob story* (how, *how* could he have believed she'd be doing that?)—what must it have done to him, that she'd given in so readily?

She hadn't even told him that she loved him too.

She'd listened to him tell her, and she'd told him nothing.

"Are you coming, Rosie?" Xander said, his cap shielding his eyes from the sun's glare. Seagulls swooped overhead. The ship's horns blazed.

She hesitated.

Not for long.

She was terrified to go back and find out that she was wrong, that Max *had* meant love all along. It would break her, break Walter, for her to have to leave a second time.

But she still had to do it.

If Max could fly headlong into bullets beneath the blazing Arabian sun, she could do this one thing for him, for them; find out if the life he'd closed off might still be possible.

She really could do that.

She could do that right now.

She was at the plantation again by five. Xander's driver hadn't brought her. She hadn't asked him to, or told Xander where she was going; he didn't need to know. But she'd found a taxi easily: a ute with broken suspension, a boiling cab, and a driver as laconic as Lance, who'd bounced them silently all the way back. *Home.*

She hadn't cared how hot it was, how uncomfortable. She'd thought only of what she was going to say to Max when she arrived. . . .

It didn't occur to her that he wouldn't be there; that he might have left himself, off to find her.

But he had.

"He went not long after you," said Esme, who'd run out to the veranda as Rose had pulled up. Walter had come too, cheeks swollen from crying, throwing himself into Rose's embrace. (*I'm never letting you go again. . . .*) It had taken a while, but eventually Hank had cajoled him into playing ball on the lawn — out of earshot, but not sight — so that Rose and Esme could talk, side by side on the porch stairs. "I spoke to him," Esme said, "told him off for breaking your heart. None of it made sense, I couldn't just do nothing."

"And?" said Rose, already feeling lighter, her heart lifting in hope.

"And he left," said Esme, "as soon as I said that you weren't going to marry Xander, and had only gone because of how much you've been torturing yourself about him loving Mabel. He'll be trying to find you now . . ."

"Should I go after him?"

"No." Esme laughed. "Wait here, otherwise you'll be chasing each other all night."

Rose did wait, just as she had for him that morning. She played with Walter, read with Walter, watched the driveway, declined the beer Hank suggested, the gin Esme proposed, ate not a bite of the dinner Hannah and Lauren made, but got changed, at Esme's insistence, into the sleeveless blue dress Esme had made her for Christmas.

"She looked fine as she was," said Lauren.

"She looks better now," said Esme. "We need to sort your hair though, Rosie."

"You sound like my brother's girlfriend," said Rose, and, anxiously resisting Esme's attempts to pin her hair, left it loose, then, unable to be where the rest of them all were, swore to Walter she'd be back to say good night, and walked down to the gate to continue waiting for him to return.

He kept her waiting.

She sat on the gate's beam, and the sun began to set, painting the sky, the land and trees, purple and pink. The beauty didn't calm her, like it normally did. Nothing could calm her. . . .

And then, there he was, driving toward her in the dusk. She blew her breath through her lips, watching him slow, come to a halt, and didn't run to him, not as she had that morning. She went still, completely still, other than for her heart, beating, *beating.* . . .

"You're here," he said, stepping down, slamming the door behind him. He was smiling. She saw his happiness, his relief, but it blurred before her, because her own eyes filled, again. "I've been looking all over for you."

He no longer wore his suit, but his corduroy trousers, one of his loose shirts; his hat.

"Where have you been?" she asked.

"Kate's. Then the port." He walked toward her. "When you weren't there, I thought you must have gone."

"No . . ."

"No," he said, stopping before her, less than an inch from her knees. "Rosie," his voice dropped, low. "Please don't cry."

"I'm not crying."

"Well, you are," he said.

And she laughed, through her tears.

The dusk closed in, softening the pink light. In the trees, lorikeets cawed. Up at the house, Esme called for Walter.

"When I first got back here," he said, "after Egypt, I thought my life was over . . ."

"It's not over."

"I thought it was," he said. "You asked me once, what I was scared of. It's been hope, that I was wrong. Believing I could be . . . enough, for you."

"That's what I've been scared of."

"You're enough, Rosie. You've always been enough." He still didn't touch her. "Mabel asked me to go with her to England, when we got to the port. She said she wanted me to leave everything. I told her I couldn't, not for her, and I never heard from her again."

"Did you love her?"

"Not like I love you."

It was the only thing she needed to hear.

"I love you too," she said, at last. "I've loved you for so long."

His dark eyes shone. "That's pretty good to know, Rosie."

"I should have said it earlier."

"I don't think I gave you the chance."

"Max," she said. "I've never felt like I have to hide. You have never, not ever, made me want to do that."

"Good."

"But I do want to look after you, because you look after me . . ."

"Yeah?" he said, and then he did touch her, running his hands around her waist.

"Yes," she said, catching her breath. "Yes. And"—she smiled—"I want to see under your shirt."

He laughed, looked down, then back up at her from beneath the rim of his hat. "Is that right?"

"It is."

His hands moved, up her waist, tracing shocks down her spine.

"I'm going to take you to Melbourne," he said. "We'll bring Walter."

"I like this idea."

"If you asked me to go to England, I'd go."

"I'm not going to ask you to go to England," she said, her eyes in his eyes.

"Thank Christ for that."

She laughed softly, raised her hand, touched his face, the scarred side, and he didn't flinch.

Her heart kept on, beating, *beating*.

Taking her hand from his cheek, she flicked the rim of his hat, lowered her lips to his, and, his arms tightening around her, finally, *finally*, kissed him.

He kissed her back.

Not gently, nor softly, but in a way she'd never before been kissed, lifting her up against him with such love, such need; the same need that had been building within her.

The kiss went on, on and on; all the months they'd waited, together at once.

They said no more.

Nothing needed to be said.

It was just them. Together, in the deepening dusk. Living.

Doing it joyfully.

Enjoying it, enormously.

EPILOGUE
29 February 1944

She hadn't wanted a big fuss for her birthday. Rationing had become much tighter, the longer the fighting in the Pacific had gone on; there was less petrol for people to travel, less sugar, less of everything. Even Hannah's Christmas pavlova had been a small affair that year. They were still so many people missing as well. Rose's father, for a heartbreaking start. He, like poor Hamish from Narrawee, had been interned by the Japanese in the Changi POW camp after the fall of Singapore, back in that February of '42. Not a second went by that they didn't think of him, hoping that he was eating, surviving, *getting through*. It was the same for Esme's Hank. He'd remained in Brisbane for more than a year, but had eventually shipped out to fight and was now on his way to England, preparing to take part in an operation that was being planned for the summer. (*A bit of a scene*, Lionel had cryptically called it, in one of his letters, *and perhaps, the beginning of the end*.) Lionel was still back in Blighty himself, still missed, every day, as was Joe, who was hanging on, not giving up, but coming home for Sarah, and their one-year-old little boy, Rose's nephew, George.

"We'll just keep it simple," Rose had declared, when the subject of her birthday had first been raised, in the packed kitchen one evening. "A picnic, or something."

"A picnic?" Walter, almost eight, had said dubiously. "It's your actual birthday, Rosie."

"That's all I want," she'd said.

"Rubbish," Stella had said. She'd been living in the annex, ever since they'd brought her back from Xander's hospital in Melbourne. She hadn't wanted to risk the waters, leave Rose again. (*I've made it to you, it's enough. Joe will just have to keep staying safe. And your father. Until this is all over.*) "We can do better than that."

"We need to mark it," Lauren had agreed. "You're not going to get another birthday for four years."

"Leave it," Max had said, "she's made her mind up. You'll never convince her."

"Very good," she'd said.

"It's fine," he'd said, "we'll do a picnic, or something."

It had been a bit of a surprise when, earlier that day, at lunchtime, she'd returned from the walk he'd taken her off for—an hour to themselves, *disappearing everywhere*—and glimpsed the trestles outside Bill's, the balloons bouncing in the sunshine; Hannah holding a cake.

"Oh *no*," she'd said, turning, punching him, softly, on the chest.

"Happy birthday, Rosie," he'd said.

Despite the gaps at the tables, plenty *had* been there, laughing and drinking in the sun: all the family, of course, including Esme and Hank's fifteen-month-old daughter, Jamie, with her head full of Esme's black curls, and smile that was as easy as her father's. Then, all the workers and their families. Walter—who'd started school two years before at the local primary—had had some of his friends along too: the kind ones, like Tina from the post office's son. And Kate, Verity, and Tim had come; Tim, who never had returned to the fighting after Malaya, but been assigned a desk job. ("Thank God for limps," Kate said.) He was, like Xander, on MacArthur's staff. It was from him that Rose had learned Xander had just recently married himself. Happily, she hoped.

"He asked me to pass this on anyway," Tim had said, handing her a bottle of champagne.

Rose hadn't opened it.

She hadn't been sure what to do with it. ("Please don't ask me," Max had said.) But she'd liked that he'd sent it.

And she'd loved the party.

All over now, though. The cake had been finished, the sandwiches eaten, and, after everyone had gone home, Rose, Lauren, Esme, and Stella had brought the children down to the river for a late-afternoon swim.

Rose sat on the bank, dangling her hot feet in the rushing water, the still-fierce sun baking her bare shoulders, her hair dropping rivulets down her back. Before her, Esme held Jamie, trying to coax her all the way into the river. On the opposite side, Walter stood, asking Rose to look, look, look while he did his dive.

"I'm looking," she said, laughing. "When am I ever not looking?"

He jumped, splashing Jamie, making her wail.

"Jamie," said Esme, raising her high. "Toughen up. What would your daddy say?"

"Don't force a one-year-old into cold water," said Max, coming through the trees, down from the house. His shirt was loose, he had his hat on, and one more little person, fresh from her nap, propped on his broad shoulder. She was still so tiny, just two months old. Her bare legs were tucked beneath her nappy. His hand covered her entire back.

She hadn't come quickly for them. There'd been a year of trying, waiting, another devastating miscarriage, more tears, more hoping. . . .

"It'll happen, Rosie," Max had kept saying. "It'll happen . . ."

She'd been born on Christmas Eve.

"Like a gift," Esme had said. "A thank-you, from Mabel."

There really had only been one name for her.

Walter, who'd never called her anything but his sister, had been very happy with that name.

"Can I hold her?" he asked Max now, clambering out of the river.

"No, mate," said Max. "You're too wet."

"I'll take her," said Rose. "She's probably hungry . . ."

"She's fine," said Max, placing her in Stella's open arms, Lauren moving beside her. "And you're getting too dry."

Then, as Stella cradled their daughter, he took off his shirt, dived into the water, and sliced through it, over to Rose, pulling her in.

She went, gladly, laughing as he dragged them both deeper and deeper.

"Happy?" he said, kissing her, his face beaded with water.

"Pretty happy," she said.

"Yeah," he said. *You look pretty happy.* "The day's not over yet, though."

"No?"

"No," he said. "Mum's babysitting later, and we're going for your picnic. I'm taking you flying."

She smiled. "I'll look forward to that."

He rested his forehead against hers and turned her around, the water swooshing. She tipped her head back, staring up at the blazing sky, such a world away from that silent freezing-cold milk train she'd sat on three years before.

Walter dived again, Jamie roared, Esme exclaimed, Stella and Lauren cooed, and he spun her on. She tightened her legs around him, and didn't close her eyes. She kept them wide open, soaking in the day, the beauty, the golden sun above, her family all around her, breathing deep. Not missing a single thing.

HISTORICAL NOTE

One of the things I love most about writing historical fiction is the re-
search. History has always been such a passion of mine, and—as with all
my books—I spent a huge amount of time delving into the period *Under
the Golden Sun* is set in, both before I started writing it, and throughout
the process, compiling stacks of notes ranging from the timeline of specific
wartime battles and raids, to what music was on the wireless, which bands
were playing in the Trocadero, and what sweets were being served in Brisbane's cinemas. I firmly believe that when reading a book set in the past,
we need to trust the facts that are woven through the narrative, and I take
getting those right very seriously. With this book, I am so fortunate to have
been able to lean on the stories of my husband's grandfather, the wonderful
Johnny Ashcroft, who lived in Australia during the Second World War. I
could happily listen to him talking of his experiences all day long. I also
discovered some brilliant works of nonfiction to help me, notably: *Aboriginal Australians: A History Since 1788* by Richard Broome; *Outback Stations*
by Evan McHugh; the handbook *Instructions for American Servicemen in
Australia; Bomber Command* by Max Hastings; *They Passed This Way* by
Barry Ralph; and *All the Way to the USA: Australian WWII War Brides*
by Robyn Arrowsmith. Additionally, I was fortunate enough to have the
valuable input of a reader on the societal attitudes of the time, particularly
with regard to the history of the Aboriginal people, and the language the

characters in the book would have used (the word "Aboriginal" itself not being a term that came into common use until the late 1960s, hence its absence in the text).

I hope very much that I have re-created the worlds of wartime London, Brisbane, and the Lucknows' cattle station in a way that does them justice.

Under the Golden Sun is, though, of course, fictional, and I have taken a few small liberties. *Dumbo*, while originally released in October 1941, was rolled out internationally in the months following, but, once I'd imagined how Walter would have felt seeing it with Rose—as he assuredly would have done—I couldn't resist having them go together within the story's time-frame. All the details I've included of Brisbane and cattle station life are as accurate as I could make them, but the names of Narrawee and the plantation are made up, as is the name of Vivian's crescent, Williams Street, in Belgravia. Finally, while there was an *Illustrious* battle cruiser at large in the Second World War, this was not the requisitioned liner Rose and Walter traveled on—it simply inspired the name.

ACKNOWLEDGMENTS

As always, huge thanks to my fantastic agent, Becky Ritchie, whom I frankly don't know what I'd do without, and of course to Deborah Schneider in New York, for being such a wonderful champion. Thank you to my amazing editors — Darcy Nicholson, in the UK, and Leslie Gelbman in the US — for all your encouragement, friendship, and insight, and to Marissa Sangiacomo, Jessica Zimmerman, Naureen Nashid, Lisa Bonvissuto, and the team at St. Martin's Press, for everything you do to bring my stories to readers. It's such a privilege to work with you.

A heartfelt thank-you, too, to the incredible community of reviewers, bloggers and Bookstagrammers I've been lucky enough to come to know. I'm endlessly grateful for the time you take to read my books, and it's always such a treat to talk with you, whether over Zoom, or email, or on Instagram; this can be a very solitary profession, but you make it feel anything but, and your support really does mean the world.

This has, of course, been a year like no other, and never have I depended more on the love, kindness, help, and wisdom of my friends and family. Thank you, always, to all of you: for the Zoom chats, the WhatsApp group therapy, the meetups in between lockdowns, and the walks (and walks, and walks). Thank you, Mum and Dad; thank you, Chloe; thank you, Iona, Kate, Katherine, Lucy, Sarra, Claire, Cesca. And thank you,

Matt, Molly, Jonah, and Raffy, my lockdown crew; I'm so glad it was with you.

Finally, thank you to Johnny Ashcroft, for sharing your memories with me, and for being such an inspiration.